DULCINEA

DULCINEA

or Wizardry A-Flute

Shalanna Collins

To order additional copies of this book, contact:
Xlibris Corporation
1-888-7-XLIBRIS
www.Xlibris.com
Orders@Xlibris.com

CONTENTS

DULCINEA'S DRAGON

This book was written for my dear husband, Don Weeks,
because he simply doesn't read anything other
than fantasy novels and computer science textbooks.
I'm hoping he'll finally consent to reread Dulcinea.

Above all, thank you, Mama and Da, for everything.

CHAPTER ONE

I was scraping orange logan-bark crystals off the coated sides of one of my alchemist's bowls—a delicate operation any time, let alone in the heat of the harvest-time afternoon—when I heard my Daddoo calling.

"Dulcinea! Ho, child! Come up front at once, my girl." Then, as an afterthought: "Be ready to have yourself bespelled. And bring my mage's-sack."

"Yes, sir." Another aspirant had turned up, I reckoned. Soon after our old Chiro's entry into the next world, Daddoo had decided that he needed a new apprentice. Preferably younger this time. Over the past fortnight, we'd welcomed a constant stream of unsuitable youths.

I kind of missed Chiro, like I'd miss a splinter after I'd worried it a-loose. And I was ready for some company around this shop besides Daddoo, who could be difficult in his way. It wouldn't hurt if I had a little help, either. In an apothecary, so many tiresome daily tasks demand attention, including collecting logan powder without scratching the precious bowls, tending the herb garden out back, and keeping the wizardchamber swept clear of majick.

These days, all the fiddly, exacting parts of making up products were left to me. Until Da could acknowledge that I was grown up—I'd turn seventeen next Colinsday, though people thought me younger because the top of my head barely reached Da's shoulders—he would keep me at this level without even testing me for majickal talent. When I'd hinted that I might make a good apprentice, he'd laughed and patted me on the head.

I grabbed Da's mage's-sack from the kneehole of his big loganwood desk, careful to touch it only by the drawstrings, so as not to discharge any wards he might've laid on it. Backing out of the wizardchamber, I quickly rewove the spellweb protecting it. I threaded my way through the stacks of supplies in our storeroom, mentally noting several items ready to be restocked, and reached the front just in time to keep Da from hollering for me again.

I pushed aside the beaded curtain separating our downstairs rooms from the shop and squinted against the bright mid-afternoon sun shafting in through our front windows, much brighter than the magelight in the back. Stepping behind the counter, I visored my hand and blinked until my vision adjusted.

Sunlight softly illuminated the merchandise lining our shop's walls, which were shelved floor-to-ceiling all around. The implements of majick and of the healing arts lay all up and down the shelves. Mortar-and-pestle sets and scrying bowls sat side by side with muslin bags of herbs and lengths of soft linen. Liquids sparkled in light amber and cobalt bottles, and powders crouched in their translucent jars, gleaming with secret power and mystery. Silhouetted in front of the medicinals that lined our west wall was the figure of a skinny young man.

In front of the counter stood Daddoo in full majicker's white, arms crossed and head tilted, sizing up the young man. Da has always been a great pot-roast of a daddy, so round that people would whisper, "He's wealthy enough to be greedy at table." But he wasn't particularly gluttonous, just generously sized all over. It was unfortunate that his ponytailed red hair had recently started to thin, backing up towards his crown like a tonsure (I kindly said he wore a horseshoe haircut) at just around the same time he'd decided to grow a graying red beard. This made him look as though he had his face on upside-down.

I bowed my head and bobbed a knee-bend, splaying my feet like a duck's and going into a momentary half-squat as a proper sign of respect. "Sirs."

Da shot me a look. "Dulcinea, you dawdler. You look a mess."

As an apology, I ducked my head toward the young fellow. His clothes seemed oddly matched: they were simultaneously prim and disarrayed. His shirt's ruffled cuffs and jabot I judged somewhat dandified; peeking out of the jabot was a silver sigil, gleaming on a satin neck-cord. Over all this he had thrown a gently worn purple robe. The robe was only knee-length, too short for his stalky frame; it hung loose on him, its satiny sleeves rolled to mid-elbow on his lanky arms and tied in place with gold braid. He must be at apprentice level two already, then, because he'd never dare wear the purples unearned. But just barely, I judged, because he looked scarcely old enough for it. Maybe twenty.

He grinned back with his big, squared-off, horsy teeth. "It is indeed a distinct pleasure to make your acquaintance, Dulcinea Brown." His deep, resonant voice surprised me, booming out of such a rawboned lad. He seemed exceptionally bony, his face all angles and points. Perhaps this was made more prominent by the way he wore his long raven hair, combed straight back and reaching down to his midback. Exactly the way that mine used to until a fortnight ago, when I'd done something I regretted. He sported bushy, surprised-looking eyebrows, mutton-chop sideburns, and a black mustache which drooped down to crescent-moon curls on either side of the smile below. I couldn't get over how much nicer-looking he was than any of the village boys, or our previous aspirants, for that matter. His green eyes sparkled with excitement, as if he actually looked forward to undergoing majickal examination.

As his emerald gaze fell on me, I wished I had taken a moment to tame my flying hair and throw off my stained apron. At least I could've cleaned off some of the logan powder with its sharp, chalky scent. I could feel the dust from the crushed crystals on my cheeks. The layer of orange powder on my hands and forearms gave me the look of jaundice, reminding me of that foolish village girl last Quitain who'd bungled turning her faithless suitor into a pumpkin. I brushed ineffectually at myself. Nothing works but a bath; the stuff's a nuisance, but fortunately inert by itself.

Da dragged over a round burlap-covered ottoman that we used for spellcasting and waved me towards it. "Sit." He reached around the curtain in our front window and stuck in our "Back Shortly" sign.

I sat, squarely in the center of the large stool. Apparently, I was to be the nellie of the audition. A nellie is a willing recipient of a spell, but the spell has to be a benevolent one, the kind of spell that won't work on a body who balks. I assumed the first devotional position, in which each foot rests on the opposing knee and the elbows fit into the hollows between the legs and the arches of the feet. It's sort of like a vertical cat-curl.

"No, no. Please kneel here for me." The newcomer wiggled his fingers to indicate my new location and position on the edge of the seat. I glanced over at Da, who nodded his approval. I untangled my legs and resettled.

"Dulcinea, this is Raz. Raz, my daughter Dulcinea." Daddoo was one for belated introductions. Of course, Raz would have known better than to give his real name; this would be his traveling name, the one he gave at inns and to acquaintances who had no need to know a man's full identity. The fewer who know a majicker's true name, the safer. "Raz shall now prove to me the level of his skills. You'll kindly behave and do whatever he tells you."

I smiled politely and met Raz's gaze. He seemed nice enough, but I was always slightly wary of doing just whatever someone might tell me. Of course, Da wouldn't let anything happen to me, the worst fotchfinger notwithstanding. Anyway, aspirants hardly ever fumbled their demonstration spells, though it could be touchy. Once I had itched for a blessed quartermoon.

I whispered a quick prayer to Saint Alyncia that Raz would be more talented than the previous three.

Raz clasped his knuckledy hands in front of his chest. "First, Dulcinea"—something in the way he said my name made it sound musical, not clangorous, as I had always heard it before; I couldn't quite place his accent, although he wasn't from around here—"I'm going to set wards on you. So I'd like you to place your hands on your ri-"

Da interrupted Raz's instructions. "Not quite so fast, please." To me Da said, "First, off with all the wards you now have."

That didn't seem to me such an outstanding idea, since it would leave me open to whatever mistakes this Raz might make. But I knew there was no arguing with Da, particularly not before a stranger.

I did need to make sure what he intended, though. "All of them, sir?"

Da's eyelid twitched. "All."

"Just checking." Wondering what Da was up to, I pulled my safestone necklace over my head and handed it to him, to go safely back in his mage's sack until he felt like reconsecrating it. He motioned for me to unlace my charged wrist-dangle as well, which I did. Between the two, I'd had a pretty fair set of physical protections.

Da wasn't satisfied. "Take off the intangibles, too." He reached into his mage's-sack and handed me the consecrated silks. Inwardly, I winced. I hated silking; it made the fine white hair on my arms stand on end, and it could itch or sting, depending on the weather. Still, I obeyed, taking the knotted bundle of silk and starting to rub it over all my exposed flesh. The stubborn orange tinge didn't budge, naturally; it merely sank in deeper.

"Not enough. Do all of yourself." Da's jaw was firm.

I gaped. "Sir?"

"All over." He spread his palms and wiggled them for emphasis.

I blinked. "But. . . ." I couldn't believe Da expected me to go skyclad before this boy—no, this young man. As though I were still a little girl. And this was hardly like changing my tunic in front of my own Da and that dried-up raisin Chiro. I felt my face go ablaze with shame.

Daddoo's left eye began winking erratically. The tic meant he was getting cranky, so I jumped to my feet and reached shyly for my buttons. But Da grabbed my hand away, then stretched behind the counter and tossed one of our burlap robes over to me. I wasn't ready to catch it, so it landed practically in my face. "No, silly porcupine. Go on back and change."

"Oh." I felt the rest of me light up with scarlet. Da made a noise down in his throat, and in his silent gaze danced merriment. Raz's fist flew to his mouth, where he bit down on his lumpy knuckles.

I'd never feel dignified again. "Of course. Pardon me for a moment, gentle sirs." Quickly I backed toward the door to the storeroom. Unfortunately, I forgot to duck, so I bumped the back of my head right into one of the bunches of herbs that I'd earlier hung from the ceiling to dry. It showered me with withered flower buds and twiggy debris. That startled me enough that I dropped the robe into a basket of assorted soaps. I opened my mouth again, then shut it because talking was useless. I knew Raz must think me a complete cudge. I snatched up the troublemaking garment and disappeared through the curtain into the back rooms, wishing I knew a spell of vanishing.

I stripped off my dusty apron and tunic, wrapping them into a ball around my leggings, boots, and dainties, then donned the ceremonial burlaps. This was a set of short-sleeved tunic and knee-length breeches, made to be baggy on a normal person, but managing to be ill-fitting on anyone. The tunic was scratchy and rode up in the back on my rear. The orange stain on my skin, especially my forearms, was so hopeless that I couldn't even see my freckles. After rubbing my hair with the silk until it practically frizzed straight out on end, like a crown of five-inch spikes framing my powdery face and ears, I supposed I was as ready as I could be. I trusted Da knew what he was doing.

I stomped back out into the front room barefoot, keeping my eyes looking determinedly at the wooden floor, and knelt again on the round seat.

His voice betrayed no suppressed merriment. "Clasp your hands together on your right knee, please, Dulcinea."

Still too shy to meet his gaze, I grasped my kneecap through the burlap. At least Raz (or whoever he was when he was at home) hadn't made some sly or smart remark, as I felt certain some of our past auditioners would have. This thought put me a bit more at ease.

Raz already had some sweet herbs cupped in his hands. He crumbled them, muttering something, and sprinkled them on my head. Then he took what smelled like pewterbark and cinnamon, mixed together and made into a salmon-pink paste, and daubed that on my Seven Holy Points: between my eyes on the bridge of my nose, on each earlobe, at the hollow atop each shoulder blade, and at the midpoint of the arches of my footsoles.

I supposed this was his invention, a new anointing he'd come up with to replace the foul brown salt Da used. This ointment smelled like hedge-roses. I knew then that it couldn't work right; certainly this fragrant concoction was preferable to Da's stinging mudsalt, but how could one expect majick without mess and discomfort?

But I sat still for the treatment, because Raz deserved his audition. Like a round-eyed toad I goggled up at him, playing the trusting nellie despite my growing apprehension. His lips formed into a slight smile, as though I amused him, yet his concentration never wavered.

He took his flint and lit a cat's-tail branch with its majicking flame. With the resulting fiery torch, he traced a majick square around me, pressing its imprint into our packed dirt floor. While he worked, he murmured something that might or mightn't have been "cherosa bisanker." Then, going sunwise—never widdershins— he traced the contained ellipse, the one you draw inside the square to focus the spell, and marked its foci. A splash from Da's drinking-jug properly quelled the firestick.

At the corners of the square, Raz marked the four runes with his sanctified blade as Da looked on, nodding. Then he took a spark of sacred flame by lighting a stick of incense off the banked flame in our brazier of purification. At the powerful points of the rune-square, he set candles—cherry, fern, cherry, fern—and lighted them in turn from the stick. Finally, he placed tapers, one black, one white, at the foci of the contained ellipse. He lighted them by setting black taper to red candle and white to green. I had to admit he seemed to know his stuff.

He gathered in his big hands the fine silver chain he'd use for my bindings. Suddenly I was filled with shame; I knew he couldn't fail, as he apparently had up until now, to notice my extra digits.

I'd been born cursed—or blessed, depending on who you talked to—with a doubled middle finger on each hand. Once people got to know me, they usually forgot about it, but sometimes at first they were afraid of me; some people believed I carried a witch-sign. Would Raz show his revulsion? Worse, he might be abruptly cowed, shrinking from my touch. I braced myself against which-ever emotion he betrayed.

Raz took hold of my hands. His expression registered nothing, not even curiosity. I let out a breath I hadn't realized I was hold-ing.

I tingled at his touch as he wrapped chains around my index fingers, crown, and big toes, then joined them with the blessed twine. I was starting to prickle with fear and excitement. Or maybe it was just the aura of impending majickal enchantment. Little shocks stung my skin all over, as if somebody were shooting stretch-bands. It was like being caught out in needle-sharp rain, yet remain-ing dry. And I could feel that the power was coming from Raz.

The familiar fiery glow began to trace round first the square, then the ellipse. A pale apricot line strengthened to dark clay-pot red as the working gathered strength. While we waited for the power-wall to peak, Raz looked me full in the face and winked. He certainly was good-looking.

"We have a moment, now. Shall we make you a personal charm?" He plucked a hair from my crown.

"Ouch!" I rubbed at the pricked place with the heel of my hand, without thinking, disarranging my tie-ups.

Raz quickly set them right again. His green eyes gleamed as he took my measure with his gaze. I felt naked as a peeled egg. For once, I found my mouth empty of words, without a smart retort.

Testing the hair by pulling it, Raz looked pleased when it stretched at least two thumbslengths before it snapped, curling. "This is delightful. In excellent condition, and quite saturated with your life-energies. May I take a proper lock?"

"Seems easiest." I shrugged, feeling a spot of apprehension, but knowing that anything he did to my head would be less damaging than what I had done to it myself a fortnight ago, and by accident, sort of. My braids had vexed me, constantly falling into the solutions as I tried to learn how to titrate herbal liquors, so I'd tried to bind them atop my head as the mature ladies of the village did—in fact, all the girls who'd already had their coming-of-age rite had developed elaborate upbraids or birdnests in which they stuck feathers or combs. Some of them, I thought, could hide a dozen eggs in their coiffures with no one the wiser.

But I had no one to show me, and Da was completely oblivious to my need for feminine advice. I had picked up a handful of hairpins and stabbed my head with it at first, ending up with a sore scalp. Then I'd gotten curling-twigs all tangled in when I tried to roll my hair into a twist like the Widder Groop's next door. Finally I'd just grabbed the knife in anger, intending to cut the ribbons that fastened the ends of the braids and start over; but, instead, without really meaning to, I kind of lopped one plait half off, where it looped over one ear. Then I had to bob the other. That made each side collar-length, but when I unwound the stubs of the plaits, I hadn't got the sides even, and had to repair that. It wasn't easy. Hair, I noticed, could not be uncut, and was strikingly easy to whack away. So it all ended up not quite touching the bottoms of my ears.

The loss of its accustomed weight then frizzed out my babyfine hair, creating a headful of ugly, angry-red twirls that cascaded down hopefully but ended too early, like an embarrassed drapery that's shrunk in the wash. It was exactly the mess that the Widder Groop's glance said it to be (perhaps I should've swallowed my pride and asked her to help, but I thought of that too late.) I hadn't fretted too much over repairing my hair, because after all I never saw any-

body but the customers and my Da. Now I was sort of sorry I
didn't at least have on a hat.

Raz snipped a lock from the front. If my hands hadn't been all
arranged in the proper position, I would've grabbed. "Hey, watch
it! That was a long piece."

"I was careful to take only from the bangs." He quirked a black
eyebrow, challenging me.

"I'm growing them out." I winced.

"Don't be peevish." He pulled away the lock of hair—quite a
thick one, and I felt another pang, similar to when I'd first ruined
my hair. Instantly repentant, I had kept the hacked-off braids rolled
in sad little coils in Mawmoo's cedar chest. A good thing, too; I
hadn't thought at the time about how powerful hair-charm was if
saved for majickal rites. I was glad I hadn't let it go to the dump,
where whoever found it could work all sorts of spells on me. Thinking
back, I realized I'd allowed that to be done with the results of all
past trims, some of them also pretty drastic, as I remembered.
Who could tell which hands that power might've fallen into? I
absolutely needed this charm.

He took the lock between his middle fingers, in the center of
its length, and twisted. The ends fanned out like little brushes.
Raz tied them with blessed thread about every thumb-joint-length
or so. "This is what mages call a 'broomstick.'"

"You don't say." I hoped I sounded properly nettled, letting
him know I knew perfectly well what he was up to.

"Hush," said Da from his vantage point in front of the counter.
I'd almost forgotten he stood there.

Raz knotted the rope of hair in the middle and threaded it
with center-drilled tiger-eye beads at each knotted station. He
fastened this into a hangman's loop, which he threaded onto a
brown leather thong and put round my neck. His tasseled sleeve-
cords tickled my ears, and I felt feathers all over the surface of my
skin. Solemnly he tapped the amulet against my breastbone, and I
imagined I felt power flowing into it, heating it from within.

"Wear this inside your neckline." He spoke so softly that for a heart-stopping moment I thought he didn't mean Da to hear; it seemed just the two of us in the ellipse, sharing an intimate secret. "Out of view. Else people will wonder what charms you fear."

"None." I couldn't help popping off when I was this nervous. "I can take care of myself."

"Quiet," said Da. "You'll scotch the working. It's nearly ready, if you please." In fact, the red glow had reached its strongest, the lines looking like rows of banked coals ready for cooking over.

"We're doing quite well, quite well." Raz's tone was mild. I didn't know whether he meant to reassure himself, me, or Da. "Charm's done. Now lift your hands in front of your face."

I knew he meant to focus the power he'd collected. Now he would lay his palms against mine and generate the field of warding. I squirmed; irrational as it was, I felt as though once we touched, he could sense all my secrets.

I hesitated, then slowly put up my hands. Raz adjusted my posture, leaning me forward by placing both his hands gently on my shoulders and moving me into the precise position he wanted. Then he frowned. Before I realized what he planned, he'd lifted me whole and set my knees on the hard dirt floor. As he stood before me, I could feel the warmth of his body; my nose filled with his strong peppermint smell.

I felt a spark of static, as though I'd rubbed my feet on a woolen carpet, as our fingers touched and our palms met flat together. Then Raz knelt on the hard dirt with me, our knees almost touching. Our gazes met. This gave me peculiar, unfamiliar stirrings around my kneecaps. For some reason, I thought of a dragon.

He raised our hands to cover my face, our forearms together skin-to-skin now, all four elbows resting on my knees as I followed his lead, doubling over. My sensations were unlike any others I had ever experienced during majickal contortions. Surely my strange reactions were obvious to Raz—and, worse, to Da. I felt my cheeks burning and squeezed my eyes tightly closed.

My ears filled with his voice and my lungs with his exhaled breath as he muttered words of power in the language of the mage. Of course I forgot them the moment I'd heard them. Still, I could feel the Words doing their work inside our ellipse. In quick succession, I saw stars, thought I would sneeze, couldn't get my breath, felt my spine go icy, had a hot rope momentarily laid across my shoulders—all illusory, of course. The power had entered us, sandwiching me between the wardings of protection. I felt myself glowing with energy. The very air was charged—and not merely with majick. I prayed the way I felt wasn't some kind of sin.

He completed the sequence with an incantation, his hot breath quietly entering—it seemed—into my ear alone:

> *By moonlight, water, rock and leaf,*
> *We ask thee, Lady of the Green*
> *that while it does remain unseen,*
> *this charge shall keep Dulcinea safe.*

The words were a frill, not required for the power's investiture, I judged. It tickled me to think he'd added a verse meant only to delight me.

Raz "read" me while I was still vulnerable inside the majick's elliptical field. "You shall have witchsight and rune-knowing." As he spoke, he broke our connection by peeling his hands free from mine. The jolt was perceptible as he separated our flesh; I felt an imaginary ripcord jerk loose from my heart. He stepped back to the very edge of the square, peering at me closely, as if to examine his handiwork. "Philtre-making. Dream interpretation. The knack for drawing out poisons."

I lit up like a Festival float. "You can see all that?" Of course, I'd shown no sign of any of these talents yet, but if Raz were correct, I could be trained in them once I had shown symptoms of majickwake. If I ever did. And if Da could—and would—teach me.

"Hush." Daddoo's admonition floated to me from afar, as through molasses. "Don't give him any sass. Or any hints."

"You also. . . ." Raz paused. "You once broke this arm"—he picked up my left to do the traces of the rune on it, then laid it gently back down—"Yes, rather badly, I'm afraid. And your right ankle, but they've both healed nicely." He clasped my right hand; I feared it felt sweaty to his cool, powdery touch. "You have kept one baby tooth that never fell out, way in back. You have a birthmark shaped like a stork bite on your—"

"Hey!" I jerked my hand away, barely able to restrain it from flying to cover my behind. I suddenly felt a whisper of cold breeze on my thigh, as if it were exposed, although I knew there was no way he could see through the burlaps.

"—On the back of your neck," Raz continued, unruffled. "And another in a place we don't need to discuss, do we?"

He was reading me like a scroll.

"You're double-jointed at the wrists and ankles. Cut your hair only last moon—and you don't much care for how it turned out." He raised one eyebrow for confirmation.

"What business is it of yours?" I bristled, feeling a bit invaded because he was so accurate.

"The child has a point, friend." Da's voice boomed out, rather late to suit me. He'd been watching us closed-mouthed, as though he were in a trance. "Should you be asking?"

Immediately Raz turned smooth-talker, as though merely to clarify an argued point. "My apologies, gentlefolk. I merely meant to say she doesn't like the way it is now; I read that in the aura around her hair, all irritated and hurt, like a recent wound that's only starting to heal. There's no harm in the knowing of that, now, is there, sir and lady?"

Daddoo stood there, looking a bit stunned. It wasn't often that he was out-talked, yet I thought he just might have met his match. I could also tell he was having trouble hiding his amazement. If my Da had ever expected all this predicting, and reading the past, and other such stuff from an aspirant during a routine

Warding, he'd never mentioned it. Even he couldn't read people as Raz had just read me.

There was more to this Raz than was immediately apparent. I wondered what other secrets he might harbor.

One thing was certain: Raz was no apprentice. He was properly a journeyman, at least a level two. If Da thought it appropriate to take him on, I guessed that was all right, though unusual in light of the beginnerhood of all of Da's past trainees. They'd all started out profoundly useless, and a few had left in exactly the same condition. What was such a majicker as Raz doing auditioning for the likes of us?

"That's all there is to the warding, at any rate." Raz smiled at me. Moving widdershins, he snuffed the candles one by one with a little silver nutshell-on-a-stick that he pulled from one of his many purple pockets. The orange glow began to fade where the tracery had been. He muttered a few more words; with his boot, again widdershins, he rubbed out the lines of power he'd drawn in the dirt. All traces of the glow were instantly gone.

The majicking was over.

Da shook his head slightly, as if to clear it. "That's it, is it?" From his tone of voice, I judged he was headed for a major grump later. Light-headed from the majick myself, I hoped this was the end of our session. I needed a long drink of cool water.

Da uncrossed his arms and wiped his hands on his dingy robe. Clearing his throat, he met Raz's gaze; then his expression softened. "You'll do. Take him back, Dulcie, and show him the basics of our business. Let him start by helping you with the herbs. In the storeroom, I mean."

I knew that meant not to take him into the wizarding chamber. Daddoo needn't have worried; I had no intention of letting on that it existed, not after the show of power we'd just seen. And maybe not ever, even after Raz was bound as an apprentice, at least until I was certain Raz would be loyal to us.

Raz looked happy, though drained. "Thank you, sir." He made a shallow bow to Da. "I'm honored to be selected. I only hope I can fulfill and even exceed your expectations." That loose smile again. Then he winked at me again. I clasped my hands over my heart as though to hide the pounding.

I smiled my best smile. "Welcome to our shop and our home. And merry met, Journeyman Raz."

CHAPTER TWO

It turned out that his name really was Raz. Raz Songsterson, of Marwell. Marwell was Ladenia's nearest neighbor and closest ally, but it was still a foreign country, all the way across the mountains. I should've guessed this from his slight accent, a Marwellian burr that lilted as if he were talking in birdsong.

I'd never known a majicker to reveal any part of his real name or wizard-name when he first entered our shop, even for accredited alchemistry. I wasn't certain it was wise, especially not until after Daddoo held Raz's binding ceremony to seal their agreement as apprentice and majick-master. Raz's fearlessness impressed me.

Having studied him while he'd bespelled me, I knew now I had been mistaken about his age earlier. He wasn't weathered-looking, but he had a certain maturity about him; he was at least twenty-three, I was sure of it.

We started stuffing herbal poultices, and I saw he was a quick learner. Raz's knobby fingers were swift, and he knew a knot I'd never seen. As we made small talk, I soon learned he had been apprenticed before, to a powerful man in Marwell. He named one of their major cities, Tiria, near where my Da's people had always lived, where what remained of our kinfolks must still be.

Raz sounded so wistful when he spoke of the place that I thoughtlessly asked, "Why did you leave there?"

Raz looked away, seeming uncomfortable. He shrugged. "There was a little misunderstanding."

I felt like the tactless Widder Groop. "Sorry. You don't have to tell me."

"I don't mind." He closed one eye. "I suppose I wasn't very wise. I squabbled with his wife. About the way I made up dream pillows—they're a type of sweetherb packet."

"Oh?" I knew what they were; I'd done them myself.

"She didn't like the way I did them. Thought the ingredients were too expensive and cut into her profits. You see, I prepare them my own special way. Mine were far more effective than the old man's. When customers started asking for mine instead. . . ." He shrugged. "Some people get the green-eyed monster, or simply can't deal with change."

I nodded, knowing just the kind of person he meant. In fact, we lived with one. "How were yours different?"

"Here, I'll show you." He took one of the small muslin squares off the pile in the center of the table. Turning to the glass jars on the shelf behind us, he lifted several lids in turn, sniffing the contents. From nearly every jar he scooped up a handful of ingredients, some of them expensive.

As he turned, I caught the scent of peppermint again. Near him, I savored the heat of his body as I sat close beside, watching his long nimble fingers. He sprinkled the ingredients on the muslin, dripped the oil over sparingly, mumbled a verse over it all with the proper finger motions, and tied up the sachet. All the while, he kept up a running patter of explanation, most of which I already knew, but I enjoyed hearing him talk. His Marwellian accent enchanted me. Though Raz had obviously traveled, he hadn't lost his hometown way of talking. It was similar to how traces of Da's Wrennish brogue still hung on, because he was born over in Blackwren-on-the-sea, despite his having lived here in Ladenia since way before I was born. I hoped I didn't sound too unsophisticated when I talked to Raz. I must've looked a little moony, because Raz finished up by giving me a concerned look.

"There, now. It's ready. Did you catch all I did?"

I had.

We made up a few of the new packets, which, in addition to the normal sweetherb and logan, included orange-feather and a crumbly white dust. Later that afternoon, I sold them to the next few biddies who wanted to recall their dreams. The way it works is that the sleeper tucks the packet into her pillowcase so as to breathe in the scent all night; when she awakes, she has only to breathe it in again to remember all. At least that was the idea. Since I seldom remembered my dreams anyway—and suspected I might be better off for it—I'd found it didn't always work for me. But then I'd never tried one of Raz's packings.

The very next day Daddoo bounded into our workroom, beaming. "I always knew it. The village's finally coming to realize the superiority of our goods," he said to Raz. "Two customers already this morning told me our dream pillows smelled heavenly, and took an extra sack. Two!" He turned his gap-toothed grin on me. "Mark that, daughter. Always use fresh ingredients and do them the way I showed you every time. People know value when they see it, Dulcinea."

"Oh, indubitably, Magefather Brown." Raz pursed his lips and brought his brows together to show he respected the old man, then glanced at me. "Reputation is everything in this business. Eventually, the fact of our products' superior quality will get through to the most selective customer." He twinkled his eyes— meaning he crinkled the corners of his eyes and made them brighter somehow; I could only think of it as "twinkling." I looked away, but then our gazes met behind Da's back, and I barely suppressed a snicker. Da turned to me questioningly.

"I'll remember, Da." My innocent expression must have fooled him, for he went away happy.

I was glad Da hadn't noticed the difference in the packings himself. Da had a habit of quarreling with his helpers, including me, if they deviated from The One True Way To Do Things—Da's way. I hoped Raz would never do anything to make Da send him away, as had happened with a couple of upstarts before we'd settled in with Chiro.

Raz's binding ceremony that afternoon was private. I worked on cooking a nice supper, complete with fruit and a steamed pudding for dessert, while listening for any sounds that might escape our wizardchamber, but I heard not a buzz. It was of course a secret ceremony between a majicker and his aspirant, one in which they would swear loyalty to one another and to the four aims of majick, which I knew were "to control, to influence, to predict, and to explain." It was legally and morally binding, meant to tie the majicker's apprentice to him in a vow to honor their bond and to seal his lips about what he has learned.

Raz and Da emerged from the back sober-faced. Their somber mood lingered, making our house and shop seem uncharacteristically quiet until evening. Raz was finally bound as an apprentice, for real.

# # #

That evening I was lying on my back out on the terrace, looking up into the velvet sky at the stars. The changing of the winds into the season of leaffall was bringing my old friends back around the skywheel: the Dancing Bear, the Dragons' Circle, the Praying Hands. I gazed for a while, enjoying the cool night air. Then I started tootling on my flute, as was my custom. I almost jumped out of my skin when Raz's voice came from behind me.

"Ah, music to soothe the most savage breast."

Startled, I couldn't help but overblow the next note. As its screech faded away, I twisted around and squinted into the darkness, toward his voice.

Raz stepped out of the shadows behind our carriage-house. The grass crackled faintly as his soft shoes crossed the back garden lawn. He came close, settling down next to me on the grassy slope. I shuddered with my delicious secret of liking him that special way, and pressed my arms close to my body, careful not to look at him until I could get myself calmed down.

"You're fairly respectable on that flute."

I felt too shy to look up. "Thanks."

"Just a pastime?"

"Yes. Well, not really." My stomach tied itself into a knot; thinking that Raz had been listening to my playing made me feel funny. I both wanted him to hear and didn't. Had I played well? Or was he just being nice? "I do love fluting. I only wish. . . ." I swallowed hard, unwilling to reveal something I didn't want Daddoo to guess or overhear.

He cocked his head. "Wish you could what?"

"Oh, nothing. It actually is just a pastime." I fiddled with the soundholes and pulled out the mouthpiece a hairsbreadth, as though fine-tuning my instrument.

"You sound as if you've practiced more seriously than that." He rolled to his side and propped his head on his hand, his elbow pressing into the dewy ground. He was too close for my comfort. "You're sure you don't secretly wish to become a flutemage? It's a type of dramaturge, you know." He needn't have defined the term. I'd heard of them, even thought I might have caught sight of a full-fledged dramaturge last year when a theatrical troupe passed through our village. A flutemage was not actually a majicker, but an illusionist who worked with music to create effects for the stage and for entertaining crowds. Anyone who majickally made scene-setting effects for the stage was called a dramaturge.

"I never thought of such a thing." Hadn't I?

Raz wiggled his eyebrows.

He was making me nervous. "Well, I suppose I'd like to be one, of course, but. . . ." Should I be telling Raz this? Could I trust him?

His emerald gaze gleamed at me.

I babbled forth, filling the yawning silence. "Some say the dramaturges are witches. That they aren't like us, that they call on strange powers foreign to a white majicker." Why had I blurted that out? "And . . . well . . . I . . . ." I dithered.

"It is also said that Dulcinea was the name of the ancient Archwitch of legend. Perhaps you'll want to fulfill your name-prophecy and become a true witch." He winked, and I wasn't sure whether to laugh or cry.

"It's not a prophecy, is it? It's just a legend, a superstition." Witches were not like us, I knew; most people believed they used diabolical majick. I'd been taunted by the village children for being double-jointed and for having hands—well, hands like mine; some called me a witch-child. But I knew I was a good person; I'd even joined the church last year, as soon as I was old enough. But the legends had always worried me. Suddenly filling with shame again, I spread my fingers wide and studied my hands. "You're making fun of me."

"No, I'm not. I promise." He reached over and took hold of my right hand, working the doubled middle fingers slightly. "I can see you are made differently, couldn't help but notice it when we first met. But your fingers are functional." Gently he probed the back of my hand; my skin burned with hot blood at his touch. "Full tendoning—you actually have a beneficial adaptation, Dulcinea." Without changing the angle of his head, he shifted his gaze towards mine. "Your mother have it?"

"No—not that Daddoo ever mentioned." I'd never known much about my mother, who'd swapped the rest of her days for the first of my own. "They tease me in town. They say I'm a birthwitch who's bad luck, or a changeling who was swapped for my parents' real baby by the fairies. They say it's a witch-sign. I've wished forever for a majick to heal it properly, without ruining my hands." I had always felt like a six-toed cat, a jinx.

He frowned, stretching out next to me again on the damp grass, heedless of his fancy clothing. "Those superstitious whiflings. Polydactylism is neither a witch-sign nor a curse." He spoke with the force of belief. "No, banish any such idea from your mind. It is, instead, a rather lucky accident for one who wants to flute."

I breathed out heavily. "So you don't think it's. . . ." *Repulsive. Hideous.* "Unsightly?" My hand in his was beginning to perspire. It felt rather warm and kind of tingly.

"Of course not." He caressed my fingers again, this time favoring my left hand with his attentions. It took effort, but I kept from squirming with pleasure. "They're not just extra weight for the hand, like most of the others I've seen. Very unusual. And of course wonderful for a flutist. Gives you options for easier fingerings. That's one of the things I noticed as I watched you from the upstairs window."

He'd watched me?

"You're definitely skillful at what you do in the shop, too." He released my hand and leaned back; he looked up, studying the sky, and I followed suit. "You seem to know a lot about the business as well as the products."

"Thank you for noticing. I wish Da would notice." The complaint burst free of its own accord. "He made me waste my entire morning counting wizardberry sachets when I could have been helping him up front." I knew I sounded sulky, and hated myself for it.

Raz laid his hand on my shoulder. I shuddered at the deliciousness of his touch and at the forbiddenness of my feelings. "He doesn't realize how helpful you are to him. He appreciates you, I'm sure." He squeezed my shoulder blade gently. "You may be feeling frustrated because you take after him, you know. Have you had any sign that you will be a majicker?" The gifts, at least the ones Raz had predicted for me, were inherited, the first signs of majickwake appearing before the age of twenty, in those who were lucky.

My mouth had gone so dry, as if in response to the warmth radiating from Raz's grasp, that words would hardly form, but I managed to squeak out, "Nothing has woken in me, I'm afraid— as far as I can tell." Granted, I could by now do several everyday webs and cantrips, just from imitating what I'd seen all my life; I was the one, for instance, who kept the dust-away spells going throughout the shop and our living quarters upstairs. These, however, required no innate talent. "I mean, I've had no particular signs that I'll develop talents." Even I could hear how disappointed I sounded, which was embarrassing. I tried to make my tone light. "No spectacular indications so far. I haven't suddenly awakened floating three feet above my mattress or anything."

"How disappointing." Raz tilted his head and removed his hand from my shoulder, although this didn't cool me down. "But it seems to me that you are already burdened with many of the regular duties proper to a beginner in our profession. It appears that you are already well versed in poultices and potions. You also undertake with some skill the worrisome tasks involved in preparing medicinal packets, right alongside the plain drudgery of dusting and attending to the accounts." It fascinated me when Raz broke into fancy talk. He seemed to have a great propensity for it. "Yet as I understand your Daddoo, he has not made you an apprentice."

I shrugged, carefully not looking over at Raz. "There wasn't anyone else to do it after Chiro died, not until you arrived. Da says I'm too young to be useful, even though he sat in the front pew three moons ago and watched me be given my responsibilities in the Church. He thinks of me as a child."

Raz's eyebrows bounced. "It only seems that way to you, Dulcinea. I see him relying on you in many instances, and he knows he's entrusting you with important matters." Weaving his fingers into his hair at the nape, Raz settled the back of his neck on his hands and gazed at the sky again. "I suspect he has already taught you a great deal, even though he refuses to call you his apprentice."

The words burst forth unbidden. "As if I'd want to be. Not for all of Ladenia, nor for all the sweet-cakes in Blackwren." I hadn't meant to sound sulky, but I couldn't help unburdening myself on this matter, and Raz's ear seemed sympathetic. "I almost feel sorry for you, having to be Da's apprentice." I wasn't in the least jealous.

"Oh?" Raz said lightly.

"Truly." I forced a casual laugh. "Too much studying and too much lecturing before you actually get to try any workings. It gets so boring when you have to recite and memorize things out of books and can't get your hands into an example."

His voice mused. "It can at that, I suppose. And you'd be studying under your own Daddoo, which could be trying, at that."

Raz shifted onto his side to face me again. He put on a thoughtful expression, the very tip of his tongue captured between his front teeth. "You don't suppose it has anything to do with your being female?"

I pretended to consider this a moment. "Probably. I don't know why Da pays any heed to those old superstitions—when he'll tell you he's not superstitious at all—but he does." Generally, Daddoo honestly didn't hold it against me that I was a mere female; I often suspected he didn't even realize it. "He'll eventually teach me anyway, I'm certain, and claim to all the town that he had to do it because I'm unmarriageable."

What I did not say—what hung in the night air between us—was what we both knew, that most marriageable girls my age were already farmwives or ladies, long away from their fathers' households.

I wiggled my six-fingered hands, reason enough no man would want me. "Not that I care. I don't even know if I want to mar—" I caught myself just in time. "To rush him along on it," I completed lamely.

Raz cast a sharp glance in my direction. "You would refuse an apprenticeship if he offered it, then?"

I sighed. "I guess not." I knew I would not. I had a secret, selfish desire to be something different, like a street performer, or maybe a traveling majicker, one who went from town to town solving problems for people who had no apothecary and no citizens schooled in natural majick. Or even, as Raz suggested, a dramaturge. But wishing didn't cancel my duty, which I knew was to carry on the family business. So what if, in the evenings, I played at being a flutemage, and dreamed of enthralling crowds with the stories in my music? It didn't hurt to dream.

"But you're out here under the stars fluting." Raz's eyes twinkled.

Despite this clue that he was teasing me, I felt warm and flustered, tongue-tied. "I just flute by ear, only for pleasure."

"An artistic outlet. Everyone needs one, to be sure. It's nothing to apologize for. Especially when you have talent."

I didn't know for sure what he meant about being artistic, but I didn't care. I liked the sound of his voice, a rich tenor cutting through the sounds of the night, crickets and night-flyers and wakeful birds.

Raz stretched out his long fingers for my flute. "Here, let me see that. How did you come to have it?"

I rolled over on my side and handed it to him. "Da took it as payment from a customer a long time ago. When I showed some interest in it, he says, he gave it to me as a toy, and I've been experimenting with music ever since."

My little silver flute was made in two parts and heavier than it appeared. He ran his handkerchief through the length of the tube, then polished the mouthpiece a bit. "Nice. Well cared for."

Almost carelessly, he began a sweet song with perfect breath control.

I couldn't have produced such a tone on threat of banishment, and I couldn't tell when he took a breath. The music poured forth without pause. Somehow, Raz made the proper tones continue while he drew in as well as when he blew out the air. Perfectly joined notes, each sliding into the next as though it were the only possible next note, inevitable and flowing. I let the music wash over me as I closed my eyes against the stars.

Listening, I saw the meadow the composer had meant, and then the young girl who went into it to meet her secret lover, and then the beautiful lover who came in and laid her down on the meadow flowers in the dew, and their sweet time together in the secret cool of the afternoon, and their heartbreak at their evening separation, and their pledge to come again on the next appointed day, and then the return to their normal lives, each nursing the sweet secret. All this happened without words, of course, as a dream the tune evoked, played out in my mind. I felt as if I were being majickally entranced. When Raz stopped, I felt as though he'd shown me a titillating picture. Judging from the burning in my skin, I had to be blushing all over.

At last I opened my eyes. He met my gaze and raised an eyebrow. To cover my real thoughts—surely he couldn't read them now, even as loud as they'd seemed to me—I asked the first question that came to mind. "Wherever did you learn that kind of playing?" It was the kind of dumb question people like the Widder asked as they twittered around a traveling bard, and it embarrassed me to have said it. "Why aren't you a minstrel, or a player in a troupe? You make music more beautiful than many I've heard at festivals."

"Well . . . I guess that's a fair question, Dulcinea." My name, made pleasing again. His eyes glittered. "I suppose you'll eventually ferret out most of my secrets, so I shan't make you wonder. For you alone, I shall relinquish my enshroudment of delitescence."

When I'd first noticed his liking for long and expensive words, I had become determined that I'd figure them out from the context rather than ask and appear a chowderhead. Sometimes I suspected he made them up, just to see if I'd ask. "Yes, please do tell."

That easy smile, warming me to my kneecaps. "I learned fluting right along with ciphering and reading, at my Daddoo's knee." He knitted his fingers behind his head and leaned back again. "My daddoo is a flutemage in Marwell. He used to travel with a troupe of players before I was born. He made and sustained the bardic scenery for the plays they put on." He sighed, presumably with the sweetness of nostalgia. "Since we boys came along, or at least all my life, he's made a living leading his ensemble of musicians at our tavern—that's what Mawmie's family does, runs the tavern. They haven't ever purely approved of the bardic calling, so . . . He still entertains a little, but now mostly he teaches and develops songs. Students travel from all over just to study with him." Raz glanced at me briefly, then looked away as though embarrassed; he must've felt he was boasting.

"You mean you gave up studying music with him just to learn practical majick from Da?" I couldn't fathom it. I just stared at Raz, dopey-faced.

His hooded gaze prevented me from discerning whether he was fabling or truthful. "What can I say? Like you, I wanted what

I couldn't easily reach. I flute for pleasure, but I've always wanted to be skilled as an alchemist."

This didn't ring true to me. Who would choose a boring life casting everyday household spells when he could make music and thrill crowds with its majickal visions? But I let it pass. "I wish we could have traded families." I was only halfway jesting.

"Maybe when you're grown you can come to Marwell and hear him." Raz glanced at me fondly—or maybe just indulgently.

My heart sank as I realized he, too, saw me as a mere child. "I am nearly grown."

He turned serious. "I can see you are. I only meant that you won't have to take your leave of home for some time yet. And so you're at an advantage over me. Younger people learn faster, didn't you know? You just learn all you can from your old Daddoo. A person can't have too many skills."

I agreed. I also heard his unspoken thoughts: stay with my old Da as much as I could while I still had him. Da was getting on in years, and I was still young, a surprise baby who had killed my Mawmoo being born kicking and "upside-down, ass-first, backwards." I'd always felt guilty and regretful about that, for obvious reasons.

"You're so right. If only a lifetime weren't half the length of time it takes to learn a craft." I rolled my eyes. "If only I knew exactly where my best talents lay."

"I ken some of them from right here." His voice was just loud enough to hear. I felt my hands start trembling. For some reason, I thought he might reach out to me, which thrilled me somehow, yet at the same time made my heart pound.

But then he said, "You're already playing fairly well, you know. And, as I said, progressing toward expertise as an alchemist and herbalist. Turning into quite a proper young lady."

I felt like a fool for misinterpreting his intentions. Covering my embarrassment made me wry. "A young lady who hasn't even taken the first Rite of Wo—"

The blood rushed into my cheeks as I realized what I'd almost said aloud. I'd forgotten, flustered with attraction as I was, that Raz was still virtually a stranger; our acquaintance was barely a quartermoon old, yet I felt I'd known him all my life. That I could talk to him about anything. Why was I being such a dunce? I had enough sense to know one did not discuss that kind of thing in polite company.

"Taken on the first of the Robes of a majicker, I mean," I finished, knowing it had to sound as lame to him as it did to me.

Raz didn't seem to notice my slip, or he chose not to acknowledge it. "Ah, Dulcinea. Don't rush to be finished with your childhood. It ends soon enough, and is regretfully lost, I can attest to that." He sounded thoughtful again. "Many's the time I've wished I didn't have to be the grown-up, that I still had Da and Mawmie always watching over and taking care of me." He shook his head, grinning ruefully. "But why am I going maudlin? Pay all of that nonsense no mind. I only meant you were right to appreciate your youth, and your Da."

Raz smiled. I felt warm down to my stockingtoes.

But then I took his full meaning, and terror at the images briefly struck my belly. Anytime I thought about losing Da, it twisted my stomach. I swallowed hard. "When I was mewling and puking age—as early back as I can remember, anyway—I used to think that if I didn't learn anything useful, then Da'd have to stay alive to do it all for me. Now I know better." I thought of old Chiro, happy until the end of his days, although he was wrinkled and nearly toothless. I sighed. "What I could have known already if I hadn't been a little fool! I only wish I hadn't wasted so much learning time."

Raz must've read it in my face, for he only said, "Patience brings all things."

"Yes." I didn't trust my voice to do a longer speech.

He lay back, pillowing his head on his interlocked fingers behind. "Pray, and trust the Lord to bring about your true profession and purpose in life, in good time."

"I do. Every night." I meant it.

"People do have second trades, you know. You're just getting a start on both at once." He grinned at me, showing his uneven teeth. For some reason, that smile made me feel happy.

"Thanks." I did intend to learn a secondary trade, even one as frivolous as fluting. Someday—even if not until the apothecary was mine, and I had shop assistants I could trust—I could go find a master, maybe even Raz's daddoo, and apprentice myself. The better I already was, I figured, the more likely they'd take me. "'Til then, I'll just practice a lot, and learn as many songs as I hear." I managed a smile and hoped my other longings were my own secret. I felt like the girl in his tune, returning home with her hidden life stashed away in her heart's treasure chest.

"If you can learn all the pieces you hear, you'll be doing something no one has ever done before." He looked at me and chuckled. "Why, with that kind of mind, you could be both a flutemaster and a Gold-Robe Mage by the time you're my age."

"You needn't be snarky about it." That kind of remark made me feel like a six-year-old. And so did my figure, for that matter. I crossed my arms over my disadvantaged breasts and hugged close my embarrassment; I wasn't a good sport at being mocked.

"No, I really mean it. You might be the one to discover how to combine the two majicks and make a new, more powerful majick." He winked, and for a moment I feared he would reach out and tweak my cheeks the way aged Mistress Cockrum in town did to everyone under twenty planting-seasons. He thought of me as a child, I could tell that, but he still treated me with respect, as he would an intellectual equal. I loved him for that—loved him even harder.

"Oh, go on. Do you really think there is such a majick, waiting to be discovered?"

He caught my amazement and grinned, ducking his head. "Why? Do you think you've already got some ideas on how you're going to do it?"

I went along with him this time. "Oh, positively. But I won't be ready to start tonight, and not any time soon. I meant someday, I'd just like to try."

"I knew what you meant."

We shared a companionable silence, watching the stars spin in the murk overhead, holes in the velvet-lined jewel-box lid on our universe that revealed the Heavenly glory-light just beyond. Presently he began again to tootle softly on my flute, which I'd laid down between us. I turned on my side, raising myself on one elbow, to watch his fingering. He saw I was learning, and nodded, looking pleased.

"You can teach yourself a goodly amount by watching and listening, you know. Listen to your own playing. And hear the tune you want to reach before you begin, in your head." He showed me the fingering for the first (he called it the "A") theme to the piece he'd just played, and soon I was tweeting it tentatively out. It didn't hurt that I could pretty much remember and pick up a piece I'd heard. I could visualize the meadow and the lovers here and there in snatches, but it wasn't a rolling picture show the way Raz's was, like proper flutestory.

"Mine doesn't sound like yours."

I must have looked sulky, for he reproved me. "Don't pout; it makes you homely." He winked. "If you expect to master something in one go, you'll always be disappointed." He tootled the "B" theme, and I copied him. Accurately, it seemed.

"See! You can do this." He nodded, as though the matter were settled. "A bit of applying yourself, and a smidgen more patience."

"I'll try." I heaved a heavy sigh from my shoulders, thinking of the practicing ahead.

"You can learn it. To start with, just get the notes and rests, and watch your rhythm, because it's nigh-unto impossible to unlearn something you've committed to memory incorrectly. Then I'll help you work on your dynamics. You know, playing soft or loud." I knew that gave the tune character. "More will come as you develop an interpretation. But memorize the tune first; that won't take so long."

"Oh, sunrise-sure it won't." I knew I had much to learn about producing a tone sweet as his with my breath and tongue, and about varying soft and loud in the music; all my melodies seemed the same volume, namely screechy and loud. "Maybe by then my hair will even have grown out."

He reached over and tousled it, throwing red curls into my eyes. My heart somersaulted and my nape went gooseflesh; I trembled so that I could hardly reach up to wipe the hair out of my eyes. "It looks fine, better already."

He smiled, and I felt funny in my stomach. "I have to get inside and to bed." What a dumb thing to say. I thanked him again and scurried in, imagining I could feel his eyes on my retreating figure. Especially the too-generous posterior I'd reputedly gotten from Mawmoo's side, like all of her sisters, but with which Da was also afflicted. I whispered a quick prayer to Saint Alyncia about that, then quickly added the more demure and devout wish that I wasn't tempting Raz into any kind of sin in his heart.

Impossible, I reassured myself as I passed the looking-glass in the hallway. I was flattering myself with that notion. He was merely being friendly to the child of his new master. A sensible person, was Raz Songs. I hoped I could remain as sensible as he about our new association.

# # #

The poultice business doubled in the next moonsphase. My Da was ecstatic. Until the day after inventory at the end of the moon.

Daddoo came into the workroom ranting. "Hell's bells. Damnation! That jackal's son. The cunning double-faced sneak. The worst kind of rascal." He looked at me with fire-jewel eyes. "He's stealing!"

I started, scattering the flaxseed I had so carefully weighed out for stuffing the pillows of ache-easing and fluid-drawing that Raz had shown me how to make. A stickyfinger? In this village?

"Who?" I double-blinked and tried to make my freckled face look child-innocent. Sometimes looking younger than one's actual seasons proves advantageous. Not often, but sometimes.

"You know who I mean. Your sneaky friend. My precious new apprentice." Daddoo scowled. "He uses too much to pack those poultices for the customers he takes. Furthermore, he knows they suspect, and they're taking advantage." He started pacing around me, making a claustrophobically close circle.

"Oh, surely not." My role as placater was not a comfortable one, but I had years' worth of practice. "He only means to make them eager to shop here again, Da." I knew our customers had, within the last fortnight or so, begun to betray a preference for Raz, asking him to make up their poultices and do the wardings, but I hadn't realized Daddoo had noticed—or would care so much.

"We're also missing two sacks of orange-feather, and I can't explain how low we're getting on talcmetal." He whirled on me. "Would you know anything about that?"

I made my expression as blank as I ever had.

He searched my face a moment with his gaze, but apparently found the nothing that I had carefully put there. "I didn't think you did, lass. That sneak. He's probably up there in his room, under my own roof, majicking away with my rare and valuable stores of orange-feather."

I suddenly had a mental picture of Raz teaching me, and of us packing the sweetherb packets that had sold so well. The collar of my tunic was suddenly tight, uncomfortable and scratchy, and it was all I could do to keep my finger from running around inside of it.

Daddoo stomped round the room for a while. "I'm going threadbare keeping this store honest, and now this. What a waste of supplies, and right under my nose. The boy can see we're on the edge of hungry every month, can't he?" We weren't, but we certainly weren't wealthy, either. "What kind of thanks is that to show to your new majick-master?"

Not for the first time, I wished I had a Mawmoo.

Other people's mawmoos calmed down their daddoos when they got into an uproar like this. All I could do was continue chopping the sweetherb stalks and murmuring "Yessir," praying he'd calm down before he hurt himself.

Finally he stopped ranting and pacing, and put his palm gently on top of my head. "You're a good girl, Dulcinea. And I know you enjoy having that young scamp around. He serves the purpose of a cousin, I reckon, or the kinfolk you never knew, what with your mama's family all gone." He shook his head wearily. "Over the years, I've thought about that. I've regretted many times our decision to settle over here when you were born, but we were already away from my people because of the war front." I knew all this, but I let him moo and moan, knowing he was calming himself down. "Ah, it's true, gal; you need a friend. A role model other than just your creaky old Daddoo. I see you two are fond of one another, and it's helped you, as well. You might even have learned a few manners and a little music from him."

The last part he added rather grudgingly. I hadn't realized he knew about our flute sessions, but now I was sure he'd heard us at least some of the time. I grinned sheepishly, merely nodding to everything he said.

"So. For your sake, I'm going to put up with him a bit longer. But these antics of his must cease." He waggled his forefinger at me; I tried to look meek and obedient. "As they say, 'fine words don't butter the bread on either side,' and I'd add they don't put it on the table, either. Maybe if I talk to the lad, I can wedge a little sense into his head under all that fine and fancy hair." He socked his fist into his other palm. "If he'd just quit wasting supplies, I'd have no quarrel with his other different ways. But I'll brook no more waste. All his newfangled, citified ideas about customer satisfaction be damned." Da maintained that we were the only useful apothecary this side of the mountains, and this village should be glad to have him.

I suppressed a grin. I could only hope Raz would soon learn to pinch the bottom of a sack at least a bit before loading it, and crumple the paper patterns before cutting the fine silks we sold for mages' robes and the lengths of lace-linen for ceremonial dress. He needed to know the little tricks of the merchant's trade, not in order to cheat good customers the way some unfair wagon-vendors did, but to be used only when times got tough, or when Da began putting on the poor-boy act. And to be profusely apologetic and quickly correct the "error" if caught, of course. I'd ease Raz into it. What did it really hurt? Everyone knew most merchants kept one surreptitious thumb on the scale; it was simply part of life. And it'd make Da happy.

# # #

Yet the trouble continued. The real problem was not the merchandise, but the customers. They liked Raz, some of them more than they liked Da, truth be told; and they weren't bothering to hide their new favoritism. If only old Widder Pidgeketl hadn't needed a Warding to reconsecrate her house, Raz might never have had to leave us.

But one day Widder Pidgeketl came in, intent on finding Raz, whilst Raz was busy in the workroom titrating mell-weed distillant. Problem was, she hung back at first and made it too obvious, putting off Da's increasingly insistent queries of could he help her, what was she looking for, was everything all right at home, had she brought something back that displeased her. Finally she came out and said it.

"Thank you kindly, Alchemist Brown, but I honestly came in to get your Raz here to come out and do a warding on my house. The other'n has wore off or something, probably because of the new roof and all the repairs on the house this season. The mischievous fairies keep getting in, they do, and my daughters are havin' dreams again. And all I need is him to come do like he done before. Worked like a charm—what I mean is, a charm's what I need."

"Well, why didn't you say so?" Daddoo grabbed his cloak. "Mind the store, Dulcinea. I can do that for ye, Widder—been warding since I was a boy my daughter's age."

"Oh, n-no, no, no," the Widder stammered. "Please don't trouble yourself." He looked at her questioningly and she blurted, "No need for the master of the place to do it, when it's something his assistant can do."

I looked on guiltily from behind the counter, biting the inside of my jaw and shifting nervously from foot to foot.

Despite her protests, Daddoo pressed doggedly on. "There's no cause for concern, good lady. It is, after all ,my honored duty to secure the village. I wouldn't think of having you do without the best of advice." He'd got his cloak and cap on before she could make herself speak up again.

Now her arms were crossed in front of her ample chest. Blocking his way, she swelled herself out by sheer force of will until she seemed like a fairly good barrier. "Goodfellow Brown. I'm sorry to have to tell you again, but I insist that you send Raz with me. He pleased me last time, and I'm intending to have him do the very same again. Isn't the customer the best judge of her own needs?"

He blinked. "Why, I suppose so, under normal circumstances. But in this case, I—what's that you said? Last time?" Obviously Da hadn't known Raz ever went out on calls.

I ran and fetched Raz to the front, hoping he could spirit her away while I found something to distract Da. Raz and I arrived to find her backing up and dancing around Da, trying to make her refusal sound firm, but polite.

She finally perched herself on our spelling hassock—I caught Da silently wincing at the disrespect—and tapped her walking-stick twice for attention. "I really prefer to use Raz, thank you. I'll just wait for him to finish up whatever he's doing, if you don't mind."

Da deflated like a pin-punctured air bladder. Raz immediately handed me the tangle of items he was holding and gathered his traveling miscellany. He and the Widder squeezed through the front door past Daddoo, who stared after them, dumbfounded. I wished again I had learned a spell of vanishing.

"I can't believe it," Da kept repeating as he wandered the shop, putting little things right here and there, brushing imaginary lint off bottletops. He looked at me with the hollowed-out gaze of a scorned suitor. "She actually prefers the boy to me."

He continued waiting on customers, but distractedly. I studiously scraped and measured and stuffed packages for everyone who came in, all the while avoiding Da's gaze.

When Raz got back, he apologized before he even hung up his cloak. But there was no settling it that way.

Da stepped to block Raz's path as Raz made for the back room. "What's the idea, taking over my services to my own customers behind my back?"

Raz blinked twice and cocked his head to one side. "Why, I can't bring to mind what you mean, sir. 'Tis true, I did go on a few calls in your stead when you were otherwise occupied here. But I thought I was aiding you." He blinked as innocently as a bottle-babe. "Is there anything wrong with honestly endeavoring to help your master in any way you can, to lessen his workload? Can you truly fault me for that?"

When Da didn't answer immediately, because he was too busy spluttering, Raz stepped closer. I thought he was about to punch a finger into Da's chest for emphasis, but luckily he didn't do it. "Moreover, if these goodwives enjoy my company, that is good for business, is it not? If they like for me to put some spice in their lives by joking with them, letting them make lolly eyes and flap their hands at me, saying, 'Oh, you flatter me, Raz,' where is the misdeed in that?"

They glared at each other, then at me. I sizzled inside like a snail trying to glide through hot ashes. I stood perfectly still so neither one would think I was taking sides.

Da picked up a commonplace book and length of twine-wrapped lead, flipped the notebook open to a fresh page, and scribbled. Raz folded his arms, waiting.

"Never do that to me again." Daddoo didn't look up from his cipherings. "Never do that to a man your senior. You should have learned that already, when you first became an acolyte at your first tutor's knee."

Raz ducked his head, just as if he were a little bit remorseful. "I swear, sir, I meant no disrespect. I accommodated a few of your loyal customers when asked, true, but that was merely to take some pressure off you, that was all." Raz flourished his sleeve in an elaborate gesture of concession. "Next time I shall refuse her."

"That's not what I meant!" Da's eyes flashed. "Just be certain she doesn't ask for ye again."

I glanced back and forth between their two dear faces, both wrinkled in anger. How could Raz both keep them from asking for him and do a good job?

But Raz said, "I will. I will do so. Thank you, sir."

Without responding, Da brushed through the curtain to the stockroom, still staring at his notes. Raz heaved a sigh and disappeared off into his room upstairs over the carriage-house. I didn't see Raz again for the rest of the day.

I was not privy to whatever lessons my Da gave to Raz in the ways of spellwork and herbalism and majicking, but I did judge that Raz wasn't the only one who needed to learn a bit of manners.

For a few days after the blowup, Raz wouldn't even look at either of us. I went on treating him normally. Eventually, after a few days of heavy silence, Da started speaking to him again. I was glad for the peace, but Raz didn't seem comfortable. Presumably the matter had been settled between them, but I wondered if other problems weighed on Raz's mind. Something he was hiding? Some shadow over his past?

I had sensed lately that Raz had come to us for reasons other than those he'd given. For one thing, Raz already knew more than he let on about preparing medicines and majicking materials. Even

I could tell that he already knew the answers to some of the questions he asked us, but I wasn't sure why he felt he had to hide some of his knowledge, unless he thought himself too advanced to be a mere aspirant. But then what was his real reason for coming here? And for staying so long?

Despite all our evening flute sessions, I never asked straight out. Maybe I should have, but I never did. I couldn't bear Raz to be angry with me. I was doubly overcome: by longings I couldn't or didn't want to name, whenever Raz was near; and, always, by a terrible craving for more skill on my flute, a deeper understanding of the music, the kind that only Raz could offer me. What's a girl to do?

CHAPTER THREE

I soon discovered why my back had been ailing, a dull ache that had kept me from sleeping and had hampered my sitting for extended periods on the stool behind our counter.

I didn't realize at first what was happening. I'd been troubled for a few days by a red rash across my forearms and the small of my back, aches and pains in my knees and elbows, swollen fingerjoints, occasional pinpricks of light behind closed eyelids, and some trouble falling asleep. Yet I hadn't connected the symptoms until a few nights after my birthday, when two bright, unbearable flashes of light behind my eyelids woke me from troubled dreams.

Another dazzling flash brought me fully awake. I sat up, blinking, expecting to find a lightning storm outside or a lantern in my face, but it was quiet and I was alone. My bedchamber was still perfectly dark, lighted only by the dim moonlight filtered through my curtains; Celeste was at quarter, and Lunette the follower scudded behind murky clouds. It was the quietest hour, halfway through the hours of the night.

I found myself scratching an irresistible itch on my leg. When I looked down, I saw I had been clawing my arms and back in my sleep until I'd bled on the freshly laundered bedsheets. The rash on my legs was so bad that when I checked it closely I found it was weeping, beads of fluid seeping slowly out of the worst of the mushy bumps. My stomach seized up with fear. What disease had come upon me in the night?

All at once something occurred to me. Each of the symptoms I'd suffered, taken together, might be characteristic of the impending development of majickal talents. My heart sped up a little. Maybe, as I'd anticipated for some time, I was finally maturing. I would soon know if I would manifest any majickal talents. Or was I imagining a connection where there was none?

I knew nothing else to do but go to Daddoo in private first thing in the morning. After dabbing some salve I kept in my nightstand on my bumps, I lay back and tried to relax. I tossed and turned, waiting for Daddoo's morning clatter in the kitchen downstairs, and finally fell into a fitful sleep just before dawn.

# # #

I interrupted Da just as he was recharging one of our globe-lights along the staircase wall. The glass globes provided the light throughout our residence as well as inside our shop. First he stopped the globe, which had slowed down so much that it hardly glowed as bright as a flash-tail bug, and plucked it out of its sconce. He held the ball between his palms just so, muttering proper words of power. Then he blew across the surface of the glass, as smoothly as the West Wind blows to billow sails across every sea. The tiny winking lightball inside grew gradually brighter; he set the globe a-spinning again above its sconce-mount, urging it along with his fingers just above the surface until it reached the proper speed. The amount of light each globe gave was relative to its speed, the faster the brighter. Da was obliged to recharge them this way about every fortnight, or they'd lose their spin and our interiors would gradually dim; I'd never seen him let them go dark.

This was one of the majicks I longed to learn. Only majickers had such light against the darkness, light that didn't depend on smoky torches or flickering candles that not only deposited soot on your walls and furnishings, but also could catch fire to your draperies or clothing the instant you were inattentive. Again I felt a burst of excitement, in anticipation of possibly developing some talent at last.

He finished speeding the last globe-lamp along our staircase wall before he turned to answer my worried entreaties. As I described my symptoms, he didn't quite look up at me, but he glanced sidelong so that I'd know he was listening. I was careful to draw no conclusions and make no references to majick, because I didn't want to influence his guesses. Digging my toe into the rug, for some reason unable to look him in the eye, I finally asked, "What do you make of it?"

"You know what this probably means, don't you, baby?" He reached up as though to ruffle my hair, but dropped his hand before actually touching me. He was rueful and tentative, and seemed almost reluctant to make contact with me. Finally he laid a hand on my shoulder. "I'm not making any guarantees, but this could be a precursor to majickwake, to my mind. Have you noticed anything else unusual?

People kept asking me that. Weren't these symptoms unusual enough? "No, Daddoo."

"It's nothing to worry about, of course. If that's all it is." He laid the back of his other hand across my forehead for a moment. "I don't think you have any fever. These aren't particular signs of illness, if they soon pass." He pulled me directly under one of the lights and examined the rashes closely. "It doesn't look like an infectious disease. Perhaps you got into something." He frowned. "I'll have Raz do the herbal work for a few days, and see if that clears it up. Does it pain you?"

"Sort of. I don't want to scratch it."

"Come along behind the counter, then."

I padded along behind him in my lapinette-lined slippers, rubbing my aching back with the knuckles of my right hand. Da jerked open several drawers in our largest apothecary chest before he found what he had come for.

"This should help." He gave me an herbal remedy—two, actually; one packet of large paper tea-bags (or that's how I thought of them, anyway, although they were packed with herbed cottony fluff instead of tea leaves) that he said would help ease the rash when dampened and laid across it, and one poultice, a large plaster that I should saturate with warm potion base and lay across my lower back to ease the cramps. That one I especially welcomed.

Da cleared his throat as I took the remedies from him. "About the other. The majickwake, I mean. If you do have other signs, you must come to me immediately."

My heartbeat sped up. This was scary, but exciting. "What kind of thing should I watch for, Da?"

"Any unusual manifestation, especially while you're doing a working or handling majickal preparations." Why couldn't anyone give me more details? "It's different for everyone."

Naturally. Nothing good can ever be easy.

"If I were you—" He broke off and restarted. "My advice is not to tell anyone about this, not even Raz. It should be a private matter between the two of us while we watch you. Discreetly."

I blinked. "Why must it be such a secret?"

Da cracked his meaty knuckles. "If you develop powers as Raz predicted—even a fraction of those he listed when he was reading you. . . ."

"I know, Da." I had already worried about this. "The idea of some of those powers scared me a little."

Closing one eye, he rubbed his beard. "You cannot afford to be mistaken for a diabolical witch instead of a natural talent. Especially if your power is great. While one may practice folk remedies and natural majick like ours quite openly, sorcery is another matter entirely."

I knew it.

Da looked earnestly at me. "You must let me advise you. It's one thing to go among the public to bless dwellings and put protections on things, and quite another to—well, to use other majicks. Sometimes we have to conceal powers that are not commonly held, because the church and state might surmise that you draw on diabolical forces. Of course, you know enough to tell the difference. But not everyone does."

I could quote the Majickers' Tome verbatim. Natural majick was "the use, for benevolent reasons, of natural phenomena and possibilities, usually by the manipulation of material components supplemented by suggestion or incantation, to produce rare and unusual effects by methods neither superstitious nor diabolical." The energy came from a natural source called the Web of Majick, which circled the world with lines of force in all directions, the same invisible lines of force that migrating birds followed when they sensed the approach of the cold weather and left mountainous Marwell for the milder valleys of Ladenia. Like the globe lights, this power-web was accessible to talented majickers only, and there were strict moral and physical limits to the amount which could be drawn for use within a given time. Although some people believed all natural philosophy was actually majicking, it wasn't; for practical household works, we merely gathered special items known to have energy potential and converted that potential to majickal energies. Conversely, a majicker had to take care that no one mistook practical workings for sorcery, especially if the results resembled diabolical majick in the effects produced. I'd memorized that passage ages ago, but only now did the words actually unscramble themselves into advice applicable for living.

Da cleared his throat. "You can see why we don't parade our talents around. Even by accident, which can easily happen if you are just coming into your powers."

"I understand, Daddoo." I shook my head. "We're probably imagining things. I have really had no mystical signs at all."

"This may well be a false alarm." He smiled and patted my hand reassuringly. "We'll have to wait and see. You may have simply developed an allergy to one of the herbs, and hence the rash." He still seemed ill at ease. "Everything else all right?"

"Yes, I guess."

"Good, good." He turned and busied himself with rearranging the shelves, not looking back at me. "I expect it'll bother you at first, if you do come into some powers. We'll deal with that should the need arise." He harrumphed a couple more times, never meeting my gaze. "If this rash and the pains don't go away in a day or so, come tell me. Let me check you tonight to be sure the remedy's proper." He met my gaze at last. "Need anything else from me?"

"No. I'll go take my remedies and have a mug of hot tea with honey. And thank you, Daddoo."

Daddoo could still fix everything in my life.

Well, most things, anyway.

# # #

My birthday came all too quickly. I'd planned all year for our special celebration.

After attending the brief Colinsday ceremonies in the town square with Da and Raz—this year I had far fewer regrets to put on my mental list than last year, but I had more misdeeds and sins of omission to confess than ever before, and I couldn't stop fidgeting as we meditated on Saint Colin's ancient sacrifices for the freedoms we enjoyed in Ladenia, so I felt briefly guilty about my lack of devotion as the ceremony kicked off a week of religious observances— I spent the rest of the morning doing the last of my marketing.

Back home, I disappeared upstairs to my room to put the finishing touches on the thank-you gifts I had for Da. I needed to work a little on the poem I planned to recite. I had made him a book of my handmade paper bound in birchbark for writing his receipts or notes, a packet of lace-trimmed linen handkerchiefs, and several silken tassels for his keys. I'd even made tassels for Raz, although it wasn't strictly necessary. But because he'd taught me and helped me grow this year, I wanted to show my respect and appreciation to him as well.

On impulse, I tucked into Raz's gift a hankie out of my collection of silk fancies; I never used the things, and Raz loved to be gaudy. Even as I wrapped the package, I hoped Raz didn't misunderstand the gesture. I knew that in Marwell they did things completely upside-down: it was an odd Marwellian custom to give the birthday celebrant gifts, instead of allowing the person who had already been given the gift of life to reciprocate with poems, recitations, expressions of thanks, and token presents. I thought our practice made eminently better sense; every year, I couldn't wait to tell Da all the things that he'd taught me or helped me with during the previous year, and to renew my thanks to him for giving me life and a proper upbringing.

After wrapping all my gifts, I went down into the kitchen and shooed Da out, warning him to stay away while I prepared our birthday feast. On tonight's menu was a pork loin stuffed with dried fruit, carrots in butter sauce, snap beans, yeast rolls, pudding with currants, and honey mead to drink. And, of course, a birthday cake. It would make a fine dinner. I'd gathered up the special ingredients during the past couple of days, affording it easily because I'd socked away a little bit of change during each of my trips to the market for the last fortnight.

Around noontime, I had my elbows in the dough for the rolls. I'd proofed the yeast, and I was checking it for rising.

"What shall I do about lunch?" Da poked his head in with a twinkle in his eye.

I was ready for him. Handing him a basket containing the fixings for several sandwiches, a round of hard cheese, and some almost-too-ripe fruit I'd managed to scrounge up, I said, "Go on a picnic in the shop. You don't want to overeat or you'll ruin your fancy dinner."

He winked at me, because this meal had been part of our yearly ritual for as long as I had been old enough to cook. "Well, be sure you fix a decent supper for us. We're having to do all your work today, you know."

"That serves you right, and now you'll know how hard I have to work every day. Now go on, get." I grinned back at him as he retreated toward the shop.

I had the table linens on and candles lighted before I called them in to supper, a little later than I'd hoped. My centerpiece of flowers from the garden was a trifle wilted, but the food was all piping hot, coming out just right. I'd made them wait until I was completely ready, the table set with the pottery that we sold to the wealthy and never used ourselves except when I insisted on pulling it out.

I walked into the keeping room where they were working on some papers, probably the store's books, with pen and ink. They both looked up expectantly. I thought I heard Raz's tummy rumble. Suppressing a smile, I curtseyed to the floor. "Honored guests. Please come to table. I welcome you to my birthday celebration."

As they entered the dining room, both of them broke into wide grins, settled at the table, and spread their napkins across their laps. Da asked the blessing, and I noticed that Raz kept his head properly bowed. He caught me peeking, and winked.

"It has smelled heavenly all day in the shop, Dulcinea." Raz gestured grandly with his spoon, a special silver piece out of his own pocket. "I have had to chase away customers who wanted only to purchase whatever it was that was baking."

"Even though our kitchen is in the very back of the house?" I winked back.

We feasted and laughed as they told of the day's events and I related my small crises in the kitchen. At last we were finished with all but the dessert.

"These victuals were superb." Da leaned back, patting his stomach contentedly. "I've trained you as well as any wife, if I do say so myself." He looked over at me, beaming with pride, and I at last felt he thought of me as a grown-up lady.

Raz's belly protruded as I had never seen it do. He rubbed it, saying, "Your daddoo's not merely swelled with fatherly pride. Good fare, Dulcinea Brown."

I stood at the table's head. "I would like, sirs, to present you with my thanks for your help this year." First I recited my poem to Da, telling all about the things he'd done for me, and bowed. "Sir, thank you for giving me a fine upbringing." I presented him with his gifts. Was he blushing, or just reddened from the warmth in the room from the cooking and the company?

Then I gave Raz his tassels and handkerchief. He looked surprised, but seemed pleased as he accepted them. He put the hankie in his pocket, arranging it just so. "It matches my cloak perfectly,

Dulcinea. Whenever I use it, I shall think of you." For some reason that made me blush, and I turned my face away quickly.

I rushed to the oven to pull out the cake. I'd kept it warm; it was full of dried apricots and frosted with apricot jam. It was heavenly.

I kept thinking Da would mention the rite of Womanhood that I now qualified to receive, but he said nothing about it. Nor did I; I wanted nothing to ruin the specialness and camaraderie of the evening.

# # #

I continued growing fonder of Raz, while learning by stages to hide my foolish and inappropriate reactions towards him. I couldn't be sure, but I believed Raz saw me as a sort of younger sister. He continued to help me with my flute technique, showing me a couple of techniques for sounding two and three notes at once using your tongue and breath differently. He even gave me an old wooden whittle-flute he'd brought from home; it had eight holes and could blow several more notes, and was called an octarine or ocarina. I never could tell exactly which, because it was a Marwellian word, and its pronunciation was strange to my ears. I learned a crazy tune Raz had made up for it, and kept it tied on a cord on my belt next to my flute. At the end of every session, Raz always told me to keep at it, for someday I'd be able to make music-pictures almost as good as his own. It was nice of him to say that, but I never really believed it.

Then one day I noticed something that renewed my excitement and made me see the flute in a whole new way. It happened when I was out fluting in the barn. I'd climbed up to get away, to keep Raz and Da—especially Raz—from hearing me while I experimented. There were sure to be mistakes and screeches that they didn't need to hear.

Up in the hayloft, I practiced making up tunes and seeing what the fastest fingerings were for particular notes. Some fingerings were easier, but it was touchy not to overblow when I tried them. I usually ended up with a note a whole eight-notes above the one I had intended—or, worse, with a screech or hoot like an injured hooty-owl. I was just getting the hang of dynamics, the loud and soft, on a tune I had made up that I liked, a palindromic one that played the same forwards or reversed, when I noticed the mice fleeing the loft.

A swarm of them. Or a pack of them—whatever you call a bunch of mice, running like the ones in the nursery rhyme, scuttling away as quickly as I'd ever seen them. But why? They'd never feared me before. A quick check of the loft turned up no cats. I sniffed myself to see if I reeked of cat, though that seemed unlikely. Was my playing was so bad it hurt their ears?

I shrugged it off that first time, but I couldn't ignore it when it happened again the next day, and again the next. The following few days, I experimented whenever no one was around. I found that if I concentrated and played the kinds of tunes that seemed the right shape for the task—and I don't know how I knew what those were; each shaped tune was spontaneous, led by a kind of intuition that simply came to me as I tootled along and thought of various notes and chords—then while I played, things would happen. As I thought of effects, I could shape them in the air and then play them into being. I used a tune to untie my bootlaces, then figured out how to influence the path of ants coming out of their hill. I chased away several more mice, one and two at the time. Once I believed I had even brought my horses Tickie and Packy in from the fields, though I wasn't certain; for all I knew, it was actually my concentration on them that called to them so strongly. But the other things I was fairly certain about. I had caused them, or at least helped them along. I had done some flute illusions. No, real majick, it seemed. Real majick?

I wasn't sure whether or not to take this to Da as a proof of talent, at least not yet. The idea that this could be majick fascinated and enchanted me in one way, but in another it worried me mightily. Had I a special talent for the flute, as I'd like to think?

Was I truly doing something unusual, reaching another dimension that not every street entertainer could reach? Or was I just so inexperienced that I was overly impressed with my own accomplishments?

I hadn't thought to ask Raz what kind of breakthroughs I might make as I gained more skill. For all I knew—since I wasn't, unlike Raz, the son of a minstrel, but merely the daughter of a quiet, bookish seamstress and an impulsive red-headed apothecary—this could be laughably simple stuff. Perhaps everyone who fluted gradually accumulated more bardic skills. These tricks might be part of their showmanship, what they used to help people make picture-stories in their minds. And the more I thought about it, the more likely I considered this the explanation.

The dilemma was how I could subtly make Raz disgorge the answer. There was no one else to ask, and I hated to ask him out-right—in fact, I flatly refused. "I'd rather remain ignorant than have him laugh at me," I told a stray cat as it leapt onto the hayloft ladder; it looked at me blankly until I tootled it a go-away, and it scampered off through the barn. I'd hate to let Raz know I hadn't expected to learn—er, whatever this knack was called. I'd feel like a fool if he cracked his smug little smile at me. He'd puff out his chest like the big city fellow explaining to the hayseedy farm girl what coins were, and I didn't like that, didn't deserve it. What a vexation it was to have wish come true in an unexpected, wonky form.

I sighed as I pulled the drying-cloth through my flute and put it away in its velvet carry-bag. I threaded the loop of its drawstring through my underbelt, where I kept the case between my under-muslins and my tunic for safekeeping. As I climbed down out of the hayloft, I strove not to be too impressed with myself.

Clearly I would have to find out somehow what types of developments I should expect. What might be the next surprise, for mercy's sake? Perhaps music could do many things, unusual things that would frighten me if they started happening unexpectedly. Saints, I might wet myself if I suddenly levitated into the air or turned a rope into a serpent.

I'd have to tell Da about that, if it happened. I giggled at the very notion.

But I wouldn't want to claim I was majicking and have them get all excited, then watch my tricks and dutifully shake their heads, all the while secretly laughing up their sleeves at my naivete. I would have to consider this a bit more before I brought it to either of them.

The dilemma was still on my mind when I sat down in our supply room to do some chores I'd been putting off. I was musing on how to bring the subject up with Raz without risking sounding like a dunderhead (I could imagine his "Why, you mean you didn't realize that was commonplace, Dulcinea?") when his voice floated into my mind. It took me a moment to realize it was reality and not part of my reverie. I was startled, but I cloaked it with a false stretch of my cramped arms. My elbows creaked audibly.

"You know what to do with those, don't you?"

I looked up as casually as I could manage. Raz, who'd sneaked up behind me, stirred with his forefinger the little pile of moonjewels I'd made, scattering them across the polished wood. I was busy drilling through the roundest ones with my charged needle to make stringable beads. I played along, played dumb. Sometimes I'd learn something interesting that way. "I'm going to sell them, of course."

He gave me an amused glance. "Don't say 'of course,' dear. Everyone knows it really means 'as any jackass can plainly see.'"

"I notice that hasn't stopped you from using the phrase."

He grinned.

I crossed my arms. "You figure you have a better suggestion for using these stones?"

"Actually, I do." He swung his leg over a stool and perched, his hands grasping the wooden seat's edge. "Take some for yourself and wear them. They'll help you in all ways, especially at night. They assist your natural senses. Night vision, night sounds, all of it."

"I've never heard of them having such properties."

"It's said all over Marwell."

"Oh." That meant it was probably a myth.

"Then there are the other effects I've discovered, ones that aren't nearly so obvious. But utterly wonderful." He waited, and I knew he wanted me to wring the information out of him. I decided to continue playing indifferent.

"Well, I appreciate the suggestion, but I think not. Da wants to see some profit this quartermoon, and I shouldn't eat into it by keeping pretties for myself."

He shrugged. "Suit yourself. But if you do hang on to a few. . . ." He shook his head, grinning. "What's the use? You aren't superstitious."

I broke down. "Yes, I am. A little. And you have me curious. Besides, you do know about it for real—you know so much lore." I knew Raz couldn't resist flattery. "I've figured folks were buying these for some reason, but I never paid any mind to what that purpose might be. Go ahead and tell what I should do." I gave him my best ignorant-girl look.

Raz gathered a handful of the opalescent beauties, smooth and round and glowing with a subtle inner light. He let them flow through his long, delicate fingers back into my intake basket. "All right, I shall. You must first activate them. You know how to charge your moonjewels, don't you?"

I resisted making a pun on paying for things by installment versus having the coin. "Just how is that done, O Wise Master?" I didn't mind letting him know he was a little snotty.

He opened his arms expansively. "Lay them out on a smooth silk and put it on the windowsill, some night in the full of the moon Celeste, to capture her energy. That will increase their grounding. Enable their powers, if you will."

Even I knew that. "Then what?"

He paused for effect. "They're delicious with milk, or mixed in oatmeal with syrup poured over for dinner." He smiled his rabbitty smile and wrinkled his nose.

I cuffed him on the arm. "Be serious."

He swung one foot off the stool's crosspiece, crossed his arms over his chest, and settled himself back. "All right. First, measure a length of silken cord or leather thong that will comfortably slip around your neck. Wait for the night of the full moon in Celeste— that's best; at least one of the moons should be full. A double-full moon will mean twice the charging, of course. Lunette isn't as strong as Celeste, but you'd be surprised if you devoted yourself to studying the little follower moon. She bestows her own subtle powers on those who believe."

He waited for me to nod, then continued. "With your hands and heart under the beam of the full moonlight, tie thirteen knots in the cord, evenly spaced along its length. Between every two knots, slip on a bead. As you knot and string, think of capturing the energy of the moon in your hands. Tie the cord into a loop when you are done, and leave it in the moonlight. Before sunrise, gather the necklace into a silk bag. Keep it in a dark place till the dark of the moon; it should be the new moon in the dominant moon from your moonbath. Then wear the cord around your neck, and its powers shall surely become available to you."

"And what powers are those? How do I call upon them?" I gave him the questioning look I'd perfected on Da.

He gathered his long hair between his smooth hands and shook the snarls out, then swept it back over his left shoulder. "They will make themselves known soon enough. Why not try it, and then come discuss with me your findings." He got up and ruffled my hair with one hand, scooping up a handful of my completed beads with the other, and ducked out of the workroom, deftly sidestepping all my majickal webbing with nary a spark.

"Hey!" I felt obligated to shout after him, but actually I was grateful for the mock theft, because it helped me not to think about the feelings electrifying my skin from his touch. I needed to stop thinking about that. Ever.

I made the rest of the usable stones into beads, then at the last minute slipped a baker's dozen into my pocket. I knew I had a length of silken cord around somewhere. Not that I ever intended for Raz to know I'd made up a silly old lucky necklace. But I was curious. I couldn't wait to try out the working and see what happened. If anything, I reminded myself. If anything.

CHAPTER FOUR

My Daddoo has always loved to sing. In the early morning, at the edge of dawn, we usually checked our inventoried stock just before opening the store, and he serenaded me, or we sang together. I fitted my voice around his in harmony as best I could if I couldn't match his pitch; my range didn't approach his two octaves. His sonorous baritone, so different from his normal speaking voice, resonated and echoed against all the hard surfaces: polished shelves, glass jars, and silver bottles.

"At eee-ven-tide, when the wind blows East, and the birds rise to their nests, la ta . . . our private starrrrs wink at us, and the da-da-dum. . . ." Daddoo never could remember all the words, though he had the tune. "I'll always remember the way you loooook, how we aaarrrre, to-night—"

I harmonized as he alternately sang and rolled R's, and we hummed when he was too lazy to invent words to substitute for the ones he'd forgotten. Together we worked until we had all the shelves dusted and marked, and all the goods sorted and replaced in their proper places. We finished just in time, too, for the sun was all the way up. It shafted sneakily through the spattered windowpanes to reveal escaped dust motes floating all above my newly organized shelves. Raz would be down soon, decked out in his purple apprentice's robes and covering his frequent yawns with the wide funnel sleeves.

Da reached for his cloak and cap. "I'll be back shortly. First I'm off to market. Then I've got a warding." He shot a dark look back at the storeroom, where Raz would soon be making up flaxseed pillows. "For once, that rascal hasn't stolen a customer. My oldest patrons still know better, mind you. I'll do this job up

brown, and they'll come to see what knot-heads they've been acting. . . ." He was still muttering about it to himself as he banged
out the front door.

Daddoo never returned "shortly" or even "directly" when he
went into town. He loved to dawdle, taking several hours to do his
marketing and visiting. I knew it was up to me to mind the store
today. Up to me and Raz, I corrected with a little thrill. My feelings for Raz had only intensified as the moons wore on. Now,
sometimes, when we two were in close quarters, I tingled all over.
It was becoming more and more challenging to hide my physical
reactions, as I knew I must.

Dame Trudgeon arrived shortly after Da's departure. She
clucked her tongue as she ran her gloved finger across the top of
the stacked glass balls just outside the window, the green and red
water-filled globes that signified our status as a registered apothecary.
Examining the dust she'd dislodged, she sent me a significant glance.
"One is judged by how clean one's storefront is kept, you know.
Good morning to you, Dulcinea Brown."

I fought off the urge to stick out my tongue and smiled instead. "Come in, good lady. I am just finishing up your order."
She was finally marrying some Duke or another; I never did know
why she had me do the floral, when she could have hired some
fancy herbalist from Lad City. Da was horribly puffed up when he
found out. I had made an arm drape for her aisle-walk, all white
flowers bundled into a floral message: white roses, white glads,
white stocks, and long-stemmed white strawdots, all wrapped up
and down their long stems with wide white ribbon. Bundled in was
a lengthy string of herbs, arranged to ensure the couple's future fertil-
ity and wealth, braided into a fancy chain and trailing down.

Even she couldn't resist it, and scurried over to catch up a
handful of the ribbon-tails and let them flow through her gnarled
fingers. "Ah, that's what I had in mind. Though you're obviously
still untrained, you're talented in a primitive way despite it,
Dulcinea Brown." Coming from her, this was high flattery. She
snapped her gaze up to meet mine. "And when are you to be

pledged in marriage yourself, young lady? It seems to me about high time, it does."

"I haven't even thought of taking a husband." I knew I would shock her by inverting the usual phrase. She proved me right by raising her unruly eyebrows a notch. I cocked my head and smiled sweetly. "I'm deciding whether I want to be apprenticed, actually. And to whom." I rather enjoyed the way the Dame's brows ratcheted up higher every time I said something outrageous. A muffled cough came faintly from the stockroom.

"By all God's little frogs and fishes!" She spluttered for a moment, then found words. "My stars, child. I must speak to your father, and soon. He thinks he's far ahead of us all, but he's got rocks under his cap. Imagine, teaching a girl to mind the shop and work up potions instead of learning what all a girl should learn." She waved a hopeless hand over the bundles on the countertop as I gathered up the rest of her household's standing order, stacking it in front of her and nodding politely. "I imagine you know the rudiments of keeping house, but little else about real life. What I want to know is, when is that man going to do something about teaching you the feminine wiles and wisdoms? When will you stop wearing the tunic-and-pinafore of a youngling and step into the cinched waists of the woman that you have become?" She rolled her eyes and waggled her fat crooked fingers. "I cannot believe you haven't even started putting your hair up. It's shameful what he's done to your head." I didn't correct her impression of whose handiwork had fashioned my coif. "And look at the condition of your clothes! You're obviously not one for mending and sewing, though I shan't say I expect you to learn the needle with no womenfolk to teach you. And that's completely aside from the problem of your personal cleanliness." She tsked.

I clamped my lips shut between my teeth to trap the retort that'd almost escaped. I might have the dust of the shop on me, but I was basically bathed. I certainly wasn't a dirt-under-nails, nor was I urchin-filthy. And I knew I didn't reek of cheap scented waters, the way she always did.

Heedless of my reaction—which was surely obvious; I felt my face burning all the way down to my breastbone—she carried on her tirade. "You poor child, with no woman in the household, and not even a nanny to teach you about—" She coughed. Evidently, she'd barely stopped herself from saying something awful, judging from the look on her face. Then she huffed up, straightening her stooped old spine as best I'd ever seen her. "Well. Suffice it to say Hector Brown had better get a sensible woman to talk to you about a certain *something*"—her voice italicized the word in the air between us—"before it suddenly happens, and scares you to death."

"I'm sure he'll take care of anything that comes up." I had to grin, thinking to myself how ironic it was for her to bring up that particular matter; what would she think if she knew the very thing was going on in secret right that moment. Maybe it was in my aura, something in the air telling even the customers that not only was I physically a mature woman, but I'd also had the first sign of becoming a real majicker. "Will you be needing anything else to-day, good lady?"

"No, that's all." She scrabbled in her pouch for her coin-bag. "But heed me, child." She looked at me hard. "You tell your father to find some woman to go over the—the *facts* with you, and soon. Else you'll be in danger of coming of age without the Rite, and you know what happens then." She paused. "Why, it's the same as going out and shouting for the Evil Eye."

My heart hammered in my breast. "I don't believe in all that." I managed to say it without choking, though my throat tightened up. "Only those without faith would take such a thing seriously. We trust the Lord to attend to our needs and protect us, just as we ask Him to in prayer." I hoped I could muster a spiritually superior glance of disdain for her. I passed to her all her wrapped parcels in exchange for the silver she'd stacked on the countertop. In spite of my conscious effort, my hands shook with agitation. "Da says that's just superstition."

"Superstition?" She spat into her palm. Three times. "Never say that aloud again, child! I swear I cannot fathom what Hector has in his mind." My eyes must have grown big as dinner-plates. She took advantage and leaned closer, across the worn countertop wood. "Mark me, girl. He'd better do something for you, and be quick about it. Or some of this 'superstition' he doesn't believe in might coil around his legs and bite him in the—" She broke off. "In the hindquarters. *Then* let him sit and say, 'It's all superstition!'" She glared at me, then at something over my shoulder, before she hugged her parcels to her. "Good day. And remember what I've said." She banged out the door, still muttering to herself; I imagined she was repeating some sort of anti-curse charm.

I felt Raz's presence over my shoulder before I actually looked to confirm he was there. He must have been the Something that Dame Trudgeon had graced with her parting glare. "So." I managed to make my tone of voice light-hearted, if a bit shaky. "How much of that little display did you get treated to?"

His gentle hands fell consolingly on my shoulders from behind. He began squeezing lightly, obviously intending to relax me, rather than increase my tension, as was the actual result. His peppermint scent warmed my innards and filled my senses with the essence of Raz. The heat from his hands burned a brand into me and I only prayed he didn't realize how crazy he could make me. But how could he not know?

His mellifluous voice with its bewitching accent made things worse for me. "That superstitious old biddy has scared you."

"No, I'm all right." I hoped my trembling was only on the inside. "She made me feel like a street waif, that's all."

He wasn't fooled. "But you are upset. Did that astoundingly rude little conversation trouble you so much?"

I nodded. Let him think it was only the evil eye that made me so unsettled, and not his nearness.

He came around to the front of the counter, allowing me to cool off a couple of degrees. "There's no need to suffer fools gladly. Let me help you, Dulcinea."

Again, somehow, the way he said my name made it musical, a melody, not the way I normally heard it. My heart skipped a couple of beats in its excitement to catch up to happy-speed.

"How?" I deliberately made my voice light. "By clouting her overhead with a staff the next time she comes around? It wouldn't help business any."

"See my locket?" He pulled on the leather thong around his neck. From under his tunic and layers of robes appeared a large charm, a silver ball with a thumb-tip sized glass crystal window for viewing the contents. I held it up to my eye in the light, but could not tell what was inside. The orb seemed big enough to hold a small field mouse, and I wondered why I had not noticed it before, if he'd indeed been wearing it.

"It's nice."

"Very." He smiled. "Because it keeps me safe. From evil eyes and all manner of unwelcome admiration." He didn't sound as if he thought it was all superstition, either. "I've an idea." He pretended to get a brainstorm, although I was certain he had come up front with the notion of doing something like this. He laid his finger along one side of his nose and wiggled his eyebrows. "Let me construct one for you."

"Oh, would you?" I would have worn a frog on the end of my nose if he'd wanted me to.

He stepped around me, selecting a few components from the shelves as he spoke. "Certainly I would, for one of my best companions. In fact, I know what I'll do. I'll not only make you a locket, but I'll make it do double duty. Give you something every young girl needs around the time of her majority."

"What?" I readied myself to blush or flee, depending on what he next said. Surely he wasn't bold enough to tease me about that . . . .

"What I'm talking about," he said, holding up a bag of pink powder, "is how I can help you quiet those gossips."

"Yes, of course." I took a deep breath. "But how?"

Raz's eyes sparkled with mischief. "By giving you the first token you'd have, had you actually gone under the Rite."

"But the Rite . . . they'll know I haven't had it." Not because
it carried with it any physical evidence, such as the scars in which
the barbarians of the sea across the Marwellian range were reputed
to take pride, nor the Mark a sorcerer wielding diabolical majick
was said to receive from his master the demon. No, only because
everyone in town would either attend or hear about any Rite given
by the church. "We're not wealthy enough for me to have a closed
ritual. And they'd know Da would never bother to haul me up to
Ladenia town to do it."

"How shall they know you didn't have a private Rite?" He
raised his eyebrows. "It doesn't have to be expensive if one doesn't
hire a hall, throw a revel, and have a crowd to feed afterward."

What status could such a private Rite lend? Would that even
count? I doubted it. But I trusted Raz—or, truth be told, I didn't
care. I nodded as though I followed his logic.

He patted the orb. "It doesn't matter much if you've put on a
public ceremony, you know; you mature and change whether
people acknowledge it or not. But they'll jump to the usual conclusion, and you won't hear any more rot about it from them.
What you need . . ." He grinned. "Is a love token."

It was my turn to stare. "A love token." I knew I sounded like
a cudge, repeating after him like that, but I was recovering from
the wild fantasies that I'd briefly entertained. Rather, I was trying
to recover. It wasn't working terrifically well.

"It's fitting, really, if you consider it for a moment." He stroked
his chin thoughtfully. "You know, because of your name and its
traditional meaning."

I gulped. "Dulcinea," of course, means "sweetheart."

What, under the endless, uncounted stars, could he be getting at? I'd thought one exchanged love tokens only after . . . well,
never mind what. I felt my cheeks warming up.

But Raz pressed on, heedless of my embarrassment. "We can
make you one right now, in fact. Flip the OPEN sign around to

CLOSED, and they'll think we're taking tea for midday. We can go up and use my altar." He twinkled his eyes.

I shuddered deliciously. It was hard to keep the excitement out of my voice. I hoped I sounded casual, noncommittal. "Your *altar* . . . . In your quarters." I'd never been in Raz's rooms, of course; it would be highly unseemly for a single girl to enter a single man's domain. "And we're going to . . . you're going to mix up a love charm?"

He nodded. "You could think of it that way. But this isn't a child's toy. The token I build you. . . ." He opened his arms in a typically overdramatic gesture. "Will bring your first true love."

My first true love? Surely he didn't suspect. He was making fun of me. Or was he making reference to us getting together at last, in some oblique way? My mouth went dry. I squeaked out something that was supposed to have been, "Really?"

He smiled. "Well . . . not right away, of course. It's intended to be a long-acting charm. But they'll know exactly what it is, and they'll start asking around to find out who gave it. The rumor can be that a distant suitor has sent it to you." He winked. "You can tell them anything you want about where it came from. That should put a jolt through the nosey old bats in the village. As for its immediate efficacy, well, as the lady who anointed the squashed toad with iodine said, 'It couldn't hurt.'"

I closed my eyes and took a deep breath to bring back my common sense. "So your plan is to make them think I'm already taken, and then they'll let me alone."

"Precisely." He smiled as though he'd taught a dull child to skip stones. He seemed glad that I was finally catching on.

I opened my mouth to tell him that Da would never hold with this plan. Rumors flying around the village about me and some distant suitor? Ridiculous. Unthinkable. And if Da should see this thing himself and recognize it—as he surely would, if ignorant old biddies were going to be able to see what it was . . . . I meant to thank Raz and then gently turn down his offer. But nothing came out of my disobedient mouth except, "Um . . . all right."

Raz reached over and grabbed one of the burlap robes we kept behind the counter in a bushel basket. He slapped me on the shoulder as if I were his ale-guzzling buddy. "Go change. Come find me upstairs when you're dressed."

#

In the back room, I adjusted the folds of the skimpy robe several times, feeling indecent and thinking about the last time I'd worn one, during Raz's spellcasting audition. I couldn't even get the belt wrapped properly, my hands were so unsteady. A love charm? Surely he was jesting with me, but I couldn't resist finding out what he planned to do.

Truth be known, I knew better than to go upstairs alone with Raz. But I told myself it was perfectly all right to be curious about your friend's living quarters. My teeth tried to chatter until I gritted them tightly together. Da would never, never approve. Of course, he must never know. And perhaps my saints would accommodate me by being busy watching someone else, someone who wasn't ready to, well, commit just about any sin that Raz might propose. It didn't mean I wouldn't feel guilty about it, but what else was repentance for? My hair was sticking out and wouldn't smooth down properly, crackling with static. My thighs dripped with sweat.

Upstairs, I found my way into the hall leading to the small apartment Daddoo had carved out of the attic of our carriage house. I'd never been up there since we'd cleaned out old Chiro's things, and I wondered why I hadn't been eaten up with curiosity about the new contents. When I hit the edges of the spell near his doorway, I realized the reason.

Briefly I wondered who else Raz might be hiding from.

"Your pardon, lady. The presence of my defense system had momentarily slipped my mind." Raz brushed aside the threads of the away-spell and reached across the threshold for me. "I am loath, however, to let my guard down, so to speak, even for a moment. If you'll come through with me, though, you'll have but the briefest moment of strangeness and then you'll be fine, once you're inside." Before I could object—not that I'd been about to—he folded me inside his arms and whirled me into his protected space.

I felt more than a moment of strangeness, but I suspected that it wasn't all sorcery's fault. I was pressed up against Raz, with his arms hugging me to him, and I could feel his body heat through our thin robes. He put me down lightly, safe inside his majickal barrier. Dizzy from the dose of humours that had rushed to my various organs, I staggered a few steps away and looked around.

The apartment was basically one huge square room with large windows facing the four winds. Windows of real glass, not spun-webbing or thin transparent oilskins. They were floor-to-ceiling panes, not tiny squares joined by wide wood grids, and they opened on a blue-and-green panorama that was not what lay outside. I knew perfectly well that our carriage house had wooden walls with no windows. I could feel majick as sure as I felt the scratchy burlap against my skin.

The better part of discretion was to say nothing about this, which is why my mouth stayed shut for a change.

In the center of the floor there was, etched in silver glittery stuff, a pentangle. The altar, I supposed, was that rosewood table smack in the middle of the pentangle's inner pentagon. The polished surface held a bowl, a chalice, some herbs, a blunt daggerlike knifeblade, and several things I didn't bother to examine closely.

An altar. Raz had a personal altar, but not to my saints. I felt ice creeping up the backs of my calves, and I couldn't help but shudder and pull my robe closer around me. Practical and natural majick, I knew for certain, proceeded from manipulating the natural physical laws as they applied to the web of majick that underlay all matter, not from supernatural powers that watched altars.

Still, I didn't feel the presence of evil. The saints would have turned my heart away from Raz had he been dedicated to the dark powers, I was sure. No, this was not evil, but some power greater than any I'd seen called upon.

As I turned, Raz faced the east wind and bowed. Subtly, he motioned for me to do the same. Holding the burlap robe tightly around me, I did so. A breeze from nowhere circled my knees. I felt stripped of my burlap, exposed before all these windows.

"Raz, people can't see in, can they?" My voice was a reedy whisper; I cleared my throat.

Raz smiled. "Worry not."

He pulled on a cord just over our heads to open a sort of roof window. The sky came into view above as our only ceiling. But instead of a sunny midmorning, we were here at dusk. I felt as though we were out under the year-wheel, lying on our backs in a meadow. Then, all around us there appeared tall bristlecones and buttonwoods; I breathed in the mossy smell of the forest. Under my feet, I felt the soft leafy floor of the deep woods, pungent with the smell of moist earth and decaying leaves. My feet sank into the pine needles up to my ankles.

"Ready?" Raz's voice dispelled my strange vision and brought me back to the present. We were back in his room, my bare feet on the marble-like pentangle. The sky was back to blue, and the breeze had stilled. I took a deep breath.

I wrapped up tighter in the burlap and settled myself carefully on the padded stool he'd produced, acutely aware of his nearness. I briefly wondered why Raz had no physical responses himself, perhaps no humours for it; it was obvious that he must not. Or maybe I was repulsive. I probably wouldn't qualify after the legendary Marwellian beauties he'd grown up around. And, of course, my hair. Oh, well. I was mostly relieved that nothing was going to happen after all, except for strange and unusual majickings, which ought to be enough for any girl. I squeezed my eyes shut and waited for instructions.

"I forgot about the something personal that I'll need." My eyes popped open, and he frowned. "Let me see your fingernails." He examined each hand briefly, then shook his head. "Bitten down to the quick, as I should've expected. Pity—they're so much smaller and less obtrusive. Well, there's always the hair."

I would be mistaken for a shorn priestess of Biba if I had to undergo many more of Raz's rites. This time, though, he took only a scant lock with his blade, cutting so that it was symmetrical against the last one he'd taken. I thought maybe my poor hair would get a chance to grow out after all.

He started the rite. As always, he cast his majick square. But this time he centered it on his altar, making that one of the foci, a thick tall pink candle on the floor the other. An ash rod, stripped of what bark it should have had, lay at his feet.

He lit the pink candle with his flint, and then used it to light a pure honey-wax votive on the altar.

"Hear us as we call upon you, O Lady." He made runic gestures in the air, then sprinkled pink talc on my forehead; some spilled down my face. I sneezed. He glared.

"It tickles," I whispered.

His eyebrows drawn together disapprovingly, he continued tracing the symbols in pink on my Seven Points, as before. The feel of his finger on my skin was exquisite torture. I bit the inside of my jaw to keep from reacting. Still, I felt the hair on my arms standing up.

"Quiet," Raz mouthed. With the same finger he traced a pink heart on his altar's white marble top, leaving pink talc to form the figure. It glistened as I watched, dazzled by its beauty.

He slipped his index finger into a quartz bowl on the altar. As if by some mystic attraction, a crystal jumped to adhere to his fingertip. It was small, an icicle of pink about a finger-joint long and half as wide, yet it glowed with an odd inner light of its own.

He twisted the lock of hair, as before, but instead of making a loop, he knotted it once around the crystal. "Smile upon our token of first love, O Lady." He stared into the flame of the candle as he spoke.

In a moment he turned to face me. Once again, our palms went flat together. As our elbows met, I felt a kink in my backbone, and straightened up my posture. This brought our faces close together, our noses nearly bumping. But instead of looking stern,

Raz tilted his face just a bit, so our noses were out of the way, but our lips were so close that I imagined I felt his on mine. The room and its trappings disappeared from around me; I hung in suspension over the Universe, waiting to see what might happen.

I thought I read a strange expression in Raz's eyes, but they clouded over and he pulled back, smoothly parting our arms elbow-to-fingertip. Just like before, I felt a string snap as we separated. The room snapped back into focus for me. As Raz reached into his pocket, he broke our eye contact. Whatever that feeling was, I had either imagined it, or it had been a momentary insanity. Whichever, it was over.

Now he held in his hand a charm-ball smaller than the one he'd shown me, but still large enough to accommodate its own little crystal window for viewing the innards. He fingered it aside and popped the hair in. Spitting on his finger, he closed the window again and I heard it click softly into place. He put its thong around my neck and stepped back, nodding with pride at his handiwork.

That was, apparently, all there was to making the token itself. He motioned for me to stand, and I knew that was the beginning of putting the majick into the object. We would ask—of whomever it was that one was supposed to ask it—for true love, and then he would invest the prayer into my new charm.

"O Lady of the Green Wood, we call to thee. We beseech thee for your blessing as this woman comes of age."

He took the ash wand from the focal point and held it vertically before him like a sword. Then I knelt, instinctively sensing what he was about to do. He knighted me with it by tapping first on my right shoulder, then on my left, and finally on my head. It didn't hurt or even feel heavy. I tingled from scalp to sternum.

He'd placed a chalice on the heart shape he had traced with the pink chalk. Now he lifted it, and I saw the gleam of liquid inside.

"Lady, as we drink to thee, we ask thee: send true love to this woman who loves ye." He poured a shallow draught into a goblet—no, it was a silver chalice—and held it out to me.

Should I sip? I drank. He kept his hand over mine, so that, I assumed, I wouldn't drink too deeply. It was wine, dark purple stuff made from some sort of berries as well as the basic grape. It tasted like Heaven's own water fountain.

I felt somehow that if we'd drunk together, or one after the other, this ritual would suddenly be over, and I would have found my first true love. But instead, Raz shifted position until we were side by side, holding the blessed vessel.

We stood with the chalice clasped between us and watched as the votive burned the rest of the way down. The candle must have been fast-burning, or maybe the herbs he sprinkled on hurried it. The smoke lingered only a moment after the flame winked out, and then it too was gone in a final gray curl. The air felt charged, and I smelled sulphur.

Raz tapped my charm and thereby invested it with the power we'd summoned around us. I felt the power go in, like a strange finger tapping on my breastbone, with a resonant chime just barely audible; then the room grew slightly dimmer.

The ritual was done.

We both stepped instinctively back, finding the majick square no longer glowing. All that was left was the glittering silver star etched into the floor, and the altar in the middle of it. And Raz.

And me.

I cleared my throat quietly, trying to dispel the mood of reverence so we could return to normal. "Is that all?" I stroked the ball I now wore around my neck. "True love." I whispered it, knowing I had already found it in the boy—the man—no, the sorcerer—before me. Did he have any idea how I felt? Was this his way of telling me he felt the same?

"Well, that's done." Raz's matter-of-fact tone startled me, after what we'd just evoked together. It was like a cold blast of air into my face. "I hope you're feeling better now. Upon my word—don't you look earnest petting your new jewel."

I looked up. I hadn't realized Raz was watching. He stood, tilt-headed, with a sappy grin on his face. The charm fell from my hand, which had gone limp as he spoke, and landed with a dainty thud on my breastbone.

"Sorry. It's just that you looked so sweet, sharing your secrets with your new love charm. I'm so glad you're happy with it." He smiled at me. Then he actually patted me on the head again, like I was some bunny he'd fed a carrot. "If you truly believe, then your true love should come to you soon." He looked as though he'd like to see that, as if my whole problem had been merely a little story out of a bard-tale. He looked positively patronizing, as bad as Daddoo at his worst.

I should have been angry. I had every right to be. Instead, I burned with shame. And humiliation. If a head could burst from the pressure of self-loathing, mine would have. I kept my head down, staring at the still barely-glowing ikon marring the polished wood of the floor, fiddling with the charm, staring anywhere but at Raz. I didn't trust myself to say anything. Friendships could be ruined by too much honesty at the wrong time.

"What's wrong?"

Trust him to know something was.

"It's just like mine." He held his charm out again, so the ball rotated only thumbs' lengths from my eyes. But the majick was gone. I had been taken in by a mere charade and a copper's worth of dust.

"It is." I managed to look up after another moment and made a grimace that apparently passed for a smile. "I love it, Raz. Thank you. I think I'd better go now."

His expression of relief told me he'd been completely taken in by my simulated appreciation. "Oh, this is excellent. I did hope that'd make you feel safer. You *are* safer, is what I mean to say. Well, well. I'll carry you out—"

But I'd already reached the edge of the majick field, and though I didn't care to think what it would feel like plunging through it alone, I also couldn't stand for him to touch me, let alone squeeze me against the length of his wiry body as before. I'd rather have died right there than want him ever again.

"No, no! You mustn't break through it yourself. Don't take another st—"

I stepped across the doorway into the barrier field.

The sound of his voice abruptly stopped, leaving a hollow echo in my ears. Tingling all over, as though stung by a flock of crystally snowballs, I froze in place. I couldn't lift my feet—no, I couldn't move my leg muscles. Stuck the way I sometimes found myself in a quicksand-molasses dream, I panicked. I shouldn't have come here! I should never have seen what was inside this room! Who did I think I was? Now I would be punished! I must forget what I had seen . . . .

The weight of my guilt was unbearable. I felt my breakfast moving around in my stomach, the blessed wine sloshing about my veins, and I was nauseated with remorse. I deserved nothing less than a complete flogging. I might never eat goose eggs again.

I choked on vomit and felt myself falling backward. Then everything went black. Just the way they always tell you it does.

CHAPTER FIVE

I woke up back in Raz's apartment with a cold wet cloth on my forehead.

"Coming around at last, are you?" He looked worried, his rabbitty face only thumbslengths from mine. "I was getting worried there for a moment."

"What. . ." Then I remembered what had happened as I stepped into the field of majick. I could wiggle my fingers and toes, so maybe no permanent damage had been done. "I guess you were right. I wasn't quite up to breaking through that by myself." I smiled as best I could, despite the embarrassment that surged through me. "I was only trying to save you some trouble."

"Which you definitely didn't." He smiled. "However, there aren't any permanent effects. The field's a bit strong, I'm afraid, and I really didn't mean it to be so awful for someone just leaving. But I had to take the precaution, you see. Of course you don't see"—he smiled broadly—"but you can probably figure it out for yourself. Won't have any burglars, will I, now?"

I bolted upright, then regretted it as the dizziness came over me again and I had to fall back on his pillows. "How long has the shop been closed? Daddoo mustn't find it all closed up and me up here. That would be—" Words wouldn't form in my mouth to explain what a disaster this would be. In fact, words wouldn't even form in my mind.

"I can't worry about that now, can I?" He pursed his lips. "I've done such a foolish thing already that can't be undone, in bringing you up here without his permission. I forgot myself entirely, and simply didn't realize. . . ."

In that moment I became aware that I'd been a complete dolt for weeks now. A fog had lifted from my mind. Maybe it had been one of Raz's spells that'd kept me so oblivious. But as advanced as my Daddoo was in many aspects of majickal practice, I couldn't imagine what he could possibly teach Raz.

Of more immediate concern was that I couldn't quite remember what I'd been doing. "What happened?" I thought my voice was going to sound normal, but I actually squeaked. "We didn't . . . I mean, we shouldn't be up here. Should I remember doing anything?"

He held my new charm-ball before my eyes, where it twisted as if trying to dazzle me, like a puppy leaping in the air and yapping out, "Love me! Oh, be my friend and love me!" If a piece of jewelry could look wistful, this one would have. I blinked; I must've taken a bump to the head. However, the sight of my charm brought back my memory of the Rite.

"I remember now," I said, feeling weak. "Did we . . . try anything else? I hope I haven't inconvenienced you."

"Oh, you didn't." His expression turned puzzled. "That's what I'm talking about. I do hope the fainting spell in the field of power hasn't befuddled your recent memories. It hasn't, has it?"

"Of course not." There was, indeed, a blank spot in my memories just after he'd handed me the necklace. I dimly recalled being a little upset for some reason, but couldn't tell why. I tried sitting up again. This time I made it. "I just wondered how long we had been up here, leaving the shop unattended."

"Only a candlemark. A bit longer, perhaps." He amended his estimate, glancing at the angle of the sunlight as it shafted in from the west, instead of the east as it had done earlier. "Not quite two bells, I'd say."

"Two bells!" I struggled with my feet and managed to get upright on them. "I've got to get downstairs right away."

"Perhaps that would be the least bothersome course for you, though not the wisest." He reached for my arm, steadying me with a touch. "But I can't let you go down there in this condition. You're still quite shaky from the post-majickal suggestions you were bombarded with. Quite a clever trick, that, don't you agree?" He twinkled at me again, and I could only nod.

I was amazed at the extent of his majickal knowledge and powers. What in the name of Saint Alyncia's legendary enchanted rosebush was such a sorcerer doing here, pretending to need apprenticeship to my Da?

I had never been more certain that "Raz" was a synonym for "secrets."

He left me for a moment while I regained my bearings. When he returned, he bore a tray with two steaming mugs of colaaf. I had never really liked the taste of colaaf, but at this point, I thought I did need a stiff shot of something. Its stimulant properties, along with the warming one got from drinking it, were perhaps just what I needed.

"Thank you, Raz." I took the mug and warmed my hands, breathing in deeply the resuscitating steam. It quickly cleared my head of the woozy-making humours. "Do you have any cream or cinnaberry?"

"Sorry." He blew across his drink to cool it. "Can you not stand to sip even a little of it straight?"

"I can." I felt a little sheepish. "I just like it better with a little orange or cinnaberry flavor to it, and the cream is really just to float on the top as a treat." I took a sip and had to swallow quickly, before my tongue and throat realized they were getting scorched. "It's good, really. And I think I'm feeling much better."

He handed the charm back to me. "Have you learned your lesson about running through fields of majick so strong you can feel them without using majick?"

"I have." I grinned back at him as I put the cord back round my neck. I briefly felt a sense of gratitude that I imagined came from the charm, although I knew that was my imagination. "I should have known the difference between being brave and being foolish." I couldn't let my emotions blind me to good sense, ever again, especially where Raz was concerned. Not if I wasn't yet tired of living. Which I wasn't.

"Come on. I'll carry you down, and we'll get the shop re-opened before Magefather Brown gets back from marketing."

# # #

Daddoo never knew that I'd been up in Raz's domain, thanks be to the pantheon of watchful, loving saints. He didn't find out that the shop had been closed for the better part of mid-day, though he did notice how little traffic in sales we'd had. He grumbled about Raz running off the customers and about me being rude to people, especially Dame Trudgeon, who he told me had "prattled some completely incomprehensible rot about the evil eye and your hair— I think she's gone daft at last." He probably would never have known about the love token, either, if I hadn't been so careless.

I banjaxed it all soon enough, of course. One afternoon I was changing the display in our front window and impulsively pulled out the ball to examine it in the light. It glistened and sparkled as I held it at the limit of its cord and admired it in the rainbowed sunbeam. I peeked into its glassed aperture to see whether my hair-lock had really formed a protective shell around itself, as the legends said. Sure enough, an opalescent coating was beginning to form.

I pushed the crystal shield aside and worked my fingertip into the opening. The crystal itself was sticky. Without thinking, I popped my finger into my mouth and tasted sea-sweetness.

That's when Daddoo caught me.

Lost in concentration, I hadn't even paid sufficient attention to hear his footfalls; his voice was sudden behind me.

"There you are, Dulcinea. I'd like you to start working on— ho, girl! What is that you have?"

"Nothing, sir." I had no time to hide the pendant, but tried to shield it with my body. No luck. Da gripped my shoulders and turned me towards him; his mouth hung open in shock.

Da's eyes narrowed. "Is this what I think it is? Who gave you this—this curse-catcher?" He grabbed for it, ripping the thong away from my neck. I felt almost a physical pain. He held it up to the window light, his face darkening to dusk.

"That's mine, sir. I want it back." He wasn't expecting my reaction, I don't suppose, and so I caught him off guard; I snatched back the ball, dismayed at the condition of the broken cord, then cringed under Da's shadow as he whirled to face me again.

"Dulcinea Jean Brown!" Da roared. His eyeballs bulged, and I could count his heartbeats by the pulsing vein in his right temple. "What is the meaning of this?"

"Please, sir." I barely slipped out of his reach as Da's anger boiled over. He'd never strike me hard—not on purpose—but I'd never seen him so agitated at me since the time I, as a young child, slipped into the kitchen and with a spoon ate the soft middles out of two round layers of chocolate cake meant for a guest as the cakes sat cooling on the windowsill. He reached for the token again, but I had it shoved down into one of my deep pockets already; I dodged him and got the countertop between us, glad for once for my lightness and resulting agility.

I hadn't counted on him being quite so strong. Reaching across the counter, he caught my arm and extracted the prize again, plucking it out and holding it at arm's length. It dangled like a dead rat from its armored tail. "Mind me, girl, or I'll snatch you baldheaded. When I ask you for something, you give it here willingly."

I took a deep breath. I had to start standing up for myself sometime. "I mean no disrespect, Da. But I'm no longer your baby. I should be able to choose to wear a little charm if it suits me."

His eyes flashed. "A charm. Complete superstition!"

"No, just a little luck-piece." I hoped he didn't recognize exactly what it really was. I supposed that Raz had been exaggerating again when he said that any villager on the street would know it for a love-charm.

Da's eyebrows went skyward into his bald circle. He, too, took a deep breath; I was proud of him, calming himself like that. "Child, the whole idea of 'luck' is superstitious. Luck, future-telling, superstition—" He waggled his fingers disgustedly, as though shaking off something stinky. "They're all against our religion."

I wasn't buying this bill of goods. "What's the difference between this and warding?"

His eyes became slits again. "What's the difference between black majick and white?"

He couldn't fluster me with that one; I knew better. "That's not a fair comparison. Black sorcery is based entirely upon a corrupt belief system, and is completely diff—"

"Quiet, child." Da turned the ball this way and that, examining it. I could see he considered it repellent. Shaking his head disgustedly, he handed it back to me; he'd forgotten that he'd meant to take it away. I mentally thanked my guardian angel that Da was sometimes this absent-minded of purpose.

But then his eyes gleamed again. "That thing. I know what it is now. It's a love token like guttersnipes of the street wear, isn't it? To ward off the evil eye in women who. . . ." He stopped. "These things aren't sold on the street corners, although that's where they belong. You've been through a ceremony?" His voice deceptively calm as he waited for my answer, Da's hazelnut-yellow eyes clearly said I'd better not have.

"No!" I hated lying to him, but there was no other way. "I just wanted one of those because all the village women kept after me about why I didn't have one." I squirmed as his gaze pinned me down for more detail. "I tried to tell that nosy old Dame Trudgeon you said it was superstition, but she didn't seem to believe me."

His lower lip poked out a hairsbreadth. "Don't you trust me more than some meddling villager? Has your old Daddoo ever been wrong?"

Yes. "It's not that I didn't believe you." I shifted from foot to foot under his gaze, my fingers tangled in errant strands of hair that had fallen in front of my eyes. "But the whole town thinks I should already have my hair up, and they say there are all sorts of important things I don't know about. Womanly things, ladies' responsibilities. That I won't know until somebody trains me, to prepare me for the ceremony of passage into womanhood."

We shared a long silence. Finally Da blinked, and his jaw lost some of its firmness; I could see I was getting somewhere. So, of course, I babbled on, one word too far. "He only made it because I—"

"He!" Da's jaw dropped all the way down, and saliva gleamed on his bottom lip. Then I knew I'd made a major error. Da's eyes lit up, and the pupils held the rune for Raz.

My voice caught in my throat.

"Oh, ho! I should have known. Raz's influence, was it? That majicking rogue with his majicking lack of majicking ethics."

Odd how "majicking" could sound more dire than the most sinful of blasphemous curses when said in that tone. By my Da. Of my Raz.

"I'm going to find that rascal and straighten him out this very instant. Perhaps with a heavy log to the head. How dare he do a Rite on my daughter. How dare he majick you in my absence!" The peculiar gleam in Daddoo's eyes scared me a little.

"He didn't do a Rite, sir. . . ." But the doors to Da's mind had snapped closed. His expression didn't look like my kindly Daddoo. I went all shuddery.

He turned on his bootheel and went in search of Raz.

The blowup was fierce. To avoid hearing the row, I ran away, off down to the tanner's cottage, where I had often played in their neglected rosebush maze. The switch-back path that took you to the center of the puzzle was a wonderful place for solitary reflection. The roses were a soothing bonus. I stroked the petals of a coral rose against my cheek and breathed in its perfume, but it gave no comfort. I'd been hollowed out inside.

Weak from missing lunch, I slunk home at two bells, late in the afternoon. I was surprised to see both Da and Raz in the shop, working alongside one another—albeit in silence—when I returned. Raz was a little subdued and Daddoo was a bit red in the face, but I could tell they'd worked something out. Apparently my superstition had been explained to his satisfaction, for later I heard him muttering, "That Trudgeon woman—I'll be answering a few of her questions, mark my words. The nerve of her. How dare she."

Praise the merciful saints for their intervention. Raz had cheated trouble once again.

# # #

I learned quite a bit of flute in the next several weeks. There were tricks: you could whistle or even sing "loo" into the flute for a different tone, and I was delighted that I could make both of them work, to a degree. Even I could hear the difference in my playing, my purer tones, the subtlety and color I could now coax out of a musical phrase. Raz was pleased with my progress, and said so often, as we lay out on the back lawn under the stars practicing. I was becoming a halfway decent intermediate flutist.

If only the smith hadn't sent his silly wife to get a mage for a house blessing on his birthday. If only Da hadn't been standing right behind her on a stool, rearranging the products on the highest shelves, when she spoke to Raz. If only things had been different . . . .

Daddoo grabbed his coat as she explained herself to Raz. Helplessly, I stood behind the counter and tried to distract Da, but to no avail.

She saw Da, too late. "Don't trouble yourself, good master. I'll wait for your apprentice."

"I'll not hear of it. I shall attend to your needs myself, Goodwife Smith." Da stepped over to take her arm, but she eluded his grasp. "Don't think it any bother. You know Smitty'd never forgive his old dice partner if I sent an apprentice to do a master's job." He tried to smile, but she stubbornly resisted his charm.

"Nonsense. It's Raz I asked, and it's Raz I'd prefer to have." She leaned on her walking-stick and stared him down, as though challenging him to answer that one.

Silence deafened me and froze the two of us behind the counter for a moment before my Da could process what she had said.

"Blast it all!" Daddoo pointed a long gristly finger at Raz, who had already reached for his cloak and staff. "You've majicked them some way; you've made our patrons spellbound to insist on you, prefer you to me. Treason, I'd call it." Of course treason only had to do with matters of state, but Da thought of our shop as a self-contained country, with himself as king. "Disloyalty. Conniving behind my back. Breaking the terms of your binding agreement, the way I reckon it. You're a fool, Songs."

While Da ranted, the smithwife gradually sidled back. Once she hit the door, she shoved it open and ran, the string of welcome-bells tinkling wildly behind her.

"Now see what you've done?" Da boomed it out, handling the shifting of blame with admirable aplomb. I had to be proud of the way he could switch gears and think on his feet, even though this was not currently a particularly logical turn of thought. "I'll have you hanged!"

"I've done nothing wrong, fair master." Raz gathered his cloak to him and pulled himself up to his full height. "It is merely that she respects my work. You should be proud that you have chosen one with my talent and taught me so well, rather than jealous that your student has surpassed you." I closed my eyes, unable to imagine how awful that statement made my Da feel. "Now, by your leave, I'll see what I can salvage of our customer relationship with the goodwife."

Open-mouthed, Da glowered silently after Raz as he left. I cringed.

"That does it! He has ensorcelled my customers somehow, has them hypnotized." Da threw his good cloak on the floor. I rescued it before he could trample it.

I didn't have the heart—no, honestly, I didn't dare—to tell him that Raz was just more talented. Well, perhaps not, but differently gifted. Surely Da had found that out in their sessions, since three afternoons a week they went behind closed doors to

work on majicking, leaving me to mind the store alone. I didn't
know how much Da knew about Raz's abilities—it depended on
what Raz had shown him—but he had to have guessed at the
extent of Raz's talent and potential. Naturally, Raz lacked other
important traits, wasn't patient, earthwise, and hardworking like
Daddoo, I reminded myself loyally.

"This last straw broke the horse's neck." Da couldn't even get
the proverb right, he was so angry. He tore off his merchant's apron
and headed into the back room. I hoped there were no customers
for a while. I'd hate for them to see me crying.

#

When Raz returned, there was another row, the worst yet. But this
time it was over something really important.

I walked in to find Da faced off against Raz in front of the
counter, yelling something about theft.

"It's not enough that you steal all my customers." His eyes
flashed as he whirled around to see who I was, then turned his
attack back to Raz. "No, that's not betrayal enough. You've finally
done something that neither you nor my daughter can manage to
weasel-talk you free from."

"Sir, calm yourself." Raz was barely holding himself together,
I judged. His face was pasty and his eyes dilated. He gripped his
cap and staff with white-knuckled hands.

I reached to turn the window sign to "Closed." "Daddoo. . . ."

"Calm down, should I?" Da turned to me. "How about my
own flesh and blood? Will Dulcinea stick by me, or will she betray
me and take the side of this—this—" He searched for the words
on the ceiling, then looked back down at me, cunning in his eyes.
"This scoundrel who stole your own Daddoo's mage's-sack!"

"No!" The denial popped out of my mouth, and I covered my
lips with my palm so nothing further would slip. I looked at Raz
the way one looks at an egg that has hatched a serpent instead of a
bird. Could he have? Had he?

Da looked satisfied by my horror. "I'll give him a chance to bring it back before I haul him before Council. Not because I feel sorry for him"—he raised a finger in emphasis—"but because I hate to trouble them over the proper fate of such a worm. Instead, I offer him a few hours to bring it back from wherever he's concealed or sent it." He turned back to Raz and raised his hands threateningly, forming the first Runic Position. "Produce it by nightfall, without fail, or your apprenticeship here is at an end." His voice fell to a low murmur, but he still projected the words so that we understood every one. "And no one will trust ye near them after I finish writing my letters of 'recommendation.'" With one final glance at Raz, he stalked out of the shop.

I'd never seen Da like that.

I couldn't help it. I turned to Raz, the question written on my features.

His voice was unsteady. "Take another mage's personally charged effects? I . . . . I didn't. I couldn't. He knows me better than that."

"You wouldn't"—there was an important distinction I was making here—"would you, Raz?"

He glanced at me, eyelids down like monk's hoods, looking as offended as a puppy being punished for tinkling in the garden, where it has always been allowed the privilege.

I whispered, "I believe you."

CHAPTER SIX

We set out to spend what was left of the afternoon finding Da's mage-sack. I knew it wasn't where he kept it, but I tore up the house and the shop looking anyhow. Da was nowhere to be found, so Raz and I closed the shop (the sign was already turned, at any rate) and searched it everywhere. Even the garden and the front grounds, although I knew perfectly well my Da always had that sack either on his person or in its hidey-hole.

The light waned; the afternoon was almost used up, and I could see the shadows predicting impending darkness. After I finished my second circuit of the grounds in the twilight, I trudged back into the shop, halfway expecting to find Da there with his sack on his shoulder, happy again. Instead, I found Raz setting up a majick square—which, I had learned, majickers in Marwell called a quincunx—in much the same way he had when we'd first met.

He glanced up at me and laid a finger across his lips. "Don't argue with me, Dulcinea. It's the only solution."

I crossed my arms. "He won't believe you, you know. He'll say you hid it just so you could show off and Call it back. Or that the reason you could Call it is you know where you put it."

"If you're going to stand around here, you've got to stay quiet. This is going to press my luck as it is, because I'll have to draw power for the second time today, and it's going to be touchy."

"What do you mean?"

Without glancing up, Raz said, "Draw power from the Web of majick, of course."

"That's not what I meant." I had meant what did he mean about pressing his luck. However, I got the strong feeling that he was evading my question on purpose.

Raz looked my way, cleared his throat, and took hold of his robe's lapels. In a stentorian tone, he began to lecture. "Majick was discovered—or invented, if you like—in the Year of Peace 1593 (Second Fredel) by the Ladenian Dalbo Applegate when his inept assistant, Wray Little, attempting to hang a clothesline, inadvertently crossed a majickal line of power and found the string empowered with a strange force of attraction. He then—"

"I know all that." And Raz knew I knew it. "What I meant was . . . why would you worry?"

"There are rules governing the use of majickal power, Dulcinea. Agreements. In addition to the natural laws."

"And certainly you wouldn't want to violate any of them. But you have done workings before that must have been more challenging than this."

He gave me a disdainful look. "It's really none of your business, but a majicker's signature, as you know, goes out on the web of power whilst he draws from it. That's not always a good thing." He stopped short, giving me a look. He'd obviously said more than he'd intended. Who was he afraid would see his signature, around here? Before I could formulate a proper question, he reproved me.

"You're distracting me, Dulcinea. I told you that if you were going to stand around here, you'd have to be quiet."

And that would be, I could tell from his expression, Raz's final words on the subject.

He continued with his preparations. On the hassock, he had placed an empty silver chalice, the largest I'd seen among our stock. Out of it protruded a knotted string of herbs.

"It's no use, Songsterson." Da's voice boomed from the front door. I turned to find him silhouetted against the open doorway, the last of the light streaming in over his shoulders. "You're found out. You've failed to return my property, and I'm the kind of man who takes action when he's been wronged."

"Give him a chance, Da." I knew I sounded pleading, and I knew my attitude did not please my Daddoo. His eyes flashed,

but he stepped into the shop and stood at my elbow, waiting for
Raz's final working as his apprentice to fail.

Since Daddoo was practically bald on top, I wondered what
the rite's personal item would be. When Raz lifted the chalice to
the Lady, I glimpsed what lay underneath, and I had my answer.
Everything personal Da had cached behind the shop's counter was
now here, under the cloth, getting bespelled. Dunce-like, I'd momentarily confused the kind of working being done; for a calling
of a personal possession, there was no need for a piece of you, but
only for another of your belongings. Raz planned to use a principle of sympathetic majick; he'd summon the mage's sack by tempting it with its companions: Da's hat, cloak, rod, and walking-staff.
Silently we stood, watching Raz call the corners and begin his
majickworks.

"Along the ley lines of majick, I pull in the item that is lost."
Raz gestured, then picked up Da's belongings one by one. "Rejoin
to these what has been taken away." He laid the items at the corners of the square as he spoke, then entered the ellipse and stood
between the two foci, in front of the hassock. His fingers worked at
an invisible tangle, pulling on the figurative cross-threads that made
up the web, the lines of majickal force.

"Sweet Lady," cried Raz, holding the chalice to his breast,
"prove my innocence. Find what is lost and return it to my circle."

The lines forming the square and the ellipse turned to flames,
but Raz wasn't even singed. The flames leaped to kneecap height,
and I feared for our shop, full of flammables as it was. I made a
move to bolt, thinking I should douse it, but Da restrained me,
the pressure from his fingers letting me know he wasn't worried
about the majickal flame. I closed my eyes for a moment, then
heard a great crash, as though a rock had been hurled through our
front window. When I opened my eyes, I saw Raz kneeling in
front of the hassock, the chalice still clasped to his breast.

From the throat of the vessel there now protruded two long
silken drawstrings.

"Look!" I ran to the edge of the enchanted area, intending to grab the sack the moment the last of the majickal aura faded away. Raz's face was sheathed in a thin veil of perspiration, and his eyes looked tired, but he grinned at me. "Don't try to talk to Da yet," I said quietly, hoping he'd understand. Then I turned to Da, expecting to see his familiar grin.

"That's not mine." Da strode over to us and straightaway breached the majickal lines. Blue sparks flew to singe the hem of his robe as he stomped his foot right down on the last of the flames and reached for the drawstrings. Raz tilted the chalice towards him and looked the other way.

Pulling out the sack, Da still looked disgruntled. "Can't be mine," he muttered, dumping a few items out of it. My forgotten safestone necklace bounced onto the packed dirt floor. I had never seen him so careless, especially with a bag he claimed wasn't even his.

I reached out instinctively, then jerked my hand back before I could be stung by a spark. "Daddoo. What if there had been wards on that?"

He waved away my concern. "He'd never dare pull it in with anything on it. No, this might be my sack, but"—he pointed at Raz, who stared back at him in disbelief—"this was all his doing. He hid it from me some way, and now he's just playing out the scene. He's no hero, believe me."

"Sir." Raz cleared his throat, then reached for the vessel. He lifted it clear, then pointed at the hassock. "I took the precaution of preparing a signature trace." It sounded as if he needed to cough. He cleared his throat again, then continued. "So that we'd know who had dared to disturb your private belongings, I set a trace to pull in the signature of the last mage who'd touched them. If you'll only read the mark of whose work it was. . . ."

On top of the hassock, traced out in some kind of silvery glitter, was Da's own rune, the one with which he signed his name, the mark that was on his sigil that he used with sealing-wax on important packages.

I knew then that Da must have hidden the sack himself.

I felt the universe shift inside me. It was as though I saw Da through Raz's eyes. And I didn't like the picture. For a moment I saw the Da that Raz knew, a pompous, jealous, silly old man. A man who was too possessive, too domineering, who couldn't take pleasure in the success of his students because he couldn't bear to see them surpass him.

My voice was strained. "Is that a real working, Daddoo?" Through my shock and disappointment, I remembered a parallel. We'd once used a similar working to track where our lost cat Piggy was and who had put him there; we'd gotten the cat back, and the first-initial rune of our unfriendly neighbor was burned into the dirt, along with a sketch of the barn he'd shut Piggy up in. We always figured he believed our cat was a familiar, although Piggy was just a good mouser and our pet. Anyway, majick couldn't lie.

"You've set a trick to do that." Da brushed at the glitter, but the stuff didn't budge. It reminded me of whatever Raz had used to trace the pentangle on his room's floor. "Some manner of tomfoolery. Done in advance."

"It looks like legitimate majick, Da." I couldn't keep my voice from cracking. "Now will you believe him?"

Da looked from one of us to the other, then harrumphed. "What shenanigans. It's barely possible—mind you, just barely— that I forgot where I put my bag. Can't imagine why you two are making such a fuss over it." He peeked at me from beneath half-closed eyelids, then winked.

Disillusionment filled my breast. I had imagined my Da would do the noble thing and admit he'd been wrong, if not apologize. My hero's clay feet gained several new cracks.

Raz had kept his gaze averted. Now he stood and swept the dust off his knees. "Under the circumstances, I believe it would be best if I took my leave earlier than intended. We have almost reached the goals I set for myself when I began our association, at any rate. I shall end my period of service today."

Their gazes locked. Then Da said, "You know best, of course. I'll get your final pay."

"You can't let him do that. Why are you doing this?" I addressed both questions to both of them. Rushing between them, I put one hand out toward each. "Raz, we can work this out. Daddoo, we were only doing what you told us."

"What I told *him*." Da pointed a no-nonsense finger, almost poking me in the nosetip. "Not you. I'll be having a word with you later, little miss. But first to the business at hand. I'll make out the document releasing this young man from my employ." Da slung the mage's sack over his shoulder and swept off, mumbling to himself, to disappear into the back of the shop. Without even shaking Raz's hand.

Raz glowered silently.

I burst into tears.

Raz stalked toward the exit, but he stopped when I called to him, although he didn't turn around. I couldn't help snuffling. "Don't you have things to pack? If you'll only wait 'til morning, I'll make you up a basket. You need food and supplies to travel."

He turned to reply, his features cloudy with thunder. "No. I won't be waiting around."

It was full dark by then, and I hated to see him leave. Through my tears, I managed to find some travel-ready food, like honeycakes and jerky and the last of our cinnaberries. A hard loaf I'd just baked and some tea bags, too. I threw in some common majickal components and a few spices and, on impulse, a large sack of sleepherb. I wrapped it all in a cloth and packed it into a small over-the-arm basket. Then I ran out to meet him.

I caught Raz looking fondly back at our place from the corner of the village square. Daddoo must have already given him his papers and his pay, for on his belt there was a new pouch that looked suspiciously familiar. I handed him the basket, and he shook hands with me solemnly.

"It isn't right. It isn't right at all." I couldn't believe it, but I was sniffling again, just like a child. "Sorry. I don't mean to blubber all the time."

"It's all right." He looked back up at the carriage-house, shaking his head. "Sometimes these things happen. It's all for the best."

"What will you do?" I shifted from foot to foot, digging a ditch with the toe of my boot in the soft dirt. "Where will you go?"

He squinted into the distance down the black road. "I'll make for the Dragon's Head Inn in Ladenia City proper. I have contacts in the area, people I needed to get in touch with eventually. I just didn't know how soon." He took a deep breath, and I thought he might be putting on a brave face. "I must get some silks and other things that can't be had around here, and now I realize I've just been putting off going into Ladenia City proper. There I'll gather my thoughts for a few days and decide what I need to do next." Almost to himself, he murmured, "My mission awaits, at any rate. Soon someone would have called for me, I fear, so I should have already moved on. This is for the best, really, Dulcinea." His eyes already had a faraway look; in his mind, he was already gone, set off on whatever mission it was that I'd known about in my heart all along. "I must stop procrastinating and over-preparing. I know I'm ready; I can fight any of them, meet any challenge they throw at me."

He sounded so vague, yet foreboding, that it frightened me. "Oh, Raz. You will be careful, won't you? Eat properly, keep dry, and stay out of danger." I didn't even know what I was saying; I was just blathering. "I mean. . . ."

He smiled and met my gaze fully. "Dulcie, you're a sweet girl. It's kind of you to think about my welfare. But there's no need to worry, I promise you. I can take care of myself." He patted me on the shoulder. "You just take care of yourself. And take care of your Da."

Raz was really, really going.

Now I knew what I had to do. "Wait here a minute. Just for a minute, and I'll be back. Please?"

I ran up to my room, pulled the hacked-off braids I'd kept out of Mawmoo's hope chest, and ran back out to Raz.

He realized what I wanted to do, seemingly from the first moment. I ran up, panting, and handed my prizes to him. Solemnly, he rolled one up and put the resulting fat curl into the locket he wore around his neck, his own hair charm, the one that I hadn't figured out what it was for. Then he reached for my love-token, and with a twist he opened its window and somehow stuffed in the other rolled braid. This time, when he pressed the crystal window closed, I heard it click as though it had locked. The charm snuggled itself back up against me. My chest went all fluttery, and I knew Raz and I shared some special—ethereal—bond.

I reached up and caught his hand as he was taking it away from the charm. My gaze met his, and he smiled sadly.

He patted my hand. "Until we meet again, then."

"Yes." I swallowed something lumpy and bitter.

I wanted, more than anything, to throw my arms around him and squeeze. Never to let him go. Maybe even—if he must go—run away with him. Fall to my knees and beg to come along, wherever he might roam. Of course I did nothing of the kind, couldn't do anything but stand there helpless.

"Well." We shook hands awkwardly. "Keep practicing that flute."

"I will."

He slung his pack over one shoulder and went off without looking back, like the hobo angel in the legends. I watched until he was out of sight down the curving road.

I knew that someday our paths would cross again.

CHAPTER SEVEN

Da's booming shouts woke me early. "Confound it. I simply will not stand for this kind of goings-on right under my own rooftop. I won't have it, I say!"

His baritone roar echoed through our rooms. I forced my eyes open to a squint; only a tiny sliver of pre-dawn light squeezed under my window's curtain. It took a moment before I realized my father wasn't standing over me, but was stomping around downstairs in our storeroom, which lay right below my bedroom.

"Daddoo? What's wrong?" He probably hadn't even heard me. I'd slept on my hair, and could feel it sticking out at all angles as I wiped my ex-bangs out of my face. Granules of sleepsand stuck to the corners of my eyes, and my mouth was cottony from sleeping with it open.

"By the damnation of Titivillus!" I blanched inwardly at Da's curse. Titivillus, in the legends, was a devil who'd tempted mankind and led us into each of the seven deadliest sins. "This is an outrage."

I winced at the crash as Da knocked something over, presumably a stack of my so-carefully arranged cartons of goods. He continued banging around and carrying on as I wriggled out from under my tangled covers. "It can't have just gone missing. Not again."

I pulled on a clean robe over my nightdress and stumbled downstairs, rubbing my bleary eyes. Padding into the storeroom, I followed his voice to find him leaning over a hopelessly tumbled stack of crates. "Daddoo, calm yourself. You know the sisters of the galen-house said shouting wasn't good for you. What is it you're looking for?"

Da's back was to me, but I could see he was still bed-rumpled, with pillow-static in his hair. The ruckus he made dropping an armload of buttonwood twig bundles in order to rummage through the scattered goods around his big bare feet was my only answer. It was so early in the morning that I could barely think. If it hadn't been for our globelights rotating gently in their sconces, I wouldn't even have been able to see him, the daylight was still so dim.

I rubbed my palms together, fighting the morning chill. "I've just straightened up in here. If you'll only tell me what you want, I know right where everything is."

Da clasped an armful of crumpled paper to his chest and twisted to look up at me with a ruddy face. "Not this, you don't. No, you don't keep track of this." He was still in his sleeprobe and reeked of catmint; he used a tincture of it to rinse out his mouth first thing upon awakening. Since he still smelled of it, he couldn't have been down here long. He was always impatient if whatever he wanted didn't come right to hand.

"I'm sure that I could find it for you." If only he would stand aside out of my way. And maybe even tell me what it was.

"It's all that boy's doing. That scoundrel. The bosom-serpent. Why I ever trusted him—" He broke off, glowering, and started rooting through a box of wilted herbs I'd intended to haul out to the compost heap.

I knew who Da meant, but I didn't intend to get into a discussion of what Raz Songsterson might or mightn't have done. I wanted to pretend, if only for a while, that Raz was merely off to town on an errand. That he'd be back soon, and we could flute tonight out under the stars and talk about the future. I always felt so optimistic whenever we sat side by side.

"At least let me help you look." Da was making a mess of my neatened-up supplies on the storage shelves.

He cleared his throat. "Girl, you still don't ken me. I'm telling you, you can't know where this is. But I think I do." He tipped back his head and practically roared. "Hell's bells, I surely do. And I'm going to track down the villain who did it. That rapscallion.

That scalawag. Oh, mark my words, Dulcinea. When I catch up with him. . . ." Words failed him.

It worried me when Da went so red in the face. "Don't take on so, Daddoo, please. A few deep breaths instead, for my sake. And just tell me what it is you're trying to find."

He whirled around, suddenly looming menacingly over me. Involuntarily, I hopped back a couple of steps, like a child dodging a slap. "It's my mage's-sack, child, my priceless, inviolable personal magebag." Da had, I surmised, picked up some of Raz's twelve-coin words. "Just as he did last night, that rascal has spirited it away. But this time, he's gone off with it." Da's eyebrows seemed wilder than ever as they lowered over his sparking eyes. "He's taken what doesn't belong to him again, no better than a common cutpurse. And he won't get away with it."

I squinched up my face, trying to think of reasons why Raz couldn't and wouldn't have pulled such a stunt. Couldn't possibly. Could he? "I thought you had it in your hands last evening."

"I did, I did." Da waved me aside and pushed through the bead-curtain into the shop proper.

I followed, noticing a little more light through the front windows as dawn broke. I was certain Daddoo would come across his sack directly. He'd just upset himself brooding all night over Raz's sudden departure, that was all. All this uproar helped him not think about his role in it. "Anyone can forget where he's put something, Da. Especially if it was in a new place for safekeeping. There are things of mine I've put away like that and haven't seen for moons, they're so safe."

He didn't deign to answer me. He plucked off the countertop a stack of empty burlap bags, ready for whatever stuffing our customers might decide to put in them, and snorted. Of course, his mage's sack wasn't lurking underneath.

I decided to brew us some sweetleaf tea and leave him to his task. Even from the kitchen, I could still hear him shoving things around in the shop and tossing aside whatever wasn't what he was looking for.

When I got back with the tea, Da had started pawing through the detritus of last night's conjuring. Our hassock was dusty with the remnants of the herbs Raz had used. Thank goodness the rune had faded away, its glimmer either sunk into the hassock's feathery innards or risen to join the general atmosphere of majickworks in the room. I set the teacups out on the counter, knowing Da would get some whenever he was ready, and determined I should clean the seat before stains could set in.

As I daubed the spots with a mixture of white vinegar and possumweed poured on a white cloth, Da continued tearing up the shop in his search. To no avail. Finally he stomped off to the back room, where I heard the popping of majickal sparks as he barged through his own webs of protection without even waving them aside. "Hellfire and damnation!"

I called after him in my most placatory voice. "Please, Da. Just try to relax. I'm certain your sack is around here somewhere. It wasn't taken." The image of Raz departing, disappearing downroad, was indelible in my mind's eye; I was convinced he could not have had the sack with him. How could he have, without my seeing it? The answer came unbidden to my mind's ear: well hidden in his baggage, you little fool. That would mean he'd planned ahead, maybe forethought the entire fracas, so he'd have time to get away with the sack and its valuable contents. It was a possibility I didn't want to consider.

I had trusted Raz completely. I thought I was a fair judge of good character, and he'd never done anything to betray my trust so far. But was he a conniving rascal? Had our friendship been false, all an elaborate ruse?

No, but perhaps he'd wanted to taunt Da for the jealous fits he'd thrown. Could the sack still be here, but under an illusion of Raz's making? Or had he decided at the last moment to steal from his own employer? It seemed unlike the Raz I knew—thought I knew—the Raz who would regard it as one of the most dishonorable betrayals.

This was not a good thing to stand around thinking about. I straightened up the shop as best I could, trying to keep back tears that had no business squeezing out and trickling down my warm cheeks. When Da emerged, hair still flying everywhichaways, to flip the CLOSED sign over and grudgingly unlock the shop, I escaped upstairs, leaving him to his sulking. I was in the mood for a good housecleaning, in more ways than one.

Naturally, I first tackled Raz's room. I hesitated a moment as I approached, but then I marched straight in. There wasn't the least twinkle of majick, nor were there any mental effects on me as I crossed the threshold. All of his wards and turnbacks had gone with him; Raz's majickal domain had been returned to its familiar musty self. There was no sign we'd ever had a tenant, what with the cobwebs stretched across the windowpanes and the dusty trunks from Da's young years stacked about.

Raz must be a consummate illusionist. Or perhaps he'd actually attached this room to a secret majickal apartment, no telling where. I'd been right to suspect he was more powerful than Da realized. Poor Da.

Thinking about it gave me the shivers. Standing in the knee-deep dust, I remembered the forest and the marble floor, both of them apparently Raz's conjurations. Or else when I'd been here before, I was not really here at all; I should have bolted to tell Da about it. Why hadn't I? The wards and no-tell spells, of course. I supposed I must have been compelled to keep that secret; I hadn't even had a fleeting thought of telling Da, although now it seemed completely obvious that it was the first thing I should have done.

My mop clattered to the floor as I released the bucket handle and took hold of the doorjamb; my knees had gone weak. I felt creepy-crawlies of unease under my skin as I looked back on the situation. My allegiance, I saw, had been with Raz instead of my own Da. Our connection had been unnaturally strong despite the brevity of our actual acquaintance—even in my thoughts, I wasn't free of him: like Da, I had picked up some of Raz's expensive words. It hadn't been like me, because I'd always known my first loyalty should be to Da and to our combined welfare. But I had been completely under Raz's influence (I dared not even think the word "spell" in this context). I'd have approved any kind of evildoing, as long as Raz smiled and encouraged it.

Certainly he was nice-looking, an excellent dresser, and his voice held its charms—not to mention that he'd helped me with my music, or rather flattered me while I tooted away on my flute, probably amused that I could be so silly as to think he was serious. But I thought of myself as a sensible girl, not one who could be so susceptible merely because a fellow was easy on the eyes and occasionally tossed off a few fawning compliments. What conniving majick could put me under a spell like that without my knowing? It could only have been done with the diabolical majick to which Raz publicly swore opposition, not with natural majick that by its very nature honored the natural order of things, including one's free will. I had of course known Raz kept secrets, but I'd expected they were personal, the type an honest man might reasonably have without reflecting on his character.

I shook my head to clear it. Had his very presence suppressed all my instincts, made me ignore common sense? At least now I was back in complete control of my own mind. I hoped.

But I couldn't control my emotions any more. Hot tears were coursing down my cheeks unbidden. Roughly I wiped them away, angry at myself. So perhaps I had been a fool. I'd learned a good lesson, and I wouldn't be fooled that way again. At least we were well rid of Raz and all he'd brought with him.

Almost all. I spied a necklace still hanging on a peg on the wall. It was Raz's sigil, the silver rune-shape he'd had around his neck the first time I'd met him, and which he'd worn for house calls and any time he'd wanted to dress up a bit.

Well, I definitely didn't want him to be able to say we had any property of his. I stomped heavily over, enjoying the way the floorboards rattled and squealed underfoot, and jerked it down. It was heavy and cold in my hand. Its silky purple cord coiled around my wrist as if by its own volition. I plucked the cord off my skin

straightaway—feeling little shocks of cold, as if my very blood
vessels had twisted away as the fiber parted from me—and held it
pinched between my fingers as I would a mouse by the tail. The
sigil swayed like a pendulum. My mental mage-light clicked on:
If—when, I meant *when*—I found Raz, I'd use this as leverage, to
trade even for Da's mage's-sack. If Raz proved innocent, then I
could claim to have wanted to return this.

Not that there was much chance Raz was innocent.

Impulsively, I threw the cord over my head. The heavy carved
rune hit me on the breastbone. I stroked the silver absently with
my forefinger, luxuriating in its smoothness. The pendant warmed
to my touch. It must be worth quite a pretty stack of coins, and of
course he prized it. I grinned with the irony of how irate he'd be if
he knew I had it on. *When* he knew. If only he could see me now.

All at once, shame washed over me, and my heart softened.
Raz could still be innocent. I should consider him so until I was
absolutely convinced that the sack was gone.

Never let it be said that I didn't give a man a fair chance; I
decided to look as thoroughly for Da's sack as I ever had for anything, and be certain of my accusation. Where else could Da's bag
have got to? Where would I hide, if I were a sack of majickal implements? Where had Da gone last night that he might have laid it
down in his irritation over their confrontation?

I searched as many more places as I could think of, even outdoors, revisiting the bushes and grounds where Raz had so recently sent me on a similar snipe-search. The more I looked, the
more vexed I became. The answer—the only possible answer—
was that Raz must've made off with the sack, like a benedict; what
was more, he had made a complete and total fool of me. Of us. Of
our whole trusting relationship, and of his oath as an (ex-)appren-
tice.

By the time I flopped down in the dining room for a belated
bowl of porridge with cinnaberry powder and a slice of
brambleberry jam on bread (accompanied by a cup of cold tea), I
was thoroughly convinced that Raz Songsterson was a wicked de-

ceiver. And I was equally determined to go after him and catch him publicly in the lie. That would show that fraud he hadn't fooled me for a moment.

I made myself eat, although I felt no hunger pangs, only a bit of nausea at how badly I'd misjudged Raz's character over the past few weeks. Besides, I needed a hot meal in my stomach to travel on.

Ladenia City was barely a quarter-day's journey a-road. Now I was doubly glad that I'd found out where the rogue intended to go. I could easily find some pretext for disappearing down that direction this afternoon, and though I wouldn't overtake him before he reached the city, he would almost certainly take a room where he'd said, or nearby. The Dragon's Head, or its bowels, I didn't care which: I would find him.

By midmorning, I was dressed for the journey, my knapsack packed and hidden behind the cedar chest at the shop's back door. I'd left a note on Da's pillow apologizing and explaining where I'd been in case I was delayed, though I didn't expect to be. He wouldn't see it unless I wasn't home by bedtime, and with luck I could scoop the note out from under his nose myself.

My Da scraped into the kitchen the moment I sat down to eat, plodding over to his own stool and collapsing onto his elbows on our table. He raised his eyebrows at me, then moaned.

Of course; he must be ravenous. "Here, let me get you some porridge. Or would you like me to make you some oat-cakes and barleycorn pudding?" I jumped up to wait on him. He deserved a little extra effort from me.

But Daddoo shook his head glumly. "No, Dulcinea, nothing. Well, maybe just a ladleful of whatever you're having there."

I rushed to get him a serving. But he only stirred pointlessly for a minute, then pushed the blue bowl away and laid his head on his folded arms.

"It's no use, gal. That hagborn coxcomb. That bell-cracking knave. He's done-and-fooled us good this time." Rousing himself, he seemed to come to his senses a bit and took on a more parental tone. "But don't you worry about it any, child. It's a matter between grownups, it is, and I'll take care of it. I shouldn't burden you with my worries. Oh, woe is me, and who cares but the fiddlers three, as they say." He feigned a grin at me as he quoted my favorite old song, and my heart tore in twain.

I would get that bloody varmint Raz before the sun set, or I wasn't worthy of the family name.

"Haven't found your mage's-sack just yet?" I made my voice bright and my face dopey, so he'd think I wasn't too worried. Da mustn't know my intentions, of that I was determined; he'd never let me go alone, and I didn't want him traveling while he was so tired and upset. I decided I might get by with a lame ruse, what with his mental state at the moment. "Well, I expect it'll turn up soon. I'll look some more. I'm sure it's here. But first, may I go into town and get myself some eyebright? We're fresh out, and I would wait, but I need it now. I was up so late last night."

He nodded without looking up. "Take the afternoon off, lass. I'll tend to the shop and close up early." He rubbed his callused hands up and down his face in the manner of a man agonizing over a decision. Hands still cupping his bearded chin, he began muttering, more to himself than to me. "I need a plan. I must make a plan of how I'm going to catch him so's he'll ensnare himself in the deed. Can't confront him directly, of course. Too blasted many things could go wrong. Can't contact the city guard—not for a crime done by one majicker against another. They'd laugh me out of the station house. Wouldn't touch it themselves, and I don't blame them. Besides, he'll be away already, into the next district." He rubbed his beard. "Letters. I'll write letters to the Councils at every point where he might be headed, so as to warn others off of hiring him. Especially from taking him on as an apprentice, I should say. A shameful thing it is when one can't trust one's own apprentice. And then I'll. . . ."

I left him to his musings. Poor Da. He'd never outwit a young scamp like Raz. He might never catch up with him. And what if their confrontation developed into fisticuffs? Daddoo could get hurt. And a majickal fight wouldn't be wise. Neither of them would be so foolish as to invoke obvious majick out in the open, but if they struck at one another at all, disaster could follow. Besides, I wasn't completely confident that Da could win. No, Daddoo was too old to go after a young man. If anyone were going to get back the honor of this family, it would have to be me.

I opened the door stealthily, as I'd learned to do in years of sneaking out. Best if Da didn't know exactly when I left and when I returned. It might take the whole afternoon, longer than a quick trip into our own village, but he mustn't worry.

I would be home before dusk. I'd slip the recovered sack into some apparent location upstairs and pretend to suddenly find it, saving face on all sides. Da would never know what I'd done.

CHAPTER EIGHT

Once on the Ladenian Road, I tried to think which fork was fastest into the city, and which route Raz would be most likely to have taken. Why hadn't I listened when Da talked about tracking?

I kicked pebbles along in front of my boots as I trudged, already weary from frustration. I considered going back for my horse, Tickie, but then Da would suspect something; it was an easy walk into the middle of town, no need to ride. In the sobering light of the afternoon, my quest seemed hopeless, futile. Where had I come up with the notion that I could catch up to Raz, and who said he was even following the road?

I regretted not having found out more from that deceiver as he was leaving. But he could have lied, anyway. I'd have to trust what he'd said and hope for the best. How could I ever have been such a stupid little fool?

I sensed a slight vibration underfoot. Gradually it became road noise, and finally resolved into the sound of approaching hoofbeats. At a pretty good clip. Wheels squeaked. I veered to the side of the road, out of the path of the wagon I anticipated. Maybe the driver or riders would offer me a lift.

I stuck out my thumb just in case. The day was bright and pleasant, but no sense taking longer than I had to.

The two black horses didn't even slow. The attached wagon rattled by, throwing pebbles into my face. I caught a brief glimpse of the driver, robed in dusty black. Probably some fat, lazy farmer on his way to market, careless of me and other travelers on foot. I sneezed several times before I got the dust out of my nose.

"My thanks, sir," I called after him, rubbing my eyes with the hem of my sleeve. "Blast you for being inconsiderate, and blast

this dust, and"—I shouted an afterthought into the sky—"especially blast that dunce-cap Raz Songsterson, whose fault it is that
I'm out on this road." I wiped my eyes and flopped down on the
roadside grass. I needed to get control of myself and plan what I
was going to do, not yell random insults at passersby. I hadn't had
the least effect on the driver, I was sure. These types had no shame at
all. Down the road, did the wagon hesitate? No, I had imagined it.

I yanked off my new boots to reposition my heel and toe plas-
ters. The leather had proved out, marking my feet with angry red
spots in the places where I needed to cushion them further. They
were beautiful black cowhide, which must have cost Da a fortune,
and I had just started getting them broken in: the worst kind of
shoes for a foolish girl to wear on a long walking journey. Rubbing
my sore feet, I decided to cool my toes for a moment. Checking
my pockets and pouches, I found only a partly stale honey-cake. I
ate it anyway.

Knowing I ought to get back on the road, I pulled the boots
back on and started off again. Overhead, a flock of birds decided to
land en masse with an irritating flapping and shedding of feathers;
alongside the road, stinking squirrels with fluffy tails flew between
the trees, jostling the branches and shaking acorns down on my
waiting head. I hated the birds for singing and the chittering squirrels for being so blasted happy. What did I think I was going to do
when I found Raz? Shout out, "Shame on you," and have him
hand his booty over immediately? I shook more of the wagon's
dust out of my hair and off the front of my tunic. Raz still wouldn't
feel under any obligation to tell me the truth or give the item
back, any more than when he'd left. I'd have to appeal to his honor
and pride. But how?

Lost in my thoughts, I didn't realize someone was behind me
until I heard the gravelly voice.

"Pardon me, miss. Might you happen to know the way to the
nearest armourer?"

I turned. A few farthels behind me waddled a monk in a brown
muslin robe. Dough-faced, he was as fat as a man could be and

still get around on foot. His tonsure shone with salty sweat above the too-long graying wisps clinging to his dirty neck. He was coming up the road as fast as he was apparently able, huffing and puffing and clutching at the skirt of his rough robe.

Da taught me always to be polite. "In Ladenia City, sir. Down the road about another two hours' worth."

"May I ask, are you headed in that direction?"

He smelled strongly of many days on the road. I tried to keep from wrinkling my nose as he came closer. "Generally." It seemed best not to share too many details.

"Oh, praise the one God. I am so pleased to find a traveling companion!" He beamed, revealing a row of variegated teeth on the top, with holes on the bottom row. I tried not to inhale, fancying that I could feel the thick staleness of his breath.

Now, how could I politely let him know that I wouldn't allow him to walk with me? Since I didn't know his order, and couldn't tell from his attire, not to refuse him would be not only unseemly, but unwise. However, one must take care not to anger strangers. "I'm in a sort of a hurry." I increased my speed, easily keeping several paces ahead of him. "Just continue on this road for a bit, taking none of the branches. Always stay on the wider part of the road, and you'll glimpse the spires of Ladenia's churches soon enough. The town's actually just over the next good hill."

"Ah! It sounds as though you know your way. I'll come right along with you, then. I'm also in kind of a rush, truth be told." He huffed and puffed a bit as he spoke, but he kept right up with me as I increased my pace.

I wished I could figure out how to stay upwind of him. He was humming a simple little tune, just under his breath; the noise made me feel itchy and irritated, the way bees buzzing circles around my ears would. I walked faster, but he paced me. Somehow he stayed right there at my left elbow, humming that simpleton, idiotic, tuneless . . . whatever it was. It wasn't even a song, but just a throbbing of air pounding my eardrums. It did seem to grow less irritating as we went along, or else I started getting used to it. I was almost at my maximum comfortable pace now without breaking into a gallop.

I couldn't seem to outdistance him. Despite his heaviness, the pursy cleric wasn't slow: I would bet he could outpace me.

"And what is your business in Lad City, gal?"

My hesitation betrayed me. "I really don't have any business there. I'm just visiting." After a pause, I blurted out, "You can follow me there if you like." Now, why had I said that? I could have bitten my unruly tongue to punish it for working on its own.

"Thankee, I think I will." He huffed a while until he caught his breath. For some reason, we synchronized our gaits, me taking smaller steps and hesitating, he striding spraddle-legged to keep up. I felt like Mama Swan with an ugly duckling she couldn't shake off. "Headed to the city with no particular business there, you'll pardon me if I find that strange. What brings a lass your age out here on this road alone?"

"Looking for somebody." I'd blurted it out involuntarily, lulled by our companionable silence.

"Are ye? And who might it be?"

A drop of perspiration beaded up between my shoulders. I knew better than to speak freely to a stranger. On second thought, I couldn't see how it could hurt. If I explained, I might learn something important. This traveler might well have seen Raz, mightn't he? As likely as anyone in the taverns of Lad City had. He could set me on the proper trail.

"Oh . . . only a visitor who stayed with us and took away something he shouldn't have. An innocent mistake, I believe. But still we need it back, and so I hope to head him off and ask him to look through his belongings and find it for me."

"Seems like your parents would have sent a boy." He raised a wild-haired black eyebrow.

"I'm the only child. Of the apothecary in the village back a ways." I bit my lip. Why was I spilling so much, even before being asked? I shook my head, trying to clear it. For a moment I had even lost track of the direction. East, that was the way we were headed.

"Still feeling all right, aren't you?" The monk blinked, looking concerned.

"Yes, I'm fine. Just a momentary confusion."

"Mayhap I should walk closer by you, and that would make you feel safer."

" . . . Okay."

He put his arm across my shoulders solicitously and murmured to me in low, peaceful tones. "There, dear. Everything's going well now, I can assure you. Yes, at last you're with someone who can help you. Truly help you. And you'll not mind helping me in return, will you, now?"

What a charming fellow. "Of course not, sir."

"Brother Mag, dear child. Brother Magloather of the Order of the Stones. But all that formality's unnecessary, isn't it, dear, between two like us, friends who share everything." I found myself nodding. This made lots of sense. "Here on the road, where we break bread together, and trudge the dust and wipe each other's shoes, and weather the storms for one another. Eh?"

"Um." My tongue was stuck to the roof of my mouth with road dust. I only smacked my lips a bit, not knowing what he wanted me to say. And, for some reason I didn't quite understand, I desperately wanted to please him, to tell him what he wanted to hear. For Brother Mag of the Stones was my new friend. That was what friends did for each other, wasn't it?

"Tell me," said his mellifluous voice—the lovely tones of which I had barely noticed until now—soothingly. So soothingly. "More about this person you seek. A young man, is he?"

"Yes." I tried to remember what Raz looked like, why I was looking for him. "Tall, buck teeth . . . black hair, mustache, tall." Had I already said that? "Plays flute." That seemed important. My new companion nodded encouragingly. "Very smart. Dresses like a dandy. Older than me."

"How much older?"

"Oh . . . I don't know for sure." I felt flustered. Immediately he soothed me again with a pat on the shoulder.

"Dark hair, eh?" He made a mysterious little noise. We ambled along in step for a few moments. "And what does this person call himself?"

I knew I shouldn't, but I couldn't help myself. "Raz. Raz Songsterson."

His sharp intake of breath scared me for a moment, and I stopped short. Quickly he resumed his soothing patter, and I felt inexplicably better, even though the content of his conversation was unsettling at best. "I thought I'd heard you shout it earlier." He patted my shoulder and we started walking again. "At last. I've found the turncoat. And what luck to run into another of his cronies. Or should I say his victims, from the sound of things." He chuckled and I felt all warm inside. "Yes, Raz of the house of Songsterson." He made the face of someone who has just been struck with an idea. "That necklace of yours—that wouldn't belong to him, would it, now?"

"Actually. . . ." I patted the heavy rune fondly. "I suppose it does. I was taking it to him."

"Ah, yes, yes. May I see it?" Before the words were out, he was slipping the cord over my head, lifting it past my ruffling hair, and then putting it around his own neck. "The sigil of a mage. Powerful thing to have. I think I should hold on to this for you, just to be sure it stays safe, don't you?"

Of course I should have thought of that. It would be so much safer with someone like him. "All right."

He ran his finger around the outline of the rune lovingly, as if testing the edge of a blade. I could have sworn I saw a line of glowing blue fading behind his fingertip.

We walked companionably on. He fell silent after a time, as though musing, though he never took his arm off my shoulders. I felt sweaty under my cloak, but I didn't object. There was something soothing about my new friend's touch; at the same time, it was somehow disturbing.

Our boots crunched through the dry gravel and fallen leaves and debris that is on every road. Other than that, we walked in a pleasant silence. To onlookers—if there had been anyone else on the road, which there wasn't at the moment—we would seem father and daughter, spiritual leader and young initiate, or perhaps even husband and much-younger wife. I didn't care. Everything was so very peaceful. I could see the spires of the local church already looming near, just beyond the next bend in the road.

But instead of following the curve of the road, he swerved and led me off the main road onto a footpath that was all overgrown with weeds. Dodging potholes, we headed toward a rest area with benches. "Let us rest for a while, dear."

"But we're within a few minutes of Ladenia proper. Don't we want to get into town?"

"Oh, certainly, certainly. We'll get there directly. It's merely that I ken you need some rest." We were just behind a stand of hedges that screened the park-like clearing from the main road. "Your feet are getting so heavy, aren't they? Yes, they are, dear. And your legs—they're like lead to lift. It's all you can do to put one foot in front of the other. And you're feeling so contented and sleepy."

I couldn't imagine how he could predict my moods so perfectly. For just about then, the fatigue kicked in, and I could hardly walk another step. I sank down quite willingly on the blanket he spread out. "I believe I will take a short rest before we get into the city." I was so winded all of a sudden that I could hardly catch my breath.

"Let me just help you get into a relaxed position." He helped my cross my ankles and wrists, and then bound them with a soft cord. "This is just to make sure you don't hurt yourself, of course." I knew he was right, but somewhere within me it seemed not quite sensible to go along with him. Yet he was a monk, a man of wisdom, wasn't he? I must just be stubborn.

"My old back isn't what it used to be. Hold on to this, dearie. If you'll just roll to your left, now—"

"It's too hot." I had to protest as he rolled the blanket around me, tucking it in all over. I felt a sudden pang of panic, claustrophobic at the thought of having the blanket cover my face, as he seemed intent on doing. He produced another rope. "Please . . . don't make me stay bundled up."

"It's such a shame that you're losing your voice," he murmured. With a growing sense of panic, I realized he was right. I could hardly croak out my protests as he trussed me up inside that woolly cover as though I were just another rug going to market. I tried to kick and thrash, but only succeeded in becoming more tangled in the damp mass of wool. Wool, I confirmed, stinks when it gets damp.

He slung the package containing me over his shoulder. I felt like a side of meat headed for the stewpot. We walked for a short distance, and I heard and felt the bushes rustle as he pushed them aside. Past the hedge or whatever it was, he lowered me to the ground again. I managed to crane my neck all the way up so as to peek out the top of the tube I was in.

He muttered a word I couldn't hear. Before my eyes his great bulk reduced, weight falling away as he shrank down to an average size; I realized what was happening as the illusion fell away. The monk was false, actually a mage. Or else he served a spirit of evil who granted him illusory powers. His robes shrank with him as he became a younger, lean, muscular man. It had been no real effort for him to keep pace with me, and now I knew why.

He stood among the branches, throwing aside a tarpaulin and a cover of fallen branches to reveal the wagon that had passed me earlier, concealed here from the road. Whinnying, snorting, and pawing of the ground told me that nearby were its black horses. I thrashed back and forth, but I was too light to budge my wraps. What would I do, anyway, if I rolled under the bushes? He'd just haul me right back out.

His meaty arms wrapped around me again, and he slung me up across his shoulders and over them. I hit something hard and creaky; my shoulders and hipbone would be bruised by morning.

Things went dark at the end of the tube. I figured out that I'd been stuffed into the back of the wagon, hidden among his wares. If I didn't panic, I wouldn't suffocate, though the air was musty and dust-scented.

I hoped I wouldn't wet myself.

"Go ahead and take yourself a little nap for a while, until I call you to awaken." *I am as dumb as anyone who ever walked*, was my last coherent thought as darkness gathered within me. I fell into a deep, dreamless sleep.

CHAPTER NINE

When I awoke, it was dark, and I was not in any familiar place.

The stone floor was dusty and cold. I sneezed as I twitched awake, stirring up a virtual carpet of dust bunnies that lay all around my head. At least that blanket was off.

I looked around. Surrounding me were stacks of wooden crates and tied-up sacks that smelled of something musty and rotten. My wrists and ankles ached, and I wished I could rub my hands and feet. Testing them, I found they were bound. Still secured with the cords, I figured, they were all tingly on pins and needles. Added to those bonds was a spiderweb of ropes covering me from the chest down. In all, it held me fairly tightly. Also, I'd been stripped down to my muslin underthings; my good green cloak, tunic, skirt, tights, and boots were all gone. Of course my coin purse had also appealed to them. Oddly, they hadn't bothered with my "Rite necklace," actually Raz's token. At least they'd not been reprobates who might've left me back here naked.

I thought I heard something scrabbling in the dark around me. What if it was a rat? Only my heart pounded louder than the sound.

Then I heard voices at the very limit of my hearing; if I strained, I could just make out snatches of conversation. I lay perfectly still, listening.

"She won't be any use to us. I say we just get rid of her."

"No! I don't take without a reason, and I don't waste a useful hostage while there's any possibility of making use of her."

"You keep her long, you'll have to feed her some. Waste of food." The grumbler was a deep-voiced man, probably young. I immediately despised him for his hateful attitude toward an innocent young girl he didn't even know—let alone that it was *me* he meant.

"We won't be feeding her enough that you'd even miss it." The cunning voice was familiar. I figured it for my kidnapper's. "She won't wake for hours—at least not for a day. Not until I call her awake."

"You sure that web's enough to hold her?"

"She's just a girl, a mere child." They'd been fooled by my short stature and slender, undeveloped body. "Completely untalented and untrained in the ways of majick." I was insulted at the confidence in the voice's tone. "Nothing to worry about."

"I can't have some runny-nosed urchin lying back there among my wares for days. You've got to—"

The second voice cut off the protest. "And this won't go on for days. I need whatever she knows about Songsterson. I have a feeling she is the key, the one who'll lead me to him at last."

The voices were moving. "Nevertheless, I'd worry. What if she needs . . . wouldn't want to have . . . and furthermore—what about nature's call. . . ." I caught only snatches of the reply, and heard receding footsteps. They were headed away from me. Nevertheless, I held still as I could be.

The first voice echoed louder for a moment. "I assure you, I won't delay that long."

Fragments from the other voice. "What if she sees—rules about keeping a captive—get rid of—what use she'd be to us—if only traces."

A stronger statement floated to my ears. "I give you my word. I will have the information quickly, and it will not be useless to us."

The voices grew softer again, though I strained for them. Finally all talk faded completely.

I tested the strength of the ropes again, but only succeeded in tiring myself out. I lay there, tears of frustration spilling down my hot cheeks and running into the curves of my ears. I couldn't believe how stupid I had been.

Why had I gone along so willingly, spilled my guts to a stranger on the road? Let myself be trussed up and taken without a struggle? What kind of religious brother seeks out an armourer, for Heaven's sake?

My villain must be the master of some powerful charms, to cast a web of spells around me without my even realizing it. His very voice had hypnotized me while we walked along the public road in broad daylight. And now he had Raz's sigil.

Think. That was what I must do. Think more successfully than ever I had. I could imagine the wails of hopelessness that idea would bring out of Da and Raz. Well, I would show them they'd underestimated me. If I ever saw either of them again.

The first thing was, where was I? The wooden boxes stacked around me let only a little light seep in between the boards, so there was no use trying to see anything. I knew we might have traveled any distance, short or long—it might be that I was inside Ladenia proper, or we could have taken a majickal journey far away from anything I knew. Although I had understood the language spoken by my current captors. I ticked this off on my mental fingers as a positive aspect.

Another thing: I had awakened on my own, I believed; the mage hadn't called me to awaken, as he'd claimed he would have to. That might mean his spells were wearing off, or that my underbrain was cleverer than I was.

I sniffed again, making a conscious effort to discern anything that might illuminate my circumstances. Around me was the scent of moldy, wet grain. I felt a sneeze lurking in the upper reaches of my nostrils, and tried to loose it, but it wouldn't come. Then I was thankful I hadn't done it, remembering that any noise might alert someone. There could be majickal alarms on me, for all I knew.

As I shifted my weight, I realized that some of the ropes that held me were sticky. I thought I recognized it after a moment; it was sticky majickal webbing, the kind that expanded and contracted so as not to kill any of the extremities, but held fast when there was any sudden movement. That meant I was in the clutches of a great majicker, indeed. This kind of flexible roping was something Da had worked on forever, but never quite perfected.

I closed my eyes to think as more hot tears squeezed out. I must have fallen asleep crying like a coward. It was dark as I came back to wakefulness, and quiet except for the scritching of mouse claws somewhere beyond. My hands and feet were freezing and stiff, and my back hurt. My cheeks felt raw from blubbering. I felt the beginnings of panic, so I forced myself to breathe slowly and deeply. I took a breath through my nose and held it for eight counts, then slowly released it from my mouth, repeating this sequence for each alternate syllable of the childhood rhyme, "the elf ran up, the elf ran down." Finally the pounding of my heart slowed and stopped filling my ears with its noise.

There in the quiet dark, alone, I began to feel a tug at the edge of my senses. Like someone gently tugging at the ends of your hair, or tapping the foot of your mattress. The vibration was more something I sensed than actually felt. Just a misty perception, like an aura.

Raz had told me, so long ago, that I would have the witchsight. Could this be it? I held my breath and tried to concentrate, then stopped thinking and opened to the feeling.

But it faded.

I'd sensed a sort of breeze down around my bare feet. Yes, there was definitely movement. It was like ice down my neckline to realize that I wasn't imagining it.

I felt a wet something dabbing—no, pecking—at my big toe. Then I felt more pricks. Sets of tiny claws, running across my feet. I trapped a scream in my throat as more tiny toenails poked into my calves and knees.

In the semi-darkness, I could not tell what they were, beyond warm furry things with pointy noses that probably overhung sharp little teeth. Mice would be the least scary option. I tried to roll away, thrashing back and forth, but the majick reacted, holding me still. My bonds tightened as I moved—they must be enchanted to tighten up briefly at any abrupt movement. The outer webbing in particular drew itself in, molding itself to me the moment I flinched, as if it felt my every movement. The net of ropes bound me fast.

It was all I could do to keep from screaming. I was sure my muslin garments smelled like the oats and cheese and cereal that had originally filled the goods-sacks they'd been sewn from; they were brand-new. I was going to be picked clean, like a carcass under a flock of hungry crows. Shaking all over, I prayed that it would be quick, and that I'd be dead before they got to my face.

But as I thrashed, ready for blind panic, my left wrist snapped into its other position. My brain snapped to attention. I'd been tied after I fell asleep, so my joints had been relaxed into their natural positions. Now I could snap them deliberately into the other notch. Maybe I could shift all my doubled joints, and thereby loosen the non-majickal ropes. Gently I started to readjust my other wrist.

As I moved, my hand brushed a bulge beneath my rough muslin undertunic. It was my flute, tied underneath at my waist for safekeeping on the journey. They hadn't taken any notice of it, or else had dismissed it as a toy.

Recalling how I had persuaded the field mice in the barn to scramble to and fro according to my flutesong, I wondered whether I might influence these as well. But I couldn't flute yet, not until I could work my hands loose. And I knew from experimenting in the hayloft that I wouldn't affect the animals' many brains without my flute. I could, however, try something on the inanimate ropes.

I began to whistle. As I formed the tune, I talked to the ropes around my wrists. They were not ropes, but normal elastic bands like the ones that held hair. While I visualized this, I worked at my double-jointed trick, clicking my wrists back and forth a few times. It burned and hurt and I heard them snap like someone cracking her knuckles, but I kept at the gentle pressure until the ropes slipped. I could move my hands!

The same trick worked for my ankles, freeing my feet. My toes wiggled in relief. Still, I had to be careful, for the netting around me still gripped firmly. Raising my heels off the ground and jiggling around, I managed to slip the flute out of its case. I stopped it with my pinky, but when I tried to slide it upward, it wouldn't budge. What was it caught on?

I raised my head slightly, long enough to see the thread that held the flute before the netting disciplined me. My bonds were designed to keep me from standing up, not to stop my blood circulation, so if I moved slowly, as if still asleep, I thought I could fool the net.

I tore the knot loose and worked both my elbows back and forth until they were in position. The net stretched just as I'd hoped, since it was made to prevent strangulation. As long as I moved inch by inch, I could get into position. Gradually I brought the flute to my lips.

The voices were long since quiet. I would just have to take the chance that my tune would attract someone.

Softly, as softly as ever I had, I managed to begin a quiet tune. It was so subtle that it was little more than echoes bouncing around my boxed-in chamber, but it did move the shadows, so I knew it was enough.

No one as far as I knew had ever tried out flute-show on animals. I started picturing them anyway. Mice, pointy-nosed and fluffy gray handfuls, as I mentally composed them, intelligence shining out of their beady little—er, charming round black eyes. I felt a slowdown in the creatures' activity even as I exhaled softly down the silver tube.

Then I grew bolder, blowing a few more cycles of the repeat, making up a story about friendly mice who wanted to help a big clumsy girl, the notes chasing themselves around me, flying up and down the silver webs like drumbeats of the heart. It was working: I could feel my tune tapping into the majick contained in the web of my bonds and resonating inside, gathering strength, capturing the energy of the original spell itself.

I started piping a tune about chewing, gnawing, the beaverish desire to chomp on ropes. It made even my teeth itch. I painted a

watercolor of the ropes around my ankles and knees, and the ones
that held my upper arms tight against my ribcage; these were
delicious hemp, the finest scented smoking stuff, and would be
fabulous to bite. Up to my waist padded some tiny paws, and sure
enough I could feel them gnawing at my bonds, hundreds of them.
At least it seemed that way, little wet noses hitting up against my
flesh under the muslin. Accidentally, I let that thought distract
me, and a wave of revulsion ran though me and my music. But
then I felt the confusion and doubt coming from the mice, and
quickly turned my whole thoughts back to the story at hand.

Chewy, gnawsome, delectable hemp. I felt the ropes unwinding,
snapping strand by strand, dropping to the ground. My tune turned
to how mice needed to drag the ropes away. The net would open
for them to take the rope, as it had to let them in. I drew the
musical painting of how they each dragged the ropes away to their
nests and lairs, the happy smiles of their families and nestmates
greeting them with nose-wrinkly smiles, crinkly, sniffle-y, snuffling noses, as they brought home the bounty to be unraveled for
nesting material. And, of course, as a great delicacy for chewing,
chewing, chewing . . . .

The last of my ropes pulled out from under me, sliding away
behind the mice as their little nails tapped oh-so-quietly away
across the hard stone floor. I had done it! I blew one last trill and
stopped for breath. I found I was breathing rather fast, my heart
tympanning at my success. I quivered all over under my skin.

The question remained—had anyone heard? I lay still quietly
for a long moment, wondering whether any majickal alarms might
have been triggered. I heard no voices, no footsteps. I judged myself safe enough for the moment. All I need do was keep the volume down.

Now all that was left was the electrified web, a living net pul-
sating up and down with sparks of majickal energy. Could I control it? Wasn't I already moving more freely, controlling it?

The confining net quivered and shimmered in the dark, alive
now with my majick and its own. I started another circuit of soft

echoes, keeping the majickal current alive and moving around me so as not to lose control of the net while I thought of the best way to get rid of it. Why not make it useful?

I would have it knit itself into a cloak, a majickal cloak warm enough for sneaking out in the night. Maybe the monk would not even recognize me dressed in it. Ha, I knew better.

The cloak. I imagined it: soft mohair yarn, its fuzzy pliable fibers stretching out, tying themselves into knots like in the crochetwork that fell from Dame Trudgeon's talented fists. I could feel the strings, like rubber-tree bands in a way, rearranging themselves and braiding into the kind of weft I intended. Weaving itself into a garment to hug my body, but not keeping me bundled and confined the way it had. This hugging would be to protect, to insulate, to cover and hold—I paused for a moment, trilling to gain some time to think. Um, also to make me look taller, less slender, and more shapely; even to give the illusion that underneath lay beauty.

Lights like tiny diamonds raced around the fibers of the net, illuminating my little cavern like so many fairies flitting about me with needle and thread. Winking under the cloth they were "weaving," the glimmers tingled and made a sizzling noise, though there was no heat. I tickled as the net's threads moved like so many tiny worms, making all around me a majickal kind of coating. As my fingers moved, I felt the excitement someone must feel who is working an entirely new kind of spell. I had never known I could control this much power—and not all of it my own.

I piped until I felt the net rearrange itself and give one last satisfied twang. It now covered my legs as tights, wrapped around the waist as a twisty belt and attached wrap skirt, and continued up to the bodice of a stretchy kind of camisole that ended in cap sleeves and scooped around my neck front and back. All this connected by cords to the cape that it had made on the outside. I couldn't see the colors exactly in this murk, but I was dazzled by the lights that still danced faintly inside the fabric. The bodice was snug, but not tight; the tights now allowed my legs the freedom of movement I had been denied. The skirt was generously long, covering any evidence of the ropes that had bound my ankles.

I ended my tune with a quavery minor-second trill that petered out gently, just in case there was no way to tie off the majick. I felt the threads tying their final knots; the majick simmered down, fading away just as I imagined it. On impulse, I envisioned the rest of the majick going to sleep, not dissipating, but waiting to wake again when I summoned it.

I waited a few breaths, and my new garments didn't set me afire, nor suddenly tighten to strangle me. I gentled the flute out from between my lips, trying not to think of the evil things that could have happened. It wasn't safe to think that way until well after I'd quelled the sound.

I still didn't understand why the majick did as I told it, or how I could do this without specific majickal training. All I could think was that Fortuna of Luck was with me, and the saints were watching over me.

I hoped my blessing or luck continued to hold. Could I sit up? Carefully I raised up on my elbows, then on my palms, still leaning back. I was a little winded from all that fluting, but also exhilarated at having made it work. I bent my knees, then sat fully up. I think I was as surprised as the netting itself must have been that it had obeyed my song, and was now mine to control.

I sobered a bit at the thought of still having to escape. Where was I?

CHAPTER TEN

The kiss of majick tugged at me all at once in the quiet. A prickling disturbed the skin on my forearms and cheeks. I hadn't bitten anything sour, but my inner cheeks would argue for it. I felt a questioning tug at the edges of my aura. Could it be my own residual energy damping down to ground around me? Or did I only imagine it?

Gradually it faded away, though something remained to nag at me, something familiar. My hair was all staticky, the shorter pieces standing out, but that was to be expected, after working with strong majick and struggling to gain control over the majickal thread. I couldn't wait to tell Da about my amazing skill; he'd be so pleased that something had come from all my "tooting on that whistle." Somehow I had to get out of here, if only to brag to him.

Now I could see that I was in an alcove surrounded by wooden crates. There were no boxes over my head as I had thought, but instead a storage loft. Was this a warehouse, or were there people? I slithered on my belly to the end of the row of boxes, hardly daring to peek around the corner. Down that way led a corridor where I judged the shaft of light was coming from.

The corridor was formed between two rows of stacked wooden crates. Beyond I could see a maze of similar corridors, all lined with boxes or crates. I suspected one might lead to a door or window I could squirm through unnoticed.

I pretzeled into a squat, wincing as my ankles creaked and my knees popped in complaint. Every joint snapped back to first position, protesting loudly. Double-jointed people were accustomed to it, but it sounded awful. I'd only been tied up flat on cold stones for a few hours. What was I, old lady Trudgeon?

Standing up, I tottered a little, but found my feet still worked fine. The stone floor was rocky and uneven, and I only hoped I wouldn't step on a loose pebble and make a stone bruise. My majickal webbing was thicker across the bottoms of my feet, but wasn't like shoe-soles for protection.

The mice hadn't managed to drag away all the heavy rope. I looped a couple of longer lengths around my left elbow, just in case.

I flattened my back against a row of crates and followed the impromptu corridor left, right, left. I'd reached a dead end. I back-tracked and took a right. This time I got about halfway to the next turn and thought I heard the echo of a voice.

I froze in place and waited, and again a voice wafted to me. Muffled, but definitely speech. Then another voice, answering it. I chanced heading toward the voices to see what information I could get.

As I drew closer, I made out a conversation. It was talk that befitted some kind of a men's game, one of those where unmarried men or men who worked at not working would gather in fours or sixes to throw the dice or deal the cards. I heard coins striking wood and decided they were either pitching coins or feeding the money kitty for the next round.

"Come on, double ducats. Come on, doubles." This one had a country accent.

A whoosh of breath, then a clanking. "Damnation!"

General rough catcalls, then men's laughter. "I told 'im, didn' I? I told him not to wager!"

"Aah, quieten yourself down before I quieten you!"

The voices got louder as I tiptoed through the maze, threading my way around sacks of grain with chewed-away corners and their goods spilling out, boxes tied securely closed with lengths of twine, and lots of weaponry: quivers of arrows, crossbows, even suits of chainmail. At the end of the aisle, I could see bright light through a break in the boxes.

Wishing for a hand mirror, I dared to poke my head around the corner.

Six men sat around a heavy oak pedestal table, casting runes. No, they were pitching runestones, but not for fortunetelling, only some kind of a game. One man had his head buried in his elbows as if dozing; another was blowing on the stones, shaking the felt bag, ready to cast. I memorized the faces I could see, wondering at the idea that this place warranted six guards. Probably these wares were majickal or stolen, or both.

The most wonderful sight was the door propped open behind them. I could smell the fresh, cool evening breeze. A few moths flitted in, attracted by the gamers' lanterns, one in the middle of the table, several hanging by thin chains from hooks in the ceiling boards. There were, however, plenty of shadows.

But I wasn't a thief, had never studied shadow-skulking. Besides, my joints were still creaky.

I could dash past really fast. Who was I kidding? As if they'd never notice their prisoner, if they knew about me—or a thief, if they didn't—running by. Even if they were absorbed in the game, it was too risky.

Maybe I could charm them with the flute. But these were men, not mice, even if only in the most strict sense of the word. I'd never tried flutework on a person. It took a moment to get the pictures going, so I dared not risk starting a song, because at the first sound they'd rush for me. The sound wouldn't be muffled as it had been in the back under a bunch of boxes. I supposed their game had drowned me out before.

That left crawling out under the table, right among all their clumsy feet. I pictured myself slithering past on my belly, feeling for all the world like the cursed serpent. Still too dangerous. I knew somehow that I'd suddenly feel hot breath down my neck and hear an "Aha!" Strong hands would haul me out. "What have we here? She'll be a fun scrump!" I winced inwardly.

No, it was far too chancy.

But perhaps the answer stood by my elbow. A tall ladder leaned against the stacks of crates, a makeshift wooden affair lashed together with cords. Meant for stacking the crates, I guessed, and plenty tall to reach the top row. I tested a rung with my hand; it seemed sturdy enough. Looking up, I saw that it led to the top of the boxes, within reach of the beams of the ceiling. Could I go up and across the beams, right over their heads, then climb down boxes on the other side? I'd have a better chance if I were closer to the door.

For a moment I closed my eyes, dizzied by the thought of crawling along the ceiling beams, precariously balanced all the way across like a long-tailed eliuku in the woods, constantly worrying that a rotting beam might crack under my weight. Remember climbing trees, I told myself. Just like climbing trees.

I eased myself up on the ladder's first rung and heard the wood creak. Holding my breath, I waited. No sound from the table except the normal clinking of the stones, clanking of the coins, cursing of the losers.

Up another rung, then the next few rungs. I moved in slow motion, as if pushing through molasses, or when you've dived to the muddy bottom of a cold pond and you're kicking, trying to bounce high enough to break through to the surface. Somehow I reached the top of the ladder.

I put both hands on the top crate and sent up a short prayer to the saints, then made ready to boost myself up. Would the boxes hold me?

They held. I scrambled over quietly as I could, but still made what I considered too much noise. The stacks of crates swayed and squeaked under me. I held my breath. No reaction from the gamblers. I started to pull the ladder up after me, then thought better of it; I might need to make a quick retreat and descent. Quietly I got to all fours and crept forward.

The ceiling sloped lower here; I flattened and dragged myself along the tops of the wooden crates, snagging now and then on a nail. My belly would've been peppered with splinters if it hadn't been for my clothes, which didn't seem damaged—the cloth just rewove itself and healed any punctures. I had to duck to keep from banging my head on the exposed beams of the roof.

Light struck my back in stripes from overhead. I looked up and couldn't believe my luck. A cord dangled from a trapdoor leading up and out, presumably to the roof. I must have been living right. All I'd have to do to go out was cling to the interior roof beams, swinging across four of them in turn, and crawl along until I reached the trapdoor and pushed it open. Assuming it wasn't nailed shut. I would've swallowed hard if my mouth hadn't been full of dust.

Something creaked below. I froze in place, then dared to glance back down. The door had blown closed, or one of them had pushed it. No turning back now.

I whispered a prayer and swung up onto the beam overhead, pretending it was a thick branch on a buttonwood tree we had in the back garden. I used to monkey-clamber across the thickest limbs, shinnying along until I could swing from the strong flexible one on the west side, then jump to the rowan oak on the other side of Aunt Mina's Creek. This was just like that branch, except it was half again as narrow and hung directly above a circle of blackguards who'd like as not kill me soon as look at me.

I crossed the first beam without any problem. About halfway across the next, a tuft of my hair caught in a crack in the roof. I jerked it out, biting my lip at the pain. My poor head. On my numb feet and battered elbows and knees, I crept on across two more. At last the door was within reach.

I pushed, and a ceiling window quietly fell open. The stars had never looked so beautiful.

# # #

Standing on the sloping roof, I knew what people meant by "ecstasy of high places." I had always been a little tottery and afraid of heights, but from here, where I knew I was safe, I felt euphoric. I had done it—I had gotten away.

The only problem now was how to get down.

I shivered in a sudden cold breeze. I surveyed the flickering stars overhead and could tell nothing about where I might be or which direction I should head; I was still close enough to home that the sky looked the same. I made out some lights at the horizon that might be part of a city, but far away. The rooftop was the only one among the treetops as far as the eye could see. I was in the middle of a clearing in deep woods.

I let the ropes slide down my arm. Both lengths tied together still wouldn't reach the ground, but I judged they would go halfway. I could probably take that fall; it was only about the height of Da standing on the shoulders of a second Da with me on top.

Again I would've swallowed hard, but I still couldn't muster any moisture.

Where could I secure the rope? The thatched roof was built on a network of boards. I felt around for a thick one and laced the rope's end under and around. I tied the best knots that Da had taught me. Tugging, I decided it would hold me. It had to. I let the rope down. It was a little shorter than I had figured on.

It was a long way down . . . .

"There she is yonder. Avast!"

I twisted around, and my blood turned to ice water. One of the villains was sticking up out of the hole in the roof, up to his chest. He seemed to be having a little trouble boosting his bulk through the trapdoor. Perhaps it was the influence of the ale I could smell all the way down here. He fumbled and his hands slipped, sending him partway back down. "You, girlie. Stop right there!"

I knew I should've hauled that ladder up after me.

No time to waste being afraid. I clambered to the edge of the roof, hanging halfway off. The tall oaks beckoned to me in the wind, and they were almost close enough to reach. Grasping the rope, I lowered myself a few lengths; it was tougher than I imagined to hang on, the hemp burning my hands. Halfway down, I kicked the side of the building and swung out. I reached for the nearest tree with my foot. Somehow I found a foothold on a branch.

Swinging myself on the branch, I went hand-over-hand to the trunk. I climbed down several more branches before I found no more handholds. I steadied for the fall, and let myself drop.

Eight kingsfeet down, I landed on the soft grass, rolling. I kept rolling until I was well under the trees into the dark, hoping there were no snakes and that the shadows would conceal me from immediate discovery. The landing had knocked me breathless, and I felt a little twinge in one rib, but there was no time to worry about it. After only an instant I hauled myself to my feet and ran into the woods.

Through the forest I went headlong, crunching across twigs, pine needles, and rocks, sticking a splinter into my foot more than once, but afraid to stop for a moment. I kept imagining I heard twigs snapping behind me or felt fingers plucking at the back of my robes.

The sounds of the night forest soon damped their fading shouts. I was in the deepest part of the woods, where the canopy of limbs blocked most of the sun and the oaks fought the maples for root space on the ground's surface. Branches slapped my face and tore at my hair and clothes. I dodged or sideswiped dozens of large trees that I missed seeing until it was too late to dodge. Heedless, I pushed myself forward until I thought I would burst. At last I slowed, pounding to a stop in a small clearing circled by skinny braidwood trunks, heavy with the need for breath.

I stood panting in the ankle-tall sticker-grass, wet and cold up to mid-calf, and listened. Not a sound. Not even the whispering of the wind in the branches or a dove cooing. It was the sleeping time of the forest; even the owls seemed quiescent.

"Dear namesake, Saint Dulcinea—if you're really a saint now—hear me," I whispered. "Protect me in this wilderness. Intercede for me and ask the Lord to save me and bring me safely home."

CHAPTER ELEVEN

I was deep in the wild forest without even one moon to guide me. Tonight should be the night of the new moon in Celeste, I recalled from our majickal calendar, yet I couldn't spy her in the skies. Lunette had not yet risen, or was hiding behind the puffy skating clouds. But it was dim out, nearly as dim as a completely moonless night. Surely Celeste would rise soon.

I shivered, drawing my cloak closer. It hugged back, alarming me a little. But when it didn't get snugger than I wanted, yet just enough for comfort, I breathed a sigh of relief. I caught the faint scent of vanilla beans and sleepherb.

Then I remembered my moonjewels. I drew the string out from where I'd hidden it in the hem of my undertunic, and it glowed with the light of the hidden moons. I'd charged them, and the moon lady had heard me. The glow was bright enough to see the ground beneath my feet. Now I could watch my path for sinkholes and snakes.

The dark damp air swirled with mist around me. I felt very alone, yet in another sense I wasn't alone at all. Still a bit exhilarated by my recent majickal success, I was still in tune with the majickal grid that hugged all the material world in its hands, the web of majick, source of the power of natural majicking. I fancied I could sense the world-base turning and the skywheel spinning all around it, the dim stars like insects on the spokes of a wagonwheel. I felt certain that soon I would receive divine guidance, that the saints had heard me and mask me from the sight of the wicked ones. Though I knew I was lost, for the moment I was at peace. I found my mental center and listened for the answer to my prayer.

The pricking at the edge of my senses returned, a prickly feeling like your foot waking up after being numb because you sat on it . . . or when it's just barely falling asleep again. This wasn't the evil mage, though, for the presence was benevolent, gentle, almost familiar.

I held my breath—then realized that was exactly the opposite of what I should do. I reached for my flute. Softly, I started one of Da's favorite songs. The song we'd sung earlier in the week, "At Eventide." As softly as I could, as if I were just another drowsy bird in the sleeping wood . . . .

Majick was afoot, for sure. In between phrases, when I paused, I could pick out faint sounds in the majickal ether around me. Whispers of a compatible melody, harmonizing with mine; then a low rumbling, vibrating my footsoles as if it came from the very center of the earth. Yet I felt no dread, as I would expect if I encountered evil or black sorcery. This was a happy and centered energy.

I played one long trill, a phrase of Raz's that I'd been practicing every night for weeks. I slipped in a minor ornament, then trilled the melody again.

"Dulcinea!"

It was a faraway echo, but the voice was my Da's.

My voice cried out involuntarily, incautiously loud. "I'm here, Da!" I was a bit hoarse.

"Dulcinea Jean! Can you hear me, girl?"

I realized I wasn't hearing him aloud. His voice spoke in my mind.

"If you can hear me, keep still and think of a pink unicorn. Send me a picture with only your thoughts. I can't hear you talking, mind—only the thought. Put all your concentration into the mental image."

The unicorn. He was an image from an old bedtime story that I'd loved, wearing Da out telling it night after night. It was a tale from legend, yet I as a child had held fast to the notion that somewhere one or more of them lived. In a wood much like this one. I'd painted the portrait in pastel chalks and wax colorworks endlessly. I squeezed my fists in effort as I visualized my imaginary pet.

A lovely soft pink all over except for his snowy-silver mane and tail, he was stocky and short, yet elegant and dancer-like. Built more like a goat or donkey than a horse, short and muscular and quick and lithe, his fur like a rabbit's that you'd long to pat, sparkling eyes and a little goatee, and of course the spiral horn . . . .

"All right, I'm too optimistic. You still have the majick attached to you, gal, but you're not practiced in this working from this far a distance. I suppose it has been a few years since I searched for you in the marketplace." We used to practice mental picture sending when I was a child, so when I got lost in hidey-seek or at the market, he had a way to find me, but I'd been too young to wonder how it worked. I'd almost forgotten. I heard his weary wry grin. "Quietly, now, quietly—pipe for me."

Softly I began to blow. What would be the song of the unicorn? His tune came to me as la-tra-la, trills in thirds, like a song on wheels. The elusive mighty Pink Unicorn. The only one left in the world, the song told me, and never seen before by any living human. His blue eyes twinkled out at me, silver mane sparkling in a new shaft of moonlight, and he nickered as he strutted in a spiral path around and above me. The music played in circles around itself as if on a carousel ride, but he wasn't part of it, running wild and free through the glade to the shallows of a mountain stream, where he delicately stepped across on the rocks of the waterfall, easy as you please, and over. He switched his silver tail and looked back over his shoulder at me, coquettish as any mare, his opal translucent horn spiraling at me from the middle of his forelock . . . pink forelock . . . my pink unicorn . . . .

"There you are, girl, there!" I heard relief in Da's voice, even though I heard it only in my mind's ear. "That must be you, I know it. Stop the tune, baby. I'll be sending to you now so you'll be able to tune in to me." His words turned serious. "You have to help me, Dulcinea. It's been a long time, ages since I—well, never you mind about all that. Now sit tight while I cast the scrying."

The pink unicorn faded from my inner eye and was replaced by a view of Da in the casting circle, back in our shielded chamber. I had never seen him like this, confident and secure in majick higher than he'd ever allowed me to monitor before. My jaw fell open. What else did I not know about my own Da?

"Found my magebag, of course." He filled something just out of sight from a crystal pitcher and I heard crackling. Cold water into the scrying bowl, I reckoned. "Silly of me to involve you. I should have known you'd go running off like that. I'd not taken to heart your liking that boy so much, and never imagined you'd try to go after him. Of course I should've known how deeply you felt, from watching you two." My cheeks warmed; had my feelings been so obvious? "Well, all that water's under the bridge now."

That was as close as Da could come to saying, "I'm sorry."

He paused a moment. "Let's see, here. Send again, not with music, just with your mind; we're linked, so it ought to work. Send, now, so I can be certain of your exact locus. I've marked you from the attic and now from here. Next I need your bearing from downstairs, and then I ought to have you."

I knew of the method: he would draw a triangle in his mind, each leg leading from me to points he knew. He could measure the distances by comparing them proportionally to the crossings they made of ley lines. Then he'd use the lines' crossings to find my approximate position.

I sent. As hard as I could manage.

The picture of Da snapped back into focus in my thoughts. Now he was sprinkling a handful of herbs to float on the water in his scryer. Could he snap me back into the shop as easily as Raz had done with the magebag?

"You've been gone all day and evening, you know." At least it had only been one day. "I was worried sick. Lucky I had you on my mind, or I might not have been paying such close attention to spurious signals of majick." Before I could send a thought in answer, he added, "Your piping, that's what. It took hold of the

majickal web and entwined itself in a working of mine. Our signa-
tures are that similar." Pride shone from his statement. "Still, it's a
true wonder I could find you, even with that trace. I don't know
how you got into that place—no, no, don't think about it; agitation interrupts my signal. But there surely is some strong evil nearby
you. Wait until I have you back here to explain. All right, now
. . . bear with me while I . . . gads, it's dark where you are,
lass."

"I know." I whispered it aloud, instead of merely thinking it,
but I couldn't tell if he heard.

"I'll cast a light for you. Harrumph—aw, stinking rats' nests, I
can't from here. I've just wasted that energy."

Then, just over my head and to the left, a ball of glow popped
into existence, like some baby moon he'd pitched at me. I reached
toward it and found I could direct its movements by moving my
flattened palm, but could come no closer than a forearm's length
near it. Which was just as well, I realized; it could be cool majickal
light, or it could be made of fire.

"Ah, I see you got it after all."

I knew he was smiling, although he wasn't sending his image
any longer. "Like a glowing candle. Thank you, Da." I took a step,
and the lightball moved just ahead of me. "Will it track me?"

"Should. It'll follow you from the front. You'll walk, and push
it along."

"But which way do I go?"

"Well, there's a good point, lass. I might be able to send it
directions for you to follow, once I know where you are in the
greater scheme. You see, I found you, but I can't read the terrain."
His brief silence scared me. "You're west of the city somewhere.
No, north."

"Which direction should I go to get to the road? Can't you tell
where I am?" My innards crunched up in a sinking feeling for a
moment, as I thought about what it would mean if he couldn't.

"Give me some landmarks. Look at things around you and tell
me about them."

"Trees." I sighed. "It's no use, Da. I'm just in the middle of the woods, where I fled." I sent him a brief series of images, stills from my recent adventure. "I believed I saw the lights of Ladenia City from that roof, to the south, and I headed towards them as best I could. But I can't say for certain."

I felt his consternation. "This may take a moment." After a pause he said, "It occurs to me, Dulce, that you had best stand around there as brief a time as possible. They may still be out looking for you, and that villain is likely to be listening for our majick."

"The guards weren't majickers, Da."

"You'd not think so, or they'd already be busy trying to trace us on the web. Best not to pipe any more, though. It might be that the mage who owns the guards is listening."

No more fluting. No more majick, save folkmajick with herbs. I could always whip up a great little aromatherapy remedy for gout from all this moss and pine bark. Oh, the irony. "Please hurry, Da." I sniffled. I wasn't going to cry. "Sorry. I think my nose is tickled by all the weeds and leafmold out here."

Daddoo seemed to understand. "Aha. I've got your position and some of the area around now. And I don't think they can hear my majicking. Nothing like a shielded chamber for keeping one's majick in, I always say. Still, I'd best use as little as possible. I can't sustain this whole image while you wander through the woods. Quickly, study this."

A map appeared below the lightball. Then a pinkish dot moved around on the map until it landed on a place in the middle of a lot of green stuff. Apparently that was supposed to be where I was. "I knew this working would find you." I fancied I could hear him chuckling, despite the limitations of the mind's voice. "That red line's the main road. We want to get you on it. And to that little tavern—you're quite a ways northwind of Lad City itself. That place is on the outskirts. You can make it there, and I'll set off at the same time to meet you." The map faded gradually. My heart pounded against my lungcage.

"Wait! Don't take it away. I haven't had nearly time to see which way, and I don't know the obstacles." I had to stop breathing in gulps this way; I knew it could make me faint. I leaned over, clapping my hands on my knees, and putting my head down so it wouldn't be totally deprived of humours from panic. "I'm trying to be brave," I added, to head off his scolding.

"I know you are, I know you are. I won't scold you, child. What you need is a living map. Here—why didn't I think of this before? Simple, simple. A sorcery-light came to mind first, but this is even easier, since it'll constantly be in contact with the ground, and I can make it draw from the ground's energy."

I didn't know what he was talking about, but my heartbeat was coming under control, and I made myself take slower, deeper breaths. The winking stars before my eyes began fading, and I straightened up. There was more light in my general area.

Now, in addition to the glowing ball, there was a long-haired fluffy cream-toned cat with long whiskers. She blinked her blue eyes at me, lifted her tail regally, and started off on the mossy floor of the forest onto a path that looked just like all the other dead-ends.

"Follow the cat, Dulcinea. Follow her out."

I gathered my wits on their tentative string and padded, stockingfooted, after her. She seemed to be able to go as fast as I could, but didn't outpace me. She even looked back over her shoulder as I lagged, climbing over low branches and jumping stones. "She's very real, Da. I didn't know you could do things like this."

"Hush, lass. I'm setting off to meet you now. I'll keep a thread of awareness on you, but I won't be able to help you. So use all your wits and get yourself to the people and lights. Make haste." His voice faded even as he finished his sentence. "I'm coming to get you, Dulcinea."

Fleetingly, in my mind's eye, I could see him covering the cauldron and scrying bowl with silks, throwing on his cloak and grabbing his staff, and making his way out of our wizardchamber

. . . but then all I could see was the cat, staying just ahead of me, and the brambles that tore at me again.

Where had Da learned this? Raz Songsterson. This was his kind of doings. He must have taught Da as much as he learned. Or, perhaps, there was a lot more about my own Daddoo that I'd spent years oblivious to.

My majickal clothing continued to amaze me; now it never tore or pulled as I wove through the brush, even though thorns constantly ripped at it. It protected me without allowing anything to penetrate, and without sustaining damage itself. Even my stockinged feet were fairly comfortable, though I could feel the forest floor. I wondered at the powers of whomever had created it, and knew that if I weren't careful—and perfectly lucky—he would draw me right back into his web. He might even be aware of my escape, allowing it as a way of drawing Da into this. Should I worry about being traced by the clothing I'd woven?

I headed off those thoughts by concentrating solely on the fluffball ahead of me and on the spot of light that danced in front, a positive pole that I the negative end pushed ahead; I could never get closer than just out of reach. Soon, but not soon enough to suit me, we were in sight of the road. Civilization at last.

The cat vanished at the wood's edge, before I had my feet on the lovely main road. I stepped onto the packed dirt lane and followed it up a hill and around a curve. It led me safely behind the first lighted tavern at the edge of town. Feeling antsy, I walked around and sat on the tavern's front steps to wait for Da.

CHAPTER TWELVE

The carved double doors to the Winged Horse tavern stood ajar, and a steady stream of people flowed in and out around me. Just as steadily, a thin stream of smoke leaked out from the billowing clouds of tobacco inside. A robust song reached me, a beer-drinking sea chantey about dozens of flasks of ale falling off a wall or something. Laughter made the rest of the place boisterous. I supposed this must be quite a festive night spot.

The string of glowing moonjewels was still wrapped around my wrist. I slipped the string back into my muslins' hem. I was a ball of nerves again, even under the city's torches. Fidgeting, I started to feel thirsty, but resolved not to move, only to watch for Da. I didn't want to miss him or make him worry more.

I hadn't been sitting there but hardly a candlemark before a young man stepped out of the tavern. He ran lightly down the steps, then threw a coy glance over his shoulder at me. Digging his toe in the dirt at the side of the steps, he wouldn't meet my gaze. He plucked a handful of grass to chew, swung his legs a moment, and finally approached the steps again. Taking a seat on the other end of the step next to me, he looked over at me and cleared his throat a couple of times. Must have been choking on the smoke inside, and no wonder.

Not wanting to be rude, I nodded. With a tentative expression on his face, he nodded back. He turned red as a chokeberry and cleared his throat again.

Perhaps tavern people were rather simple. I craned my neck and looked down the road, but no travelers rode. My foot started tapping. How long would Da be?

A couple of coughs later, the youth cleared his throat and said, "Um." I glanced over, thinking he might need a pat on the back, but his face wore its customary (so far) idiotic grin. He extended his hand, full of silver and even a couple of gold-toned coins. "See?"

I scooted closer to the other edge of the step. "Very nice." I didn't know what the blazes to say, and I was on the verge of turning rude.

"How much is it, then?" He looked at me hopefully.

How should I know the price of drinks in the tavern? He was the one who'd been inside, not me. "I don't know."

"You—" His voice cracked. "You don't know?"

"Ask inside. I really have no idea." I turned firmly away, wondering how soon I could get a glass of water and some clean muslins.

His mouth gaped. Was he an idiot, or was the lateness of the hour affecting his judgment? For that matter, I supposed my judgment might be slightly impaired. I shouldn't even have spoken. I tried to figure out where else I could sit and wait, but the only well-lighted spot around was right here.

Finally, he croaked out, "And who should I talk to in—in there?"

"The man behind the bar, I would imagine." Honestly, what a little fool, not to know how to buy a drink. His parents must have been hermits or invalids, because they hadn't taught him a thing. I stood and folded my arms, turning my back to him. Still no dust downroad, and no sign of Da.

"I'll talk to him. You'll be here?"

I couldn't believe the boy was still trying to talk to me. Hadn't I given him reason to leave me alone? Well, now I would. I turned back and slowly gave him a cold stare. If he'd been a flower, he'd have surely withered under my gaze. "I really couldn't say. I think you need to go on inside."

"I'll be right back." He bolted into the tavern.

I sank back down on the stoop, shaking my head. People like that might be dangerous. It simply wasn't safe to be out after dark in the city, just as Da had always told me.

Within moments, three other young men, even stupider-looking than that last one, were gathered around me. My heart pounded and a high-pitched ringing started in my ears. Could these be associates of my abductor? I spoke as roughly and abruptly as I could manage. "What do you want?"

The tallest of the three giggled, then hiccuped. The short one next to him leered at me. "You know what we come after, Girlie. D'you have a room, or do you want to do it right here?" At this, all three burst into nervous laughter.

"Excuse me." I leapt to my feet and dashed inside the double doors. Raucous laughter followed me inside, damped only when I kicked the doors closed behind me.

This city went crazy after dark with moon madness. I hoped patrons indoors would make better sense.

Inside, the air was dense with the odors of colaff, molasses, and thick, dark tree-sugar. Not to mention a wealth of other smells associated with unwashed, road-weary bodies. And the stink of ale-burp. I approached the barman with trepidation, scanning the area so that I could avoid that first youth whom I'd inadvertently sent inside. Thank the saints he didn't seem to be around.

Patting the spot where my coin purse should have hung from the silk belt I no longer had, I frowned. I realized I couldn't even get a tankard of water; I had no money. I was so dry. Maybe someone had abandoned a waterglass somewhere. I slid onto the end of a long bench filled with revelers deep in discussion and tried to make myself inconspicuous.

"I'll wager the Society gets hold of him and fixes him good." A customer raised his tankard to this remark, and several more applauded. "After what he's stolen, why, I shouldn't wonder if they don't poke his head up on a stick!"

"Majicking and witchcraft and sorcery, it's all the same," said another. "Ought to string all of them up so they can't bother hardworking honest people."

This kind of talk made me shaky. It occurred to me that they could as well be talking about Raz, in light of what the evil mage had said. Raz would keep his distance from these types, surely. I slid off the bench as quietly as I could and flattened myself against one of the double exit doors. Peeking out, I satisfied myself that all the strange youths had dispersed, then slipped into the night.

I spent the rest of my time waiting for Da hidden around the back in the bushes behind the privy. It wasn't the most splendiferous situation I could've hoped for, but everyone but those with specific business in mind stayed wide away from the area. I clothespinned my nose with my fingers and sat back, waiting. I think I dozed off for a while.

Much, much later, I heard someone approaching on horseback. "Tickie!" I'd know that clop-clop anywhere.

I ran to the roadside, and there was Da in his black traveling cloak, dismounting, tying Tickie to the hitching post.

"I was never so glad to hug your fat belly."

He squeezed back, as though I weren't almost too grown-up for hugging. "I was seldom so glad for you to, even though sayin' so is sassing."

"Let's go home."

Da had in his pocket a little sack lined with slickleaf. He handed it to me and started untying Tickie. "Thought you might like a midnight snack." It contained two small hard rolls, a round of soft cheese, and a few handsful of berries.

I was so grateful for it. "I hope you have your waterskin."

He did.

I drank deeply and wiped my mouth on my sleeve. "I'm sorry I was such an idiot, Da. I thought I'd be back before nightfall." I shook my head. "What do you think of that fellow knowing Raz? Or at least having heard of him."

"What I think, lass. . . ." He took a long, meditative pause. "Is, that boy Raz wasn't quite what he seemed. Of course, I knew that right away." He got into Tickie's saddle and held out his hand for me. I mounted behind him, needing no boost.

"I knew it, and once we started studying together, he couldn't hide from me that he had other powers. Powers more sorcerous than practical." Da's voice lowered, his words meant just for me. "But once I was certain that they weren't drawn from the dark side, I kept quiet, because I wanted to exchange wisdom with that rascal. He taught me things that . . . well, best not to discuss these things until we're safely home. Are you up solidly?"

"I'm fine." I wriggled around on the back of the saddle, not caring how uncomfortable it was, and patted Tickie's side.

Da was very amused, for some reason, when I told him of the youths who'd approached me at the tavern, but he wouldn't explain his mirth, just said I'd done the right thing. As we rode toward home, I filled him in with all that I had overheard about Raz. I skirted the edges of the story of my kidnapping; no need to worry him overmuch, since I had made out fine. He said very little, merely grunting at appropriate points during my convoluted tale.

We topped a hill and the town proper came into view. It was dark again away from the torches that had lined the outlying row of taverns, and I reckoned we approached Ladenia City from the wrong side, the side I wouldn't want to walk through after dark alone. Suddenly I was bone-weary, my crisis-granted energy having worn off completely.

He could sense it. "Are you tired, child?"

"You know I am, Daddoo."

"Why don't we find a room and stay in town for the night, then." He rubbed his eyes with the back of his hairy hand. Why hadn't I thought how weak he must be from all that majicking and worry? At his age, too.

"Maybe we ought," I said tentatively. "We haven't had a night away in ages."

He made an effort to sound jolly. "There's a really nice inn here with a wonderful late-night kitchen, if I recall correctly. And we'll make a day of it in town on the morrow. You can go to all the shops with me. How would you like that?"

I hugged him from behind. "I'd love it, Daddoo. Yes, let's."

CHAPTER THIRTEEN

We stayed in the cheapest room of the Fat Badger, a fancy rich-man's inn high on a hill overlooking the lake, right in the middle of town. Da winced at the cost, but we both felt it was worth it for the luxurious surroundings. They had, the desk lady assured me, washtubs that they would haul to your room and fill with heated water for you to bathe in. It sounded like a hedonistic, wasteful pursuit, and quite enjoyable. I couldn't wait to try it tomorrow. Imagine the luxury of your own pond to soak in, and heated, yet.

It was hard to believe I'd been in much danger, now that Da was here and I was tucked snugly into a booth in the Badger's dining room. We sat, fat and happy and warm, in the hoot-owl traveler's quarters where the kitchen could feed you late into the night. Still hungry, we'd reached deep into our pockets—er, Da's pocket—for service by the late staff.

I decided I'd overreacted, and felt ridiculous as I sat munching on a cool melon and some fig cakes. I was even more sure that I'd been silly to panic as I accepted the extra blankets the kind innwife offered and trudged up to our room on Da's heels. The monk—wizard—whatever he was, whoever he was, must have realized the whole thing was a mistake. He'd left me in a warehouse and hadn't bothered to track me. Probably, they'd realized I was useless to them. After all, I was merely another member of the (possibly) irate mob looking for Raz. The man had figured out that the likelihood of my leading them to Raz was low, and he'd never bother with me again.

In fact, in the flickering warmth of our room's lanterns, my misadventure seemed nothing more than a dream. I'd learned my lesson; I would be more careful on the road alone in the future. Who was I kidding—I wouldn't brave the road alone for some time. And I'd never wear any majicker's sigil in plain sight, not even my own if I made one, nor shout people's names at passing wagons. As the wag said, it didn't take me long to juggle a hot horseshoe. I leaned back on Da's shoulder and let him, as he had when I was a child, tuck me into my own separate bed, a tall carved one with an actual feather mattress. Paradise.

# # #

The sounds of the town coming alive woke me just after first light. I stretched in the pillow-like bed, luxuriating in its feel. It was especially nice after the hard floors of the warehouse. With a pang of guilt I glanced at Da, still asleep on the floor on the straw mattress they'd provided for the "extra" second bed in the room. I snuggled under the soft warm blanket, dark blue to match my eyes—maybe we could buy it to take home—pulled it up to my chin, and sighed with bliss. It was pure decadence to lie abed late, and even grander to watch Da snoring nearby, not even caring if the shop opened right on time or not. It had been such a long time since we'd come to town just for a visit, and I looked forward to our day together.

Outside the window over my bed the light grew brighter; I slid the pane open. The dewy morning air cooled my face. The breeze came slowly alive with the chirrups and calls of birds, the raucous staccato of the merchants in their shops propping open their doors for the day and calling greetings to one another, the squeak of wheels and clop-clop of hooves as coaches and travelers began their journeys. Behind me, in the innhall beyond, fellow travelers started trickling downstairs, some of their voices lowered in foreign tongues which sounded to me like the songs of insects.

As the capital city of Ladenia, Lad City, as it was nicknamed, hosted many exciting events. The Fat Badger might be on the hill above town, but I could still tell there was something important brewing, just from the mood of the travelers around us, and from the feel of the tavern last night. Perhaps a fair or a caravan was coming into town. I could hardly wait to stroll the colorful streets on Da's arm.

I dressed quickly in the clothes Da had brought, including clean muslins and stockings—heavenly—and my red tunic. On impulse, I rolled my majickal garment into one of Da's empty drawstring bags and stuffed it underbed with our luggage. I plopped his empty waterskin on top. Less chance the chambermaid or staff would pilfer it. I'd explain about its origins to Da later.

He was still resting wonderfully, his snoring having subsided to the basic kawk-choo I was so familiar with. I'd let him rest as long as he wanted, or up until mid-morning, anyway. I flopped back down on my bed. Then I raised up on one elbow and arched my stomach to be taller so I could see more sights from our hilltop window.

Ladenia City stood bare and bold on the high grasslands overlooking the deep footprint of Lake Ossyme. Footpaths of reddish clay, looking like raw gashes in the hillside's blanket of wildflowers, led down to the rocky shore. Below, a gaudy sail sank into the distant mists on the horizon—headed, I surmised, for the corresponding coast of Marwell, where it would next see port. Away from me bobbed the softer taupe-and mud-toned sails of a fishing fleet, the sailors' skill gentling them out with the tide that flowed up the broad mouth of the Langarou toward Ladenia's border with the Dwarflands.

The river Langarou—a Marwellian word, Da had once explained, meaning "snaketail"—had cut a gully through the hills that separated us from our neighbors in Marwell, but on this side of the range, the river had liked what it saw in the valley, pooled here, and become so contented it had made a wide lake. From here on south, the flow was quieter, docile. Friendly, not like where it ran over rocks on the Marwellian crags and got strangled between mine shafts in the Dwarven ranges.

The city's southern edge was outlined by the Langarou's bends. The houses dotting the hillsides looked insignificant from here. I could understand why city folk thought our village rude and rustic in comparison to the beauty of this place.

The room's door banged open behind me. Startled, I twisted to face the doorway. My heart leapt into my throat at the sight of our two familiar—to me, at least—visitors. My kidnapper, the monk. And the first fat jackass I'd outfoxed, or at least outrun, back at the tavern last night; only today, he wore the uniform of the city guard. Two gleaming-eyed rascally faces I'd hoped never to see again, but who were, in fact, here, closing and latching the door behind them.

"There. She's the whore from last night." The jackass winked at me, pointing a thick gnarled stick in my direction. I'd thought him simple, and I'd been correct. "And who's this—your master?" He kicked at Da, who was just stirring, eyes still squeezed shut. The kick fell short of Da's ribs, but shoved him enough to start bringing him around.

"Hey!" I couldn't get the word out of my mouth. Something bitter choked me as I inhaled, and I started coughing. Words wouldn't form in my mouth; I struggled to remember what you were supposed to yell in order to summon aid. I knew it was a short word, began with "s"—no, "h"—I was sure, "h" . . . .

The monk—or whatever he really was—had his finger to his lips. "Quiet, now. We wouldn't want to startle your friend here awake." He made a few arcane gestures over Da's stirring form. I knew the signs he made were activating some kind of spell.

They must've each been preparing spells as they stood outside our door. All the while I'd lain there on my belly like an ignorant little cudge, thinking about idiotic girl things like the scenery, they'd been knitting a majickal net to throw over us. They'd bribed the desk for our key or used majick on the door. And what kind of watch had I kept? I could've smacked myself for being a stupe.

"Help!" I choked on the word, the cognates strangling in my throat. My gaze was inexorably drawn to the jackass. The stick he aimed at me must, of course, be a wizard's rod or majickal staff; it was about an inch thick and as long as his arm. The faint blue haze between me and the staff must be what sucked my voice away before I could shout for help. My throat burned with dryness, and I couldn't think of the proper words I wanted to shout. If only I could warn Da, he might be able to resist or retaliate; yet the spell was already forming around him, and I could only hope it was nothing too drastic.

"No need to alarm our fellow visitors." The monk showed his even yellow teeth in what he must have thought of as a menacing smile, but looked more like a grimace. "We'll only be here another moment, and then we're off to find out just what the connection is between you and Songsterson."

Da lay immobile, seemingly unable to move at all; I suspected a spell of binding. The monk walked over to check him. He held his palms over Da's belly for an eyeblink, then grinned even wider. "Luck's dice, this one is a majicker, undoubtedly a powerful one. I'm sure this fellow knows even more about that cunning fox Songsterson. A man like him we can use, whether he's willing or not. This is quite suitable. Quite suitable, indeed."

The monk came toward me. I waited until he was close enough and then kicked out at his groin. He dodged and shook his head sadly as he pinned me to the mattress with one strong arm. "Must I waste more valuable energy incapacitating you further? Come, now. Just cooperate, and you'll soon be released. Why are you shielding that boy? What kind of hold over you could he have that would cause you to risk yourself?"

Of course I couldn't answer because of his spell of silence. "You fool, even if I knew something, you aren't giving me a chance to answer your questions," I thought, as loudly as I could. But, thank Lady Luck, the nincompoop seemed unable to read my thoughts. I thought it stupid and wasteful of him not to just ask if I knew more about Raz. How did he know I wouldn't just tell him?

Briefly he floated his palms above my unwilling belly. "I don't know what you are." The monk patted me on the head; I cringed inwardly. "You're not exactly a majicker. At least, you're not any kind of mage I've ever known. Yet you must've used some kind of trickery to escape me before. Well, time enough to find out what when we get where we're going. Rest assured I'm ready for you this time. I shall be curious to discover whatever secrets you hide."

I goggled toward Da. The spell of binding—if that was all it was—that the monk had cast on him looked to be taking full effect now, even as he was coming awake from whatever crazy dream he'd thought he was having. His eyes were glazed over, and he didn't seem to be responding properly. He sat up when the jackass reached his way. But instead of making fists and hitting the fat idiot, Da scooped his hands as though to bring water to his face; he was like a dazed animal being led to the slaughterhouse. He didn't even struggle as the jackass strung ropes like a leash round his arms and waist and stood him up, then dressed him in his cloak and boots. The cloak covered his bonds, leaving only the ends of the ropes showing.

I hoped someone outside might hear me struggling, but I knew that with all the noise outside in the halls, and with our neighbors busy emptying out their rooms before check-out so as not to have to pay for another day, we merely sounded like a rowdy party.

The monk stood over me, striking arcane poses and chanting unintelligibly as he held me down with one hand. I decided against trying to roll away, saving my strength for a better opportunity. This felt like the same hypnotic charm he'd used on me before. But this time, I didn't react quite the same way, perhaps because I knew what was happening this time. I couldn't help drifting into an agreeable state: What the monk suggested I'd do, I would do. Oddly, though, despite the part of my mind that was in control at the moment agreeing to obey, another part of me mercifully stayed conscious, planning to figure out how to regain control and waiting for its moment to rebel.

The sorcerer draped his arm over my shoulders, while the jackass took hold of Da's leash. Da's captivity was made to look like a garden-variety arrest, done the way the Guard usually did it when they arrested someone. I, on the other hand, looked too young to be taken into custody, so it appeared they planned to pass me off as the monk's daughter or ward.

My erstwhile guardian grinned down at me jovially. Or, I should say, Janus-like. "Let's go out the back way, shall we?"

I couldn't object. Apparently, I had to sleepwalk wherever he told me to go. If I didn't exactly know which direction that was, he had to lead me, or I'd bump right into something. I couldn't control my body or my voice. Bless Saint Alyncia, protector of the foolish, though, because it had no effect on my thoughts.

We trooped down the inn's hall and the back stairs right past the other guests. The thieves marched us into the alleyway like sneaks trying to avoid paying for the night. I felt my cheeks reddening, even though we'd paid in advance.

Da's gait had changed to a sort of limping waddle, and this worried me. That jackass might have kicked him too hard. I didn't know why I was aware of my surroundings, while Da didn't seem to be. It also appeared that I had some kind of automatic mechanism to avoid puddles, while the jackass took glee in leading Da through every one of them.

The alleyway was nothing but a muddy gravel path. Back doors to the inns and shops were labeled and had bells for deliverymen to jingle. We finally reached a door with no signage whatsoever. After fiddling with the latch and with a primitive-looking lock, they unbarred the door and shoved us into a tiny room. A single lantern burned within, and I could discern some of the room's features by the dancing shadows as my eyes adjusted to the dark.

We were in a storeroom. Shelves lined the walls, climbing clear up to the ceiling and holding rows of all manner of goods in bags, boxes, and glass jars. It reminded me of our storeroom, but an exotic version. The walls of the room were painted that institutional green that people seemed to want to paint storerooms; they thought it would resonate with wealth because it was the color associated with money and growth. At least it wasn't a mossy, moldy jail cell.

The monk unlooped a rope from around his waist where it hung on his belt. "Cross your wrists one over the other."

I knew how to keep from being tied tightly by considering the way I'd escaped last time. I just clicked my wrists into the second joint position as I held them out, before he started looping the rope. He bound them and pulled on the ends of the rough hemp. It burned, and if I hadn't been schooled a bit in relaxing, it would really have hurt. I made sure everything was totally relaxed the way it must have been when I was tied while asleep before; that way, my double joints would remain in the position they'd need to be in.

They made us sit against the wall while they tied our ankles, as well. I worried about how roughly the jackass guardsman was tying Da. Da's head lolled forward on his chest, his eyelids fluttered, and he looked like he was going to sleep. He began to snore softly as they propped him back against the wall, then gave up and let him lie full stretched on the floor.

"Search him," the monk told his cohort. He proceeded to search me himself. This time he found and took my flute. He made me strip off the cloak, tunic, stockings, and boots (my second-best pair this time) that Da had brought me, which I did clumsily on purpose to make him think I was deeply bespelled, until I was down to my muslins again.

He rolled all my possessions inside my cloak and tossed the ball as far as he could, out the door into the alley. I heard a clatter as the parcel hit the brick wall and fell into the pebbles; I winced. A whimper almost escaped me, and I realized that control of my voice had returned.

"Worthless coins I must've missed," he muttered. I'd been thinking of my instrument.

They took Da's good cloak and boots, but not his pyjamas. Both of us now were in clothes too basic for much traveling, which was probably the intention. My rough muslins looked decent, if poor. Out in the streets, I would be mistaken for a street urchin, complete with dirty feet. Da, however, would be instantly obvious as a man in his pyjamas. I supposed I should be thankful that we weren't going to have to lie on the cold stone floor mouse-naked.

"Cinch that tight, now." The jackass and the monk traded prisoners, and the jackass made sure the rope seemed tight on my wrists and ankles, then on Da's. (He made sure he didn't touch my hands. Superstitious gull.) He didn't seem to notice anything unusual about my bonds. The jackass was a thief: he had Da's good boots under his arm, rolled up in the woolen cloak.

"I'll give you some time to think about how loyal you feel to Songsterson versus how you value your freedom, little girlie. And when he wakes up"—the monk jerked his thumb back at Da—"make certain he considers the same thing."

He blew out the lantern and they stomped out. For a moment I felt panicky, being in the complete dark; but then I saw that the door was so ill-fitting that sunlight came in around the edges. A boarded-up place on the wall that must have once been a glassed window also admitted some light.

The clatter outside told me they were barring the door. I heard the mage muttering a half-rhyme I thought I recognized. Yes, I was sure of it. He was laying on a warding of portal holding. I'd heard Raz do it for people's storerooms and storage sheds dozens of times.

I heard the monk's voice mutter, "That should hold them until the Master Mortogh comes." Their boots shuffled away down the gravel of the alley.

I figured we'd best be missing by the time a person named such as that showed up.

CHAPTER FOURTEEN

I was frantic to check on Daddoo. I couldn't wait to work free from my bonds. Even trussed up, I found I could "walk" around on my buttocks and move my arms at the shoulders, so as soon as my eyes adjusted enough to the dimness, I bounced my way over to him.

I shook Da by the shoulders hopefully, but it was no use. I couldn't rouse him. I could tell his humours were flowing by feeling for them pulsing through his veins, so I knew he was alive. What I didn't know was why I was alert now and seemingly spell-free, while he was not. Had the spells worn off faster since I was younger? Lighter? Less sleepy? I had been full awake when the attack started. I also had past experience dealing with the spell. Perhaps the wards that Raz had last put on me had helped. I didn't know.

One thing I did know, though, from the scent of the place: I was at home here. All around me were the herbs of an apothecary shop or herbal emporium. My heart lifted. Our captors apparently had no way of knowing this was like tossing a rabbit into the briar patch; I knew my way around herbs, and I might be able to find just what I needed to bring Da around.

I worked on my ropes, bending my wrists and popping them to and fro between the two jointed positions, the way I had learnt back in the warehouse. Soon I had my hands free. My feet and Da's took a little longer, owing to the tightness of the knots. I could have used the sharp little teeth of those mice.

Finally we were loose. I rubbed some warmth back into my feet and took Da's hands into mine long enough to reassure myself that he was all right, though I still couldn't rouse him. I put his ropes back so they seemed tied, but weren't. I figured the warding meant they'd be leaving us here for a while. I leaned back against the wall opposite the door to rest and think.

Faintly, I caught murmurs and snatches of conversation. I deduced that on the other side of this wall lay the shop proper, complete with shopkeeper. Any noises I made might be covered by the sounds of commerce. On the other hand, someone might come back here at any time, so I had to be ready to play possum.

Cautiously, I stood up. I kept my ropes looped loosely around my elbows so I could hit the ground quickly if someone unbarred the door. My heartbeat quickened at the prospect. If I was clever, I could get us out of here before anyone returned.

The first step was to see what might be on the shelves. I thought I was justified in thieving a bit, considering what they'd taken from us. How could it be so wicked to tear open a few bags in return? If I could mix a helpful concoction and get us out of here, it would be worth atoning for a couple of sins. Besides, they'd taken my purse and Da's, and knowing Da, he'd had quite a bit in his.

I turned my attention first to the back wall. On the bottom shelf were stacked rolls of expensive parchment; cheaper pulp-paper tied with bright ribbon; chalk sticks for marking runes and warding symbols; waxy crayon sticks; berry-colored inks in thick chunky glass bottles with cork stoppers; quills to be fitted with nibs to make pens; the nibs . . . nothing useful.

One shelf above lay bundles of dried herbs. I recognized wiregrass for swelling, sawtooth-leaf weed for cuts, marshcress for spitting up from the lungs, knifegrass—no thank you; a laxative was the last thing I needed—and potchbush to battle infection. At last, some useful stuff. I chose a healthy-looking bit of numbvine and snapped off a small bit of the root of a large Nodding-Tom. These two would help heal any rope burns on our arms and legs. I picked out a sack of casting herbs, meant for drawing the a majick circle, and set it aside just in case. Most wonderful were the sacks of what I realized was pureleaf; I tucked away a couple. It certainly wouldn't hurt to purify any water I found.

After a moment's thought, I pocketed a small bundle of redberry bark; I rationalized it could come in handy if Da turned out to have a residual headache, or, heaven forbid, a fever.

Still, these things weren't going to set us free. What I needed was something to wake Da. I didn't know how to get the spell off, but I knew there were combinations of herbs that could help your mind and body fight off a spell as its residual power waned with time.

Raz had taught me this much. Over time, the strength of a webbed spell waned, because the originating sorcerer departed; the further away from his influence one got—or rather the farther he traveled—the weaker the spell would tend to go. It had to fade as the power he'd fed it was exhausted. This was one limitation of web majicking, and the reason spell fixatives in the form of material components had been developed. The monk hadn't bothered with any. In contrast, folkmajick might be less spectacular, but folkmajick stuck, and was dependent not on the skill and power of the majicker but on the strength and fixative level of the herbs used in the charm.

I scanned the next shelf, which held bags and bags of dried foods and supplies intended to sustain travelers. From one of them I loosened the tie and poured out a handful of sweetherb; I also found cloves and margali leaf and mint. These four together would help Da's body fight the spell better than it could without, if I could find some water to dissolve it all in. Or tea. I had heard urine was a sterile fluid, but surely we weren't reduced to that yet. Especially when Da wasn't awake to ask about it. I'd hate for someone to dose me with something like that without at least asking first.

I got a couple of those sacks. While I was at it, I borrowed—er, stole—four more bags of various dried fruits and other travelers' foods. Maybe I was an incurable optimist. I was quickly running out of room to stash them in my undergarments' small pockets, and decided to use some rope to string them on and tie them around my waist under my skirt.

I was afraid to climb the shelves so as to reach up higher. I couldn't risk the noise of a collapse, which could be brought on by one little slip of my foot. Unfortunate, for on the highest shelf in the corner, many oddments awaited. There was a wood carving of a laughing monkey wearing a hat. A crystal inkwell and a bottle of opalescent lavender ink beckoned next to that. Most curious of all was a crystal sphere about a palm-span in diameter, perched on a base of three brass dragon-heads. The ball seemed to glow a soft, pale green from within, but it could have been a trick of the light. Probably it was just a reflection of the green wall.

I didn't have anywhere to stash those kinds of treasures, even if I could reach. They were curiosities that I shouldn't be thinking of taking, anyway. Even stealing from thieves was limited to taking back the same value you'd lost to them, if you were fair.

I turned to the lowest shelf on the back wall. Nothing interesting, just papers and old ledger books. The top books held a thick layer of dust.

Above that stood the medicinals. Bottles and jars, amphorae and tittles, phials and opaque containers of all shapes. There were cobalt blue and molasses-toned glass containers, corked or sealed with dripped wax or paper, each filled with any kind of decoction I could imagine. All with labels inked in a careless hand, but in Wrennish, and perfectly readable despite the blotches and smudges. Easy as peppermint for digestion.

I held my breath as I ran my finger down the shelf, looking for the label I needed. I found the purple powder in a jar three from the corner. Lifting the big glass stopper was a sensual experience; the sweet savory odor of the sleepsand was unmistakable.

Sleepsand would render any sleep, even a majickally induced one, easy and healing. Conversely, it would help you wake normally from a spell-set sleep, stopping a spell's effects by turning you to natural slumber. I thought anything it did would be bound to help Da.

I had what I needed.

Except for the simplest thing. Where would they keep a bottle of water?

Da stirred behind me, and I rushed over to check him. He moaned, and his eyelids fluttered slightly. Worried, I blurted out a standard test question he'd taught me to use in case we were ever in this situation.

"Listen to me, Daddoo, and think before you answer. It's important. Do stones eat their young?"

He opened his eyes all the way and frowned at me. "What's wrong with you, girlie? Rocks are earth. They're not living creatures."

So he'd passed the thinking test. "Just testing. Now let's see your tongue."

"Huh?" He lowered his eyebrows, puzzled.

"Stick out your tongue. No, leave it out." It looked fine in color, if a bit coated, but I needed to test his reflexes. "Can you hold it out for a minute?"

He grimaced. "Certainly I can, but why?" Talking around his tongue, the words came out garbled, but loud.

"Shhh! We have to whisper. I just wondered." If he couldn't do it, it would've meant there was danger of damage to his thinking. So far, all appeared well.

"Now, take this." I cupped the sleepsand in my palm and tilted it toward his mouth, hoping he'd take it without questioning me. It was more palatable in a drink, but it could be swallowed by dissolving on the tongue.

He knew what it was right off. Recognizing its nature was another good sign his mind was intact, although a bit addled by that spell. "For what? I'm already nodding off."

"Just do it, Da. Please, sir." It would help him sleep naturally so that he could wake having thrown off the spell. He coughed a bit, but sucked the powder in; I managed to get it all down him without making too much of a fuss. His eyes closed and he relaxed, his features going slack as in normal sleep. He'd probably doze the better part of the morning. If it was still morning; I couldn't be certain how much time had actually passed.

Now to find the water, or something equally neutral that wouldn't react with my four-herb cocktail. If we were both dosed with this, we could recover from the effects of the spells gradually but naturally.

I found some dried apricots mixed with shelled nuts in a tiny muslin bag and couldn't resist eating them. I decided to fill the resulting empty bag with more sleepsand to tie on my makeshift belt. Then I fixed everything else back on the shelves the way it had been so my burglary wouldn't show. I was soon sorry to have eaten the dried things, though, because I still found nothing that looked safe to drink. What could I dissolve the healing herbs in? And what to use for a vessel?

Just then I heard a noise outside our door. I shoved my booty behind some papers on the first shelf, then scrambled down into the position I'd been left in. I hoped I didn't look red-faced from all that scurrying around. I twisted my ropes together loosely and made sure it looked like I was tied up tightly. It wouldn't do for them to know I could get out of them. I'd had no time to retie Da, but with him asleep, they might not inspect him so closely.

Presently the door rattled open. A short, stout youth with a pimply face banged it open and plonked down a tray. He, too, wore the uniform of the city guard; but he hadn't come to rescue us, as I realized after an initial moment of excitement. He'd brought us water and gruel and bread.

He rubbed his head back to front, mussing his cropped hair so that one cowlick stood straight out. "Here. Make it last you."

"Thank you, sir." I thought it clever of me to act the little fool, and flapped my hands about flirtatiously as best I could without risking my bonds falling off. I batted my eyelashes at him. "How lovely! I was getting so thirsty, too. But how are we to eat, all tied up like this?"

He blinked, then stepped in and leaned against the door frame, regarding me. "The boss didn't think about that, I figure, little lady. Guess you'll manage." He shifted his weight to the other foot. "You're an awful young one to be in this much trouble, I reckon to say." He seemed a bit bemused by this. Then he saw Da. He jerked his thumb in Da's general direction. "He alive?"

My heart paused, but then I composed myself. I had just checked Daddoo a moment before, and his chest still rose and fell steadily, if shallowly. "Certainly he's alive. He's just been knocked out, that's all." I shrugged, thinking it best to play dumb—er, even dumber than usual. "I guess he'll wake up afterwhile."

A look of pity (for my obvious stupidity, I surmised) flickered in the kid's eyes. "Let's hope so."

"I'm sure. He does this sometimes when he's real, real sleepy." I tried to sound like a typical idiot girl, like the ones in the village who wove ribbons in their hair and giggled inanely at the sight of males. I tilted my head to the side coquettishly. "Mister, how long will it be before we're released?" In response to his look of incredulity at the very suggestion, I added, "At least they must tell what it is we're being held for, so we're given proper procedure by the council. I know they're men of the law who'll follow Council rules." Not that I expected them to do anything of the kind.

He shrugged. "All's I know is, keep you here until the Mast— the boss comes." He leaned forward, his shoulder on the door. "He's the one who says what's to be done. I only follow orders." He turned and backed up a bit. He seemed to be about to go, so I thought fast.

"Wait, sir! What do I do if I—well, if I feel the call of nature?" I felt my face burning, but that had been the only emergency that came to mind.

"Eh?" He eased the door back open and blinked. "You need to visit the privy?"

I had a feeling that I could make him feel sorry for me. I didn't need to go just then, but I jumped at the opportunity to get my bearings. Any information I might stumble across would help me. "Actually . . . yes." I put on my most helpless, innocent, gullible girl face.

He glanced over his shoulder. He scanned me with his gaze, and I put on the most honest look I could muster. He bit his lip, and I thought he seemed torn. "Guess it wouldn't hurt to take you, just for a moment. They didn't send a bowl or a jar or nothin', so I figger they don't know or care what's needed. Don't have any common sense. Never think about what a prisoner gotta have, say, if you're going to keep them for a while. No, ma'am, they never think, but just leave everything to me." He glanced back again, chewing at his rubbery lower lip, as though they might have heard. "Come along, then. And be quick about it." He reached down and jerked on my ropes. I grabbed them so their slackness wouldn't give me away and followed him out.

The bar across the door was a thick branch of alderwood, simple enough to break through if you were strong. No wonder they'd thought they needed the warding as well. I made sure to take a good look at the door itself as he resealed it with a few mutterings under his breath. Chalk marks on its face formed a two-triangles figure, actually a kind of six-pointed star, inside a confining circle; it was an air warding, then, and breakable from our side with a simple knock-knock, like the spell I'd used on the Widder Groop's inherited hope-chests. By the time he turned around, I had the blank look pasted back on my face.

"I appreciate this so much, sir. I'm Dulcie. What's your name?" I was playing the foolish girl to the hilt.

He wasn't as gullible as all that, to be fooled into giving his name, but he softened further. "Guess it's all right to be friendly to you—you're just a kid. Must be that feller in there who they're really after. That a kinsman of yours, Dulcie?"

"My . . . uncle." It didn't seem safe to reveal just how close we actually were, in case it might give them some ideas about torturing one of us to get information out of the other—the idea, though distasteful, wasn't impossible. Too late, I realized that making him my uncle wasn't a big improvement. "But I don't know what he did. He didn't mean to offend, whatever he said to that big fat man!" I clapped my hands over my mouth, as though I'd just realized I'd insulted the monk. "Sorry, mister—um, mister. But that man was very large and pudgy, and I'm sure we didn't mean to say nothing nasty."

A look of understanding came into his eye. "Ah. Well, I wouldn't worry too much, then. They're just tryin' to put a scare into ya. Though I can't see going to so much trouble."

We walked down the alley, shops on either side of us, and I judged that it ran between major streets in the city, forming a "T," and ending in a blind corner at the top. I noticed a mark that looked familiar on the back door of one of the shops, three globes stacked in a pyramid, and filed the image away in my mind for pondering later.

We'd reached the outhouse, sensibly located at the blind end of the alley. "Don't take too long, now. I ain't so sure they'd like it if they knew I was doing this, but you're just a kid. You remind me of my baby sister."

I smiled winningly and stepped into the privy, closing the door on the rest of his sentence, which sounded like, "She's purty near as silly as you."

The privy was not what you'd call sanitary. I did my business since I was here, holding my breath, and stepped carefully out, holding my hands in front of me to emphasize the trouble I'd had getting my drawers back up. He pointedly avoided touching my hands on the way back, even after we'd stopped to run water over them at the pump. I splashed my nose into it, too; by now, I really was warm and uncomfortable.

"I appreciate all you've done, Mister," I said as we came back to the door. I noted carefully the mutterings he gave to pop the door open. Now I knew exactly what kind of ward it was and how to majick-knock it open. "I wonder if you might consider helping me in doing just one more tiny little thing?"

His eyes narrowed. He turned, suspicious. "What would that be?"

I eyelash-fluttered again and gave a simpering little giggle. "There's this little tin whistle in with my things. I play it sometimes to pass the time. If it's going to be a while more, do you think you could bring it to me?" I tilted my head and played the admiring chickie.

He frowned. "You don't want to make a bunch of loud noise. There are customers in the shop up front, you know."

I hadn't been sure, but it was nice to know I was a good guesser. "I won't. I promise. I'll be real quiet so that they won't even hear me. They don't hear us talking now, do they?"

He cackled. "If they had, we'd be knowing about it already. The shopkeeper ain't the type to tolerate anything. He knows you're here, but he never comes back here. It's where we always put—" He stopped himself. "People we want to talk to."

"It's no louder when I play than we're talking. I won't blow hard." Blowing harder and softer wasn't the way to get dynamic range on the flute, but that was how people thought you did it, so I used the notion to my advantage. "If you can find it for me, I'll give you something pretty that I have."

He shot me a questioning look. "Like what?"

"Some pretty stones I polished up." I tried to be coy so he'd think I might have some silichite but be moronic enough not to know what it was. "They glow in the light, especially moonlight."

"I don't need anything like that. Why would I?" He worried the few whiskers on his chin with his finger.

I worked up a tear, letting it glisten in the corner of my eye.

He worked his mouth around a bit. "I shouldn't do it, I know. But you are just a kid."

I fluttered again. "And I'm so bored. Do you think, maybe . . . ?"

He pursed his lips, one hand on his hip. "We'll see. I don't even know what stuff you have, or where they'd have thrown the stuff."

"Out that door, sir. Right into the alleyway in all the dirt and mess. My red cloak's balled up around it." I made what I hoped was the face of a prune. "But I don't care if it's all sticky. I can clean it up if you find it. And thank you kindly for looking!"

He closed the door on my words, and I heard him mutter the words to renew the Warding quickly. Da was still out, and didn't even open one eye; now that I had the water and could purify it, I would dose us both with anti-spell. I might not need it, but it couldn't hurt. That would wait until he stirred again. I closed my eyes and leaned back against the rough stone wall by the door. I wasn't the least bit sleepy.

The door opened again. "Here." The youth thrust his arm in and tossed something my direction. My red tunic, torn, covered with mud and leaves. And rolled inside, my flute.

"Thank you, mister—er—" I made wide eyes and acted the dunce.

He caved in. "I'm Orthe. Now don't screed that whistle too loud, or they're sure to hear you. And put it away before any-body comes in, as soon as you hear them out here. Maybe it'll help you pass time."

I already had my flute out of the case and was running my fingers down it to be sure there weren't any dents when he threw in the smaller of our supply bags. "That was the only other thing out there. Now, where's what you promised me?"

I remembered. I pulled the string of moonjewels out of the hem of my under-muslins and threw it to him. "Thank you, Mr. Orthe."

The heavy sound of the bar being replaced across the door was my answer.

CHAPTER FIFTEEN

I settled back down against the wall near Da, throwing off my loose coils of rope. Easing the two segments of the flute apart, I fingered it carefully, inspecting the delicate silver tube for scratches and scrapes. Finding none, I ran through the basic fingerings Raz had taught me silently, then twittered a breath of warm air through the head joint to warm it to playing temperature before fitting the parts back together.

Da opened one eye. "You back again?"

"You're awake." I breathed a sigh of relief.

"And why shouldn't I be?" He narrowed his hazel eyes. "D'you do something to me with that powder? You did, didn't you? You damned majicker."

I grinned. "Majicker! I suppose that's a compliment, coming from you."

"I surely didn't mean it that way. And furthermore, just who might you be?"

"Daddoo . . . " I gulped. "It's me, Dulcie. Dulcinea Jean."

"I don't know any Dulcinea." He frowned. "It's a trick. That was my wife's name, God keep her in His Heaven. Yet you do look somewhat like her, except for that awful mop of red hair you have on you." My red hair came from his side of the family. "But you're not she."

"Don't you know me, Da?" My voice faltered, and the flute fell softly to my lap.

"I certainly do not. And you have cast some kind of spell that's made me immobile, plus I'm trussed up like a rooster going to market." He didn't ken that his ropes were untied; maybe he still couldn't move. "How dare you. I demand an explanation." Anger flashed in his eyes.

"Da. . . ." The spell. It was more than a binding spell, then. If it had made him confused . . . . "Let's just get out of here, and I'll explain later." I pulled off his ropes and tried to help him stand.

His gaze burned into me. "Oh, no, you don't. I'll stay right here until you explain just what you're up to. In fact, I'm going to holler for the city guard."

"No! I mean, please wait a moment. If you make noise, it might attract them."

"And that's just what I want." He lifted his head. "Help! Hey, ho, help, anyone!"

I clapped my hand over his mouth in desperation. As he tried to bite me, I added, "I promise they're way worse than I am. Please, just keep from shouting and making things worse." I dug a kerchief out of my newly returned supply sack to protect my hand from his teeth. I could scarcely bear seeing him helpless, with no voluntary motion of his body below the neck. I hadn't realized they had left him in such a state. Purposely, or accidentally?

It scared me to have to hold my wrapped hand over his nose and mouth, but I was sure I wasn't suffocating him, because he kept thrashing. Only with his head, because apparently the rest of him was immobilized by the spell. I alternately prayed and hummed a soothing tune, a folktune he'd used to lull me to sleep when I was a baby.

He finally calmed down, relaxed his neck, and stopped making noises. I half expected him to shout out when I removed my sweaty palm, but he lay quietly. He seemed defeated and out of energy. "You've won for the moment," he said in a hoarse whisper, "but as soon as my strength returns, you'll find you've chosen the wrong man to do this to."

"I know they've got the wrong man." I spoke quietly, patting his hand, but stopped when he looked daggers at me. I sat back for a moment while he panted and caught his breath. My eyes welled with tears, but I wouldn't let them spill.

I set to decocting the herbs in the water. I wouldn't touch that food for fear it was dosed. But the pureleaf would cleanse the water. I crumbled half a sack of it in first, then added the four healing herbs and stirred them in with my finger. Da glared mistrustfully, and he wouldn't talk to me for a while.

And he wouldn't take the herbs, either. "You think I was birthed yesternight? Here you stand, spouting insulting lies. And now you're trying to poison me."

"All right, Daddoo. Just don't make so much noi—"

"Stop that!"

"Stop what?"

He glared, his eyes losing their depth and going flat, like cold gleaming ore-stones. "Calling me Daddoo. You're no kin to me, you cutpurse. You're nothing but a waylayer."

"But, Da. . . ."

"I have no wife. Thus I have no child. Neither have I any bastards."

"All right, sir. Just try to rest, and perhaps things will seem clearer afterwhile."

This sent him deeper into suspicion, and he fought to keep his eyes open. He kept coming just to the point of sleep, then rousing himself before drowsing off.

If I went away, he might relax. I withdrew to my corner, first retrieving the goods I'd stolen and then stuffing them into my pack. I fiddled with arranging my ill-gotten gains in their pouches under my muslins, on the rope I'd tied around my waist. Then I sat, sifting the leftover herbs from my potion through my fingers.

I left the tincture I'd already mixed in the water glass, in case he might forget and take it later. Presently he fell back to sleep, mumbling to himself.

I eased over next to Da. His pulse and respiration were normal. I lifted one eyelid to make sure his eyes hadn't rolled back. Instead, his eyes moved around under their closed lids, meaning he was dreaming. Perhaps I had overdosed him with sleepsand. Could that be dangerous? Could it be causing him to forget me, of all things?

We had to get out of here. But Da was too heavy for me to lift, his ninestone too much for my unexercised and puny fourstone.

Even if I lifted him at first, I might drop him as soon as my fear-fed strength petered out. Worse, he apparently wouldn't cooperate in our escape, even if I could get him moving. He'd get us picked up again, that was certain, either by the monk's blackguards or the city guard. Which, I knew from Orthe's uniform (unless it were false, which I doubted: that held a penalty of its own, and surely the men knew their colleagues), had probably been infiltrated by the same organization.

Either detainment would be the last thing I wanted.

I needed Da to recognize me, or at least trust me. As long as he couldn't or wouldn't walk on his own, I needed someone who could carry Da out of here to somewhere we could get the spell off, or someone who could just take off the spell.

Only one name, double unfortunately, came to mind.

Raz Songsterson would know what to do. This was all his fault, blast him. Why did he have to be a wanted criminal or whatever he was? No, he'd double-crossed or tempted these criminals, so he stood on the side of right, I supposed. Oh, my head. But why'd he have to mix us up in this? I knew I was being unreasonable, but I didn't care. Raz Songsterson owed me.

I closed my eyes and suddenly saw a picture of Raz in my mind, standing at a stable where he was haggling with a man over the price of a horse. My eyes flew open and I realized it must have been a trick of my imagination.

I took some deep breaths and visualized calming images like sleeping bunnies, hot spiceflower tea and crispy cakes, satiny peaceful pillows of herbs. I would find and bring back Raz, and everything would be all right.

It had fallen quiet on the other side of the wall. Could they have closed up for lunch? I was losing all sense of time. I had to do something, even if it turned out to be a mistake. I'd try to be as quiet as I could, but it was time to try a bit of majicking.

I traced a circle in the packed dirt floor by dragging my longest fingernail around. Then I sprinkled on the casting herbs, the way I'd seen Da and Raz do. These were stolen herbs, but there was no help for it, even if it violated a wagonload of rules. The majick would have to understand.

I centered myself and measured my breaths, hoping I was close enough to the serene attitude required for successful casting. Picturing Raz in my mind's eye, I tried to think of what he usually did next in a casting. He typically used an appropriate prop; in this case, I needed something reflective, a surface in which to see what I sought.

Of course I had no cauldron of sacred, purified spring water, nor any silver coin to drop in to represent the moon lady. But I did have one reflective surface: Raz's love token, the spherical hair charm. I jerked it over my head and placed it in the ring of calling. No censer of incense, so a sprinkle of the fragrant cloves would have to do. The majick would either come or it wouldn't.

I stared at the mirrored charmball and chanted quietly. "Raz, Raz, hear me, Raz Songsterson of Marwell." As I watched, I imagined his image forming faintly in the glass. I really could see his image faintly. No, I was imagining things. *No,* there it was. I grabbed up the charm, whispering, "Raz. . . ."

There was no picture. I'd been seeing things. I took a deep breath. I didn't know enough to do this.

I grabbed a bag of cleansing salts off the middle shelf and rubbed out my circle with my palm. I cast it over again, cleansing first with the salts. Surely I could figure out what I was doing wrong. There were two basic principles of simple majick, the laws of the thaumaturge. Perhaps one or the other was the key.

I remembered, or thought I remembered, Da trying to teach the laws to Chiro. The old man never really did catch on, but I could recall many afternoons when he'd sat in the workroom muttering incantations to himself. They were in the forgettable language, but he mixed in nonsense syllables; that was his own invention, thinking that people overhearing him would believe the rhymes did the trick rather than the power syllables themselves. Chiro had thought the precaution necessary despite Da's assurances that non-majickers couldn't remember the mage-cant three moments after hearing it. Chiro never got all the incantations quite perfect, so I heard the nonsense parts over and over, and remembered them like any child knows nursery rhymes. And always the two laws of thaumaturgy, repeated as though he'd catch on to how they were applied if only he said them often enough: "Like produces like, by the principle of sympathy; a part attracts the whole, or 'once together, forever together,' by the principle of contagion."

Sympathy and contagion: the two most basic physical laws of majick. If you could draw a parallel in miniature to what you wanted done on a larger or far-away scale, you could produce the larger effect. Provided you chose an appropriate enough analogue, of course. That was where most majickers fell down on the job and resorted to more tangible physical means to do what they wanted; analogies were tough to draw in the best of situations. The other thing was that it worked best if you had at least part of the thing you sought, thus bringing in contagion. At least I had the charm, which was invested with Raz's majickal signature. And Raz now had something of mine in his charm.

So. What was "like" the thing I wanted to do? What would attract Raz to me, or Raz's charm to mine? How could I bring Raz's charm—and with it Raz—to me? I sat back on my haunches, fists on thighs, and concentrated. I had to identify the similarities between what *was* and what *should be*. Fleetingly I considered that there was ample reason why more people didn't devote their lives to becoming majickers.

I sighed. Could a part of my shorn hair attract another part to itself? Or would it just stick to my head, figuring that was the closest piece from which it had been recently sundered? It was worth a try.

"As I bring this charm towards me"—I lifted and brought the charm to my face, stroking it as I would a frightened and recalcitrant kitten—"by extension, this charm brings its mate toward itself. Come, come, come along now; answer my call, respond to my command." I stirred the herbs with one hand and sprinkled them around the circle again. I laid the charm back in the center and made several arcane passes over it, like the ones I'd seen Raz do at the altar. Closing my eyes, I visualized my reflection in the mirrored curve, then Raz's image. I imagined Raz leaving the stable, hurrying down the alleyway, opening this door. Where was he now? "Show me what is seen in your mate's view, as you show me what is reflected in you."

I opened my eyes slowly and saw an image forming in the ball. With a sharp intake of breath, I hunkered down to see more clearly. "Raz?" I bit my lip, trying to construct a picture out of the cloudy colors I saw in the ball.

Nothing. It had all been in my fevered imagination. "Confound it all," I muttered. I'd worked myself up to a pitch over nothing. I'd have to risk making noise, if I were going to have any success.

I set the charm back in the center and pulled out my flute. Softly, as softly as I'd ever played, I started on a tune Raz had taught me. It was a palindromic tune, the same backwards as forwards, and only seven tones. It was mesmerizingly repetitive without being boring.

Nothing seemed to be happening. I thought again about the Principles of Sympathy and Contagion. Merely imagining Raz coming hadn't caused him to burst in the door. So they weren't enough; I needed to establish command over any majickal power I might gather. "I impose my will on thee," I told the charm. "Obey this tune, and call Raz to me." I was almost embarrassed to order the charm around, but I knew I'd heard Raz say the same kind of phrase.

I fluted again, concentrating on all that was Raz, thinking of our times spent together and his characteristic actions, drawing his portrait in notes. Some were dissonant; that seemed fitting.

I started hearing a few harmonics in my pipe and tried to correct it with changes in my embouchure; then I realized the harmonics weren't coming from me. I stopped blowing and reached out towards the ball, careful to stop just short of actually touching it for fear of spoiling the effect as I had twice before, by accidentally grounding the majick and sending it back into the earth through my touch.

Even from a hairsbreadth away, the charm was moving the air with vibration. I could feel it humming, thrumming power through itself like the purr of a large housecat, making the harmonics to my song. My music had set it vibrating!

This time, I was sure I could see in the mirror of the charm's reflection a picture of Raz, standing at the bar in a tavern. Raz was looking into his charm and cocking his head, as though it had got his attention. I pulled back my finger and sat on my hands so that I wouldn't reach out for it and break the spell, as I had the last two times. He stepped outside and scanned the area, swiveling his head as though looking for someone.

"Raz! Raz, it's me. Come quickly!" But the vision had faded. This time, though, I was certain I hadn't been imagining it. "Well, it wasn't exactly like Da's scrying." I wiped my damp palms on the front of my shirt. "But it does mean you're nearby. I hope."

I thought I'd recognized that area behind Raz. It looked like the town square I'd seen as we rode.

The ball still vibrated a bit as I slipped it back over my head. It tickled a little under the muslin, a second chirping heartbeat. The majick must be keeping us in touch, like a finder spell. For once, I might be doing something right.

I still couldn't bring Da around, even with a bit of the clove powder under his nose. I suppressed my worry and sent up another little prayer, just as a reminder. Not that I didn't trust the saints. But nothing's wrong with keeping the lifeline open.

My red tunic looked shabbier than my muslins, and I'd be more noticeable wearing that without a skirt than in full muslins. I'd pass for a street urchin, as dirty as I was. I rolled the tunic into a pillow and slipped it under Da's head. If he woke, he'd know I'd left it as a sign I would soon return.

To go outdoors, I needed some kind of foot coverings. I tore a couple of rags off the bottom of my muslin underskirt and tied them around my feet. I did the same for Da, ripping the hems off of his pyjama bottoms. A man his age never went about barefoot unless he'd been arrested.

I shook Da's shoulder again, but he merely snorted and turned over in his sleep. At last he seemed to be sleeping normally. Kissing him on the forehead, I promised to return. "I'll be back as soon as I can with help, Daddoo. Be well."

The knock-knock spell to undo the wards was simple, using the same syllables I'd heard Orthe utter. I could hear the slight chirp of the door's wood as it was un-majicked, and could have sworn I sensed a slight glow for a moment. I was certain that it had worked.

I tried the door, then realized it was still barred with the alderwood. I couldn't budge it with my shoulder, and I didn't think I ought to wait around, hoping Raz got my message. He wasn't listening for me to send the way Da had been, and who knew what, if anything, I might have sent?

I'd have to make the branch remember when it was part of a tree, and talk it into moving with my music.

So I blew, and the flute talked to the branch through the door. It wove a spell-melody, a song of the four winds and the light rain of a storm, the birds nesting in the crotches of the oaks, the leaves of the horse-apples rustling. Now the tree in my song blew with a strong night breeze, and next it flexed with the storm blowing in from the northlands, making it go back and forth as the wind persuaded. Its leaves fluttered and flew. I visualized the wood bending, bent, straining against the wind but finally yielding to snap. With my mind's eyes and ears I heard and saw the storm. Laying my hand on the door momentarily, I could tell that the door was bowing slightly in and out as well. Hurriedly I returned to my persuasive melody, and the branch swaying and bending, about to snap, yes—snap!

I heard the crunching of the thick wood from here. It was all I could do to restrain a shout. We were free.

I checked Da again quickly—I had become rather compulsive about it—and shouldered the door open. It popped as if it had never been latched. I grabbed the latch handle quickly so it wouldn't swing wide.

Light shafted in from the alley. I squeezed through the door and hurriedly replaced what was left of the alderwood bar, arranged so no break line showed. With luck I'd return before anyone else. Maybe I'd even find Da mobile.

"Where are you, Raz?"

CHAPTER SIXTEEN

Today was a market day in Ladenia City, as was every day after the new moon in Celeste. It was therefore traditionally the day that civil dispute cases were heard by the Council of Fair Magistrates. I remembered it as soon as I stepped into the throng.

The crowds buzzed outside in the city square and in the adjacent market area, where peddlers of all kinds of wares would have come from all around the region to set up their shops for this special day of selling. It all meant I might not be as quickly noticed, and I'd be able to hide in the crowds; the other side of the situation was that more people would be there to notice me as I ran around, basically, in my undergarments. A bushel of one, four pecks of the other.

I skulked down the alley, as self-conscious as a naked Emperor. The cobblestones from the street were wet with leakage and with what came out of washbasins and chamber-pots tossed from people's back windows; here in the dirtway, they made a sticky mess. In the mud grew some hearty-looking weeds and stickerplants. I avoided them as best I could.

I went through a few of the trash containers behind shops, but gave it up when I sensed movement at the bottoms, something skittling around inside the dirty boxes. It would've been nice to find my skirt or boots, but apparently what Orthe had been able to dig out were the only things the paupers had accidentally missed. Anything left in an alley was fair game for beggars and soon scrounged. I pushed back my dirty hair with a dirtier hand and sighed.

The backs of the shops and maisonettes formed a solid wall separating me from the main square, but I could see a break ahead.

I slipped quietly along behind the backdoors, freezing at every mouse-tail that flashed between the cartons of garbage, my heart jumping at the slightest noise or movement. It would be just my luck for the city guard to see me skulking the alleyways in urchin dress and mistake me for a beggar; sometimes beggars were disturbed, even arrested, but other times ignored.

As I got close to the end of the passage, I could hear quite a bustle out on the square. When I got close enough to peep out, I saw what the commotion was. A traders' caravan had pulled into the square, forming an interior spiral of sales wagons. That meant the market area proper was completely filled, because this was the overflow location. The throngs would be impassable today, then; but perhaps that was to my advantage, after all.

The carts and wagons looked dilapidated even from this distance, and I supposed these were Jipsies. Still, they'd been allowed to stop, so they seemed legitimate enough. They already had their awnings up and windows open and wares out and, no doubt, many urchins gamboling about picking pockets in the crowds.

Jipsy urchins—of course. Could I pass for one? I roughed myself up a little more, rolling in the dust of the alley. Much as I hated to, I splashed ankle-deep into a large puddle and made my foot-cloths into mud-crust shoes like the tramps wore, until I wore virtual socks and soles of mud. I frayed the bottom thumbslength or so of my underskirt into fringed strips, and found a bandanna (really a dinner-napkin) in the supply pouch to wrap around my disheveled head. I rubbed my buzzing charm for luck and stepped out, slipping into the crowd.

There were strange markings on the doors of these garishly painted coaches, and ragged-looking horses and people stood next to them, surveying the crowds and hawking their wares. It was like a street fair. Merchants glared from the doors of their fancy shops on the square, but there was nothing they could do to prevent this legal competition.

The shoppers here were more than tolerant. People milled around and congregated at each coach, calling out their offers on each bargain. Some people were even getting the discounts they suggested. One woman left a milliner's coach with armsful of colorful spiderweave fabrics.

Raz wouldn't be buying fabric. I headed diagonally across the square, dodging elbows. As I rounded the end of the line of wagons, my charm started to vibrate again, harder than before. I laid my hand on it and pushed it against my heart. It only got worse as I bumped through the crowd, moving with the current, being pressed to move faster than I'd have hurried by my own volition. I needed to stop when the vibrations were at their strongest, but could I stand among all these people and find Raz, even if he were in plain view? I felt like a pygmy among all the taller people.

Raz must be nearby. I managed to get turned back around and headed towards the front of the caravan. I stepped at a lively pace to keep from being knocked over and tried to make sense of the various sigils, marks, and drawings on the wagons that served to communicate what each proprietor had for sale.

Here was a fortune-teller, a milliner, a house of exotic spices, a wagon filled with preserved jellies and jams and pickles of all kinds. To my left stooped an old man sweeping in front of a sign picturing various minerals and crystals. Just what Raz had said he wanted to come here to buy.

I muffled the charm between my hands as its sound grew louder, going from a soft screeching in the middle of the scale to a louder, higher pitch. I stood still a moment, but then it quietened and started up again on a different note. Now the vibrato tone was coming from a different compass point. I traced the sound towards the direction of the West Wind; sure enough, through the multicolored crowd, someone approached, a tall skinny man in purple robes, with long dark hair under a purple feather cap . . . .

"Raz!" I couldn't suppress the yelp. He was wearing a completely new outfit: a sleeveless velvet jacket of rich violet over a ruffledy-front lavender shirt, and britches to match the jacket. Over all this, he wore a fancified silk version of his customary purple robe, open down the front, with floating sleeves. Funniest of all, though, was the floppy purple hat concealing his dark hair and the false flame-hued queue exiting instead, brought around over his right shoulder. I supposed it was a disguise of some sort. He looked like a dandy who'd just come into wealth. But I knew better than to let a giggle escape. Besides, my heart was too swelled with joy at seeing him close enough to touch again.

Our gazes met and locked. He grasped my arm and pulled me between two of the wagons, garnering irritated glances from their proprietors. "Dulcinea! I thought it was you, but I couldn't imagine. . . . What are you doing here?" He had his charm in one fist; now he held his fist to my ear, and I felt the sympathy and tingling as the two charms vibrated in synchronization. "And how'd you manage this?"

"Me?" I held out my charm, singing like a loose kiwi bird. "I thought it was your charm making mine vibrate."

He grabbed mine and stuffed it into one pocket, and then shoved his into another pocket. The tones instantly stopped; he must've had shielding in his robe. "Any cudge could have figured that out. What I meant was, what kind of majick did you work? How did you activate the sympathy?"

"I didn't. My charm just started singing like that. Although I confess I wanted it to. I kind of needed to get in touch with you." I fidgeted a bit, not wanting to confess to majicking "blind," without having any idea what I was doing; it was dangerous, and Raz would be right to call me on it.

He squinted. "You used your hair charm to call to me."

" . . . Not exactly." Why did I feel the need to fudge and conceal? "I mean, I did, but I just fooled around, not knowing if it would work, or how to use it properly."

"I'd say you did exceedingly well for someone who didn't know what she was doing." He looked doubtful but challenged me no further. "You'll have to show me later what you may have done to activate it, so that when you thought of me it began sending."

"I'll try to remember." This was not the time to break the news to him about music and majick. "I did need to see you, beca—"

He interrupted me. "Oddly enough, I had you on my mind this morning, Dulcinea Brown, just before the charm started vibrating." He scratched his head, sending his purple hat a-tilt. "Did your Da figure it out? And what does he want with me, anyway? I thought he despised me." He looked rueful.

"Raz, Daddoo's ill. Something awful." I burst out with it, not bothering to explain. "I need your help to get him home."

"He's in the galen-house here in Lad City?" Raz clasped his hands to his chest. "Under the care of the healers of Saint Alyncia? This must be serious." He looked distraught. "Are you sure? I mean, is it that bad?"

"Worse." I bit my lip. "He's not in a galen. He's bespelled, and he's being held captive."

Raz looked stunned, then searched my face with his gaze.

I bumbled on. "We were caught and taken prisoner by—well, I don't know who, but some men who kidnapped both of us on the road. And the odd thing is that they say they're really looking for you. They say you did something or have something of theirs, becau—mffff."

He clamped his hand over my mouth. "No more talk until we're somewhere more private. Here, follow me; I see we do need to talk."

"We need to get back to Da first." But Raz wasn't listening to my muffled complaint. He let go of me once we'd turned around and evaded the coaches' grazing horses, and set off in quite the wrong direction. It was all I could do to keep up with his long legs as he led me on a weaving trail through the rows of caravan wagons, dodging crowds of shoppers and merchants. The sun was hot and I judged it was the middle of the afternoon. How soon would this Master Mortogh, whoever he might be, discover me missing?

Raz led me back of a tavern where there was a wooden picnic bench in a quiet corner, under a spreading hickory. "This is a safe enough place to talk. I know the proprietor and clientele here, and they aren't the kind to eavesdrop." He motioned for me to sit, then settled down on the grass, cross-legged.

I perched tentatively on the edge of the bench. "Don't get too comfortable. We must hurry." I told him all that had happened since his departure. I tried to gloss over the circumstances leading up to my setting off to find him, but he only grinned and rolled his eyes.

"Can't a body trust anyone?" He murmured it aloud, but gestured for me to go on. I hoped the twinkle in his eye was from amusement. "Little wonder he lost that sack again, the way you two keep house." I frowned at him.

When I got to the description of the monk, Raz bit his lip. As I described the rest of the monk's actions, Raz began shaking his head. I sort of left out the part about shouting Raz's name and wearing his sigil; I couldn't quite make myself admit that I had been so foolish. His hat fell into his lap when I told of my escape. He grasped it and kneaded its purple brim, heedless of the disarray this caused in his false orange queue. His own hair went all directions and he chewed on a strand of it nervously as I finished up my tale.

"Well?"

"Well, what?" The lock of hair fell damply out of the corner of his red mouth. "What do I think? I don't know yet, although I have some idea who that might have been."

"Do you know why they're after you?"

"Let's get to that a little later. What I can't discern is why they associated me with you." I just shrugged. "But since they have, we'll act on the assumption that they have been watching me, and therefore they believe us to be together in a conspiracy against them." He puffed out his cheeks with air, then blew it out in a sigh. "Frankly, I don't know what to do about that, Dulcinea."

I grasped his arm. "I think we ought to go and get Da now, and then plan what you should do about all the rest of it after we get back home."

"That's very practical." He allowed me a wry grin. "Of course we shall rescue Magefather Brown immediately. We may have to carry him between us if he can't walk. I can't necessarily cure that unless we can guess what caused the effects you describe. There could be any number of spells, or even a physical cause."

"Do you think you can figure it out when you see it?" My heart pounded, and I talked sweet to it inwardly to quiet it down to a normal pulsation. "We've got to get him back to himself and get home."

"You say he's confused and forgetful. If it's as you describe"— Raz held up his hands to ward off my indignant "of course it is"— "which I'm sure it is—then it's most likely being caused by an ongoing spell. A wizard in the organization, probably the one dressed as a monk, is suspicious of me, as well he should be." Raz looked proud of this. "He has put a powerful glamour on various people he suspects may have heard something. The Society wants to be sure no one gets hold of any clues to the plan they have."

"Which is?"

"Something I don't want to tell you about because it would put you in more danger." Only the right side of his lips turned up into a smile. He might have fooled some, but to me he looked smug.

"Since I'm in the gooey middle of it already, I think I need to know." I crossed my arms and ankles and gave him a look of disdain.

He looked away. "Perhaps later. It will require a somewhat long, time-wasting explanation." He turned back to me. "First things first. Do you think you can find again the room where your Da is being held?"

I cut my eyes at him, hoping he sensed the total contempt in my gaze. "Of course not—I'm a complete little fool who set off with no idea where she was headed, nor how to get back to where she started from."

He sighed, raising himself up by pushing on his knees with his hands. "I didn't mean it like that. I meant, take me there now." He reached into his pocket. "Before I forget, and lest I be unjustly accused again. . . ." He slipped my charm out of his pocket and handed it back to me, first wrapping it in a silk neckerchief. "There, it's calmed. Now it shouldn't go off again until you, er, 'need it to,' as you put it."

I stuffed the charm down in my neckline.

We slipped back down the alley easily without seeing anyone. It took me only moments to verify that the wards were still off and the latch undone. "We've beaten them back, then." I breathed a prayer of thanksgiving. "Da, we're here!" I felt pretty full of myself as I opened the door—

To a plain, empty storeroom. Goods on the shelves, but no people on the floor. No Da.

CHAPTER SEVENTEEN

I stood in the doorway a moment, then dashed in, thinking Da surely must've come to himself and found a way to hide. "Da! Where are you?" I snatched up the loose ropes that lay where I had left Da, subconsciously seeing how they'd been sliced to ribbons with a sharp blade, but denying the implications of this. "There must be a secret passageway."

"For shame, Dulcinea. Is this a childish prank?" Raz began to scold me, but when I turned to him, I must've looked white and panicked enough that he recanted the approach hurriedly. "Well, where is he?"

"I don't know!" My head bounced around on its neck-springs as I looked up and down every corner of the shadowy little room. "He can't have been gone long." I rushed back to the door and looked this way and that, but didn't see fresh tracks to speak of. We had rubbed them out, like as not, in our rush to break in. And normal traffic in the alley would obscure them further as the trail led on. "I was just here. . ." This couldn't be real. Everything was going black; I blinked back the rising panic and willed myself to stay calm. I dropped the ropes without meaning to. I was going to faint. I should never have left him here alone. How would I ever find him again?

Raz shook me by my forearms. "How long ago? Dulcinea, it's important."

I stared at the scuffed-up dirt floor. "I hadn't been gone terribly long before I met you. A candlemark, maybe two."

He dropped my arms and went to inspect the doorway. "Trail's not much good now." He pressed his lips together with his fingers. I rushed over to the doorway behind him to see what he meant. "Some shoeprints lead away from here"—I couldn't make out a thing—"but within mere strides, the ground is too scuffed." Raz pushed past me and searched the shelves and floor all over again, as though Da could be concealed invisibly under dust motes. While I trembled in the doorway, consumed with the need to go, go, go anywhere and Do Something, even it was wrong, Raz tapped softly all over the rear wall, as if testing for secret doors.

"Stop that. Somebody'll hear you. There's a shop up front." I choked a little, finding it difficult to talk. Probably the dirt we'd stirred up. I swallowed dust.

Raz cast a glance circling the room. "Wonder if some of this mightn't be useful?" He slid a small packet of herbs off a shelf into one of his pockets.

"Raz, don't." I couldn't approve of his theft; they'd taken nothing from him. "I've already. . . ."

He didn't seem to care what I thought. He next reached up with his long arms, then went to his tiptoes. He could just barely reach the topmost shelf. "Ahhhh." He released a quiet sigh of ecstasy as he grasped that glowing green glass ball, the one that had tempted me. "You jewel, you. I haven't seen one of these in a month of Colinsdays. Hmm-mmm." It, too, slipped into one of the innumerable pockets of his voluminous robe.

I sniffled loudly, giving him a disapproving glare. "That's pilfering."

He looked at me seriously. "Does it matter, thieving from thieves, considering how much this will help us if—I mean when—we find your father?"

"If the shopkeeper has you arrested for thieving, we won't be able to help him at all." My voice shook with the effort of being audible without coughing or screeching. I thought of my own small thefts and shivered even more, because if they found the stuff on me, who knew what would happen? I held the door almost closed, thinking that if someone came by, we were doomed.

A light came into Raz's eyes. "The shopkeep—that's it. We ought to go round the front of the shop and see what shop it is. Walk down the alley and count doors for me, will you?"

When I didn't respond, Raz grasped my shoulders, turned me around, and led me back into the alley. I calmed myself with the thought that I could always come back and search for more clues. At least out here we were at much less risk of discovery and capture by this Mortogh and his friends.

"I think our business here is done, Dulcinea. No sense making it too easy for the next burglar." Raz kicked the door to the storeroom closed and barred it. No one, bless all the saints who watch over fools, came to see about all the commotion we'd made.

"It's got to be an apothecary," I whispered. "That seems obvious from the stock. It should be easy enough to find."

Raz didn't answer. He put his arm around me and that funny tingling I'd always felt when he was near swept through me, though more mildly than usual. Even my body was an insensitive lout, ready to betray Da and go on about satisfying its own hot blood. I had to concentrate and stay in the immediate moment or I'd lose my mind.

We walked quietly down toward the blind channel I'd found before, counting doors. The one where we'd been held was seventh from the end; seven, the number sacred to Saint Colin, Ladenia's patron. Perhaps it was a lucky omen.

I sniffled once more, then dried my tears. My feeling of hopelessness was receding a bit, and I thought now I could be strong. "I've got to do whatever it takes to get Da back. Tell me what to do, for I don't know." Raz needed to be flattered a bit to do his best work, I knew, so I laid it on thickly, for Da's sake. "I'm relying on you because you're the expert, Raz. I trust you and I'll do whatever you tell me to."

He chucked me under the chin. "That's the spirit. Let's get back to a safe talking spot."

Back in the alley, between the trash containers for privacy, Raz leaned against the stone wall and pulled some silks out of yet another of his purple pockets. He tied a few colorful lengths together and handed them to me. "Put those on so you won't look so much like you're wearing your undies." He'd seen me tie scarves together at home to make a vest and overskirt; I wasn't one for sewing all the time. Then he pulled my bandanna off my head and tied it around my hair and behind my ears in the Romany fashion. "There. That's the way it's supposed to be. You want to look more like the Jipsies."

"What good will that do?" I knew what he meant, though. Over my muddy things, I tied the scarves to form a makeshift costume. Then my pockets' contents made me look lumpy. It wouldn't do to be detained as a possible thief, so I emptied them all into the pouch at my waist. My underpinnings didn't show.

"That costume's fairly good." Raz's tone was admiring for once.

"Thanks." It should help me look less conspicuous in the marketplace. I could still hear the din of their haggling, the talk of trading and dropping of coins. "If I'm a Jipsy girl, though, I've lost my ear-loops."

He waved his hands. "You're close enough. Now, let's discuss the plan. I'll go into the seventh shop down; the apothecary, if we're correct. After all, if somebody's got a storeroom here on merchants' row in the square, it stands to reason they've got a store front here for selling. The Society must've called a favor due in order to put you two in there. And whoever owns this storeroom"— he shot me a knowing look—"trust me, they know exactly what goes on back here. And believe me when I tell you, to be 'allowed' to harbor prisoners of the Society, they must be trusted members, fairly powerful, high up in the hierarchy."

I rubbed my finger under my nose and sniffled. "You keep saying Society. Don't you mean the city guard? I told you, that one man was dressed as a guard." Probably the city guard was crooked. Government was by definition corrupt, that was well known.

Raz turned stern. "You said you'd do whatever I told you without asking questions. When I tell you it's the Society, it's the Society. Now try to listen, Dulcinea. It's important. Your Da's life may be at stake."

One thing about Raz, he certainly knew the way to keep me calm. "Don't remind me." I couldn't listen properly when my spleen threatened to send paralysis up and down my limbs as my humours turned to bile, encouraging panic. I rubbed my numbing hands up and down my cold upper arms, trying to keep calm. *Oh, Saint Sophronicles, patron of the devout, protect Da. Help me get to him.*

"Now, for the plan. I can't just pop in and say, 'I heard a noise in your back room,' because then more than likely we'd end up their next guests. Besides, what were we supposedly doing skulking around in the alley?" He squinted, then pointed a forefinger at me. "No, that won't work. It's best if I'm shopping—no, no good. I'll say I'm looking for someone specific. Someone you met who may have news you need to hear. Er, I mean, that I've met—we won't let them see you, naturally."

I couldn't follow his logic, except for that last part. "The monk and the jackass"—Raz shot me a questioning look at the use of that term, which was unlike me, but I disregarded it—"would probably know me, yes. Even with rags tied around me like this." Maybe I should just keep hidden. Actually, I probably deserved to be caught again, for not sticking with my Da instead of saving myself. I pushed my index finger across the base of my nose to stop it running.

Raz detached the false queue from his hat. "Let's see what happens if we add this." He attached it somehow to my headwrap, then braided it to hang over my right shoulder.

"I'm sure I look quite the elegant lady." I pirouetted, giggling despite myself.

Raz splashed me with water from his waterskin. "Hey!" It reeked of alcohol. "What was that for?"

He grinned. "A tad of rum. Furthers the illusion of having slept in the gutters—Miss Guttersnipe."

I sighed. "Ugh." I'd never get the stink off my skin.

"That should reduce people's desire to be near you. You're going to stay mostly hidden, but I might need you to identify someone. Actually, now you would probably pass for a street girl. You don't look at all like yourself. Except for the smearing with mud on the face; that's customary for you."

I swung, but he caught my arm. He looked right and left. "Careful. You don't want to make us memorable, the way people scuffling sometimes are."

I sobered quickly. Best if we were not remembered in the alleys or streets at all.

Raz turned back to me expectantly. "Okay, I need descriptions, things they may have said, their names."

"Names?" That struck a silver elf-bell in my mind.

"Any names, any names at all."

It came back to me all at once. "Orthe. That was the name of the young fellow who brought our food. At least, that's what he said."

He grabbed my upper arm. "How did you get him to tell you?"

"Ouch!"

"Sorry." He loosened his grip.

"I don't know. I guess I just asked nicely." I rubbed my arm. "At least I think that was it. Orthe. He pronounced it to rhyme with horsie, sort of."

"Are you sure?" Before I could give a sarcastic answer, Raz hurried to correct himself. "Okay, I know you're certain. Figure of speech. I have some idea now about the way to begin this."

"But isn't it dangerous? If they twig to your ruse, how will I know what to do?" I would play along with him the best I could, but that might not be very well at all. "How will we avoid getting caught ourselves?"

After examining his fingernails a moment, he let a smile spread across his face. "Plan two. I escape out the back way while you hide out there among the crowd. Either way, I'll come find you when I've found out what I can."

Raz was overconfident, as ever. None of this sounded safe to me. "Honest to oaths, Raz, think: what could you possibly do that

won't arouse suspicion? Just go around asking people, 'Excuse me—
did you see some wicked men carrying my daddoo through here a
few minutes ago?'"

"Why not?" Raz winked. "Oh, ye of so little confidence. I've
been round the wheel a few times, you know. I might be able to
find things out. People like to talk, even if they need a bit of persuasion to get started."

"How are you going to persuade them?" I blew my nose on
my filthy skirt.

"Through a few contacts I have in the guardsmen's guild—
those who don't realize I'm not really in the employ of the Society." His face lit up. "Or maybe this Orthe works in the store.
That's why he's close by to feed and watch the prisoners. He doesn't
sound terribly bright, but he might know where they'd take a
prisoner next. He might well be bought. Probably he's in their
employ only because they pay the best wage, not because he's
convinced of their philosophy." He knotted his one long eyebrow
in thought along his prowlike forehead. "Of course, considering
their philosophy. . . ."

"What? What's their phil—philo—" I snuffled, diverting my
tears to my runny nose.

He looked at me with level green eyes. "They're a group of
wizards devoted to evil and creating mayhem. They call themselves the Society of Mages. Only that's a misnomer; they're not
real mages, but exactly the opposite of mages like your Da and
myself, who seek to do constructive things with natural majicks.
They're the secret society that has kept alive the old knowledge, the
Old Majickings, the dangerous stuff that I wouldn't dare to study."

I sniffled again and coughed. "They're warlocks?"

"No, my dear. A warlock is—well, they don't exist; that's all
I'm going to explain, because we don't have time to argue com-
parative religion." He stroked his long Roman nose with one index
finger. "Say instead that they are practitioners of the Black Arts.
Demon-callers. Their powers are granted by the fallen ex-angels.
Diabolical majick."

I burst into tears and fell on my butt in the weeds, sobbing.

"This is no time for your courage to fail." Raz spoke sternly, yet there was a thinness to his voice that meant he, too, was concerned. He plucked ineffectually at the shoulder of my muslins. "You must be brave, my dear. Besides, didn't you just say that no one must hear us? We've been lucky not to get stopped so far. Let's get out and follow the trail to your Daddoo while we still can."

I swallowed something lumpy and bitter and followed Raz out into the hot sticky afternoon.

CHAPTER EIGHTEEN

I stumbled after Raz, keeping sight of him in the teeming crowd only because I had hold of the tail of his dark purple sleevecuff. I wiped my eyes savagely with the back of my hand, pretending they were merely irritated by the unfamiliar spices and dust from the foreign caravan. I couldn't think straight. All I could think about was how I'd abandoned my own father to the tortures of the forces of darkness, while making good my own escape. What kind of person was I? This was not the act of a devoted, loving daughter. Da would never have left me.

Raz looked thoughtful. "Perhaps I shall go in and inquire after Orthe openly. I've been away on a journey—that much is true—and I need to get in touch with the Society." He closed one eye. "If the counterman doesn't know of Orthe, or if he panics at the mention of the Society, that itself will tell me plenty."

I threw Raz a suspicious glance. "Why do you know so much about this Society?"

Raz's lips twitched as if he were suppressing a grin. "Let's just say that I used to work their side of the fence. Or at least I let them think I did."

This was disturbing. "Then how do I know you're not a double-faced renegade? I shouldn't trust you any more than they should. A man who lies to his first wife about his mistress will, after they've married, lie to her about his next mistress."

"You make everything so theatrical, my dear, that it's difficult to believe that you're not a changeling who was lost out of my family's bassinets." I remembered him saying his family was in the theater, but I didn't think this was a compliment.

That irked me, and I poked back with a sharp remark. "For that matter, how can I be certain you're not a friend of that monk, luring me back in?" I couldn't imagine what they'd want me for, but I would've liked to hear Raz reassure me. I tried to look defiant, but knew I came off more like a lost little girl.

His tone turned sardonic. "You came to me, remember."

"I had no one else to turn to." I relented. "Okay, I know you're not like them. So you wouldn't really be one of them." I hoped. "I guess I'll just have to trust you. But I don't see why you can't tell me straight out what you're mixed up in."

"Be patient just a short while longer. It will take some time to properly convince you of the moral uprightness of the Academy and about my majick-master there."

Raz had another majick-master, during the same time he'd been serving Da? That was simply not done, if not unethical. But, since I still depended on Raz's help, I said nothing. Instead, I went at it obliquely. "What is this Academy?"

"It's the school for majickers set up by the Majickers' Guild."

I stuck out my lower lip. "Sounds like another name for the Society-of-whatever."

"Quite the opposite, dear. Acceptance to the Academy is the highest honor a majicker could hope for."

I said nothing, hoping he'd believe I was skeptical.

"Come, Dulcinea. You know I'm not in agreement with the Society."

"I used to think so." I decided on a devil's advocacy bait. "Now all I can say is I don't know. The Society, the Academy, all these things you never mentioned while you were with us. Who knows what else you might be hiding?" I put my fists on my hips and stood still in front of him. "I challenge you on your honor as a majicker to tell me the truth—or at least some of it."

"The truth, Dulcinea?" Raz's intense gaze always cut through to my secret heart of hearts. "That I'm set in every way against the Society, their idea of what is right action, and most of all against what they are planning now."

"And what is that, pray tell, so that I can judge for myself whether it is so terrible?" This concept sounded hollow even to my ears; it was like saying the devil's son might be an all right sort since he'd made the honor roll.

Raz shook his head, tight-lipped.

I relented. "All right, perhaps that was expecting too much. Tell me what is so wrong with the Society, then. Other than going around and kidnapping innocent people, and so forth. What is it that they do that you don't want them to do?"

He glanced at me, then pulled me aside, out of the crowd, to a more secluded corner behind some buildings. "All right, then, the quick rundown on the Society. They are doing something—I can't say what, not out here in the open—but something very foolish to try to increase the power at their disposal. You see, honorable majickers are sworn to pull only a certain amount of majick from the natural sources on the Web within a given time period. That's done in order that the resource never becomes so depleted that it runs out. Like the water in a well, which gets depleted permanently after its aquifer has had too many demands made upon it too quickly by too many people." He raised his eyebrows, and I nodded, loosening my fists a bit (I hadn't even realized my hands were balled.) "The Society not only takes more than its fair share, but it wants even more than can be had by moral means. Hence, their choice to turn to the black arts." He looked as serious as I'd ever seen him. "Without going into details, Dulcinea, what they are planning to do may give them power for the moment, but it has the potential to tear the very fabric of reality as we know it. The Society cares only for gaining power, even at great potential risk. It is unclear whether they are unaware of the dangers inherent in what they are doing, or they know and simply don't care about the chaos that would ensue if power from—from where they are planning on taking it—began to leak into our world."

"Into our world?" What other world, save the afterlife, was there? "You're pulling my leg."

"Dulcinea, I've never been more serious."

I just looked at him. This was way over my head. I couldn't really take it seriously because it was so much bigger than I'd expected. Perhaps he was having a little joke, but he looked perfectly serious. There had to be a punch line. "And?"

"And there is no one but the few of us who know about it to fight them and stop them."

I stuck my lower lip out a bit, feeling out-talked. Raz had put things into such general terms that I couldn't relate it to today. "What does all this have to do with us?"

"The destiny of the world is everyone's problem, my dear." He gestured around us, at the crowds, the city, the everyday bustle. "Let's not argue philosophy and the meaning of life at the moment, eh what? It should be enough to let you know that there's more at stake than a simple quarrel between denominations of majickers." Then he straightened his robes. "Sand's slipping through the glass while we stand here yawping. I need to be off on our present mission."

"I'm going with you."

Again the eyebrows went up. "That's unwise."

"I don't care." I swiped the back of my hand across my eyes. "I can't stand to wait out here and wonder what's happening. What if you don't come out?" I crossed my arms and put on a fierce face. "No, I'd die waiting out here alone."

Raz began to object, then shrugged. "All right. But lag behind me; you're small, so you can almost hide in my robes. And if anyone looks familiar, make yourself scarce." He gave me a sharp look. "You're my little sister. I had to let you tag along."

"All right." I had promised to do whatever Raz asked.

"And if you get caught. . . ."

"It's my own fault." After a moment, I added, "And every man for himself."

"There's my girl."

# # #

"They said it would be a man and his friend." The swarthy man's stony, deadpan face didn't change. "They didn't say nothing about no girls."

Raz grasped his corded lapels, rocking back and forth heel to toe. "My sister is my friend."

The man grunted, not completely convinced. "I'll not allow that gal nearby whilst we transact our bidness." He insisted I be sent away before he'd talk to Raz further.

Raz shrugged and shoved me, as roughly as he'd do his true sister, toward the exit. Into my ear he hissed, "Let me go see what I can find out. You wait out here." As we hit the door, he amended his orders. "Don't stand around, though; wander a bit. It'll look less suspicious. Meet me in front of the seer's wagon."

He was gone in a rustle of purple silk.

One of these days, that conspicuous shade—the color once reserved for royalty—was going to get him noticed at the wrong time.

I bit my lip. If something went wrong, if someone recognized Raz . . . how would I know it? I'd just be left waiting here until nightfall. And then what?

I shifted my weight from foot to foot. I had to find an outlet for the nervous energy that now flooded me, making it difficult to think about anything but how to bear the waiting. *Please*, I prayed to all the saints, *please don't let Raz get caught, too.*

I stomped around the corner, studying every booth and shop. I had no idea what I was looking for until I saw a coach, one parked under two spreading buttonwood trees with their many tiny leaves and displaying a vibrantly green flag bearing the stylized symbol of a staring eye. That must be the seer.

As I drew closer, I saw a tall but stooped woman lurking about the ramp that gave access to the little coach; a dirty red scarf covered her head down to the ears, beneath which flowed tangled corkscrews of jet-black hair down to her shoulders. Her olive skin was wrinkled all over, and her fingers were lumpy with age. Her vision was sharp enough, though, for her to see me approaching from a distance. As soon as she spied me, she crooked one forefinger at me, forming a grimace that revealed all three of her top teeth. I took it for a welcoming smile and, before I realized I shouldn't, nodded in return.

"Ah, young woman! You want to know what destiny holds for you, yes? Come. Closer, dearie, closer. I see in your future a tall, dark, and handsome youth." She bared her gapped teeth at me. I found the resulting expression remarkably unattractive, though I remembered my manners and smiled back. If only she hadn't acquired the yellow tobacco stains and the discolored brown spots typical of those who chewed the addictive juice-nut, not to mention the cow's breath to match, maybe I could've kept from recoiling as she stepped closer. "And you're going to take a short journey on foot—yes?" She reached out, grasping at my mud-sodden sleeve, but instead clawing my exposed white armflesh. "Come, daughter, and let me tell you what I see in store."

I flinched and stepped back, abandoning politeness. "No, thank you."

"But there's things you want to know. Come hear your future, my girlie. I know these things. For instance." She leered at me with her flat black eyes. "You're about to suffer a great disappointment." Apparently, one's fortunes worsened the longer one resisted her offer.

I took a few steps back into the crowd, wondering why Raz'd had to pick this stupid place for our rendezvous. The jostling shoppers were too thick to break into. I was trapped under the jipsies' trees.

"I can't afford a reading."

All at once the jipsy woman paled. She stumbled and fell back, as though she were about to swoon. Her face took on a distracted expression, and she grasped for the nearest tree. I thought she was trying to keep from falling. Without thinking, I stepped forward and reached for her. I caught her by the sleeve, and she righted herself. But her eyes still didn't look quite right.

A strange trembling passed through the Jipsy woman, and then a gleam of intelligence took its place in her gaze. She grasped both of my arms. "The saints want me to warn you. You must seek he whose face lives beneath a round and shiny boulder, fringed with grass of gray. But take care when you see him, for he will be wary of you. Tell him, 'The way is long and wearying, but my spirits remain light as the weather.'"

"What?" I jerked my arms away, but she reached for them again.

Then she seemed to come to herself. "Where was I?" Distract-edly, she cleared her throat. "I must have gone into one of my trances." There was an odd glint in her eyes. "I have these spells, and they're from the saints. Whatever I told you, you be sure you do it. Hear?"

Against my better judgment, which told me not to answer, I said, "Yes." I hoped that wasn't a binding promise.

"Count yourself lucky, girl, because I normally wouldn't tell that important a thing unless I'd already been paid." She tilted her head and stroked the back of my hand with her wizened old claws. "That was a gift from the angels. Now for the reading. Come inside so's I can finish telling your fortune."

Fascinated despite myself, I almost followed her as she took a few steps towards the doorway. Then I realized I couldn't, even if I wanted to. "I appreciate the offer, but, seriously, I cannot pay." I backed away. "Besides, I'm meeting someone, and I must be out here waiting so he'll see me." I should never have made eye con-tact. What had possessed me to let her do any reading at all? She had pretended to go weak as a ruse. That silly "message from the saints" was an obvious fabrication, as well. It had only been one of her tricks.

Now her black eyes glittered brighter. "You are in danger, and so are others around you. I alone can look into your future to tell you what you needs must know."

I turned my empty pockets inside-out in the universal gesture for pennilessness. "Honestly, I have no money. I truly can't afford it."

Her teeth gleamed with saliva as she chuckled. "Too late for that, dearie. You already owes me silver coin just for what I've done told you."

I displayed my upturned, open palms. "Kindly stop Seeing for me, then. I've already told you I can't pay."

A wide, swarthy man with a dark complexion and black beard stepped out from the undertree shadows. "Have we a walkout, Mother?" He strode toward me, his earrings and bracelets jingling; he wore no shirt on his tangled black chest, but only bandannas tied on his head and wrists and baggy grayish pantaloons. He lacked only the eye patch to match the meanest pirate a-seas. I backed up a few more steps, but the jostling crowd prevented my escape. He reached out with one long arm, and I barely dodged.

"Please, sir. I didn't come for my future. I was merely passing by and only stopped to be polite." I stepped to the left and back, right into the soft belly of someone else—and knew I was caught.

Purple sleeves wrapped around me, along with Raz's familiar peppermint scent. Raz had arrived just in time, for once. I let out a long breath and counted heartbeats while I waited for my pulse to slow.

Raz's voice boomed deep. "Is there a problem, Lady Dulcinea?"

The gypsy pirate made a noise deep in his throat. "This girl's a-tryin' to run off afore payin' for her readin'."

Raz stepped between me and my attackers. "She's not old enough to come as a customer. Why, she's but a waif in my care. She didn't enter your studio, did she?"

As Raz spoke, the old woman sank back into the shadows under the trees. The man merely grunted.

"Then you have no claim on her. Outside, she's just a visitor. She has as much right to walk around the caravan as anyone. Let us make for the shops." Raz cocked one eyebrow. "Or do you try to block the trade of other merchants? I'll wager they'd be interested to hear how you're scaring customers, perhaps driving them from the marketplace entirely."

The man stepped back. "A thousand times I ask your pardon, Sir. Briefly, I thought she was someone else. Go with luck, missy. And you, sir." He lowered his head over his extended arm in a kind of bow.

Raz hustled me away from there into the midmarket, muttering under his breath. "Don't you have the sense not to attract attention to yourself? It strains belief that you'd let those gypsies talk to you."

"*Let* them talk to me?"

"Never mind, ne'er mind. It's done." He shook out his hair. "Anyway, I have good news. And I can't believe your good fortune. It's a fortuitous thing that fellow insisted he wouldn't talk in front of little girls." I winced, but knew that the saints had been watching over me again. "Guess who he called out from the back for me?"

I grinned. "My good friend Orthe?"

"Knew you'd get it in one." He chuckled, tossing a small pouch in the air and catching it deftly in his other hand. "Lady Luck was watching over you today, Dulcinea. Yes, when I mentioned Orthe, the shopkeep knocked on the wall in a peculiar rhythm, and soon he came forward out of the back, possibly that same stockroom."

"How?" There had been no back door.

Raz waved this detail away. "Please don't interrupt, dear. It betrays a lack of breeding. At any rate, your Orthe accepted me as a loyal member—nay, a Fellow—of the Society. Fact is, after the opening pleasantries and how-d'ye-dos, and after selling me this"— he indicated the pouch—"which I actually needed, and was willing to overpay for, in light of our liberation of some of their backroom goods"—he grinned—"he claimed to have heard good things about me. Our mutual acquaintance was quite helpful."

I sucked in my breath. "So he hadn't heard that you. . . ." I paused, searching for the diplomatic phrase.

Raz waved it away. "No, it's not widely known that I have divided loyalties, as it were. Discretion is the watchword in these types of situations. And lucky for me, too."

I pushed my hair behind my ears, feeling impatient because Raz was dragging the story out. "Well, then. What did he say?"

CHAPTER NINETEEN

Raz imitated the boy's high-pitched voice and struck an ingenuous pose. "In a stage whisper, he asked me, 'So you're taking the prisoner for interrogation now?'" You'd have thought he was in on the biggest secret ever from the way his chest puffed out. It seemed as if he just didn't know not to be so eager.

"So, naturally, I said I was. I expected he might have your Da elsewhere in the shop."

"And?" I scampered along at Raz's heels like some frolicking pup, excited to hurry him along in the telling. "Since Da's not with you"—I restated the obvious, like a cudge—"he wasn't there, but surely you know where he is?" I tried to keep from breathing too fast. "I assume you got something."

"I got something, all right. That dunce Orthe spilled the catch-phrase, the method, and the location for picking up the prisoner. I said I'd put in an extra-good word for him."

"You must have been living right."

He winked. "When have I ever?"

Behind Raz's back, I blew a kiss to Lady Luck in the sky. "Da's safe, then. Oh, praise the saints."

"Even as we speak, we are halfway to the place he is being held." Raz could never resist a chance to preen. "We did have a bit of good fortune back there, though, didn't we? It's the Ladenian in me—the luck of Ladenia City walks with me."

"Well, pray be sure you keep it buttoned in your pocket so it can't flee." I snatched up an apple that I spied in one of his outer pockets, polished it on my sleeve, and prepared to bite into it. Then I shot him a suspicious look. "This is just regular food, isn't it? Not majickal or blessed or anything?"

He glanced over. "Little thief. No, that's merely an apple. Have it if you like. But I did plan for us to sup at the tavern, in case your Daddoo hasn't been properly fed, as we prepare for our journey home."

I slipped the apple into my pocket for later. I felt exhilarated, astounded at our luck, and the magnitude of my good fortune was just hitting me as I realized what would've happened had Orthe come out while I stood there—if he'd recognized me. I must have shown my consternation, because Raz gave me a puzzled look.

"Are you listening? You seem a million miles away."

"I was just thinking." I skipped a few steps. No sense telling him everything on my mind. I decided to pick his brain instead. "How did you ever get involved with the sort of people who are in that Society?"

"As I told you, Dulcinea, it is one of my assignments at the Academy." He hadn't told me any such thing. He sighed. "I must've seemed rather mysterious over the past few months, but I needed to keep a quite low profile. There was nothing to be gained by burdening you and Magefather Brown with my entire story, and much at stake to be lost if someone should speak out of turn."

"But didn't you also have a responsibility to those you swore loyalty to, meaning you must let them know if you have another master you also serve, especially if their goals might be in conflict, and your loyalty would thus be divided?"

He glared. "Please don't interrupt constantly, Dulcinea. It's a sign of a lack of schooling. As I was saying. . . ."

I kept quiet, blinking femininely.

He looked daggers and kept silence until he felt he'd gotten his point across, then softened. "I did nothing unethical, and I had good reason for concealing my dual purpose. I kept my oaths and was completely loyal to Magefather Brown while I was with you."

"I have no doubt in my mind," I said dryly.

He went on as if he hadn't heard. "In any case, you needn't worry about me being on the wrong side of morality. I'm one of the goodfellows, one of the true defenders of wizardry."

"Defending it against what?"

He quirked his left eyebrow without moving the right. "Are we alone? Have we our privacy?"

"I think you're as safe from eavesdropping amidst a jostling crowd as anywhere." I made my tone rather pointed.

He glanced around, then nodded, apparently satisfied that we were among shoppers and others who didn't care in the least what we were discussing. Still, he made his tone so low that I had to bump up against his side to hear. "I'm a student of wizardry at the Academy of Mages, the school of true majick run by the Brotherhood." Before I could ask, he pasted on, "We are a guild of white majickers who have taken the Majicker's Oath: 'We shall aid any who ask, right all possible wrongs, but take no revenge, do no harm, and bear no ill will.'" He'd struck a pose, probably without realizing it, hand over his heart as though pledging allegiance to the beliefs once again. "And even as students, we know the importance of always living by that oath and upholding our honor. I am one of the few select students of the craft. The head majick-master's favorite, if I may be immodest for a moment."

"How unlike you," I murmured, but he wasn't listening.

"I shan't mention the name of my majick-master. It would mean nothing to you, at any rate, though it would mean much to those who know about such things. His reputation is known far and wide, and his face and manner are also fairly easily recognized, again by those who know such things, say, inside the community of majickers."

We were halfway across town, by my reckoning, and the nature of the neighborhoods had changed. Instead of window boxes brimming with flowers, the ramshackle houses and businesses around this area had boarded-up windows and collapsed front stoops. I hoped Raz had got the directions right. I took the apple out and juggled it from hand to hand, trying to pay attention while I waited for Raz to get to a germane point.

"But therein lies not only a blessing, but also a hazard: he is so well-known that he's too easily spotted when it comes time to go out into the cities and do the Brotherhood's business."

"Which is?" I couldn't help asking.

Raz glared at me, and I realized I'd been too loud. When he was certain no one had paid the least attention to us, he continued in low tones. "Good works and proper action, deeds to benefit humanity and discoveries that will serve mankind. Also, things we're hired to do that meet our high moral standards. I'll explain more later if you like. May I get on with my original line of thought?"

"Please." I hoped I sounded contrite.

"As I said, our majick-master is too prominent to go out and do his own research. So when it came time to infiltrate the Society, to see whether the rumors were true. . . ." He polished his fingernails on his lapel and smiled smugly. "I was chosen for the mission."

"Which rumors?"

"You mean 'what rumors,' for you have heard no rumors of the sort at all. Correct?" He admonished me with a crooking of his finger, and I acquiesced by nodding. "Rumors about the terrorist attack they've planned on this very city. During Festival Week, next moonsphase. At its height, just as people have massed to watch the start of the parade. They'll wait until the floats and dancers are all set up and people are lining the roads to watch, and then. . . ." His fist slapped into his other palm.

I plugged my mouth with the apple so I wouldn't cry out. "Attack!" I muttered into my juicy microphone.

"Yes, attack." Raz looked serious. "It's an awful thought, isn't it?"

Through my mind flashed images of the upcoming festival and the hundreds of villagers who'd be in the Square and the Park in Ladenia City. My hands went cold. "Horrid."

"It's a complex tale that I won't go into now, but suffice it to say that while I remain a student and employee of the Academy, I have managed to infiltrate the Society. I've convinced their leadership that I felt wronged and wanted to 'defect.'"

"If they're all like Orthe, that couldn't have been too difficult." I nudged him, but he dodged, prissily adjusting his robes.

"They're not, my dear. No. Most of them are quite accomplished at the craft, and quite ambitious as well. Some of the best and brightest, Dulcinea, have fallen to the temptation of power through the black arts."

I almost dropped my apple.

"They didn't start out that sort, most of them. They've forgotten themselves, of course. They don't like to think that they could fall prey to evil, and so they tell themselves that it is only a means to a proper end. They think their accomplishments will justify their methods."

I nodded seriously, as though the arrogance of Society mages was well known to me.

He patted his chest. "It took machination and cunning on my part, but I convinced them I'd joined their side, and they did finally admit me. The worst day I've lived was the day of my initiation into that organization. You wouldn't want to know what that ceremony is like."

I would, but I kept quiet.

"I tell you, my Wizard's Mark took some explaining." Before I could challenge him about the mention of a wizardmark, he continued, "Things heated up when I stumbled upon their dungeon and the secret weapon within." Raz turned to me, eyes glittering. "They have done it, Dulcinea. They conjured a shimmering blue Wyrm."

"Wyrm." I pretended to understand what he meant so he'd keep explaining, sans educational digressions.

"A True Dragon. Not like those dragonets you see some mages keeping in cages or perched on their shoulders and claim that they're familiars. A true, full-sized, free Dragon." He turned pensive. "Though, from the looks of it, still a baby, or it would never have fit in that dungeon."

"A baby dragon." I prompted him for more details. I visualized a huge serpent, but wondered if I could work up the humility to ask openly for a description.

"Yes. And blue, to boot. Isn't that something? Even if it is a mere pup." He looked agitated.

"But what's a—I mean, what do you mean by. . . ." I shook my head. "What are you calling a dragon?"

"A dragon, of course. You know what a dragon is."

"But—there isn't any such thing. Not outside of fairy tales."

Raz gave me one of his smug, brighter-than-thou looks. "Really, Dulcinea, I thought you were better educated than that. As you must know, dragons exist on a plane adjacent to ours."

"Of course." This fascinating tidbit was new to me, but I would never let on. Another mind-scrambling revelation from the world of arcane majick. I supposed that was what he'd meant when he had said there were other worlds than ours, even besides the one of the angels and the saints for which we were eventually destined. I phrased my probing question as a breezy statement. "A plane adjacent to ours, which you can, of course, get into."

He glanced sharply over. "Not so loud, Dulcinea. That's the dangerous part, as you have guessed. If the right methods are used—and this gets back into the Society's plan I mentioned earlier, and the dangers inherent in it—this particular plane is very easily accessed." I nodded as though this were perfectly sensible. "The dangers, naturally, lie in Gating back and forth without maintaining a strict balance in the power that is transferred. What you bring from that plane to this, whether in energy or material, you must pay back in kind from this one to that. Though sealing the Gate is not difficult, it must be done properly to prevent leakage and chaos. It's something that the Academy has known how to do for a long time, and that the Society has only recently discovered. Perhaps through a betrayal."

I'd figured the Society might have a man like Raz at the Academy whose true loyalties lay with the Society, but I said nothing.

"In any case, consider the chaos that would ensue if dragons began Gating over to this plane on their own, if power from the other plane began to leak into this one and feed Discordia and disorder. . . . Or even worse."

I couldn't resist asking. "What could be worse?"

"Exactly." He took it as a rhetorical question. "It's all possible, and can be done safely, with knowledge and planning. Of course we are forbidden to do so. It's all laid out clearly in the Majickers' Creed; we've sworn that we won't interfere in the other planes of existence. Certainly we're not to bring dragons and their kind to the material plane; it's far too hard on their systems to adjust, in the first place. More importantly, it's unfair to take one. It's slavery and oppression of an intelligent life form. But the Society people don't sign up to the Oath nor the Creed, not their kind." His fists clenched.

Again I took a breezy tone, in case he was teasing me. "Naturally. But what do the dragons say about it?"

He shot me a stern look. "You realize that there are many other planes of existence that we could touch—think of Heaven and Hades and Limbo, my dear, and you'll realize anyone knows it. Most merely think of them in a spiritual sense instead of a psychically dimensional sense. But all planes, save the world of the afterlife, are accessible environments supporting mortal life of some sort, planes in which we could travel and commune with the other lifeforms, had we learned to properly train our minds. There is in fact one otherwhere plane that we do touch when we pull power from the grid of majickal ley lines girdling the world, commonly known as the Web of Majick."

Raz was in fine form today. I made a little noise of exasperation, eager to get back to the dragon.

"These planes of existence, as you'd expect, contain other forms of life as natural to their plane as we to ours. It's as it is with any animal of the world that lives untamed in the jungle, following its own path. It has its own power." He glanced over, and I indicated I knew what he was getting at by pursing my lips thoughtfully. "The core of majickwork consists of directing power, the power of trained thought. Majickers develop control over their own thoughts so as to gain the ability to access power from the other planes, the non-physical planes, especially the Web that circles the world with its invisible fibers, carrying majickal power. The inhabitants of these other planes, naturally, draw on the same power, for the most part; there's enough to go around, but we mustn't interfere with the other planes in any other way. The corollary is that a properly trained mind can communicate with these beings on other planes, and sometimes can even force them to return to the physical plane with us. The morally correct thing is not to do that. Follow me?"

I decided to just accept it all at face value; it was too much to analyze in my present mental state. I felt like my mind now had about the capacity of a peanut. "Go on. I mean, I understand all that. But what happened next with the stolen dragon?"

"I couldn't free it. It was rather—undomesticated." He frowned. "But I managed to—*obtain*—from its keepers a stone that possesses some kind of power that's connected with controlling it."

Da's instinct about Raz not having many scruples when it came to "obtaining" useful items had not been so far off, after all. I'd seen it twice now. I sucked on the remains of the apple core and spat out a seed. "A rock that controls a dragon."

He turned on a side street, one that had houses with scraggly vegetation and people on the street who looked slightly unsavory. "Sometimes you sound like an echo, my dear. Yes, exactly. It is a very unusual item. That's why I need to consult with my colleagues and especially my majick-master. That's why it is so essential that I find a way to get back in touch with the Academy."

I frowned, kicking a stone ahead of us on the path. "Is that what you were doing when I, er, found you?"

"Not exactly." He grimaced. "You see, I said communication was impossible. That's not strictly true; I meant safe communication, with no danger of interception. Since my departure from school, the Society's blackguards have secreted themselves throughout the countryside to keep me or anyone else from entering or leaving our enclave. They've also laid traps to detect majick that sends an unwise tendril past the shielded gateways of the Academy's guild buildings. Any communications can be intercepted and the sender tracked. There's no telling when I might blunder into Society mages or spies."

I found myself sucking on the strings of the apple's core and tossed it into the pathside ditch. "But you're a majicker. Can't you just . . . well, fly there or something?"

He sent me a withering look. "We are not witches, Dulcinea." He rubbed his chin in his palm. "Majickal travel is out of the question, even if I were so advanced and powerful to have access to it, which I don't. They're also physically watching the Academy grounds, as I said. If I were seen approaching the enclave. . . ."

I interpreted this to mean that he mustn't approach the Academy overland because it would endanger the compound, not to mention that he might be captured by the blackguards. Also, because that enclave had defenses, if Raz triggered anything by accident, Raz might have to be sacrificed by his own side.

He shook his head. "I don't yet know how I'll get back there, let alone get the stone safely to them."

I had ideas, like sending it through the King's post, or hiding it inside a chicken brought from market and sending a food courier with it as though it were a gift from somewhere. I thought one of them might even work.

But at the moment there was no time to speak of my ideas and have them ridiculed. Raz stopped in front of a shabby-looking tailor shop. "We're here."

My heart skipped. I survived a withering look from Raz. "Do you think he's still. . . ."

"You're my sister, remember." Raz hissed it into my ear. Mostly the "s" parts hissed, but he did fill my ear with spittle as he whispered. I set my jaw. Well, I could be a bratty and irritating sister. That part I was sure I could play.

CHAPTER TWENTY

I would've missed this shop from the main road. Set between a bakery and the armourers, number 19-1/2 was marked only by a small sign hanging under the roof overhang with an arrow pointing up. The entryway to it had a half-door, a door that was barely half the width of a normal one, and from there you went up a narrow, steep stair. The door at the top was scarred, as though it had often been kicked open by someone carrying armfuls of clothing and supplies.

In the tiny tailor shop, the air was close and everything smelled like dust. Bolts of fabric lay around, and half-finished garments were lined up on pegs on the wall. I sneezed, fanning away some of the floating dust motes with my hand. The small window behind the main table was high-set and filthy, admitting little light.

A fat man peeked around from behind a black curtain when the bells on the door announced us. He was bald on top, but yarnlike strands of gray hair hung from just above his ears to below his shoulders. He stood up off his stool and took the pins out of his mouth. "What can we help you with today?"

Raz's voice boomed out, overloud in the small space. "Among the rushes floats the infant." Raz beamed and looked at the man expectantly.

The bald man looked him up and down, gave me the same going-over, then stared at Raz. The top of his head gleamed with perspiration. "Sir?"

"Floating peacefully, the rushes carry the prophet."

Still the man showed no sign of recognition. If anything, he sounded grumpy. "Look, my good man, if you've something to say, make it plain. Come out with it."

Looking at his face, I suddenly heard the words of the old gypsy woman in my mind's ear. "A round and shiny boulder, fringed with grass of gray." His head could be a boulder, all right. Could this be the man she'd prophesied?

Raz spoke louder. "Among the rushes—"

"Yes, yes, I'm not deaf. That much I heard." The bald man squinted. "But what's not coming across is any sense."

I realized Orthe had not been such a featherbrain, but instead rather cunning. He'd set a trap, and Raz had stuck his neck into it. Perhaps he hadn't the manpower to capture Raz back at that shop, but here there might be a majicker Raz's equal.

The thought of bolting for the door briefly crossed my mind, but then I'd be returned to my original problem, with no idea how to rescue either Raz or Da. I elbowed Raz in the ribs. Why didn't Raz catch on?

Raz shifted his weight to his left foot, looking uncertain. "Am I not making myself clear?"

The bald man eased his hand up towards a long pull-cord hanging from a hole in the ceiling. "I'm starting to think that you are. I think you are, indeed." He was about to grasp the rope, looking as suspicious as Da when I tried to sneak an extra helping of sugar-cakes off of the plate, when I suddenly found my voice.

"The way is long. . . ." What had she said? *Please, Saint Dulcinea, granter of random acts of kindness, please give the seer's words back to me now.* The tailor trained a sharp look of interest on me, and I knew I was on track. Prayers definitely availed much; my brain filled with the words as the memory rushed back. "Long and wearying. But my spirits are—remain—remain light as—" He had the tip of his tongue on his teeth, and looked like I was about to win the prize. "The weather!"

The tailor's fist banged down on the cabinet. "Damnation, man, you should have come across right away," he said to Raz, grinning crookedly. "I thought you were a false-face posing as our representative. A sneak trying to guess one of our catchphrases." He whewed. "Why, you oughtn't to tempt fate like that. I was about to pull the security cord." He gestured to the curtain. For the first time I noticed the doorway to the back room. In the shadow of the doorway hulked a large man looking like a tavern's bouncer. "And believe me, once they have taken you wrong, it's not easy to recover the situation."

"Rectify," muttered Raz, under his breath. To the bald man, he bowed, doffing his hat. "I apologize for trying your patience. I merely wanted to check another byword, which obviously hasn't yet been distributed. I should have told you that my sister was the actual courier and I the mere chaperone."

The tailor rolled his eyes. "Imagine, trusting a young gal like that. Meaning no offense, little lady." He cast an apologetic glance my way, possibly realizing that my looks could be deceptive, and I might wield power. "They're pulling stunts like this on me all the time these days. Here, I'll get the prisoner and be gladly rid of him. He's a burden to me, and keeps my strongarms tied up with watching him." He shook his head. "If you ask me, that man's not right in the head, muttering constantly to himself about a fight."

My heart sank, but I couldn't allow myself to break down with worry about Da. I had to act normal. I pulled a pout. "Told you he'd be one of those crazy ones."

"We do what our masters ask," Raz said in his most authoritative tone.

The tailor returned, pushing Da ahead of him. My heart speeded up. I was so excited to see Da walking around and looking all right that I nearly gave myself away. But as they got closer, I could tell Da still wasn't quite normal. He was almost zombielike, looking at Raz wonderingly. However, he still had the power of his voice.

"I know you!" He glared at Raz.

Raz had the presence of mind to play along. "Indeed you do, sir. Now come right along with me."

"I know that girl, too." He pointed at me as he would identify a playmate across the sandpit. My heart sank. Did he really know me for who I was, or was he still . . . still. . . .

"You see?" Raz worked the exchange smoothly into an acknowl-edgment of his couriership. The bald tailor grunted and turned back to his tasks.

Before Da could say anything more, Raz escorted him firmly down the aisle. Da, meek as a schoolboy, seemed content to follow orders from anyone who claimed authority. We headed out and into the street.

Smoothly Raz extracted a square of fabric from one of his volu-minous robe's many pockets; he threw it over Da's shoulders, and I saw it would pass for a traveling cloak, covering the back of his pyjamas. We made for a stand of oak trees in the square, and quickly untied Da's ropes.

A lady passing by stopped to stare, and I grinned at her—convincingly, I hoped. "Been trying a few ways of tying these robes tighter. Tailor's no good; avoid that shop if you value your money." I nodded in the shop's general direction. She tossed her head and walked away.

"Good thinking," muttered Raz.

"I'm hungry," announced a happy Da. He looked vacant as a simpleton.

"That's a thought." Raz took one of Da's elbows in his own. "Let's step into the Pig, shall we, and have a quick bite."

Following Raz's lead, I took Da's other elbow. Like the three adventurers headed down the legendary red brick road, we marched across the cobbled street to the Singing Pig tavern. Da hummed as if leading the way.

# # #

It turned out that the Pig was right next to the Dragon's Head Inn, where Raz had a room. I wouldn't have figured this as a part of town he'd stay in, but it might well be very affordable. Raz sent a boy to retrieve our belongings and Tickie from the Fat Badger across town, where Tickie'd racked up somewhat of a bill. He also gave instructions for bringing his own horse, one he'd just bought,

and his pack stuff from the stable. "Make them ready at the hitching post within the candle-hour."

He slipped the boy a handful of silver, and the boy's eyes lit
up. "Yessir!"

Then Raz turned to me. "That Orthe. The betrayer. The stinking, smug trickster. Giving me a false password so I'd be caught.
Clever, because he did know about me, but never let on. Just smiled
and smiled while being a villain." He narrowed his eyes. "How did
you . . . ."

I smiled wordlessly a moment, enjoying seeing him at a loss
for words, for a change. "How did I what?"

He snorted. "You know. You guessed, or you knew, the proper
phrase. Now it's my turn to ask how you got mixed up with that
kind of people. Who told you? Did you overhear it earlier, then
put two and two together all of a sudden?"

I felt smug. "The saints told me."

Raz looked sour. "Very funny. You can be quite witty when
you like, Dulcinea."

"Lucky guess." If the truth displeased him.

He liked that better. "You overheard while you were hypnotized,
I'll wager. You just don't remember hearing it. Fortuna smiled upon
you once again and blessed you with recall at the proper time."

That wasn't true. But before I was required to explain further,
our food arrived, hot and steaming. Better than the ploughman's
lunch I'd expected: roasted joints, potatoes, glazed carrots, jellied
winterbloom fruits, bread and melting butter.

Da still seemed vague, but set to eating what I had ordered for
him with his usual eagerness. He paused to speak only once. "Well,
this is more like it. Can't fathom any establishment staying in
business serving only the glop and water I've had so far in my stay
in this town." He bit into a roasted turkey leg with gusto.

I almost giggled, then felt solemn. He'd forgotten what'd really happened. This was awful. Today and yesterday had been like
living in a flute-story, but one that had gone into a minor key, a
dirge. How soon would Da be himself again? My gaze met Raz's.

"What if he stays like . . . like. . . ." I mouthed it silently across the table at Raz.

Raz whomped his arm across Da's shoulders affectionately, as though they were seafaring buddies meeting up again after a shore leave. "He'll come out of it. I'll take this glamour, or whatever it is, right back off him up in my room. Then we'll settle up my bill and be on our way." Da shook off Raz's arm without even looking up, returning his attention to his meal.

"You're not afraid to do majick here?" I paused, clinking my spoon aimlessly on the edge of my tin plate. "Won't they be watching for you on the. . . ." I realized I probably shouldn't mention the web of majick in public, so I made little circles in the air with my spoon. "You know."

"I won't have to draw much power. I hope." His eyebrows drew a little closer together. "At any rate, it can't be too complex. It's some simple glamour. In the short time it takes to unwork it, they won't even notice me. My signature won't be broadcast far."

"If they can somehow feel you working majick, though." I hadn't realized I said it aloud until Raz nodded. "It is still dangerous. Theoretically."

He nodded again. "Real majickings—you can feel them, can't you? You've felt them looking for you, seeking out dangers nearby, weaving their web of protection around you. But that was only when the spells were meant to act upon you personally. Well, a wizard can learn to seek majick anywhere it is, so that he eventually can track the faintest of vibrations from any spell. If he knows how, and if he concentrates, and if he has a bit of luck. And they've had a bit of luck with us lately, haven't they?" He looked grim. "No, too much majicking might scream for them and hand us right back to them, covered with syrup on a silver serving tray."

"I had no idea majicking was so dangerous." I put on a child-like, innocent expression. I hoped he caught my irony.

Raz gave me a wry look. "These risks are one reason I was interested in your Da teaching me his folk majick and herbal ways. Natural majickings don't speak as loudly of craft, because they echo nature's ways of getting things done instead of manifesting the will by drawing on lines of force, and thus can't be so easily traced."

"Oh." I hadn't really thought about that. But I recalled how, when Da was scrying for me in the woods, I could feel the majick hunting for me all around. An actual presence it'd had, bouncing around among the trees like so many rabbits, searching for its intended target. "They still might hear you."

"There are other majickers in a city of this size, you know. And I was careful never to do a working in their presence, so they don't know my signature. As long as they have no possessions of mine to read my signature off of, they're only guessing."

This was not the time to explain to Raz about the monk taking his necklace. I bit the inside of my cheek and decided I was finished with my dinner.

"It'll be all right. I might have to try a few things, but." Raz waved away any problems. "It'll be fine. Besides, we'll be away from here as soon as I'm finished."

"I hope it doesn't take too long." A sudden idea came to me. "Are you thinking what I'm thinking?"

"That is highly doubtful, Dulcinea." Raz massaged his temples.

I ignored the remark. "We ought to get out of here before dark. In the dark, we might not even know if we're being followed." I didn't even want to speak aloud my visions of being waylaid on the darkened roads. Speaking of them might make them happen. But I couldn't help myself, blathering on. "That monk. Even the thought of him scares me. If he gets hold of me again, he's sure to do something horrible. He knows us all three, and we've barely gotten out of his clutches. And we're just sitting here as though we were on a relaxing little jaunt to the marketplace, while we ought to be making haste away from this town."

When my voice went shrill, it tended to carry. Raz looked meaningfully right and left and made a subtle shushing sound. I consciously lowered my volume and pitch.

He took a bite of his meat. "Attitude is everything. Exude confidence." He swallowed, then dabbed at his mouth. "Don't forget we know our route. We'll make quick time on the road." He sounded less confident than I would have hoped. I realized he was worried. I took deep breaths to keep from panicking.

"Let's just hurry." That seemed all we could do. I offered up a silent prayer.

When I opened my eyes, Raz was again his usual cocksure self. "Don't borrow trouble, Dulcinea. We'll be fine." He stretched his arms in front of him and cracked all his knuckles, making me wince. "No one on the road will pay any attention to an old man and his children."

I wasn't so certain.

I sighed, feeling the weariness in my calves and the arches of my feet. The mere thought of the long ride home, doubled with Da on Tickie, made me ache. Right now I needed Raz, but I couldn't help feeling a little resentful. If it hadn't been for Raz coming to us in the first place, Da and I would be home safe, closing up the shop and blowing out the candles about now, tucking ourselves into the safety of warm clean bedclothes. But instead here we were, in the worst fix I'd ever been in.

And all because Raz had stolen something—a rock—just as the blackguards had said, and was now on the run from this Society, an association of obvious power.

I guessed this situation had been going on for several moons. Since Raz hadn't exactly had the funds to live off of while waiting to find a way back into the Academy compound, he needed another job in order to eat. He also needed to stay out of the Society's way. He'd decided to learn what he could as he hid out in unobvious locations. Mainly in the bosom of our family. That had been inconsiderate of him. Completely thoughtless. With no regard for anyone else. What an arrogant codswallop.

I decided there was no use being angry about that after the fact, so I officially pre-and post-forgave him.

"All right, brother dear." I smiled sweetly, determined not to betray bitterness or anger. I had to be strong and tolerant for Da's sake. "Forward into the breach, or the fray, or whatever it is."

"There you go." Raz smiled back. "All you have to remember is do what I tell you." He picked up his pewterware and slurped the last of his ale. "Ahhh. Yes, if you'll just do what I ask and not go off with your own ideas, we'll be just fine."

I couldn't stand to let that pass without a return jab. "Your ideas haven't exactly put you into the best of situations so far. I was doing fairly well until I got mixed up with you."

He quirked an eyebrow. "Ah, but now you're in it with me, you see. The Society mages now know who you are. I can't figure out how they made the connection, but they must have."

I still felt this was not the time to explain about my foolishness on the road. My face must have betrayed me.

He squinted at me. "You didn't admit to anything, did you? Of course you never mentioned my name, so it's singularly mystifying."

I kept quiet.

"Even though I expect I'll have your Da right as raindrops again before we leave, I feel a sense of obligation to him still. We never dissolved our apprentice vows properly, by the way." I made a sour face. "Since indirectly I was the cause of all this inconvenience, I feel honor-bound to accompany you two back to your shop."

How I would have loved to say, "Don't grant us any favors." But I kept my silence.

He took one last huge bite. "I'll check around to be sure there's no sign the Society might intend to come after you again. Even though it delays my greatly important main mission." Raz talked with his mouth full, although I knew that he knew perfectly well it was rude.

I said nothing.

He waved his spoon hand, dripping sticky gunk on the table-top. "They likely think you know far more about me than you do.

About where I'm headed, or my private majickal business, since, after all, you sheltered me in a majick-shielded place. Or your Da did, albeit unknowingly." He frowned. "I never intended to bring you and your family into this. I admit I just wasn't thinking ahead in sufficient detail." It was the closest to an apology I figured I'd ever get, but I couldn't even take pleasure in it, let alone gloat.

"It's all right." I twisted my ragged napkin and threw it over my plate. "I just want Da to be all right again. Once he comes to himself. . . ." I took a deep breath. "He'll surely know a way to help you get to the wizard. He might could tell you more about the stone, as well. You can stay with us as long as you want."

I still had, I had to admit, a fancy for Raz Songsterson.

CHAPTER TWENTY-ONE

We were finished dining, and I itched to get back a-road. I felt people's gazes lingering on me as they passed. Whether that was in my imagination or not, it made me uneasy. I thought of the monk and the jackass, and it was all I could do to keep still. Doubtlessly, people were wondering about us, as few Jipsy children were invited to sup with dignified-looking types like my companions. Even Raz glanced nervously about, clearing his throat as he cleaned under his fingernails with his pocket-knife, imaginary dirt sprinkling over the scraps in his plate.

It was time we ought to be on our way.

At last Raz pushed back his chair. He laid his hand on Da's shoulder, apparently expecting him to be pliant.

But Da had turned obstinate. Though his plate was empty, his spoon still scraped at syrup and crumbs. He glared at Raz irritably and pulled his pewter porringer closer to his chest as Raz reached over to move the plate away.

"Such a fine meal, companions. Was it not? Though I regret leaving this excellent establishment"—he patted Daddoo's arm—"I believe we've all finished with our repast. It's time we were gone." Raz tried to look squirrel-eager and energetic, but only ended up looking sweaty and nerve-wracked. "Don't you agree, my good fellow? Daylight's nearly spent."

Da poked at Raz's finger with his pronged fork and snorted when Raz quickly snatched back his hand. "I'm not done, sir. I'll thank you to wait until a body's finished his meal." He squinted his right eye and waggled a finger at Raz. "Who are you, anyroad? I don't know you. I'll be going noplace with you." Da set his jaw, and his eyes glistened in that way he had when he dared you, just dared you, to cross him. He could be firm as set plaster when all his bulk held its ground.

"But, sir." Raz's voice was all molasses to the eardrum. "You do recall we're to complete our business deal upstairs in your quarters at the inn." His tone implied that of course Da remembered this, though it might have momentarily slipped his mind as he contemplated other important business decisions. "I am certain that if you'll just come along with us, you'll be able to bring our transaction to a favorable close." He stood, plucking at Da's sleeve.

I scooted out from behind the table. "Yes, Daddoo. Let's please go ahead and get this over with." He loved thinking of himself as someone who finished what he started, so I hoped to appeal to that deep-seated sense of himself. "You know you're not one to leave things waiting."

"Let me think." Da seemed so uncertain that I almost came to tears. My mouth wouldn't work or I'd have said something reassuring then, if I could think of proper words.

Murmuring soothing things, Raz and I got around back of Da. We each grasped one of Da's elbows and, by sheer flattery, managed to get him a few steps away from the table. We made it into the main aisle, where the crowd carried us with it, out of the tavern. But halfway up the steps to the inn proper, Da scowled and stopped.

"I recall you now, boy. You and I've had an argument, and I haven't forgotten how you behaved." He pulled his arm away from Raz. "Shame on you, boy, respecting your elders no better than this. I'll have no more to do with you." Then he turned his frown on me. "As for you, whoever you are, please explain yourself as well."

"Daddoo. . . ." I bit back my protest before I made things worse. I had to turn away; I wouldn't let them see the tear that escaped when he stared at me so angrily, as though I were the most impudent of strangers.

Raz reached for Da again, but ended up dodging an ineffectual punch in the nose. "My deepest apologies, sir, but you do have my traveling bags closed up in your room. Can't we just proceed upstairs and pray let you hand them out to me? I shan't try to come in." The whole time, Raz was plucking at Da's sleeves in an obvious rhythmic pattern. I could only hope it was part of an effective spell.

"Unhand me, and that's my final word on the subject." Da shoved Raz's hands away and whirled on me with fiery gaze. "Both of you. Hear?"

I heard myself gasp, but Raz was around to my side momentarily, running interference.

"Excuse me, sir. Excuse me." Raz patted the air around Da now, about five or six inches away from him like a silhouette-worker, making noises of comfort. "Mistook you for someone else. Won't happen again." But in among his comfort words, he sneaked nonsense syllables. I knew from the sound that they must be in the majickers' cant, the components of an incantation. His gestures, matched to the pronouncing of various syllables, were so subtle as to be missed unless you were seriously watching for them. I hadn't seen him do that before, and the idea intrigued me. Imagine, hiding an incantation in a poem, or in every other line of a thank-you speech, or in between the platitudes of a recitation you gave before a crowd. Why, every other word of some huckster's spiel could conceal an incantation to purchase his worthless product. The possibilities boggled my mind.

Da quickly grew increasingly glassy-eyed and compliant. Thinking fast, I slipped my arm into Da's and hoped Raz would catch on and play along. I spoke loudly, for the benefit of any who might be eavesdropping. "That's more like it. Come along, Hector, dear. This youth is obviously muddled. His aims are misguided, to say the least. Let's get away to your room where he cannot follow."

Da turned his familiar toothy smile on me. "That's my girl! The only way to handle a village fool. We shall merely ignore him, and he'll grow bored and cease molesting us."

He started stomping boldly up the stairs, and I could hardly keep up the pace. Raz scurried along behind, robes billowing.

For once, I was glad to be on the disreputable side of town, where no one would question public arguments and uproars.

I had no idea where Raz's room might be, and of course neither could Da. Da reached the landing and halted, gazing about confusedly. I motioned for Raz to slip past us so I could follow him. I said, "Come along—it's right here, remember, Daddoo?"

Raz had taken a far nicer room than I had ever seen at an inn; this one had a sugarwood bed with carved posts and a fluffy overstuffed duvet, in addition to a dressing-table, a side chair, and a bench for putting your luggage. Both sides of the bed looked rumpled. I didn't know why that made me grumpy.

Da swiveled his head wildly back and forth. "Sir, I don't know what monkeyshines you're up to or why, but I've never been here before. What in tarnation's the idea?" Suddenly an expression of great weariness came over him. He sat heavily on the mattress, covering his face with his big red hands and rubbing up and down his stubbly cheeks. His face paled, and I feared once again for his health. "If only I could remember. Why don't I know what I'm doing here?" He peered at me between his fingers. "You I do know, gal. Yet I can't quite place you as to who exactly you are."

"A friend," Raz supplied smoothly as he sat lightly next to Da. He grasped one of Da's upper arms in both hands, massaging with flattened palms up and down Da's muslin sleeve. "She's on your side. So'm I, sir."

Da's face went blank as he relaxed into the full effects of the spell, whatever it was. Raz's majickal touch must have recharged it. Remembering what Raz had told me, I felt for the majick. Sure enough, it was there for the perceiving, once you know to try. I felt the majick leaking out all around Da. He was again the captive of Raz's power.

Raz exhaled his relief, then muttered. "I don't like this. I mislike putting a persuasion spell on a body just to get him into the blasted innroom, for blessed sakes." His left eyelid drooped a bit, the way it had started doing whenever he had to admit something he'd rather not. "I shouldn't have to keep doing this."

I didn't like the sound of that.

Raz dug around in his luggage. "Bless all the saints for keeping that uproar from happening back in the tavern. Bad enough we were out making a scene on the street. I hated to put out even the finest thread of majickal power in the open like that."

"You don't think anyone was listening, do you?" I clicked my thumbnails against each other nervously.

"I can't be sure, because all my attention was on the spell. But I feel no investigative tendrils. So I'm assuming we're safe." He gestured and knocked on something, and I imagined he was removing protections from his mage's bag. Sure enough, he pulled out the familiar velvet pouches with their satin ribbon ties. He kept on talking, but it seemed he was talking more to himself. "Before I do further workings, though, I'll check again. The first order of business will be to determine the scope and power of the enchantment. Second will be to slide its snare back over his head, so to speak, working easily as I can, without letting loose any of its tension before I get it completely free. That's when they'll realize it's being tampered with, you see. I'll have to get immediately out of the power grid at that moment." He worked his mouth around a bit. "I wish I could ask advice from my master. At least send them some kind of signal to let them know what I'm doing."

"While we're here. . . ." I was thinking aloud. "Can't you work a delayed spell, some kind of message that would wait, and then send itself from here to your master?" This seemed like a brainstorm. "Here in the room, you wouldn't be noticed, you said. Then when the message goes off, we'll be long gone, and if they storm the room, it doesn't matter, because they've lost us."

His eyebrows danced around a bit before he shook his head. "I like the way your thoughts are running, Dulcinea. Very high-level." His face took on a rueful expression. "But it's still too risky. It would take quite some time to set up such a spell, and the longer I'm connected to the majick-web, even with only a trickle of power required. . . . No. It could attract unwanted attention, and one of them might become curious and take time to trace such a spell, just to see who might have need of such a thing. And then they'd be sure to get my signature off the remnants of the spell, if they caught it going off. And maybe recognize it, as we said. But good thinking."

He motioned for me to stand. Together, we pulled Da to his feet. Raz put Da's hands at his sides and he meekly accepted being manipulated like a rag doll. To keep my mind off the alarm this raised in me, I continued quizzing Raz.

"I can't see how they intercept spells. If you aren't talking to them or sending to them, how can they 'hear' only you? If you're not listening for something specific, don't you just hear a majickal roar?"

He sighed. "Experienced mages learn to separate different majickal signals. They can often tell who is working a long-term spell, especially if they're studying it when you're starting to work. 'Pull a thread, let trace a thread'—it's the law of reciprocity. Whenever you pull on the majickal lines for power, then in return you are letting anyone else out there know where you are, approximately, and that you are majicking. If they can figure out who you are, as well, by getting your signature, and they've got some kind of grudge against you or have been trying to find you—then it's not safe at all." He shook his head.

"Then how can it be safe to do anything?" I reached out and propped up Da, who had started to waver a bit.

"It sometimes isn't." He helped me get Da stabilized. "I'm not planning for this to take long. Also, we're in a town among other majickal vibrations, probably in the midst of many traveling majickers whose broadcasts will interfere. They won't have time to trace this. They won't know who it is working webstrings on their spell." Raz laced the blessed chains around Da's fingers. "As long as they have no way to identify me, such as a possession of mine, or an item of clothing, something they could read my signature off of, we're probably fine."

I really needed to tell Raz about the mage having his necklace. Instead, another question came out of my mouth. "Aren't there ways to hide what you're doing? Is a signature like handwriting, where each one forms letters a little differently, and where the ink or the nib makes a difference? Can't you disguise it, the way you can your handwriting if you write with the unaccustomed hand?"

He glanced up, nodding his approval of my advancement in majickal concepts. "Again, good question. There are ways to misdirect the return path so it doesn't lead directly to you, but, again, that takes more time and more power, not to mention more cunning and more thought, and thus even more time. One can always keep others away somewhat if one is more powerful. The more powerful one is, the more techniques are available to one. But advanced work is never easy or quick."

"Mmm." Da kept slipping down. I murmured noncommittal noises, propping Da up with my shoulder.

"Majick is like anything else worth doing: it asks from you something in return for what it gives, and what you must contribute increases as you need more out of it. Covering my tracks would require quite a bit more elaborate preparations than what I have in mind to do today. And time is a luxury we don't have."

I murmured my assent, propping a sagging Da up and encircling him from behind with both my arms. I didn't know how much longer he could stand unsupported. If he locked his knees, he could faint.

Raz pushed his hair back with both hands. "Well, let's get to it. The afternoon is waning."

CHAPTER TWENTY-TWO

Raz cast his majick square as always, but omitted the corner candles. Instead, he sprinkled along the imaginary lines a white crystal that I guessed was salt. A faint blue glow suffused him, and when he grasped Da, the aura grew to enclose both of them. An elliptical blue glow started at Raz's fingertips and swirled around them, much like oatmeal swirling into the boiling water in a pot. Like smoke constrained by a soap bubble, it coalesced, finally spiraling to fill an imaginary ellipse inside the square.

Raz released Da and closed his eyes in concentration. I sat quietly on the edge of the mattress, hands folded in my lap, hoping Da wouldn't topple again. I was just outside of the effective ellipse formed by the square, and I couldn't reach in to grab him. Fortunately, he was currently standing, bemused, studying his shoes like a village idiot.

With a grand gesture, Raz broke out in a singsong chant. It was so sudden and so unusually worded (compared to what he normally said) that I nearly fell off the bed.

"Oh, heavenly lines of ethereal force, I grasp thee. I command you, the ethereal ley lines that guide all our majickal energies to the appropriate intersection of power, to do my bidding. By arcane methods prescribed by the ancients, I reach to manipulate you with my majickal fingertips, like a harper plucking her silver-coated strings." Raz struck a pose and did some contorted gestures.

I almost burst out laughing. Was this an elaborate put-on? Maybe he meant to shock Da back to reality; if he didn't wake up to correct his apprentice, he'd really be deeply ensorcelled. Or he was play-acting some pompous thing to impress me, and only some parts were of real effect. No, already I felt the questioning tingle of majick around the edges of the inscribed square. Raz must actually be doing a spell.

With effort, I suppressed my amusement. Raz continued to call on the forces by name, working his arms around like slinky snakes. Da stood like a sapling, swaying back and forth with each pass of Raz's hands. I made ready to catch him should he fall over toward me.

Raz opened his eyes and jerked his head towards me. I shot him a quizzical look, and he gestured for me to get his supplies. At least that was what I supposed he wanted, and he nodded when I got out his majickal kits and spread their components on the worn bedcover behind me. Since he apparently couldn't speak to me without breaking the spell, I'd have to try to hand him the most likely things first; I didn't know how else to find out what he wanted.

Raz kept frowning and grunting as I tried handing him this and that. I came across all manner of strange items as I continued to sort through things to give him: a palm-fitting clear glass disc; some misshapen rubbery balls about the size of eggs but heavier than seemed logical; a rough orange rock that shed grains all over my hands. At last something suited his purposes; he took from me a set of brass cubes, four of them, each face about a thumbslength square. They must have been hollow; they weren't heavy, but something liquid sloshed inside.

Setting the cubes around the corners of the square, Raz theremined his palms above like a tramp warming his hands over a campfire. I almost giggled again. The blue became more vibrant, and I caught a brief stench of singed hair. Then Raz motioned for me to hand him the item closest to my hand, which happened to be a cloth-wrapped globe. As I handed the hefty appurtenance to him, a cold wave washed through my breast. I belatedly realized what it was as he rolled it out of its wrappings: the glowing green ball he'd purloined from my prison. I heard faint growls, as if from a distance. They seemingly came from the orb.

"Raz. . . ."

He flapped one hand angrily at me, indicating that this required my silence. He cupped the globe in his palms and breathed words on it, words that could have been "cherose selanka." It glistened brightly, as though it contained green oil eager to spill out; all at once, it dimmed alarmingly, becoming dead as a spent bullet.

"That was a mistake," Raz said in an eerily soft voice as he pushed his hair out of his face again. "That's going to attract some attention, see if it doesn't."

Raz hastily rewrapped the orb and tossed it back toward me. It was all I could do to make myself catch the thing and lay it carefully on the bed. It was heavy as lead, and hot. I thought I heard Raz mutter, "See what I get for trying to save power." A majicker could only draw so much power in so many days or bells or candlemarks, as Raz had explained, though I had no idea what the limits were or how a mage could judge his progress.

Sparks of blue winked into place in the air inside the ellipse, outlining Raz and Da; an awful buzzing started up. The expression of a cornered wildcat came into Raz's eyes, and he jerked loose from Da's grasp. Sparks flew everywhere, bouncing off the edges of the majickal ellipse and ricocheting back to Raz. I was on my feet in an instant. My heart pounded and I thought I might suffocate before I could think of what to do; I knew I mustn't breach the square, but I couldn't sit by and see them destroyed.

Hurriedly, Raz "cut" the lines of his majick square with a twist of his athame blade. I'd never seen him uncast so swiftly. He seldom used such a shortcut because of his customary respect for elegance, and perhaps because it could be dangerous if done clumsily. The lines still glowed, but showed wide breaks along each side of the square. Da fell backward towards the mattress, and I managed to maneuver him onto it. He seemed dazed, but not burned.

Again I felt majick leaking, but stronger this time. Raz brought his palms close, then tore them apart. I heard a clap, and blue sparks flew from his hands. He knelt and rubbed the remains of the lines out with his bare hands, groaning softly. The aura faded quickly.

"What's wrong?" I couldn't keep quiet as I knew I should, but at least I managed to make myself whisper. "Raz? Are you all right? Were you cut off?"

"No and no." He scrambled to his feet. "We must be off. Don't ask questions now. I'll explain later. If I can figure it out myself."

"Something went wrong." I heard myself getting shrill again and clamped my lips closed. I checked Da and found him asleep. I startled him awake and he frowned, then placidly began playing the finger game about the spider in the drainpipe with his fingers, flat on his back, seemingly content.

Raz was throwing his things back into his bags, and I hurried to help. "You can say that again. But don't bother to." He looked grim. "The spell isn't a simple glamour. I should've realized. Should never have tried to work on it here. Although I couldn't have known it would be so ridiculously well booby-trapped."

"What does that mean?" My chest felt hollow and I could barely make the sound.

"The spell's linked to an alarm." He attached his mage-sacks one by one to the buckles on his stockings and rearranged his robe, just as if I were a fellow. No, it was more as though I were some servant beneath notice, and so it didn't matter if I saw his bare legs. If I'd been nobler, I'd have looked away from the scrawny things.

"You mean you can't do it right now."

He cut his hooded eyes at me. "Which word didn't you understand?"

I didn't let him get my goat. "I mean, you can try it again. Back home. Couldn't you spell-cast from within our circle, or within your old room? All the powerful workings you've done there, surely . . . ?" I brushed the backs of my hands over my eyes. Why was I so unreasonably emotional, such a silly little girl? "Because of the kind of spell that's on him?"

Raz looked stern. "The roots are just too deep. I mean, the knots are tight." He rolled his eyes. "My apologies, but I simply can't put it into layman's terms. That spell is still connected to the web of majick, that's the problem, and constantly draws a low level of power. If that were interrupted, it would set off alarms intricately woven in by the spell's caster. Or so it would if it were my spell, I'll promise you." He rubbed together his hands. "I might be able to short-circuit the accursed process, perhaps by drawing the power to some inanimate object——" He corrected himself immediately. "On second thought, it would have to be another living creature." I didn't ask him whether he meant me, or maybe somebody's cow. "But it would take a lot of time, which we don't have to spare."

"Maybe you can try something else later." I sniffled, hating my weakness.

"I don't know, Dulcinea. This kind of ongoing spell can operate on several people at once. Your Daddoo is not the only man they have under its ensorcelment, and so it makes things more difficult. To free one, I might have to free them all, which will certainly anger the originating mage, not to mention leave my fingerprints everywhere. And it'd take a long, long time, perhaps several days." He jerked the covers off the mattress and stuffed them down the linen chute (another sign of how fancy this room was.) "Just in case. Don't want them picking a signature off those. Any cloth a majicker rests on can inadvertently be infused during a working." Being a majicker held less and less appeal for me today. "At any rate, the spell is more complex than I thought. And its maker more accomplished than I'd like. Through the web of majick, the spell's caster is feeding it a trickle of continuous power to keep it active. But that also keeps him tied to the ongoing spell, which allows the placing of trip-threads and trace-threads."

Da was asleep again. "How can we travel if he's like this? We have to wake him up."

Raz bit off his words, obviously considering me thick-headed as a squirrel. "I can't try taking off a spell like this, not out here in the open." He donned his traveling cape and shook his ringlets out from under the collar. "It would be more obvious than a scream in the frosty forest after a quieting snow. Like holding up a torch at middlenight. I should never have touched their globe; that was foolish. I wasn't thinking clearly." He straightened, balling the rest of his clothes from the floor into a snarl. "Hurry and get the rest of this packed."

I started stuffing anything and everything into bags: stinky stockings, a scrap of paper, a crumbly old loaf of bread, whatever I came across. I didn't stop to consider what was garbage. I couldn't know what, if left behind, might lead them to us. For all I knew, they had sniffer spells to chase us using any rag we'd stepped on.

Raz tied a last bundle under his cloak. He had to be too warm under all those layers. "If my luck holds, they haven't already set off to capture us. Unless they've pieced together our location from the trace I felt them starting."

I stuffed the last few things into Raz's backpack and slung it across my shoulders. "I'm ready. Just let me get Da dressed."

Raz and I got him sitting up. Kneeling on the floor, I covered Da's bare feet with a pair of Raz's stockings, then Raz's extra traveling boots, hoping they didn't pinch his feet too terribly. He offered no resistance, not even clenching his toes. Raz's clothes would be too small, so Raz's extra cape over those pyjamas would have to serve. I rolled his sleeves so their flannel nature would be less obvious. Daddoo was like a three-year-old letting me dress him for church. It gave me the uneasies all the way down my spine.

"He's ready." I stood, brushing at my kneecaps. "It would be nice to wash up a little bit."

"Forget the washing up. Come on."

As we pulled him to his feet, Da came back online. He flailed his arms and grunted. "Here, now. What's all this? What are you two sneaks up to?" He was coming around, coming to himself—his new self, I corrected. When I tried to take his arm and stand him up, he slapped at me. Reflexively I released him, expecting to duck more blows. Instead, Da dug in his heels and gripped the bedpost.

"Hell's bells. Blast you, unhand me. You two are doing the devil's own work. Who are you and what is it you want with me? Tarnation!"

Raz and I both held Da this time as Raz recited a slightly different incantation. Da went limp, then pliable. He smiled.

"Can he have a reaction to having been charmed so often?" I brushed at the dirt on his face and hands.

Raz didn't answer me directly. "Maybe this persuasion will last long enough to get us home." Raz looked at Da, who followed after him out the door like a puppy. "Come along, Dulcinea." Raz held the door open for me.

Finishing up my quick prayer to all listening saints, I scurried after Raz and his new "pet," Da.

# # #

Our horses were brought out from the stables all clean and frisky (and it was a funny thing, but it turned out that the horse Raz had bought, Rapstallion, looked just like the one he had bargained for in my fleeting vision). The grooms even helped us load them and arrange our parcels and bags. I suspected Raz had slipped them considerable "gratuities," to use Raz-speak. For once, I didn't care how much of his own money he wasted. I was simply glad to be a-road.

This time I'd ride in front. Da gladly gripped me about my waist, happy as a child to be riding. I held his arms clasped in place for fear he'd fall asleep or let go. Tickie nickered and nuzzled my leg; I found a sugar cube in Raz's pack and slipped it to him.

We must have been at the failed unworking a while, for the sky had darkened. We made our escape into the crowd at dusk.

"I can't keep enchanting him like this." Raz shook his head as we pulled our reins and guided our mounts onto the road. The dust flew up from Tickie's feet, and I felt we were halfway home.

"It must exhaust you. And power's wasted, I imagine." It worried me that we had mixed majicks on Da.

Raz glanced my way. "That's not what I meant. It's too dangerous."

"What are you using on him?" My chest tightened. "Can it hurt him?"

Raz tilted his head, as though considering. "I hadn't thought about that aspect of things. What I meant was he's dangerous to us all, because he's so heavy with a majickal aura, being under both these spells. It must glow like the dickens to the Sight, but God forbid anyone should be Looking out here, anyway. I hadn't time or means to cast a majick-quieting on him before we left, and I don't dare try one now. Talk about risky. Still. . . ." He held the reins loosely, ticking off possibilities on those long fingers of his. "If we ran into someone who knew me on the road—but we won't tonight; it's dark." That didn't console me. "A knowledgeable person, even a non-majicker, might be able to detect that one of us is constantly majicked. There could be a majick leak, though I don't feel much coming off him now. Of course, the original spell might well allow traces of power to escape and leave a trail as well. And we daren't be leaking majick in any form; it could give them a perfect trail."

"Never mind. Sorry I asked." I preferred not to hear more.

Heedless of my feelings, Raz kept talking to me over his shoulder. "We're fairly safe, if none of that happens."

"I feel so much better, knowing that." Daddoo was snoring softly, heavy against my shoulder. I pinned his arms under my elbows so he couldn't slip if he let go. Clinging to Da, I prayed the rest of the way home.

CHAPTER TWENTY-THREE

The saints were listening and willing; we reached our hill without any sign of being followed. At least there was no commotion behind us, and we weren't snatched off the road.

Oh, it was grand to be home. Even in the darkness, I could see that our shop and our home above it were still there. I didn't want to go inside without Raz just in case, though, so I corralled Da in our front garden while Raz led the horses to their stalls. Da pawed and snorted as we stood, as if he were one of the horses himself. He did seem to recognize that we were home, grumbling to himself as I fumbled with his key ring.

Our front door was stuck all over with notes and orders from customers, each layer more urgent than the ones tacked beneath. I tore them down, scratching my finger on one of the tacks, and resolved to open in the morning with at least a few of the items readied early, if I could get Raz's help.

Raz came back from stabling the horses and reported that there was no sign of anyone hiding. "I threw a brief scan for majick, and felt nothing except your Da. We've escaped them, for now." He looked exhilarated. I couldn't get excited, the roadweariness finally taking effect and weighing down my limbs and back.

The shop already seemed full of dust. Though we'd been gone but four days, I felt like it had been a moonsphase. My torch fitted easily into the familiar space in the wall-sconce, and once the shadows from the moonlight through the windows were somewhat dispelled, I felt better. Our globe lights were dim, and I hurried to light a few candles so I could douse the smoky torch.

Da barged through the door on my heels. "At last, at last! I've been trying to get back home for a hen's age, mark you well. When

I find out who took me off on that useless jaunt. . . ." I found it most advisable to smile and nod, as though I agreed. He ignored me and marched off up the stairs, candelabra in fist. I hoped he would take the same precautions with the flame as he would if he were in his right frame of mind. I would check it before I retired. I'd also draw and carry up a couple of buckets of water on my way to bed.

Raz recharged a few globes for me and helped me check all the corners of the shop. Then he went through the upstairs with me, but we found nobody hiding, and no sign of mischief.

"Looks like we're safe." He sounded tired, but cheerful. "In the morning, you come down and open up the shop with your Da, and see if that doesn't bring him right back to himself. Sometimes people can shake off these things on their own, once they get back on their own ground." He patted my shoulder.

I knew he was only saying that to make me feel better.

We went downstairs so I could double-check the latches on the doors. The stack of notes from the door loomed on the countertop where I had ditched them. "Could you help catch up on the orders in the morning?"

The old Raz was back. "Certainly, certainly. I'll be down late, though. I have a few jiggs-and-jaggs to take care of." He yawned, not bothering to cover his mouth, and headed up the staircase to his old lair over the garage. He'd be unpleasantly surprised when he got up there and remembered the condition he'd left it in, I wagered. I wondered briefly what Da would say when he found Raz back in his apprentice's quarters, especially in his present mood.

# # #

The insistent banging on our shop's front door woke me before daybreak.

"Coming, coming!" I threw on my robe and trudged downstairs as quickly as I could manage, tying the belt all tangledy and stumbling over the end of it in my haste. "Who in the name of decency dares to have an emergency at this hour?"

The Widder Groop marched right in the door as I sleepily swung it open, forgetting to peek through the curtains first. I could've been in real trouble; I silently rebuked myself for my lack of caution. But she seemed less interested in telling me about whatever crisis had brought her here so early than in glancing about the shop, then looking critically back at me. As usual, I supposed, my appearance did not meet with her idea of community standards for young ladies.

"At last! Where's your father? What's been going on?" Her gray bun half escaped its pins as she turned back and forth. "No one's seen hide nor hair of either of you for days, none of the horses'd been cared for if it hadn't been for your neighbors, and not a sign as to why."

She exaggerated; only a couple of days. I wiped my hair out of my eyes. "Didn't he tell you that we were"—I improvised—"unexpectedly called out of town? There must have been some notice or someone told."

She brandished a note, which I took. Scanning it quickly, I deduced Da had left it on the front door when he came seeking me out; in too many words, he'd explained we'd be closed for a day and a half for our supply-gathering trip. What was wrong with that?

"I'm sorry we were so long—" I broke off as she marched back behind the counter. "Hey! Excuse me, but that's off limits to our customers. Even so valued a one as our nexdor neighbor." I scurried to stop her before she pulled aside the curtain to the stockroom.

She whirled on me, her expansive breasts threatening to box my ears until I ducked. "Tell me the truth, girl. Hector Otto Brown has never closed this shop for one day without giving his clientele at least a fortnight's notice, not even when he lost his wife." I sucked in a breath; it wasn't her place to remind me of that time. "I want to know what's become of him."

Before I reacted too harshly, I paused and counted to eleven, because she appeared honestly concerned. "He's fine." Whoops, better account for it if he was still acting oddly when he got down-stairs. "Though he's awful tired. We went a long way, and we were delayed in returning. But he's resting. Is there something I can help you with, or"—I made my expression as pointed as I could—"can your needs wait until I have a chance to get dressed and open the shop in a few more candles' time?"

She didn't take the point. "Dulcinea Jean Brown, I don't know what you're up to. All I know is that your father's nowhere to be seen, and here you are by yourself. You can't expect to hide whatever's happened to him. Why don't you fess up, and perhaps I'll be able to help you."

I took exception to everything she insinuated, whatever it was. "Look here, Wid—um, Missus Groop, my Daddoo is upstairs abed. Not with illness, but with sleep. I'll be certain to tell him to expect you as soon as the store opens. Then your curiosity can be satisfied. Until then, unless there's some kind of emergency in your household, I shall have to ask you to—"

"Tarnation, girl! What's all the ruckus?" A torch got socked into the sconce-holder at the top of the back stairs, and Da appeared descending in its light, resplendent in his ticking-stripe pyjamas and long-tailed robe and even his knitted sleepcap, out from under which his hair spiked helter-skelter. "Who in the devil is marching around down here making such a racket two bells before sunshine? I've got half a mind to—" Then he spied the Widder, and broke off. "Heavens, me. I didn't realize it was so late. Pardon me for not being here to welcome you when we opened, but I must have overslept." He turned on his customer-warming grin. "Never mind. How may I be of service to you this morning?"

I'd have to rush up and douse that torch soon, or we'd have soot on the wall; where had he gotten it? We only used them outside, and he had a perfectly good lantern at bedside.

At the bottom of the stairs, Da peered out the curtained window, and his brow knitted in perplexity when no light shone forth under them. "Is it raining and overcast? Where's my OPEN sign?" I winced. Wrong window, Daddoo, I almost blurted out.

"Hector." The Widder ran to his side. "I'm so relieved. We in the neighborhood shops believed. . . ." She shot me a sidelong glance and finished with what I calculated she supposed to be a more neighborly phrasing. "Feared something could have happened to you. After all, you took off without warning. There's been quite a stir, what with all the mystery about your disappearance."

Disappearance? He'd said he left to pick up supplies. Either she knew something about our situation and was testing him, or she was trying to make something else out of what she should accept as a normal excursion. Whichever way, she wanted to imply that I had something to do with it. What was she up to?

"Disappearance?" He blinked. I busied myself lighting the oil-lamps so we weren't all standing around in half-darkness, although my eyes had adjusted. Our globes had dimmed again. I sent Raz an urgent mental message to rescue me. That woman was prying, and now she . . . she . . . well, I'd known she didn't approve of me, but I hadn't realized how much she must really dislike me.

I shouldered past them, still on the lowest stairstep, to douse the torch. I could feel my stomach boiling and wished I could just run out the front door. But I had no place to go. Besides, was that fair? Why should I be chased from my own home? No, I had more right to be standing here than she. Than Raz. Than a lot of people. I tore the front curtain shoving it aside and flipping the OPEN sign viciously around.

"Yes, your unexplained disappearance." She fluttered her eyelashes. I knew she did it even though I wasn't looking her way. I imagined the wind they generated reached all the way to me where I was twisting the lamp-key on the customer counter. "You'll excuse me for being forward, but we all thought, what with the way your daughter is all you have, that you might've—"

"Daughter?" I glanced up to catch his bemused look. "Goodwife, I don't follow you at all. Are you wanting to make a purchase here, or perhaps do you have me confused with some other shop owner?"

My heart stopped and hung in the air while I racked my worthless, sleep-clouded brain for some way to salvage this situation. If he revealed that he didn't know who I was, it could be a lot worse than her merely realizing there was something incompetent about Da. Even that would be bad enough to lose us our shop at the hands of the Council, because I was still pre-Rite and thus underage—unqualified to assume control of a business. What lurked in her conniving little mind? Might she plan to put me under a cloud of suspicion and have me taken away, so that the field would be open for her to marry Da? The disturbing paranoid thoughts flickered in circles through my mind. Although I'd always planned to travel someday, this wasn't exactly the way I'd wanted it to happen. I took a deep breath.

But I didn't have to say a word. Da's expression, that of a man whose personal limits had been exceeded, was enough to stop her.

The Widder took a step back, tilting her head. "I see I've taken one too many liberties. I do apologize, sir, for being so forceful. I only thought that since we've been neighbors for so long, I might talk plainly to you. I truly meant no harm. I'll go now, if you're certain you're all right?"

She glanced back at me, seemingly worried that I'd jump on her. What did she think, that I'd cry, "Foiled again!" and stab her with a dull athame-blade? I refused to meet her gaze, and stepped aside to give her a wide berth as she reached the exitway. But instead of ignoring me, she crooked a finger at me. "Dulcinea Brown. Come over here. I want to ask you something."

I set my mouth in an angry line and stalked over, arms crossed and hugged tightly to my chest. "What is it you want? I have quite a few things to do before we open the shop." I glanced meaningfully down at my bare feet. "Including put on some clothes. So, if you don't mind stating your business quickly. . . ."

"Sorry if I jumped to a conclusion." It was hard for her to force the words out, but she reached out and grasped my upper arm with one of her pinching old claws. I flinched, but she held fast. "You've got to understand how odd it seemed to us that he'd go off without telling anyone, and not a sign of his apprentice or you or one blessed soul for six days and nights . . . well, I can't explain. You'll understand when you're older."

If I lived to be eleventeen, I wouldn't understand that old bat. Plus, by my count, I thought we'd been gone only four days.

She wrung her veiny hands. "But tell me this plainly, now. Is he quite himself? He seems. . . ."

I didn't feel like confiding in this hag. "He seems to have been roused out of a deep sleep several candles earlier than he should have been, and for no good reason, to my mind. He's weary from our long journey and from the bargaining we did during our travels, as am I. And we'd both appreciate it if you came back during shop hours." I pointed at the sign in the window, though she knew perfectly well when we'd normally be opening.

She yanked the door open, throwing the string of bells on the hinge all a-tinkle. "Very well. I'll do that. And if there's still something odd about him. . . . Mark my words, Dulcinea, I'm going to find out why." She slammed the door, and I let out a loud "Oooooh" of frustrated rage that drowned out the rattling of the windowpanes.

"Stop that, girlie!" Da had appeared behind me, scowling. Apparently, he held me responsible for driving away a customer. "I don't know how you got in here, but as you told the lady, we're not even open yet. I can't imagine how customers got in here, but I suppose I ought to be thankful it's not burglars." He yanked the door open, and, taking me by the shoulders, shoved me out before I could react. "Come back only if you intend to buy something. Good day."

The oil lamp in the window whisked out as his big hand twisted the key, and then I heard his footsteps receding back into the darkness of the shop. I glanced frantically around in the pre-dawn light. The town wasn't awake yet, and luck was with me in one sense: the Widder had taken herself off already and wasn't around to see my ejection, though I wouldn't put it past her to be observing me from a secret window somewhere.

My feet were cold. Now they were filthy. Filthier. I pulled my flimsy robe closer and marched around to the back door. Latched.

"Blast!" I stomped my foot and rubbed my eyes viciously until they wept.

# # #

There was no sense standing around out here. I tested all the windows, but I'd been too conscientious at some time in the past; they were all properly secured, tight as the drawstrings of a miser's purse when the church called for donations.

First light was seeping into the sky, streaks of purple and violet and indigo blue on the velvet of the cloudless star-ceiling. I knew I'd better get myself inside and get that shop opened up. I had to keep Da away from the clientele until they stopped asking about our absence. He could blab out something that would make people even more suspicious. I'd have to handle the explanations, and soon.

I scooped up a handful of pebbles from the garden and threw my leg over the low wooden fence that separated our yard from the vegetable garden. Clambering over awkwardly, I managed to rip the hem out of my nightdress. I jerked it loose and marched up behind the carriage house. Taking three or four small stones, I hurled them up at Raz's window. Nothing. I shivered in the predawn chill. After a moment, I tossed the rest.

The rain of stones had its intended effect. One window shoved upward and Raz's tousled head poked out. "And who comes to serenade me this night? Oh, my love, where hidest thou?"

I stuck out my tongue. "Don't mock me. And keep your voice down."

Raz cocked his head. "What are you doing out here, Dulcinea? Aren't you cold?" I pulled my robe closer. "If you wish to court me, don't you know, there are formal rules. Although I must admit I'm flattered. Or could there be another reason that you'd stand out here at"—he squinted at the sundial, but it wasn't yet

readable—"the earliest hour I've ever seen you wakeful, and throw
stones to break my window glass?"

"I don't have time to explain. Get down here and let me in.
We've got to open this shop and have Da seeming normal before
the neighbors suspect."

"You incurable romantic, you. I can tell I'm going to have to
train you better before you go out to serenade other young men, if
we hope to gain you a proper dowry." He quoted a line from some
poem or another I was sure I'd heard, then shut the window. Al-
ternating my weight between my frigid feet, I stomped for warmth
and hoped he was on his way down.

# # #

Somehow we got through the day without the Widder or anyone
else getting anything particularly nonsensical out of Daddoo. His
condition wasn't going to be simple to conceal, even though he
did seem to know how to take care of his shop duties fairly well,
and he could still handle the customers. And feed himself, and
even dress himself. I couldn't feel sufficiently thankful for these
things, although I wanted to.

Evidently, Da's confused fog wasn't just going to fade away as
he settled into his familiar surroundings, despite the cheerful hopes
Raz had voiced earlier. Da's mind worked oddly; he was endlessly
muddled and vague, hand-waving explanations and carelessness
having replaced thoughtful answers and good judgment. He was
also quicker than ever to grow irritated. It seemed he'd truly forgotten who "Dulcinea" was, for he now didn't even recall having
been married, let alone siring a daughter. For that matter, he seemed
to think he was about Raz's age, despite his graying beard and
addled bald pate.

But Raz he remembered, and he was still angry about "that
wasted jaunt into town," among other offenses, some of them imagined. However, I told Raz, "At least he tolerates your working here.
He keeps throwing me out." I sniffled.

Raz patted my arm. "Feeling sorry for yourself, I see. Cheer up. This is a side effect of the spell. Once it's off, that'll change, trust me."

"And when are we going to be taking it off?"

"Tonight, after we close. Don't worry, Dulcinea."

He reached out as though to pat me on the head, but I dodged in time. Patronizing wowser.

By late afternoon, most of the backlogged orders had been filled as I compounded, Raz dispensed, and Da wandered around switching bottles meaninglessly from shelf to shelf and muttering to himself. After we'd hustled the last customer out, I heaved a sigh. At last we were ready to free Da's imprisoned intellect. Raz gathered the majicking supplies as I coaxed Daddoo behind the shop's counter and into our shielded chamber.

CHAPTER TWENTY-FOUR

After the third abortive attempt, Da was exhausted and Raz's eyes were bugging out. I convinced Raz to take a breather while Da snoozed on the ottoman inside our broken charmed circle. We tiptoed out into the shop.

"It's no use. The moment I get in, they start a trace." Raz beat out a rhythm of frustration on his knees with his thumbtips. My eyes were swollen from crying. "I can't draw power out of the spell without them coming at me. So far I've avoided allowing them to actually complete the contact, but I can't be sure they won't find this place the next time."

My throat was already tight. Now our home itself was at risk. "How can we be sure they haven't already?"

He shot me a withering look. "I set warnings for myself in case anyone approached. My senselines told me they were coming up the ley lines, and I just got out in time, every time. Last time, he or she almost found me at the near crossing." He shifted his weight, switching his crossed legs. "What I can't understand is how they twigged so quickly. There must be other sorcery in this town, but they sorted me out within fractions of a candlemark. It's as though they know me right away."

I had waited too long to confess about the sigil. "Raz . . . about that."

He was still musing. "It's unusual, because surely I'm not the only sorcerer in the area. I know I'm not, because I've searched, and I've found a few. Nobody powerful, certainly not Society mages. But still. It's making me crazy."

"You're not crazy." Sheepishly, I confessed about the necklace and the monk's theft.

As I spoke, his hands went to his face. Before I finished my tale, he groaned. "Please, Dulcinea, tell me you're trying to scare me." He covered his eyes and mouth with his big palms.

"Do you hate me?"

His voice was muffled behind his hands. "I do wish you had found it in your heart to tell me sooner."

"Do you think that could be why they recognize you?"

He uncovered his face. "It almost certainly is. After all, when I was majicking in town, with a borrowed sphere of theirs to boot. . . ." His expression scared me, not because he looked angry, but because I'd never seen him terrified.

"I didn't mean to lose it. I never meant to hide its loss from you, either. I just couldn't find a way to tell you."

"You mean you couldn't work up the courage to tell me how incautious you were." His face reddened. "Preferably in time for us to take some precautions." Raz was a majicker, and I didn't know what he might do if he gave vent to the rage he must be feeling. Perhaps he would kill me now. I deserved it; I should have been less of a fool, less of a coward. I cringed, closed my eyes, and waited for the blow, whispering a final prayer that I be forgiven and accepted into the kingdom of the afterlife.

"What are you crying about now, you silly girl?" I heard a sigh. "What's done is done. It wasn't completely your fault; I was careless to have left my sigil in the first place. I suppose I wanted an excuse to come back someday."

Amazed, I opened my eyes. Through the blur of tears, I saw Raz staring at the floor, as though he were a bit embarrassed himself. It couldn't be that he meant what he was saying, although I knew he'd been fond of Da and might have intended someday to mend their fences. It must be that he was too kindhearted to take revenge on me, and he was finding an excuse.

"But I took it off the nail and wore it when I had no right to. It's all my fault." I blew my nose and dried my eyes. "I'm sorry, Raz. What can I do to undo the damage?"

"Very little, I'm afraid. Well, it's done now. All I can do is try to disengage from the thing and break its connection to me as soon as possible." He shook his head. "That's why so many of the spells I've done lately have needed to be cloaked in another spell, a ruse spell. Whenever I began a spell uncloaked, my warnings started up, popping off the cords of power, snapping shut like mousetraps in the grain barn." He rubbed his temples. "That's in the past. Let's think about what happens next." As he spoke, he searched his pockets for something, eventually pulling out a silk kerchief. He started to dab at his face with it, but stopped when he realized it had a lump inside. Idly he unrolled it, then glanced up at me as though he'd forgotten I was there. "I probably shouldn't do this, but would you like to see something interesting?"

Would I ever.

From the kerchief he let a stone roll into his hand. It started out as a crumbly red stone, a dull red like river rock, and I almost said, "What good is that?" Instead, I racked my brain so as to have some kind of a guess. "Is that a lodestone to divine safe paths?"

"Not exactly." He rolled it back and forth, and it gradually came awake with sparkling lights. It seemed alive, glowing from within. "It's—well, it's something that I'm still trying to figure out. It's a focus for majickal power."

I didn't know what to say. I suspected I knew what it was, but he'd obviously forgotten telling me about the stolen stone while we were in town. When I looked at the thing, it seemed that I was looking into something, into deep water, down below from a depth that pressed on me, from whence it would be difficult to surface. I closed my eyes and turned my head so I could divert my gaze. I didn't want to look at it again, and wished he would put it away.

From somewhere came the feeling that this stone not only didn't exactly belong to Raz, but it should not be had by a man at all. Not having dwelled on his status as a thief, I didn't want to think too deeply about this. Wherever this rock—no, jewel—had come from wanted it back.

I waited a while for Raz to do something with the stone, thinking he meant to demonstrate how it worked, but he only gazed at it, becoming more and more meditative. I feared he might become hypnotized, so I spoke. "Thank you for showing it to me."

"Eh?" The mesmerization broken, Raz glanced back up at me. "It is, isn't it. Very much so." I had said nothing about the stone being powerful, beautiful, or the like, so he must have been lost in his own thoughts. I was just glad he came to himself. He took more care than I thought necessary in rolling it back up and tucking it into one of his innermost pockets. I was uneasy until he had the thing stowed away again.

Still playing with the cloth inside his pocket, Raz looked up at me through his long eyelashes. "I have figured out what it must be."

I'd started refolding the silks in one of our baskets, and didn't immediately follow him. "What?"

"I can't be sure until I try it. But I conjecture from my research that I am in possession of a chunk of true dragonstone, a gem known as draconitis."

"Say what?" I chewed on a piece of my hair.

"Draconitis. A blood-red stone, opaque and veined with green, but with a light within, if the gem is still viable. One lies at the base of every dragon's brain, the source of all its majick, allowing its powers of flight, dragon breath, and the like. A dragonly pituitary, if you will."

I had no idea what that might be, but nodded knowingly.

"We call it a gem, but actually it's not a geocrystal, but a biocrystal. A unique treasure to have in hand. There are probably only one or two in our plane. What makes it rarer is that the stone—actually a gland—must be harvested while the dragon is alive, preferably asleep; if the dragon realizes it is threatened, or feels that the removal has left it wounded, it will deliberately spoil the draconite by applying a physiological or majickal process not yet completely understood. It can do this to its own gem even at a distance, you see, as a means of exacting revenge."

Without thinking, I popped off. "I would hardly call that 'taking revenge.' It seems a perfectly natural reaction to me, though of course the hunters wouldn't like it." I personally considered it extremely barbaric to take anything out of any creature's brain, living or not. I didn't even particularly like to eat meat, though I did try to for my health (not, of course, dragonsteak) whenever I could sufficiently mask its origin and texture.

He glanced sharply over again. "Are you going to listen or talk?"

I gestured for him to continue.

"It doesn't hurt the dragons. That is, the wounds are not mortal, in most cases. Of course, dragon products are so valuable to some segments of society—for the armored leather that can be made out of the hides, and the meat, which is a delicacy in the dwarflands, and so on—that often the harvesters of the gem"—oh, he meant the *hunters*, I realized suddenly—"will at that stage kill the dragon's physical body. The soul, as you can probably guess, naturally returns to its home plane for rebirth or assumption into the spirit world, depending on the particular situation and phase of the dragon's life." He spread his arms grandly, his silken sleeves flowing out like wings. "So, Dulcinea, despite your tender heart towards animals, you still shouldn't judge the harvesters too harshly. It is all part of the cycle of life, after all, and dragon products and by-products benefit mankind greatly, when put to proper use."

"Ah." I nodded dumbly. The concept of dragonslaying for such mundane products boggled whatever was left of my mind. I'd have thought the only proper justification for killing such a majestic creation would be to rescue a princess or retrieve a holy grail or some such vessel. Actually, I had never given any consideration to the morality of such a situation, chiefly because I hadn't even believed in dragons until a few days before, when Raz had insisted they existed.

Even now, I wasn't sure I should take Raz's claims seriously. My brain was far past the "full" mark.

He mused a moment, then perked up again. "Not only is the stone the seat of majick in the dragon, but also it works once it's removed. They say that if you focus your will through it, you can control any dragon."

Perhaps this majick worked both ways, I thought, considering the message I'd gotten during the brief time I'd looked into the jewel. I thought it best not to mention this.

"As you might guess, that makes it even more certain that no stone is surrendered voluntarily. And dragons recognize the stones—even if removed from unknown dragons and kept in majickers' carved boxes—for what they are, just as you'd know a human heart if you saw me brandish it at you—and you'd know I meant you ill."

"Uh-huh." Amazed, I'd now run out of all but one-syllable responses.

"Master Ouida at the Academy teaches an entire course on draconite and all the forms of dragonsbane. Naturally, it's also in the Almanack of Sorcery—or is it the Majickers' Encyclopaedia?" He frowned. "I only wish I had access to our library. But, of course, communication with home now is simply out of the question."

"But. . . ." I started over. "If. . . . So . . . ." My mind whirled. "What did you need with that stone? It seems that if you hadn't stolen it, they might not be so interested in pursuing you, and. . . ."

This part Raz ignored. "Don't you think it was clever of me to get it away from them? For that matter, you ought properly to tell me what a heroic thing I did, to take that power away from them."

"I am astounded." This much was true.

He smiled slightly, as though to acknowledge that it was proper for me to be impressed. "I'm not certain just what the other powers of this stone are. Some say it's specially majicked, that it confers the ability to summon dragons from the majickal plane or banish them back. Without the dangers of the Gating spells, or leakage, or any need to pay back."

This was obviously baloney. "Oh, come, Raz. Surely not."

"I've seen the dragon they summoned, Dulcinea." His eyes gleamed as he glanced at me, probably to check my level of awe. "I believe they're running tests on it so they can control it in the raids they plan to make on various outlying villages, starting right away. That will begin the spread of rumors and an atmosphere of fear. Then they can confidently conjure a controllable larger one, the one they plan to unleash on Ladenia City. It's a masterstroke, I'll give them that, to wait until the parade starts. This will produce the maximum possible carnage."

My head already swam. "You're making me sick. This is too hateful."

"But accurate. The damage will be considerable, and it'll leave people terrified of the next attack. People will never suspect it's not just a natural monster, come out of a lair someplace, probably with its companions, and they'll go wild trying to plan against the day it will attack again."

I was, for once, speechless. "What are we going to do?"

He shot me a sharp look. "*You* will do nothing but stay out of their way. *I* plan to help stop them." His hand cupped his chin and its index finger stroked his mustache. "Actually, I haven't planned in detail further than to take this stone back to my master and explain. He will know what we must do."

"But you just said," I pointed out in as reasonable and non-threatening a tone as I could muster up, "that communication with the Academy is impossible. Do you mean it can't be done, or it's too dangerous?"

"I'm getting to that. You see, time is running out." Festival time was a scant three fortnights away, occurring whenever the two moons switched places in the skies during a change in phases. It only happened twice a year, and it was a big event, drawing people from the outlying areas in to trade goods and get their official government business taken care of. The city would be teeming with innocents. If something happened, the survivors would flee and panic the countryside with their tales of dragon attacks. "I truly believe that, if I had access to the literature or the ear of the Academy's gem-master, I could find out enough to figure out the stone's vibrations. I would know how to use it for control. Thus, I could dispel the test dragon in time to avoid the massacre."

"Makes sense."

He preened a bit. "It does, doesn't it. However, you see, my stated mission is to bring whatever I find back to the Academy for the masters and sages to analyze. My wizard-master explicitly said, 'Don't try to work with it yourself.'" He shrugged, as if to say, who can question authority? "Hence, it is imperative that I get back as soon as possible." As though to himself, he murmured, "Time is of the essence. I simply must find a way."

I was more than ready for us to return to the present problem. "In the meantime, though. Until you do. What's our next move?" I flopped down onto a bench. "After you dis—dis—get a-loose from the sigil, can we try again with Da?"

"Let me give it some thought. You wouldn't believe how clever those rascals are." He glanced at me, then changed his tune. "But of course I'll get it, eventually."

"How soon is eventually?"

I didn't get to find out. Da trundled in, rubbing the sleep-crystals out of his eyes. He smiled kindly and inquired who the two of us were. "And what may I help you find today? I don't believe I've seen you around town."

"He remains muddled," Raz said aloud, rubbing his chin. "I'm not sure if that's part of the intention of the spell, or an unintended bonus to the caster."

Da turned to him, interrupting. "Mind your manners, boy. If you've got something to say about somebody, don't talk behind his back. Perhaps you should go home"—he emphasized "home"—"and talk to the person you're gossiping about."

I was glad Da didn't suspect he was the topic of discussion.

"Do you need some help securing the shop for the night, sir?" Raz became all business, heading behind the counter, straightening jars all the way.

"I can manage, thank you. I'd just like all the customers to leave." His eyes gleamed as he looked at me with the now-familiar dismissive glare.

"Da. . . ." I was too tired to argue.

Da folded his arms, then pointed at the door. "I grow weary of dealing with people like you. I can't run a business like this."

"I'm only trying to help you." Raz honeyed his tone, but whatever he was trying to do, he was too drawn-out or weary.

Da's eyes flashed, and he set his jaw. "I'm asking you two, please, to either buy something or leave the shop. Now."

We scurried out the front door, then around the back to sneak into our living quarters. I, at least, needed to rest.

"At least now he's not so hostile toward you." Raz said it in an upbeat manner, apparently intending to be helpful.

"Oh, that's a comfort. Now he doesn't even care enough to hate me." I burst out sobbing like a schoolchild. Raz stepped forward and enfolded me in his robed arms. Instead of helping, the hug made me feel like the devil's child: his touch set my humours aflow again, which was the last thing I needed. I should be thinking of Daddoo, and I knew by now Raz thought me completely without feminine charms. And Raz had now revealed things about himself that I didn't admire, to boot. I couldn't help how I felt about Raz, so I hated myself even more.

Now I really didn't know what to do. I couldn't leave Da alone. How could he even take care of himself? What might happen to his mind next? Even if his confusion didn't worsen, could he do all the chores, or would he even remember them? One thing was certain, though: since Da had forgotten who I was, my mere presence rubbed him against the lie of the fur, like an All Hallow'd Eve cat all arched and spitting.

# # #

The next morning, as we were opening the shop, Da tried again to rid himself of me.

"Girl, what are you doing here? I have a mind to call the constable and have him teach you a lesson about loitering in honest people's shops." He squinted one eye as he gazed toward Raz, carrying supplies in from the back room. "And that boy, too, while I'm at it. Although he's not near as useless as you are."

"Dadd—" I'd momentarily forgotten how that irritated him. "I mean, *sir*. You remember. We work here."

"Nonsense. I had to fire my good help months ago." He gave me a hard look. "For cheating me."

"But *I* didn't cheat you. It would be ridiculous. I'm your little girl, Daddoo." I saw my protests were still in vain, but some automatic part of me babbled on. "I'm sure if you try, you can remember. And Raz is your apprentice."

Now Da glared. "Please, have a bit of respect and call me Apothecary Brown or Master. And pray stop telling me such transparent lies. They're in very poor taste. My apprentice Chiro, God rest his soul, is dead. I am a bachelor, and have no heirs." His eyelid started its warning tic. "At the very least, if you're not a liar, you must be mistaken." *Or a fool*, his tone implied. "Kindly leave now. Immediately, if you please."

He turned his back and started eyeing Raz again.

I snatched up my cloak and purse posthaste and left to get some air. We needed food anyway; the larder was nearly bare. I'd had to throw out all the foodstuffs that'd spoiled while we were gone. We'd soon be living on potatoes and colaaf. Halfway down the front path, I realized I hadn't brought my market-basket, and that my purse was un-clangorously light. Empty, of course. I'd have to raid the till the moment Da wasn't looking. I sneaked in the back way—I had made certain this morning to unlatch the back doors and windows—and managed to get my basket and some funds without getting caught.

On the way out, though, I bumped right into Da. There was an odd glint in his eye, and when I dodged, muttering an apology, he dodged the same way. We waltzed for a moment. Then he fixed me with a bright tigerseye stare and began gesturing. At me. His gesticulations reminded me of some of his majickal passes, and it made me a little nervous.

"Excuse me, begging your pardon, sorry, sir." I dodged this way and that, but he deliberately blocked the doorway. I might have shoved him out of my way and escaped, but force of long habit had instilled in me too much respect for my parent to do so.

Both Da's hands went into his pockets. Starting a singsong chant, he added whatever he had in his left pocket to something in his right hand. He must have mixed up some herbs in one pocket and some kind of activator in the other, then readied himself for me, watching and waiting. Before I could blink, he showered me over the head with the dry fragrants while he chanted. "Clairion, occultia, mysteria. Tufunga, mysteria, ignorable. Hear me, O natural elements. We see her in our halls, and wish that we did not. So please take pity on us all, and force us to note her not!" He clapped his hands, and I felt a warmth suffuse me.

"Daddoo!" I froze within, my blood surging to a temporary halt in my vessels. "What have you done?" I looked down at myself, suddenly horrified at the thought that I might be invisible, or dissolving, or worse. But I could see my feet, my hands, and all the rest of myself in between quite clearly. Still, I let out a squeak.

Da chuckled. "That ought to take care of you." He glanced around, as though he really didn't notice me at all, even though I still stood directly before him. "Don't worry, child. I know it seems harsh, but I had to do something. You insisted on trying to run me madwand."

"But what did you do, sir?" My hands tingled, felt numb, had a mind of their own, were trembling; no, I was imagining things. I flexed my fingers and they felt connected, normal.

"Why, I've cast a spell on you, of course." He smiled in a satisfied way he had, as though to himself, as though I were already gone, banished from his presence. "It's a form of the Ignorable enchantment, one that's simply meant to make you easier to ignore, unless someone should desire to look for you." His eyebrows bounced. "Though I can't imagine what someone would want with you, poor confused waif. It won't hurt you, but the village will be pleased not to have to pay heed to your constant idiotic chatter." He'd turned and was already wandering away; thus, I could hardly hear these final insults.

"And what does that mean, sir?" I pursued him into the stockroom. Though I stood right before him, he glanced right over my head more than once before he found me. He seemingly had to look closely to see me.

"As I said." He cleared his throat and looked a little sheepish, waving one hand in dismissal. "It's a mere Unnoticeable spell. To make you easier to ignore. Doesn't hurt you."

I supposed there could be such a spell, though I hadn't heard of it before. Daddoo's logic was twisted, but unassailable; he still remembered being bound by his Majicker's Oath. As Raz had noted, all white majickers swore it. Its tenets included directives to harm no thinking creature save in self-defense or to save the life or limb of another. And since I'd done nothing to him except hang around waiting on him and cleaning up his shop, he couldn't honorably justify doing anything that might damage me, praise be to the saints. But this was probably permissible, I thought miserably. This kind of spell, if it'd really worked—which I couldn't tell until I got out among others—was merely irritating . . . unless you didn't mind being able to avoid notice.

He blinked and glanced around, as though he'd lost sight of me. "Now, where have you gotten to? Oh, well. She's run off." As an afterthought, he added to himself, "And good riddance. Pathetic little thing, must be an orphan. Look at that hair. But it's not my business, no, sir. I have my own work to be done." He wandered away, as though he'd put me out of his thoughts already.

I squashed my knitted cap on my matted head and stalked out the back door, hoping to regain at least a bit of my dignity, if not my self-estimation. I headed off down the road aimlessly, then took the fork toward the village. Was there truly some stupid, unheard-of spell on me? I sighed.

I walked towards the marketplace, ostensibly for groceries, but also to distract myself. I couldn't believe it, but people completely ignored me, even when I was in their paths, to the point of side-stepping me just in time to avoid a collision. The boys who normally either made catcalls or vomiting noises as I passed now took no notice at all, not even looking up when I walked past them. For some reason, this did not please me in the least.

I hoped I could think of a way to wheedle Raz into taking the spell off me, if he could—and if he didn't laugh it off as a good joke at my expense. It didn't seem to be harmful, but then it hadn't yet been active long, either.

At the marketplace, I thought about practicing at being a stickyfinger, but unfortunately my internal honesty-cricket was working too well. I still felt guilty about the herbs and bark I had pilfered from that storeroom, even though the thieves had kept my purse and all my traveling clothes and oddments—save my flute, thanks to that nice gullible rascal, Orthe. If I stole, I'd only be emulating my erstwhile hero, the clayfoot Raz. But I felt bad anyhow.

I bought some ladyfingers and sweetcakes for a treat, and then a basketful of greens, and a sack of porridge to boil up later, and dried tartberries and almonds to put into the porridge, and some fragrant bark to flavor it with for special if I got to feeling low. At the last minute, I decided to buy some eggs and bread, but I could never attract the attention of the vendor. Finally, I threw my coins down on his counter and took a basket of eggs and a couple of crusty loaves. Nobody tried to stop me.

Ignored, I trudged toward home. No one bothered me on the way, and even the Widder next door, out raking her garden, didn't take any notice.

The effects of my Unnoticeability were interesting, to say the least. Over the next few days, I experimented a bit, and found that I could completely escape people's attention if I put forth a bit of effort. Oh, I could get myself noticed when I spoke directly to someone using her name, or if I tripped someone up or bumped into him. Yet if I were merely present in the shop, I could fade into the shadows easily as any elf—or so it seemed to me. Also, my footsteps and breathing faded into the background: even when I wasn't sneaking around, people appeared to pass off my sounds as mice or the creaking of the walls. When I hummed a tune, it amused me to watch people glancing around, trying to figure out where the noise was coming from. I had to speak, sneeze, or move something around before they'd finally startle and turn my direction, immediately looking sheepish, and often muttering something self-deprecating like, "What's the matter with me? I must get myself some spectacles."

At least I didn't have to wait on the customers or endure Da's brush-offs. And I could live right there underfoot in the house and shop and still have complete privacy to do whatever I wanted, happily ignored. I could see how the effects of the spell might come in handy. I stopped worrying about getting Raz to take it off.

CHAPTER TWENTY-FIVE

During this time, Raz was secretive, spending most of his free time upstairs in his old rooms over the carriage house. Da apparently decided he must've hired Raz, for he ceased fussing about him being in the shop. As far as Raz's residency, Da kept forgetting about him. Perhaps he hadn't quite noticed that we were actually living in the house, for he said nothing about houseguests beginning to reek like sardine stew after three nights.

Da wandered at night, though, and I ended up having to sleep in the front room of Raz's quarters instead of in my own cozy room. I didn't want to be tossed out in my sleep. Raz cast a private loft for me that looked out onto the treetops—he'd put his rooms back the way I remembered them, all majicked-up—and I felt I was sleeping in a treehouse. The birds sang me awake in the mornings; without curtains, the room brightened gradually and less painfully than my old bedchamber, and I didn't mind so much getting up early. I had my own entrance and complete privacy from his rooms, which he was careful to keep me out of these days. Being so close to Raz in the evenings agitated my humours and increased a certain feeling that I preferred to avoid, but my new quarters were comfortable, and I enjoyed everything else about them.

I still couldn't very well wait on the customers, because of the Unnoticeable, and if I made myself obvious, it agitated Da. This left me to work twice as hard in the back room, but at least Da seemed normal in front of our patrons, still able to do his tasks properly, as far as I could tell.

About a fortnight later, Raz stopped coming out of his rooms entirely. Three nights after, in the middlenight, I heard quite a bit of noise, like pounding or knocking, intermittently coming from his quarters. I fell back into a fitful sleep. In my dreams, I saw Raz building a treehouse and dancing in a fairy-circle of huge mushrooms as tall as he and wide enough to be umbrellas. The dragonstone gleamed over his head like a ruby sun, then fell under his feet as he pounded it into a puddle, which solidified into a thousand tiny crystals. He sifted them through his fingers, laughing. When I awoke, hearing him still at work in his chamber, I couldn't help but wonder. I tossed until morning, and fancied that Raz might be readying a fantastic spell to make everything all right again.

In the morning, Raz came downstairs wearing the determined expression of a man who has made up his mind. I decided I'd try to make conversation and pretend I didn't notice the secret roiling just below the surface; that way he was more likely to spill it, rather than hold the promise of telling over my head.

"Dulcinea? Dulcie. . . ." At the foot of the rear stairs, Raz paused, looking bemused. He glanced around, looking right past me as I knelt by the cookfire in our big fireplace, stirring my pot of breakfast porridge. "Dulcinea!"

"Right here." I smiled and waved, exaggerating the movement. "No need to shout."

He spotted me and grinned sheepishly. "Sorry—didn't notice you there at first. Which, in point of actual fact, is precisely what I wanted to talk to you about."

I ladled another helping of porridge into the pot and added water, throwing a handful of dried fruit on top because I felt generous. "You do look pleased with yourself this morning. Like a bowl of this?"

He pulled out a chair and leaned his elbows on its arched back. "If you insist. Though it smells a little scorched."

I rose above that remark. Serenely as I could, I answered. "That's just old grease sputtering down below on the coals. Da isn't maintaining the cookfire the way he always used to, for obvious reasons. It's the same with the light globes; they're slowed and dimming again. He doesn't renew them at all." I stirred the plumping fruit and then paused, as though the next sentence were just an idle thought. "Have you come up with any more ideas about how to help him, by chance?"

Raz accepted a bowlful, pulled his silver spoon out of his pocket, and started polishing it on his sleeve. "No, I haven't. I was thinking about something else this morning."

"Oh?" I sprinkled a taste of powdered cinnabark on top of my serving and sat down next to him with my simple tin spoon.

"Worrying, actually." He folded his fingers into a knot and leaned forward over his bowl. "It's quite serious. I haven't been able to keep myself completely secret while I've been investigating that spell, and now I think the Society may be on my trail."

I almost knocked my good blue bowl to the floor. "Oh, no. It's the sigil, isn't it?"

"No, I did manage to disengage from my sigil right after you told me they had it. Though I will reiterate that had I known to do that right away, evading them would have been simpler." He gave me a look, implicitly scolding me again. If I'd been snow, I would have melted. "It only took a couple of attempts. Pity, that. The signet had served me in good stead."

"Sorry again." I'd never live that one down. "I guess I deserve the Society to come crashing down on me, though, since that was my fault. But not Da. He has done nothing to deserve me and all my mistakes."

His eyebrows bounced into his hairline. "Oh, give it a rest, Dulcinea. Besides, I said they'd found *me*, not your home. The shop is in no danger, as long as I leave."

"How do you figure that?"

"They're not barbarians. I figure they've discovered you weren't in any conspiracy with me. You two were only a way to get to me. They have no use for you if they can get me. It's me they've been after all along."

That arrogance of his again, rearing its head. "But what if they think we know where you've gone?"

"All the more reason to leave here before they trace me. And I believe I have a couple of days; their methods, as far as I can tell from my investigations, are rather more primitive than I'd thought, and all traces of my presence should fade before they get a bearing on me. By then, I should be well into the Hidden Trails."

Whatever those were. I didn't know what to say. "That's all very well for you." I hoped he was right, that they'd forget about us if they thought they could get Raz. That they had no reason to bother with me. But the thought of them capturing Raz and torturing him made me sick, too.

"I'll be leaving right away."

My heart sank.

He grinned, exuding the air of someone with a secret. "But wait until I tell you the part that I think you're going to like."

I pushed my hair behind my ears irritably. "How could there be any part to it I'd like?"

He leaned back and pillowed his head on his hands. "I think I'll take you along. I'd like you to see the Academy, and I have a little job for you."

It was my turn to quirk an eyebrow, hiding my excitement as well as I could. My heartbeat sped up and I felt my hands begin to tremble. "Oh, you do, do you? Have I no say in the matter?"

Between generous mouthfuls of porridge, he talked with a full mouth. "Come, Dulcinea, let's not be coy. I am aware of your admiration, as you must know"—my face started burning—"and I know how much you'd like to travel with me."

I stuck a spoonful of porridge into my mouth and swallowed it, along with my illusions and my pride. "I don't know where you got that idea. You're such a humble soul." I grimaced to let him know I was mocking him. "Thanks, but no thanks."

He made a stern face. "Let me at least outline my plan before you reject it out of hand, would you?"

I fell silent, stirring my cooling glop, as he explicated.

"First of all, since you're effectively unnoticeable, it might be worth letting you try to sneak through the Trackless Forest, right under the noses of the Society's spies, and enter the Academy compound."

"What?" My spoon clanged against the side of my bowl.

He held up his palms again. "Just listen. You might be able to slip through the trapped sections without attracting attention. Once you get inside, you can tell the Majick-Master what has been going on, and then have him figure out how to make contact with me."

One tiny detail remained. "And what if I can't slip through without their catching me?"

He waved his hands, erasing that possibility. "Highly unlikely they'd pay any attention to you. We'll dress you as a beggar again, not like a messenger or someone important. You haven't got a majickal signature and you won't be of interest to them; I can tell from my studies of the majick-web that there are no feelers out for you or your Da, so even the monk has lost interest. Just like that." He snapped his fingers. "Besides, be reasonable. The Society will be watching for someone like me, somebody stinking of majicks, not for a waifling hiking through the forest. They won't waste power on chasing you."

I bristled inwardly, but kept quiet.

He took my silence as agreement. "I see you follow my reasoning. You'll take a route I'll outline for you—you'll study and memorize the map, so as not to be caught with it—who knows what they'd do to you if they caught you with that map, let alone what I'd do to you for revealing one of our hidden trails. We have methods of punishment that compare favorably with those of the Society for those who betray us." He looked stern. "Not that you'd do that on purpose, of course, but as I have to keep reminding myself, you are still a child."

My spoon clanged to the bottom of my bowl.

"Once there, you'll get in to see the Master by using my password—I do hope you realize just how sensitive this information is." He scowled, pinching his lips shut with the fingertips of the hand that wasn't busy stirring his food. I wished they'd suddenly tighten and rip those rude lips right off. "It may be some time before they trust you, but once they hear of your long journey and verify some of the details about me—which I'll probably have to bespell within your head to keep you from inadvertently blabbing it—"

"Are you certain you want such a dunderhead child to accompany you?" I picked up my bowl, thinking of slopping the rest of it over his insulting head. "Who knows what kind of thing I might let slip? I might do more harm than good."

"Don't be so sensitive, Dulcinea." He slurped the dregs out of his own bowl. "I'm merely thinking aloud, if you will. Straightening the details of the trip in my mind. This is somewhat of a large undertaking, you know, and I'd hate to waste a lot of time on something I wasn't quite certain we could make work."

I slammed down my napkin. "And just how long would all this take?" My appetite was gone; I carried my bowl over to wash it out. I still felt reluctant to go jaunting off for any reason, leaving Da alone. Even if the blackguards didn't come, he might get worse, even to where he'd forget to feed himself.

"Only a few moonphases or so."

My bowl clanked into the washbasin. "A few moons! And what happens to the shop while I'm away?"

"Nothing." He cocked one eyebrow. "Your father seems capable of doing all his daily chores. It's just us he can't deal with."

"For now, you mean. What happens if he loses more of his sense?"

"What happens if we manage to reach the majick-master and get help taking the spell off?"

That prospect was sufficiently appealing that I closed my mouth and thought about it a moment. "You mean it?"

"Sure. You help us, of course we'd help you." He pushed his empty bowl aside. "I'd have to plan, but we have a little time. We'd want to leave tonight. I don't know the details you'd need to manage, but at any rate, you're not exactly popular around here."

"Don't remind me." I sighed. "All right, suppose I go with you. Who's going to take care of Da? You know he needs someone to keep an eye on him."

"Hire somebody. Get one of the neighbors. One of the regular customers who comes in all the time, or somebody who wants his son to earn some coin. Put a sign in the window. You'll think of something." Raz patted the table, getting up to leave. "We'll leave as soon as you can make your arrangements, then."

"You're taking a fearsome number of details for granted." I called it after him, but he was already halfway up the steps. That egotistical snip. He knew I'd fall for his idea.

As much as I hated to, I knew who I could get to come and work for free just so she could be around Da. Maybe it would appease her enough that she wouldn't pursue having me declared illegitimate, or whatever her ambition was.

I enlisted the Widder Groop to keep an eye on Da. I had to explain his mental state, so I told her that he'd had a shock—emphasizing that she should not refer to it nor ask him about it, for this could set him back—and therefore was a bit forgetful, but that this should wear off soon, and his former personality would then be restored, as long as he stayed in his routine at home and had no more upsets. I figured the best way for her to do this was by working part-time in the shop.

I thought she'd be pleased, and she was. That designing old biddy. Da accepted this arrangement as "very sensible, getting me some better help." I rolled my eyes as she clung to his arm with her shiny claws in his sleeves, trailing him and flattering him while pretending to learn the ropes of waiting on folks and dusting the shelves. Just as well I wouldn't be around to see all that.

CHAPTER TWENTY-SIX

The road wound through the wood at the edge of Ladenia City, veering away just as we'd have entered the city limits proper, skirting the edge of town. This was the eastern rim of Ladenia City, a crescent of woods leading up into a mountainous region that was unincorporated all the way across to Marwell. Under the trees, it was degree-marks cooler. Light dappled our path, and the horses seemed to be enjoying our brisk tempo. I was deep in self-doubt, wondering if I really should've left Daddoo, when Raz spoke. I imagine he was just talking to himself, thinking out loud; he'd probably forgotten I was even there, riding beside him and all ears.

"If only there were a way to evade their dratted tracking system, avoid setting it off. Or of breaking that lock on the locators, even for an eyeblink."

Raz had been muttering things like this to himself intermittently for several miles, ever since we'd left the shop at dawn. He hadn't waved back the way I did, as the Widder clutched Da's arm and beamed. He'd said nothing to me, even though I'd tried to make conversation a couple of times since midmorning.

The only words I could make out consistently from his monologue were "blasted wizardlock" and "unethical blackguards." Before we left, Raz had gone into great detail about how quick our journey would be once he got us onto the Hidden Trails, the majickally maintained shortcuts across the country that were created by and known only to majickers, and which were findable by using a navigational method on the majickal Web. His Academy's masters had made them, and they were a source of great pride. The only trouble was we could not locate any.

Raz had planned for us to get into this area the first or second day at the latest, or so he'd led me to believe. He'd expected to find an entry point in this forest. Once on these special trails, we would make good time while remaining safe from the spies, highwaymen, robbers, and blackguards that Raz expected to see under every unturned stone; from the way he'd ranted, I'd envisioned every roadside bush stuffed full, bulging with elbows and knees and sticking-out swords all awaiting us. But so far we'd had an uneventful trip.

I would have felt free and buoyant with excitement about this pleasant journey if it hadn't been for Raz's obvious concern. Raz alternated between looking angry and worried. The latter scared me most.

"I'm convinced, Dulcinea, that one of the Hidden Trails has an entry point right around here. I can feel the villains' majick guarding it. They've got protection all around." He finally slowed, deigning to look in my direction. "They're bound to have left a break someplace. Mark it well, they surely have. Everyone makes a mistake here or there. Simply a matter of finding where, that's all. All I need is a spot of luck."

I refrained from asking whether he'd kept his pocket buttoned.

He kicked a couple of times and then reined Rapstallion in; confused, his new steed speeded and slowed a few times. I expected he'd turn and bite Raz if he could figure it out, or else bite my Tickie in the rump, so I backed off my distance a bit. That was my first mistake of the morning. Major mistake, that is.

"Dulcinea?" Raz's voice rose unwisely. He looked wildly around. "Dulcinea! Where are you, you silly—" Then he spied me. He frowned, as though it had been my fault he'd lost sight of me.

It hadn't been any such thing, of course. He knew about the Unnoticeable spell, so I frowned back.

"Take care you keep close to me, hear? This isn't a pleasure trip."

"That much is obvious so far," I muttered.

"What? Speak up, if you're going to talk."

"You've no call to be snappish. I'm always listening." My lower lip popped out, and I pulled it back in and chewed.

Dust rose from the path as he reined sharply and crossed in front of me; I sneezed.

"Plans have changed. We're going to come to a streambed soon, and I want you to wait for me there and tend to the horses a bit."

"Where are you going?"

"I need to get away by myself so there aren't any distractions or"—he glanced at me meaningfully—"negative influences."

The morning sun shone on our heads as we came out from under the protection of a leafy chimetree grove onto a treeless path; wheeling above was what I thought was a soarwing, or perhaps a hawk. This should have been such an enjoyable part of our journey.

"What is it you need all this privacy to do?" I didn't feel like a negative influence. Something was; Raz had been like a different person since we entered the wood. If I hadn't known he was keeping majickal feelers out, I'd have suspected a spell of crankiness.

"I'm going to cast, Dulcinea. I'm searching for our hidden path, of course. But before I start, I'll have set my own traps on the ley lines. Then let them trace away. See how the Society mages like a taste of their own medicine." He laughed bitterly. "If they do find me, I'll soon be gone from the locator spell's circle of certainty. We can take evasive action. But at least I'll have taught them they're not the only clever ones around."

"I don't think you should." Tempting fate, or testing the saints, whatever you liked to call it when somebody taunted majickers, sounded dangerous.

"And is that your decision to make?" Raz's eyes turned dark.

" . . . I suppose not." I covered my shock by ducking my head and studying the bells on Tickie's harness. He shook his mane as I did so, as though he'd heard and understood, and was as taken aback as I at Raz's irritable reply.

An ominous silence ensued.

The breeze blew cool, and I lifted my hair off the back of my neck. It was growing, defying all obstacles. I twisted it up experimentally, then let it fall again.

Pebbles crunched under the horses' hooves as we wound through a weedy meadow and forded a shallow stream that seemed to be trying only half-heartedly to flow. We came slowly up and out of the flatland as the road ascended toward the mountain plateau. Both the horses were breathing hard when we reached the top. Raz pulled his reins and 'Stallion obediently headed to the side of the road to let him dismount.

"How far away are you going?"

"I'll be back."

I kicked the stirrups off my feet as Raz tied Rapstallion's holdings to a nearby chinaberry and stalked off into the forest. Even if he wasn't yet starting a working, I was afraid to follow, for fear he was merely doing his business behind a bush somewhere. I'd already crossed Raz by mistake several times, and I wasn't eager to get into it with him again. We'd quarreled so often already, and I figured he was sorry he'd brought me. For that matter, so was I.

I jumped off and tried not to take my irritation out on the innocent horses. I'd asked Raz if we could buy a pack animal, but of course he wouldn't hear of it; so instead we led along Packy, my smaller horse, having me alternate riding her and Tickie, and all three horses were overloaded with supplies. He wouldn't admit it slowed us down.

I redistributed the saddlebags the way I'd meant to earlier but couldn't while Raz was watching. I splashed a rag with some of the cool water from my waterskin and patted the horses down, getting off the gallop-foam and some of the road dirt, mopping them up as best I could.

I started to fume. Had I known he had a side trip in mind, we could have stopped by the stream. He didn't give proper thought to the comfort and care of my horses; he'd even made fun of their names, and I'd turned defensive, telling him the truth, that I'd been allowed to name them in childhood, but he just snorted. I wasn't sure he deserved Rapstallion, a nice-looking horse who would require this same kind of thoughtful care that Raz might not think to give.

The horses really should've been brushed again, but I gave them each a carrot instead and a pat on the nose for the time being. There's so much you have to do for a horse on a journey that you never think about until you've forgotten to do it. At least I got them cleaned up a bit. Then I stomped over to sit and sulk under a spreading serviceberry tree. Why should Raz hold the monopoly on bad moods?

It was no use. I couldn't rest while Raz was away somewhere. Plus I was now certain that he'd lied to me about the kind of spell he meant to cast. Or even if he was casting. It might be doom to cast out here in the open, and he knew it. Didn't I have any say in our safety?

Whenever he felt like it, Raz expected me to dance through a hornet's nest of booby-traps, and expected me to hop to doing it. And, unfortunately, I was such a dunderheaded cudge that I would usually start stepping. Was that sensible? I sighed. Probably. We'd come so far. And since Da was lost to me, all I had was Raz; for whatever reason, I still strained to please him. I was such a feather-brain. Getting just like a stupid village girl.

When Raz at length returned, I was still under the tree, stretched out on my stomach and gnawing on the jerky we'd meant for lunch. He wore a foul expression and was obviously in one of his newly discovered moods. Without a word, he hurled himself up on Rapstallion, and I scrambled to catch up.

Our journey through the forest should've been pleasant. We were on a rather well-maintained trail, almost a proper road, which curved attractively through some interesting pebble-covered hills and green valleys. Above my head, the gold-rimmed leaves, red and green hanging side by side, fluttered in the soft breeze. It wasn't quite snowtime yet, but I could feel the seasons' changing in the air. I might have even been able to enjoy it if I hadn't itched to ask Raz about the paths and the spell. I had no idea how much further into the woods we could go without entering the Society's sphere of influence. When would it be too late to find one of the hidden pathways? Were we already past the point of no return, reduced to riding out in the open like a couple of goony-birds flapping around during target-practice?

Raz should at least tell me things were hopeless so I could prepare myself; that was the only decent thing to do. I could keep quiet no longer. I pulled alongside Raz and spoke loud enough that he couldn't pretend he didn't hear me. "Raz?"

"What!" He snapped at me over his shoulder, and I ducked involuntarily. Tickie shied.

I'd finally had it. "I'll tell you what. Everything, Raz Songsterson. Our predicament, whatever it may be—you don't tell me anything—it's not my fault. This whole thing is not my fault." He snorted, but I ignored that. "I want some answers from you." He glared. "If you can't figure out where we can find these trails—if they really exist, I mean. Maybe they're gone, or your wizards quit maintaining them, or they now belong to the Society. We might do better just going another way, if there is one. . . ." I trailed off, because his gaze rose in temperature and threatened to flash with fire.

"You know nothing about this, Dulcinea, so please don't presume to advise me. Leave the majick to the majickers." He let out a deep breath. "It is not that I can't find the trails. I am merely trying to establish directional signals, which is the first step in locating them." This certainly seemed to me the same as not being able to find them. "I can't manage that because of the deliberate majickal noise. It's unethical, is what it is. Those blackguards have bollixed up the entire directional system for farthels and farthels around. Look at your compass."

I pulled the lodestone case out of my waist pack. Horrified, I stared as the charged stone spun wildly.

"It is one thing to mess with other wizards, but they have no business interfering with every innocent merchant and traveler. Have they no moral compunctions at all? No, of course not."

His shoulders slumped forward, and I felt a desperate pang at the thought that he was about to lose heart. I also wondered how the deuce we'd find out way out of the forest if we lost this path. I certainly had no sense of direction, at least until the sun began to set or the stars came out to point our way. Maybe not even then.

Raz was thinking along the same lines. "We must stay strictly on this trail and trust that it proceeds as I remember it. One of these times I'll find a spot where their influence has weakened, and I will grab a string of the Web and jerk it as hard as I can just to spite them. Just wait and see if I don't."

Where was his concern for our personal safety? If only I ever got out of this, I resolved to avoid the whims of Raz forevermore. I sent up a prayer, this time pointedly omitting Raz (sinful as it was) but asking for safe passage for myself and the three horses.

I would now be entirely in the hands of the saints.

Raz and I rode the rest of the day without exchanging five words. We camped in sullen silence, me doing all the work and taking care of the horses as Raz withdrew to spellcast. He went off several times briefly, always in a different direction, but returned with renewed anger.

# # #

The fourth day along the journey, we were still not on any majickal pathway. But we'd come safely out of the forest onto the King's Roadway, a wide graveled highway that ran straight to the horizon. I knew our deliverance was due to the intervention of my saints.

We'd had no problems so far on the public road, other than Raz's silences and shortness with me. We had seen few travelers on the road in either direction. Raz apparently found even this disquieting.

"The open roads are most dangerous. Bandits and highwaymen are desperate and reckless when there's slim pickings with few travelers. We've got deep woodland on either side. At any time, without warning, we could be set upon and devoured by wild beasts." He gestured grandly around us.

We rode alone in the sunny morning light. The only hooves I heard were our mounts'. Other than ourselves, the wide road was completely deserted. What scared me was the reasonable tone in Raz's voice. I ventured a comment. "Other than that, we're perfectly safe."

He shot me a warning look.

I said nothing more.

Just after dark, when I was starting to worry about the condition of the road surface—the previous road had turned into a narrow gravel path meandering between villages—we stopped in a clearing well off the main road. I was afraid a stray chunk of stone could lame one of the horses, and breathed a sigh of relief when we stopped uneventfully.

We dismounted without a word to each other. I started dinner with the last of the oatmeal. Fed up with doing most of the drudge work, I had pains in the backs of my knees, and my temper threatened to flare. I brought up the subject of the quick majickal trails again as I ladled the cereal. I was only thinking aloud.

"Do you still think we have a chance of finding any trails? Because I need to have some idea how long this will take if we never find any. What about if we hide alongside the road where you think one might be, and sort of wait to see if somebody else disappears into the underbrush and follow wherev—"

He cut me off with a wave of his flat palm. "Dulcinea Brown, you do realize who's in charge here, don't you? And who has taken this route over and over again? If you want to make this a success, you have to do what I tell you."

"I wasn't questioning your authority." I let resentment come into my voice full force. "I was merely"—I noticed how much I had started to sound like Raz—"suggesting a possible alternative that might be workable."

"Oh, indubitably." Raz inconsiderately dipped his hand along with his bread into the gruel hanging over the fire that I'd set and banked, even though he'd already bitten into that end, and threw me a look of contempt. "We'll simply tarry around where I think a majickal portal ought to be, and wait however long it takes for some mage to wave his staff and crash into the bushes, presumably disappearing to where we want to be. Do you seriously think that's how one enters the Hidden Trails?"

My temper finally clawed its way out of its rattling cage and flew at Raz. "Well, I don't know. I'm just guessing. I need to know how close we are and whether I should lose heart." I pushed my wild hair out of my sweaty face. "I'm trying to get along with you, Raz Songsterson. You don't tell me anything."

"There are things it is better you didn't know—"

"I'm tired of hearing that." I flailed my arms at him. "You don't want me to know anything because you won't admit how smart I am. You don't even really like me, do you?"

"If only you realized." His eyes burned with what I could only interpret as anger. "I must control myself. You're too young and inexperienced to comprehend. You're still only a child."

"A child, a child. I know, and completely useless to you." He didn't like me, and at the moment I didn't like him much. "Well, let me tell you something, Raz Songsterson. I left my cozy home and took risks to come along with you. I didn't have to come and help you, you ought to remember. I wish I'd stayed home where I belong."

And that's when Raz made his mistake. "Home. Yes, indeed. Your problem is that you aren't welcome there any longer, either, remember, dear?"

I threw down my bowl, heedless of denting the pewter, and turned to stalk away. On second thought, I reached for the gruel pot where it still hung, intending to hurl it at him, but he grabbed my wrist.

"Let go of me, or I'll. . . ." I couldn't stop the tears, and I no longer cared what he thought of me. Baby-mind or not, he'd said he needed me for this mission, but now he was about to lose me, as he deserved.

"You'll do what?" The arrogant sparkle of power in his eyes made me even madder.

I jerked my wrist away and rubbed it. "I'm going to leave. You don't need me, and you aren't even civil, so I've decided you can go on ahead without my help."

He quirked an eyebrow sardonically and spoke in an amused tone. "You're going to walk off into the forest by yourself after sunset, or are you heading back down the road to be waylaid again?"

I threw the facts at him. "I'm taking both my horses. They belong to my father, after all."

"That's partially correct."

"Balderdash and brimstone, *partially*! They're ours, plain and simple. In fact, I should take all three of them." I knew he'd bought Rapstallion with money he'd earned from my Da, and right now that made me furious. "The money you tricked us out of should be returned; you came to us under false pretenses, never telling us how dangerous it was to shelter you. You hid in our home and ex—ex—" I spluttered to a pause.

"Exploited." He supplied it blank-faced.

"Exploited our hospitality." I picked right up where I had left off. "You took advantage of us in every way. If you hadn't come, we'd still be fine. It's your fault Da's mind is ruined. I'm calling the loans in. Therefore, Stallion is merely on loan to you—WAS on loan to you." I knew I sounded wild-eyed, but it didn't matter to me.

"All right." He spoke quietly and calmly. "Let's say that I should take some of the responsibility for your father's predicament. I don't agree with your assessment entirely, but for the purposes of argument, I'll temporarily concede that rationale. But working from that premise, even if I returned my salary, which wasn't terribly generous"—he wasn't winning me over with that detail, because he had lived as well as we had—"I'd still own the horse. And more."

"More of what?" I was light-headed with anger, and bewildered that he had given a soft answer to turn away my wrath.

"I am now a silent partner with a financial interest in your shop." As he informed me of this dubious fact, he crossed his arms and leaned back. "Hector Brown signed one-third over to me in exchange for my teaching him certain—skills."

"Liar." That couldn't possibly be true. Could it?

Raz's lips curved upwards in a nasty facsimile of a smile. "What you don't realize, Dulcinea, is—well, never mind. It's no use."

I just stared at him, thinking a hundred insults, but unable to articulate one. Once spoken, a slight could never be unsaid. And I for whatever cause didn't want to hate Raz forever as much as I felt like hating him right now.

Undeniably, that was a smirk on Raz's face. He leaned forward again. "But go ahead—do take the horses, if you can handle all three of them. And run headlong down that road wizzy-prissy right into trouble, from which I may or may not choose to extricate you. Or you can sit down and try to talk sense to me, and I'll tell you whatever it is you wanted to know." He flapped his eyelashes at me and grinned toothily. I thought again how much he looked like a tall, misguided rabbit. "Perhaps it was a mistake to bring you. But since you're out here, we might as well make the best of it. Shall I turn back and take you home, losing time in the bargain, or shall we continue with our quest? Only if, naturally, you agree to cease making a scene that could attract undue attention."

He was baiting me, but I ignored that. I even ignored the absurdity of saying I would attract attention way out here in the woods, when he was doing most of the talking. I knew I should ignore his offer and ride straight for home, but I also knew I wouldn't. Also, if what he said were true—if he'd majicked Da somehow to turn over an interest in our business—I might have to tread softly to protect myself. Time for a deep breath. "All right. I'm sorry I lost my temper." I pushed my hair out of my face again and mopped my brow with my sweaty sleeve. "But you haven't played fair with me since we left home. You've kept me completely in the dark about where we're headed and what you're doing. I don't feel secure any more." Trust was the issue. "I never did anything but what you've told me to. The whole reason I came was that I wanted to help. If you—er, if we"—I determined to be more diplomatic—"can't find one of the Hidden Trails, does that mean we can't get into the wizard's keep?"

He looked solemn. "Not exactly. But the problem is nearly solved, Dulcinea. Have a little confidence in me. I've found a minor nexus near here already, while we were riding; that's the reason I kept pushing ahead, going until I started to feel the pull of the ley-crossing weaken. It's some distance crow's west of here, but it's about here in the ley-across direction."

I knew the grid of majickal ley lines went "up" and "down," the way directions on land went east and west, but I wasn't sure which way he really meant. I just nodded. Suddenly I was very tired.

"It is taxing. I'm afraid majick-weariness can make one very disagreeable." That was the closest he'd come to making amends, I knew. "After we rest, I'm going to try an experiment, and then we'll know which way to go in the morning." He stifled a yawn. "Perhaps I'll wait until early morning to try it. I think we should try to get some sleep."

CHAPTER TWENTY-SEVEN

The next morning—I knew it was morning merely because the dew had formed on the tips of the grass all around my head, where I'd rolled off my herb-plump pillow, but it was still before dawn—I caught Raz skulking around getting dressed. I conjectured he'd been about to slip away without my knowing.

"You shouldn't sneak off, Raz." I rubbed the sleep-sand out of my eyes as best I could, but everything was still a morning blur. I'd had my bed on a patch of dawg-grass, I discovered too late, and now I was suffering for it—strings of mucus in my eyes, a haze over my vision, itchy face, runny nose. Raz was a splotch of purple. "Remember, we talked about being more fair with me."

"I didn't want to wake you." That was also Da's typical excuse when I caught him sneaking around. I glared at him, and he ran his hand through the tangle on his blurry head as he thought up the next fib.

I raised up by stretching my hands behind me. "Never mind the pretense. What if you'd gone off and never come back? You could be snatched away by any kind of predator, and I'd be snoring here, completely unawares."

"From what you said last night, you might think you were better off." I knew he was grinning because the ends of his mustache moved. "But seriously, if that were to happen—which it will not, I assure you; I know what I'm doing—there's something you ought to have."

He pulled a parchment envelope out of one of his innumerable pockets. "This contains a report I need to deliver to my Master. On the front of the envelope, you'll find a map and brief directions overland to an alternative destination, a tavern in Marwell where you should be able to find some of my fellows. If I were to disappear, you would go directly on that route and deliver this. Anyone there will know me and can find the proper person to take you to. Wait there until the message is understood, and go with whoever it is so that he can give you something for your trouble. If you'll promise to do this, I would appreciate it in the extreme. After that, your responsibility to me would be ended."

"Raz. . . ." I sat up, my pallet of blankets tangled around my legs. "You're scaring me."

"It's merely a contingency plan. Nothing to be concerned about. Grown-ups, Dulcinea, do have to speak of the worst so they can plan for it." He smiled again, and handed me the envelope. It made my fingers tingle, and I thrust it into the bottom of my pack.

"At any rate, I'm off to try that experiment I spoke of." The word "experiment" felt like an untruth inside his sentence, but I couldn't wrap my mind around a reason; it was just intuition or imagination. For some reason, I thought again of that odd stone he had shown me. "To do this properly, I need to be well away from other people, so don't try to bother me. I'll be some distance to the west wind. With luck, when I return"—my eyes must have been focusing better, because I could tell he winked—"we'll have our entree into the Hidden Paths."

Before I could blink, he had rustled off into the woods, his majick-sacks jingling under his robes.

When I could no longer hear his feet crunching the pine needles and serviceberry hulls, I sat up and pulled the envelope out of my pack. Unfortunately, he'd foreseen my curiosity. No matter how I tried going at it, I couldn't open the envelope. Either it would change as I tried to work my index finger under the flap, or I couldn't tear it, or I would forget what I was doing and start putting it away again. He'd ensorcelled it so I couldn't get at whatever was inside—at least not until I became a far more knowledgeable majicker.

"Drat." The letter went into my innermost pocket for later. I untangled myself from my bedclothes and rolled them up. I even rolled up his bedroll and loaded his supplies back on the horses. They were securely tied, contentedly picking at grass.

As I dressed, I grew more and more suspicious. What did Raz mean, an experiment? He'd never had to be away from people to do majicking before. Maybe he just didn't want me to see how he did it; no, that made no sense, since I had seen all manner of spellcastings. And it couldn't be concern over my witnessing his failures, since I'd attended plenty, and heard the cussing afterward.

Maybe he was doing diabolical majick. He would hide to conceal that from me. Despite his many disclaimers, Raz still might not be the completely white mage he claimed to be. He'd misrepresented himself—all right, lied—to me before, hadn't he? Proven himself a petty thief when it served his purposes, much as I hated to admit it.

Perhaps now he'd brought me into the woods to trade me to that Society for—what?—something he wanted to ransom. Even now he could be with them, negotiating. Maybe he couldn't bring himself to turn me over into their hands personally, but he was even now receiving his three sacks of copper for my life. . . . Why anyone would want me I couldn't say, but that explanation held as much appeal as any I'd thought up so far.

I had automatically trusted Raz ever since he came into our lives; he had seemingly proven himself over and over, but perhaps it was only convenient for him to do these things because they served his own ends. Had my special (and unwise) liking for him blinded me to his true nature? He stole that dragonstone, or whatever it really turned out to be, after all. And it wasn't something he should have hold of; it had let me know that itself. Perhaps it was gradually running him mad. It might be all the same to him if he abandoned me in the woods when it suited him, or once my usefulness to him as a workslave was over.

That seemed extreme. Perhaps he'd simply decided after last night to just take off and depend on me to get myself home safely to Da, who didn't any longer want me. It would be like Raz to do that so I wouldn't have to run away from him and desert the mission. But he'd said exactly the opposite.

My breath came shallow and I felt my face burning. I sank to my knees on the grass and squeezed out a few tears, but I couldn't make myself believe in either theory enough to become truly afraid, only upset over the disintegration of our closeness and our mission.

I jerked a few blades out of the green carpet and chewed on a seedy stalk. Raz might be a rascal, but not a ruthless betrayer. I was a more sensitive judge of character than that. He'd given us his true name from the beginning. Also, he had come to our rescue. And Da used to trust him, had him in his complete confidence—up to a point. If Raz could be believed, he now even shared my inheritance. That still rankled. But something there was that he wasn't telling me, and on purpose. What, by the Stones, could be his next secret? And why had I been such a little fool as not to find it out before leaving home?

# # #

The horses seemed restless; somehow, they sensed my anxiety. I knew of one way to calm us down. I found a comfortable perch on a hill in the grass and sat down to pipe.

I made up a song about a gently flowing stream where horses and sheep safely grazed, and the trees dropped sugarcubes. Tickie and Rapstallion settled happily, while Packy searched the ground for sugar until I explained (musically) that the acorns and filberts he kept finding were the same. Without realizing at first that I was doing it, I segued into wondering what was in the letter. I saw myself reading it and understanding everything. If only the thing would unstick at a corner. . . . I imagined it popping open to reveal all Raz's secrets.

Abruptly I felt a cricket or grasshopper hopping around in my inner pocket. I broke off the song and jumped up to shake them out. I leapt around, jerked my tunic off, and shook out my pockets.

The letter fell out, all unscrolled.

It read:

My dear and honest Master, Madare of Alorraine:

If you receive this letter, I am surely gone to the afterlife or soon will be, having been captured by our adversaries the Society. Although most of my personal business is settled and was put to rights before I left your citadel, there is one more matter I wish to turn over into your capable hands.

The young girl bringing this to you or your associate is an extremely talented untrained majicker. She has great though unmeasured majickal potential, and must receive training. I know that once you have examined her you will agree to take her underwing. Please take my prepaid tuition and the monies I have left with you in safekeeping and use them to train Dulcinea Brown. She will amaze you with her natural fluting ability. She is also a herbalist and can already do some things I have never yet seen done by someone so young. You will be pleased with her quickness. She also knows of the outcome of my mission; ask, and she will tell you what she knows. I think you will find my discoveries interesting.

Once you have heard her talent, think of me and what I should have done; my choices may have not always been right, but I made them with a pure heart as far as I was able.

I trust you to take proper care of your new protégé and to let her replace me in the plans I am aware you had made for my maturation in the discipline of majick. Know that I would do it if I were still here and do it in the same spirit, as I know you will.

Your faithful and regretful-to-leave student,
<a signature inkblot scribble that I knew read>
Erasmus A. Songsterson

My cheeks were wet with tears. I hurriedly rolled the letter back up and stuck it into my innermost pocket. I felt horrid, wicked, snoopy, and as mean-spirited as I ever had. Raz had spoken accurately earlier: some things were not meant for me to know. That letter was something I should never have seen.

Conflicting feelings fought and swirled around in my head like tomcats staking out territory. It dizzied me until I had to lie back and breathe deeply. Although I hadn't meant to snoop—hadn't really realized what I was doing—I should have known better than to give in to the temptation to read the whole missive. Still, it was wonderful to know that Raz did hold me in high esteem. I experienced a wave of that odd feeling for him again, twice over. At the same time, I felt angry that he hadn't told me just how dangerous whatever it was he was going to try today might be. And why did he write the letter at all if this journey were safe—and how could he be so sure I was going to survive him? I didn't know how I felt.

When a few more candlemarks had passed with no sign of his return, I was convinced that Raz was in serious danger. He hadn't said how long I should wait before panicking, had he?

Besides, I suddenly didn't feel comfortable alone out here in the wild woods.

Raz had a good head start, but I didn't have to worry as much about being seen, so maybe I could catch up. I hurried to get water in our buckets and put one within reach of each of the horses. I hid our packs and supplies in a hollow tree.

It wasn't hard at all to follow Raz's trail. "Either he has no sense of covering his tracks, thinks me a complete incompetent at following, or trusts I will tarry like an airyhead whilst he goes off however long he feels like," I muttered.

The sloppy shoe-prints and broken branches soon led me to the top of a small hill. I climbed the tallest tree halfway, and suddenly I spotted Raz on the downslope, ducking and dodging from behind one tree to the next as though keeping undercover. He wasn't skillful at it, but then again he didn't have the advantage of being bespelled to escape notice, as I did.

I supposed that explained how I'd managed to catch up: he'd been slowed down, taking care not to be seen by our presumed watchers. I trusted I was still beneath notice, and besides I was tinier and quicker. I thought I could follow along in sprints and sneaks, always keeping him in sight. I decided to follow from as far a distance as I could handle, which turned out to be several horses' lengths.

I was getting rather good at this business of skulking around.

Raz led me through the deep woods to the bend of a river, likely a tributary of the same Langarou we'd been closely following all along the road. I could hear running water just before the expanse of blue came into sight. Rather than come to the water's edge, I scaled a thick oak and climbed high enough to survey the area.

Just on the other side of a rickety-looking bridge to a midstream island stood a large castle—no, a walled compound, complete with posted guards. Every turret and stone fairly sparkled with the blue aura of majick. I stifled a gasp as I realized what it must be: either it was the wizards' school, in which case Raz had led me along for completely different reasons than he'd given me, or else it must be the enclave of the Society of Mages.

The castle had turrets like the grandest in all Ladenia, and had the entire river for a moat. A footbridge went across to the castle's entrance maze. The surrounding trees, bushes, and plantings were so dense that you'd tramp around forever before you found a way in. Come to think of that, I couldn't see any doors in the building. There had to be some way in, but it wasn't on this side.

Raz popped out of his current hidey-place. He strode across the bridge bold as anything and continued hiking the path leading through the woods, as though not to bother with the castle. The guards appeared to pay him no mind. But then he ducked into that garden-maze of bushes. They must have missed him completely—or was it just that they figured it was mazy enough to lose him? Perhaps they'd allowed him in on purpose. Perhaps they were illusory.

From my vantage point, I could oversee Raz traversing the maze. He didn't try to cover his tracks, and he seemed to know just which turns to make. As I watched, he dropped a tiny, glowing bead. Before he dropped the next, he breathed on it between his palms as though to warm it, much the same way some dicers blow on the spots to make lucky faces turn up on the next throw.

Once Raz reached the center of the maze, he jumped and twirled three times. In front of my amazed eyes, the ground swallowed him up, and he fell out of sight.

"Raz!" The sound of my own voice shrieking startled me. I nearly lost my grip on the oak. Then I realized he'd dropped down through some type of secret door, a trapdoor. And now I knew—unless there was another component to the key that I hadn't heard or seen—how to open the door for myself. If Raz could land safely, at his size, I should be able to do it as well.

I decided that, either way, it would be worth my while to slip in right behind him.

CHAPTER TWENTY-EIGHT

My Unnoticeability was still in force, so I didn't bother to sneak around. I sauntered nonchalantly across the bridge, down the path, and into the maze. I saw no guard pointing me out or raising an alarm or even waving a fist towards me. No one took any notice whatsoever of me. Or at least they didn't let on.

There it was, the first of Raz's little glow-pebbles. I followed the trail to the center of the maze and stood staring at a pair of wooden trap doors, looking like barn doors, but set into the earth.

I hesitated, although I knew the next step would be to jump three times, turning, as I'd seen him do. But the question was, had there been some additional component to his actions that I hadn't been able to see or hear from a distance? A whispered Word of Power, an enchantment, an utterance I didn't know? If there had been, would I fall into a trap when I didn't do the key of the spell just exactly right?

The doors looked like rickety wood, but as I stood on them, testing my weight, I knew it must be an illusion, as the guards themselves must be. Not a creak came from the boards, and not a peep came from any guard.

Holding my nose in case water lay beneath the trap, I jumped and spun, thinking positive thoughts.

The doors popped open, and I was falling.

Before my stomach could even reach the bottom, I had landed in a haystack. When I could breathe again, I mentally checked myself: no broken bones, nothing sprained or bruised. The hay had broken my fall. I felt lucky that Raz nor anyone else was beneath me.

The doors eased themselves closed overhead. I waited while my eyesight adjusted to the dim illumination from two flickering torches on the wall above. From here, wide stone steps led downward even farther. I couldn't see much past the first three, but now I could hear footsteps—Raz's or someone else's, I couldn't tell. Burying myself in the hay, I held as still as a runt-kip until the steps retreated and faded away.

Even reminding myself of the Unnoticeable spell didn't make me any braver. But I had to know what Raz was up to, and probably rescue him from whatever he was getting into.

I took the path that I judged the footsteps hadn't. Torches placed in sconces at intervals lighted the way just enough. From the lack of smoke and sputter, I decided even these were majickal.

I made my way down by torchlight until I came to a corridor. Spying one of Raz's beads to the left, I knew that was the proper direction to take. I scooped it up, juggling and weighing it as I hesitated; then I pressed on down the corridor.

It was quiet, and my footsteps echoed in the shadowy dungeon. Instead of being the narrow stone passage I had expected, the passage was four men wide and lined with smooth river stones. Either someone—many someones—had laboriously hauled and placed each, or it had been done by majickal means.

The path curved to the left. As I approached an archway, sudden flashes of light dazzled me. Something glittered off the polished stones on the walls. Too bright for a torch.

Beyond the arch lay a cavern, a ragged oval about fifty king's-feet in diameter. The castle must have been built over a natural cave. The ceiling loomed high overhead.

In the center, where the ceiling reached its apex, stood a huge cage, approximately ten by twenty king's-feet by my eyeball. Inside the cage a majickal fire burned. At least that's what I thought at first, that there was a fire—majickal because it seemed non-consuming, and fire because of its dancing points of light, although they were a brilliant blue. It took me a second look to realize it wasn't inanimate, but was . . . an expanse of lizard covered with shimmering scales.

A dragon!

By my estimate, the monster measured about eight king's-feet tall from ground to crown, or five and a half from dirt to shoulders. It stood on its hind legs, digging its talons into the dirt floor with both jackrabbit-built, four-toed feet. Waving in the air near Raz's foolish face were two taloned five-fingered hands—er, front legs and paws. Its head was about the size and shape of a large wolf's, and it had a long snaky giraffe neck that was also quite thin, looking as though it had no business trying to support its much-larger member. It seemingly could swivel that flexible neck most of the way around. Supporting its long S-curved neck was a stocky compact body with a relatively large sternum—the muscles, I imagined, needed to support flight—its barrel chest wider than the footings on which it sat. Its glittery scales shone, throwing off the sparklies of light that I'd mistaken for sparks from flame, looking like some exotic blue blade-metal.

The most fascinating thing about the dragon, of course, were its wings, which it had partially raised and extended in an attitude of defensiveness, but which were hampered by the metal bars of the gridded cage. Sprouting out of its midback, the two giant wings were partially translucent, batlike; each had a "hand" consisting of four wing fingers clawed at the ends, with a short free claw where they joined, and those claws grasped the bars of the brassy cage as though they were mere toothpicks to be torn away.

Why did its head bob and weave so on its snaky neck? It was looking at something just coming into view. I followed its gaze, and quickly covered my mouth as a gasp escaped.

Raz stood before the cage in the Majicker's First Stance. Muttering a power word that he must have had all prepared, Raz reached for the cage door. I couldn't believe it, but as I gaped in wonder, Raz swung open the cage door and stepped inside.

The giant Wyrm started making a questioning noise. "Hrrr, hrr, hrr?"

Raz stood in the beast's very shadow, swaying drunkenly back and forth like someone under a spell, both his hands raised in the classic "I am enchanting you" stance. In his left hand he held something aloft. Shafts of multicolored light hit the cavern floor and ceiling from something within his fist, as though he channeled sun with a prism. I could guess what Raz held, and I sucked in a breath. The beast stared at Raz's hand, and I could have sworn it was shocked, mystified, or dazzled by what it saw. Why didn't it attack?

I crept forward as far as I dared, to the very edge of the cavern. As I watched from behind a column of stone, Raz began muttering words of power. I couldn't understand them, but they seemed different from his usual majickal cant. They hung in the air, glimmering invisibly, for a moment after he enunciated them, then dissolved like glittery dust and fell useless to the dirt. The language didn't coalesce, refused to obey, wouldn't form an aura or beam of any type of majick that I could feel. The entire display of power—attempted invocation of power—seemed to succeed only in irritating the dragon.

In fact, Raz's very presence seemed to be making the dragon crazy. Its questioning "hrr?" gave way to a sound like that of cymbals clashing. Its jaws gaped, and I counted rows and rows of efficient-looking teeth. It looked like a cobra watching for the precise moment to strike.

A jewel that gave control of dragonkind, my auntie's derrière. I knew Raz intended to work power through it, but something was wrong. I couldn't feel even a bare thread of majick yet. As I watched, the brilliance of the jewel went dull, and the stone's lights began to fade.

Raz opened his hand, looking uncomprehendingly at the dead rock. The stone had been a faceted jewel with strange lights dancing within. But now it had changed; it was no more than a dull red rock that held but a dim glow.

As Raz swayed, confused now, the dragon thrashed and flailed about at the very ends of his ropes. Skinny ropes, I now noticed.

Chains would've suited me better, but of course on a majickal creature, iron would either cause it unbearable agony where it touched, or it would instantly rust and crumble; iron couldn't be used on them, any more than a majicker could escape iron. This was a major paradox vexing majickers and their conjurations. What it meant to me was that the dragon was truly a majickal being.

Raz stood, looking dazed, as claws waved close; he swayed out of the way almost by chance, like one end of a lodestone repelling the similar end of another. As I watched, the dragon flushed—that was the only way I could interpret it, as though he were blushing from rage. Its scales went through a part of the rainbow as they warmed to a darker blue, then purpled; my jaw dropped as it finally turned an angry red all over. A puff of smoke escaped its nostrils, and I feared it would breathe out death. A faint scent of sulfur filled the air.

If Raz had dared to come so close to it—with its killing breath, if the legends and storybooks were truthful—that meant there were limits on the range for working power through the dragonstone. He'd have stayed back the maximum distance. It seemed natural that the dragon instinctively wanted to destroy that stone; that a dragon would hate it made perfect sense, if it was truly a stone that could bring dragons to this plane or send them away. In any case, this dragon was about to take revenge (this time the phrase seemed fitting) on Raz for whomever of his kind had given up his gem.

Raz must be enchanted by his own tool. Drop it, I wanted to say, drop the accursed stone and run! But my voice was frozen like my legs, cold against the stone column.

The claws lashed out at Raz. The tail wrapped itself around the cage bars as though for balance, and I noticed a blue opal speartip point tipped it. Raz barely dodged the left claws aimed at the side of his face, and I muffled my scream.

My voice was back; my legs would move. I leapt up, but I couldn't make myself clamber down and become the dragon's dessert. Confound it, I was a coward. I covered my eyes, unable to watch.

Abruptly, I heard a series of loud pops. My eyelids followed suit, popping wide. The dragon, frenzied, had snapped the ropes that had bound its lower limbs. Raz was cornered. The dragon surged forward; in a motion, it would have him pinned up against the metal grid of the cage.

"I command thee—hold! Halt! Hold!" Raz's voice had lost none of its power. It startled me such that I stood perfectly still, my body automatically responding to Raz's bossing. In a frozen moment the dragon obeyed, and Raz stood edging toward the cage door, holding the Wyrmbeast off as if by sheer force of will. Everything was as quiet as the inside of an icicle as the dragon and Raz eyed one another, wondering who would make the next move.

A ruckus of footsteps from the corridor behind me loudly shattered the nervous silence, and I ducked as far into the shadows behind the stalagmites as I could. Guards stomped into the chamber, several guards.

A gap-toothed short one squawked first from the archway. "Here, now! What's all this? Well, looky here. Our monster's done caught us a prowler, he has!"

I feared I might burst into giggles of hysteria and ducked lower. At least the dragon hadn't killed Raz. I didn't know whether the guards had heard all the commotion, or if they'd headed this way when they detected the stone's release of uncontrolled majick.

The dragon started, its neck whipping around and its head swiveling back and forth as it studied the new presences. Raz whirled as they approached, their boots clacking against the rock floor. The stone popped out of Raz's hand and cracked against one of the bars, then skittered across the dirt of the dungeon floor. One of the guards slapped his boot down on the stone. I heard Raz's groan as the man bent to scoop it up.

Instantly the dragon began to fade from its angry red shade. The sparklies stopped, muting to a jewel-toned glow. Before my amazed gaze, the dragon quickly faded to a placid turquoise blue, its underbelly simultaneously becoming a normal lizardy apple-green.

I was looking at a chameleon dragon, one whose color reflected its inner turmoil or rage as well as serenity and joy. Not only did it turn to a beautiful seashore tone with apple-green underside, but also it calmed visibly around the lips, covering its double row of teeth. It cowed down and mewled "hrr, hrr," like a happy kitten, resting its head peaceably on its rump.

"Muchly obliged," said the guard, grinning so wide I could count his missing teeth from where I hid. "That'll about do it for you, won't it, then."

It was a simple matter for the guards to enter the cage now. Two of them easily re-tied the placid dragon, checking their knots carefully this time. The other three promptly collared Raz, throwing him onto the dirt in another nearby cage.

"Your cell is close to the dragon's to let it smell its next dinner. They love fresh meat." The taller, snaggle-toothed one cackled as the others chained Raz hand and foot to brackets set into the stone wall. A wizard bound in cold iron can't spellcast. "Not too long now until dinnertime."

"Curse you, and may it follow down to your children's children and so on forevermore," Raz cried. He received a faceful of spittle in answer as the guards stomped away.

CHAPTER TWENTY-NINE

After the guards were well down the corridor, still cackling, I climbed down into the cavern.

Raz wasn't properly appreciative. "What's the idea, following me?" Then he looked remorseful. "I suppose it has worked out for the best. Can you get me out of these?" He waved his poor little wrists as helplessly as any flirting girl, and I had a brief feeling of power over him, which I was ashamed to admit that I enjoyed—a little.

"I'll try."

He let out a sigh. "They ought to be gone a while, although there's no way of knowing. How I'd love to study the beast further"—his chains clanked as he pointed at the now-placid dragon, whose faceted eyes studied us cagily from afar behind its bars—"but I can't risk it. Just see what you have that's like a rod, a skinny piece of metal, something that you can use to work at these locks. I'll direct you as best I can."

I started searching obediently through my pockets, a reflex in response to one of Raz's commands, before I realized I had nothing. What I did have was my flute. I could hardly suppress a grin at the thought of how my talent would surprise him. I'd forgotten that I'd never yet had his ear long enough to broach the subject; we'd had so many problems that I'd had no opportunity to explain to him—more to the point, he hadn't given me a chance to tell him—about my new ways of fluting. Raz might be pleasantly shocked into a rare quiet. I played it coy.

"I think I know how to do it, Raz. What I'm worried about is climbing out of here. It's certainly a long way up."

He shook his head. "There's a different turn you can take at the top of the stairs to reach the carriage doors around back. It's where they used to store their coaches. I've marked the way leading out of the maze." Rubbing his wrists, he squinted in the dragon's direction. "What a creature. What an opportunity for study. What we could learn from it! But first things first, and quickly. Can you get me out of these?"

"I can't find anything to pick locks with. Besides, a *child* like me is so *useless*." I couldn't resist teasing him a bit as I drew out the flute. "I have an idea, though." I enjoyed the mystified look on his face as I began to pipe about locks and keys and the satisfaction of fitting them into each other perfectly. Click, click, went my flute keys against the polished body, and click, click went the imaginary locks in my song. I envisioned the iron melting, bending, turning soft as candy-taffy and stretch, stretch, stretching to release Raz's wrists and ankles. I sang along internally, watching in my mind's eye his cuffs open and his chains drop free.

"I see you've continued to teach yourself fluting." Raz's tone was dryer than sand. He worked his wrists a bit, and the cuffs seemed looser. Out of the corner of my eye, I could see the dragon rocking back and forth on its haunches and looking at me with curiosity.

I studied the dragon a little closer. Two little spiral horns like the inside of a pretty pinkish shell poked out of its face just above the eyes, over the eyeridge. A spiny, rayed fin ran down the back of its neck. Its ears were pointy like a cat's and positioned similarly on its head, their outer surface of hard blue scales and the inside edges dark blue that faded into greenish-yellow as they entered the ear canal. On the underside of its chin were a couple of whiskerlike antennae.

He was the most beautiful and fearsome thing I'd ever seen. The more I looked at him, the better I liked him. In fact, he seemed to be thinking the same about me. As I watched him, he seemed to actually bob his head in time with my tune. He? Yes, I decided; though I had no clue as to sexing dragons, this one I intuitively knew to be a "him." His emerald eyes were dodecahedral, glittering with a majickal light. I could think of nothing but the light; how beautiful the creature was, despite its fearsomeness.

I'd forgotten to think about the iron and was in tune with the dragon. In my mind, images began to form. A tall, tall mountain poking up through the white fluffy clouds. The glistening ocean breaking onto the rocks at its base. The lovely, damp, dark caves riddling its innards, where not only could you find cozy, homey spaces lined with warm mud just the right temperature for sleeping and lolling, but also hoards of bright, sparkling jewels. . . .

It occurred to me that these were pictures of (for lack of a name to put to it in my language) dragon land. The flute-majick had spoken to it! And this must be its way to communicate.

Now I saw an image of a jail cell, bondage, slavery . . . suffocation, and my wings tied! I couldn't move my wings . . . I couldn't breathe, in sympathy with whatever was being sent. Gasping for breath, hunger gnawing at my insides, and all I could think of was escape from this cavern, claustrophobic and dry as a boneyard. . . . I ran out of air and couldn't blow another note. All at once I comprehended that this was the dragon's way of telling me he wanted to get out and go home.

I'll take you home, I thought. I sent him pictures of free flight in the wild clouds, not knowing how I would do it, but now completely simpatico and convinced I could somehow find a way. I sang softly on a trill, drawing a road and path out through the wood, but when it didn't respond, sending only confusion, I realized why: it was used not to walking, but flying. The huge wings and the stubby little feet, of course; I was such a featherbrain. Immediately I shifted to a bird's eye view of escape, showing him the as-the-crow-flies way. I was flooded with light; he sent a feeling of joy and flapped his wings. Even at this distance, the wind almost knocked me over. The flute slipped loose from my lips and my hair blew back.

"Dulcinea. . . ." Raz woke me out of my reverie. "Nothing's happening to the shackles. Please hurry; as you can see, the dragon is getting restless."

"Sorry." I'd forgotten that what I thought about, my music acted upon. I brought my mind back to the story of softening metal.

But the more I talked to the metal, the more my dragon became agitated. This music seemingly goaded him; he reddened again and flew into a rage, flailing all his limbs. His cage door popped slightly ajar because of the vibrations he caused as he clawed and danced, weaving his little head around on its skinny neck like a charmed snake. I hated to know he was upset, but I almost had the metal softened, almost, almost. . . .

Then I heard footbeats. And two guards shouting to one another. "He's found another toy, has he? We'll find it quick enough."

I leaped behind a stalagmite as Raz snapped his hands free from their irons. But they'd seen me or heard the dying tones of my last tune, and at least one of them had spied me.

"There's another burglar! The music came from there." One of the guards pointed right at my position, and headed my way. I thought I might be able to dodge behind the dragon's cage. As one of them got close, I scuttled sideways along the wall towards my saurine friend.

Sure enough, they each approached me, then looked confused. They were having a difficult time finding me because of the "unnoticed" spell. Just as I was feeling cocky, I backed into the dragon's cage accidentally, and the bars bent like soft ashwood. I realized I had inadvertently softened its cage metal along with Raz's shackles. The brass bars smushed like potters' clay as my lardbutt rear pushed them aside. I fell back, practically into the dragon's waiting hug, the ends of my hair tickling his broad underbelly. I found myself flat on my back, staring upside-down right into his curious face.

"There she is! But she's no trouble for us now." They pointed and stepped far away, laughing, obviously thinking it would surely kill me. But as I lay eye-to-eye with the dragon, I didn't get a claw across the abdomen. Like a worried hound dog, he looked at me quizzically, unable to commune with me without a majickal "carrier" such as the musical wave.

I sat up and began to pipe. He sighed his "hrr, hrr," and laid his glitter-scaled head on my shoulder. It wasn't any heavier than a large goose you'd carry from the market in a market basket. The guards gasped in wonder as we secretly communicated our predicaments, he explaining that he was ready to leave, and me agreeing, but telling him what we needed to do and that we must get Raz.

Soon as I'd completed my pictorial instructions (if you've never tried to translate all manner of abstract concepts into images a foreign intelligence can grasp, and do it on the fly, you've never yet lived dangerously), the dragon backed happily out of the cage, crushing its rear wall into brass toothpicks.

"What the blazes?" shouted one guard.

"Sod it, he's gone mad! Run!" the other shouted back.

The guards scattered as he came directly for them. Apparently they knew their weapons were useless. One of them had a sudden brainstorm and pulled Raz's dragonstone out of the top of his dagger case, but he was apparently only a guard who'd had some luck calming the dragon with it the previous time, not a mage who would know how to wield its power. The stone remained cold and dark. My friend cornered him in short order and made the guard drop the stone, which the dragon promptly swallowed.

Raz sighed heavily.

"Good boy!" I shouted as I made for Raz's side. His foot shackles had softened, and all he had to do was pull lightly to loose his ankles. Brightening, Raz cast off the iron into the dirt with a loud clank.

"Let's go," I sang out, trilling on the flute to signal my friend that we were ready for the next step we'd discussed. He obediently chased the guards up the dungeon stairs and out the carriage doors Raz had described. I felt the saints had made it possible for Raz to tell me about them and how they were reached so I could tell the dragon. They were the only part of the castle wide enough to accommodate a raging dragon.

Raz and I were right behind him. He broke through the door frame (all right, they weren't *quite* wide enough to accommodate a dragon, especially if he had his wings spread) and rushed out onto the grass. We had just barely time to race after him, climb up his neck, and hang on as he ran down the impromptu runway. We took off over the river and headed windward.

I got my bottom settled on his back's toothridge with difficulty, hanging onto his neck with both hands and trying to be sure I wasn't squeezing. It was nothing like riding Tickie, even bareback. "I hope I'm not hurting him." Then I realized Raz, behind me, was awfully close to my squirming tailbone. My butt was pressed right up against Raz's belly; I felt a rush of thrills even as I was overcome with embarrassment. "Or you."

"Forget the niceties, Dulcinea. I don't know how you did this," Raz said into my ear over the wind and the wing noise, "but I'm certainly glad you managed it."

CHAPTER THIRTY

It seemed I sat astride silky skin instead of upon interlocking, clicking scales. This natural body armor was soft but impenetrable. The dragon's back was plated with shimmering silvery-blue scales. Up close, I could see his scales were each a little smaller than my palm. His tummy side was covered in smaller scales—about the size of Raz's big thumbnail—tiny, pebbly scales, which sparkled green. His back feet beneath us were webbed like a duck's between the four toes. His front paws and back feet were greenish-yellow on the palms and soles and the underside of his toes. The inner surface of his wings, between the bones or "fingers" that were plated with scales, was transparent silk skin, not glittery.

As we soared, he kept looking back at us, craning his neck and making moony eyes with those glittering jewels in his head.

"He wants to know where to go, I think." I didn't know how I knew.

"Well, then, tell him," came Raz's voice, thin and blown-away over the wind.

"How am I supposed to tell him where to go? I have to keep hanging on with both hands."

"I'll hold you." He slipped his hands under my upper arms, wrapped his hairy arms around my waist, and clasped his big hands firmly on my belly. He pressed me up against him. My shoulders involuntarily went up, and I had to breathe deep a few times. "Just imagine we're at home, on the grassy garden knoll, and you're on my lap, where you can safely pipe."

Safely, indeed—on his lap! "I hope I can trust you to hang on tight." And I hoped my blood didn't heat up too much when he clasped me close. Who knew what might happen up in the air if the driver were overcome with *those* kinds of thoughts?

I brought the flute to my lips as Raz tightened his grip on me, and I considered what kind of song would make a proper travelogue.

I sent him home to our shop. I just thought a picture of it, and then imagined what it must look like from the air, nudging the dragon in the proper direction of the King's Road. If we flew along the Ladenian road, as I imagined in the picture I was sending, we could return to my store—er, my lair—where he would get a treat. At the mention of a treat (I drew a picture of a fuzzy gray woods-mouse, much enlarged), he seemed perkier and the scales on his neck practically stood on end. I felt that we'd clomped halfway up a shiny metallic rope dangling from the sky and were hanging on, suspended above a tiny city built from child's blocks.

All the while I piped, the dragon's head wavered and nodded on the end of his long neck, a graceful dance that I took (hopefully) to mean comprehension and agreement. The sunlight danced on his scales as it does on the water as your canoe cuts through the still lake, and I felt we were both hypnotized by the beauty created by the other. Thank goodness for the circular breathing I'd practiced back home, so my song was never interrupted. I trilled a last trill as a please-and-thank-you.

Once I'd finished showing the way the only way I knew how, the dragon rotated his head back at me as though to see whether that was all. His eyes shone with excitement; I imagined it was at our mutual understanding. I nodded encouragingly. After a moment, he turned his head back and sent his neck through an arc, seemingly gaining his bearings and the lay of the land. Then our ride grew bumpy: he rotated something in his right wing, which made my hip joint pop until I got my thigh re-settled (my damp limb's underside had stuck to the glistening scales like you'll stick to a leather saddle on a warm day), and I felt us gain a bit of altitude. Then the end of his tail came around near my foot as he coiled it, spiraling it tight to our right-hand side, er, starboard side, then slung it quickly to its full length towards the left (west), er, aft side. We circled and soared with the East Wind, headed for home.

"That's right. Perfect." I crooned and patted the dragon's neck. The bumpy ride smoothed out.

"Perhaps a bit more to the North Wind quadrant." Raz leaned into my hair and muttered near my ear, but I could tell he was pleased and flummoxed and maybe even a little jealous—of me!—all at the same time.

I tootled a bit more about nudging us to the north, and the rush of the wind increased as we moved through the air currents. We went through a sparse cloud, which chilled me a little, but didn't wet us down. It was like holding on to a balloon's string and taking a ride through a cloud.

We glided smoothly into a corrected vector, taking us towards Ladenia City and home. "As the crow, er, dragon, flies," I murmured.

Raz craned his neck around to speak into my ear with his warm breath, and I dodged the slap from his flying hair. "What amazes me is that you managed to conceal your true abilities from me for so long." At least that was what I thought I heard; it was difficult to listen over the noise of the wind.

"I didn't." I shouted it backward and was rewarded by having to clutch at the dragon's slick neck again as he flinched. "Sorry. I said, I didn't hide a thing." I felt like scolding him a little; it helped keep my mind free of inappropriate physical desires. "You just never had time to listen, never paid any attention."

From the tone of Raz's voice, I knew he was scowling. "I have watched you. I have seen you in action. What I simply haven't seen is anything like this." He waved a hand, then grabbed for solid dragon neck again as we hit an air pocket and dropped a few handspans suddenly. "Charm Critter. Whatever you'd like to call it."

"I've tried to tell you before. You were always too busy." I shrugged, knowing he didn't see things from my perspective. "It was never the right time to explain."

He cleared his throat. "At any rate. Assuming this is not just a fluke, and that you can do again what you did in there . . . we have something important on our hands, Dulcinea." He paused. "In fact, it's something that I've never seen before. And I've studied quite widely. Effects like this gained only through music is not mentioned in any of the literature nor in oral majickal tradition."

"Isn't this just flutemagery, as you do, but taken a step further?"

"I don't think so, Dulcinea." He heaved a sigh I could feel down to my bones. "I really don't think so."

"Oh. So?" I didn't see why that should amaze him.

"So. It's such an important discovery that I propose you accompany me back to the master Madare specifically to let him see and evaluate this wonderful new majick."

At first I didn't know what to say; when words would again form in my mouth, I stuck my foot on top of them. "You know I can't leave Da for that long."

"I was getting to that."

I crossed my arms, but had to grab back around the dragon's neck again. I forgot I couldn't balance on a moving dragon the way I could on Tickie. *Tickie!*

I gasped. "Raz, we forgot—I forgot. The horses!"

I felt, rather than heard, him sigh. "The horses *what?*"

"Our three horses. They're still out there in the middle of the wood, in—" I realized that I really didn't know where they were. "Oh, Raz. I've left them to die. And your new Rapstallion, too. Oh, how long has it been? They'll starve. They'll dehydrate."

My rational side said I hadn't been gone but a few bells. But Raz had said there were predators, and for sure there were thieves in the world. What bothered me so much was that I'd abandoned them without a second thought, happy to ride off on some strange dragon, deserting them to starve. I couldn't believe how awful I was. I sniffled, then choked on a sob.

"Take it easy. You're just coming down off the excitement in the dungeon, and this is a reaction. It's natural to feel exhausted and let down, and thus overreact. Especially as I imagine we're in a majickal field generated by the dragon itself, one not familiar to us, and you may be feeling its effects. We'll send someone for the horses as soon as we land."

It wouldn't be soon enough. "But we don't even know exactly where they are—"

"Seriously, Dulcinea. You can't worry about them."

Raz didn't care about the horses; Tickie and Packy weren't his pets. "There's no one to send for the horses. Da can't go, and we don't have anyone else. It'll be days journeying—"

"I'll take care of it."

"You haven't taken care of everything too well so far." I knew I was being nasty, yet I couldn't help it. I couldn't stop crying. I didn't know what had gotten into me, but all at once the entire trip seemed so unreal. I just wanted to get the horses and take them home. Yet I knew I couldn't fly them home on the dragon; I'd just have to hope they'd be all right. And Da might not be thrilled to see us, and we couldn't take the spell off of him, and what would he do when he saw the dragon? I knew I wasn't rational, but emotions had overcome me.

All at once, a shrill screech startled me. "What's that?"

The screech trailed off and turned into whimpering. We dropped several feet and started weaving around and around, into a downward spiral. I tightened my grasp on Raz. "What's happening?"

"Dulcinea." Raz's voice was solid and stern. "Quiet your thoughts and think again of the map to the shop."

I couldn't imagine why Raz wasn't paying attention. "Never mind that. We're falling!" I clutched at Raz and tightened my thighs as best I could on the slippery scales, but I felt as though I'd fly off into the clouds any moment. The treetops tickled my feet, their branches practically grasping my toes. They were getting closer all the time, waving their leafy fingers, waiting to consume us like an ill-fated kite. "Do something!"

"It is you who must do something. As I said." Raz kept his voice calm, but he grasped my hands in front of my waist and squeezed my wrists hard enough to start pinching off my circulation. "Our steed is agitated because you've upset yourself. You must have transmitted your confusion and panic to him. Now you must correct it. Reassure him that you've figured out how to make it all right, and that all he needs to do is fly to the shop. Show him where it is again. Do it now, Dulcinea."

He raised my wrists to the flute. I hoped he hadn't crippled my playing, made my hands too numb from squeezing to finger the notes. I started whistling a soothing little tune with minimal scale movement, and soon Raz was humming along with it. Still, we were slowly losing altitude.

I hugged the dragon's neck and squeezed closed my eyelids. I sent confidence that my other pets, the horses, were being rescued. I showed boys from the village crashing into the clearing, bringing feedbags full of oats, and the horses dancing for joy as they were led towards home. Then I concentrated on our altitude, imagining the dragon flying straight and smooth again, soaring with a happy expression in his eyes. Then I imagined the path to home, as detailed as I could. I played this without thinking consciously of the melody, only of the pictures I was making in my mind.

The whimpering quieted. Gradually, his flapping resumed, and his waving neck straightened out. He flattened out our flight path and climbed again.

"Now, please," Raz said in controlled tones, "watch what you're thinking. He's very sensitive to you for some reason." I hadn't even been fluting when I'd panicked about the horses. Had my brain and his met on some wavelength, and he'd been able to make his way there even without the music? "Let's just get on the ground safely before you start making any further plans, shall we?"

I tried to visualize, think of nothing but the map to home, just in case. "You said when we got there, you had an idea. But what about Da?"

"I was getting to that. He must agree to accompany us. My master Madare may be the only one who can figure out how to take off this spell—since it's not likely we will convince the head of the Society to do it. And that's who I think the original caster is."

The thought upset me, and then I realized I mustn't be upset. "Oh, no!"

"What?" Raz's arms tightened around me deliciously. I tried to throw off the warm feeling that he was enjoying my proximity along with the ride; I knew that was my imagination. I tempered my tone before I spoke again.

"I almost thought of the monk and could've upset the dragon. Why is he picking up so easily on anything I think?"

"You've connected with him on some level. He feels only you can 'talk' to him. The reason he's so sensitive, of course"—again that phrase he'd warned me against, for obvious reasons from his tone of his voice—"is that he's only a baby dragon."

"This is a baby?" I shouted back, belatedly sorry and hoping it didn't offend the dragon.

"By their standards."

"That means hatchling?"

"No, but might as well be as far as reasoning power is concerned. Their wisdom and knowledge is gained slowly, through gradual experience. Years, I mean."

"How can you tell? He seems plenty grown to me."

"But he's very young. Barely three seasons out of hatching, and remember how long they live and how slowly they develop." Raz's voice floated just over the sound of the wind, for the prevailing breezes had changed. "I can tell, because he doesn't even have his sharp spines on his backridge developed yet, and these horns are so tiny."

"Tiny!" They looked fearsome enough to me.

"His horns are bumps compared to what they will be." Raz pointed with one of his forefingers, without unclasping his hands from around my waist. "There would be a circle of spikes on the end of the tail in a mature dragon. And a hexagonal mound would have risen in the center of the forehead to support further spellcasting. Now it serves as his compass and controls his breath weapon. That will enlarge as he does." He took a pensive tone. "I was surprised to see that he doesn't have spikes along the back like the ancient sauruses—they're after all Wyrms—but he does have a rudimentary backbone ridge."

"I'd noticed that. It's not terribly comfortable when you're riding bareback."

"It's safe, though. The scales can shock you, however, because they're just a little electric with majick. If you aren't careful when you're brushing up against them all the time, I mean."

"I'll remember." I knew that wasn't going to happen here. I was already all a-tingle with excitement from everything that was happening, so I wouldn't even notice if I were shocked with more majick. "Look—I think that's the spire of our church!"

We were in sight of home.

CHAPTER THIRTY-ONE

We sank groundward gradually and smoothly as a bird, but more quietly, with no flapping. I directed the dragon to the village square on which our shop stood.

Only a few people were in the square, notably a gaggle of young children playing a game of tag. Widder Pidgeketl stood still on her front walk as we came into sight; her eyes opened round as dinner plates as we approached. I couldn't help feeling pleased that I had finally impressed her.

We landed in the center of the village square. Dust flew up all around us, and my dragon swiveled his neck, surveying our little town. "Hrr?"

"It's okay." I patted him on the neck and visualized him in a muddy cave, then superimposed an image of me ensconced in the shop. "This is my lair, and you must wait here while I go and get your treats."

"Hrrrrr!" He settled down into a squat on his thick haunches, and I turned to the children who had gathered around.

"Would you like to pet him?" To the adults around I added, "He's perfectly tame."

"Dulcinea, we don't know that!" Raz shook his head, and everyone stepped back again. "I'm going to get us some supplies. Quickly, find your father." Raz disappeared around back, heading, I supposed, for his rooms upstairs.

The Widder Groop emerged from around the corner of our shop, looking mystified, pushing her hair back up into its sagging bun and wiping her hands on her merchant's apron. One of Da's, I predicted. "Dulcinea Brown!" I guessed that when you rode a dragon, all Unnoticeability was nullified. "You've come home at last! What are you doing with that monster?" Hands on hips, she looked ready to scold me, Wyrm or no Wyrm.

"It's kind of a long story. Where's Da?"

She shook her head. "I'm sure he's around somewhere. He doesn't wander far. But I'm getting more worried by the day. I had intended to send for you, if you'd ever left word anywhere. I couldn't find you at the taverns of Marwell, where that rascal said he was taking you, though the messenger boys said everyone knew of the rascal there. You've got to do something about Hector."

My heart pounded. "Is he all right? I mean, physically."

She waved a hand. "His body's fine. It's his thinking parts that worry me."

"Let's discuss that. But wait a moment." I turned to the dragon. "Stay right here." Obligingly, he cocked his head. Then I slipped out my flute and piped for the dragon about how friendly the citizenry was. I let a couple of the braver children pet it on the neck. "See, he's happy. Would you boys go and find me some field mice—not anybody's pets, but some that are vermin, large ones— for the dragon?" A couple of them ran off towards the fields. I felt fleetingly bad on behalf of the mice, but pushed it out of my thoughts, because I wanted the dragon to enjoy his snack.

I piped a restful tune, thinking of taking a short break abed of an afternoon, curled up with one of my books, Raz working in the room behind me, the sun on my bare feet. The dragon yawned hugely, causing no little panic when people counted his double rows of pointy teeth and dodged the puffs of smoke that escaped. I caught a faint smell of burned toast. In a moment he turned around three times like a big dumb hound, twined his neck around like a snake, and pillowed his head on his rump. He seemed perfectly contented to rest while people gaped.

Raz emerged, carrying three thick ropes and a couple of soft blankets. "What did I say, Dulcinea? We must fly soon. Find your Daddoo."

"I am, I am." Allowing Raz to get around to the dragon's side, I grabbed the Widder's arm. "Take me to wherever Da goes. I need to find him right now."

We found Da wandering around the Widder's back garden, whistling and smelling the flowers. She clamped onto his arm and he docilely followed us home, muttering something about herbs and pillows. I wondered if he would ever be my comfy old Da, or if his mind would never work properly again.

# # #

Raz had fashioned a kind of harness for the dragon out of the ropes, and the blankets were artfully arranged so as to cushion where a saddle would have been on a steed. We would weave our legs under the ropes to help anchor us, and we could hold ropes instead of grabbing at his scales. Raz reached for my arm. "Come along, you two. I smell majick, and not a good strain of it, either."

I felt around with my majickal mind and indeed did sense malevolent majick in the air. I laid a hand on Da's shoulder. "All right, sir. I have someone I want you to meet. Wouldn't it be fun to fly with us on the dragon to meet him?"

The Widder gasped, but Da disengaged from her and tilted his head at me. "Ride on a dragon?"

"Yes, on this one right here." I gestured grandly and winked at the dragon, who raised his head and posed. Raz patted the "saddle" area and smiled encouragingly.

"I don't believe I want to meet your friend," Daddoo said. My heart sank. His voice perked up. "But I couldn't refuse a ride on a dragon." My spirits rose again, and I grasped Da's arm. "May I truly ride on this dragon?"

"Indubitably." Raz beamed.

"There's room for all of us." I hoped there was.

"Then let us fly." Raz extended his hand to help Da get on.

"Fly!" Da's face was wreathed in smiles, like a baby's. Raz and I boosted him up.

The dragon took to him instantly. "Hrr, hrr, hrrr!"

Da laid his cheek against the dragon's. "And we're a good boy, aren't we, boy? What a sweet tempered beast you are." Out of his pocket he pulled a cube of sugar and a sweetcake and held them flat on his palm as though offering them to our horses. To my astonishment, the dragon delicately picked them up with his lips and smacked greedily. "Hfffrrr!"

Da turned to me. "See there, gal? That's how to make friends with any steed, right there. Show them you like them first, and you're fine. Aren't we, boy?"

The dragon purred.

Raz boosted himself up on the dragon's back. He gestured for me to get up.

I glanced around home one last time, shooing the children back. "We need room to take off." I only hoped he could lift us all. "Wait a second." I arranged the ropes so they held Da's legs against the dragon. On impulse, I started to go inside after a change of clothes; I couldn't meet Raz's majick-master in rough traveling garb. What kind of respect would that show?

The Widder gasped. "Oh, my stars and little fishes. Would you look what's coming now. Get back, children." The children scattered as the Widder signaled frantically.

I turned to see men running up the street towards us. Townspeople as well as ex-soldiers. Brandishing sticks, spears, and swords. Shouts of "There! Get him!" reached me. Simultaneously I realized that either spies had been set around our shop by the Society, which explained the presence of malevolent majick I'd felt, or that the moment we'd landed, fearful townspeople had organized to defend themselves against the "monster."

"Hurry, Dulcinea." Raz grabbed for me, and gaily Da caught me up. They placed me between them on the dragon, so that I was sandwiched tightly.

"Remember your orders!" The shout came from one of the frantic front-line torchbearers headed towards us. Probably a leader, though I noted that he now seemed to be bringing up the rear of the group. "Disturb no citizen other than the dragonriders. Leave be the shop itself. That's specific orders. Get those three." A warrior in full armor shook his spear as he approached, and three more took his cue and headed our way.

Raz and I got our legs in the ropes and clasped each other about the waist.

"Go, go!" Raz pushed my hands toward my flute, which still hung loose around my neck on its silver chain.

I trilled a song of panic and hurry, all about jumping into the air as the meadows blazed with fire and the woodland beasts flew for cover, finishing the opening image-phrase just as the men reached the square. The dragon bowed his neck and puffed smoke at them copiously. They scattered, dropping back, and we rose into the air. One of the bandits was brave enough to snatch at Da's shoe, but got only a handful of mud for his trouble.

"Take good care of my place, Juleida," Da called to the Widder. *Juleida?*

She nodded, looking pleased, but her wringing hands betrayed her upset. I felt sorry enough to wave at her. *Juleida, eh. Rats.*

"Fortuna, sender of luck, be praised. The dolts don't realize he's too young to have a functioning breath weapon." Raz sighed relief as we flew higher, the people turning into ants beyond our feet. "Hang on, everyone. Next stop, the Academy."

I continued my tune with a dousing of the flames, so the forest was saved, and all the animals cheered as the dragon circled high over the treetops. He obligingly went into the pattern, waiting for further instruction.

I would've grinned, but it would have ruined my flute tone. "Which way to your fortress, sire?" I piped on.

# # #

Since this time we were laced together, tied onto the dragon much as a brown paper parcel is tied up, I could pay more attention to the scenery and less to hanging on tight. I played a melody of high flight for freedom, and sent the dragon a picture story of how to fly to the Academy's compound, using a map Raz produced out of a pocket and Raz's verbal directions. He flapped happily away, our combined weights as nothing to a dragon's back.

"Well, sir. You indeed did what you said, and we are flying on a dragon. What is of interest about this place we're headed for?" Da sounded jolly, as though we were his drinking buddies, and we were on an outing to find a new pub.

"The Academy of Wizardry, Magefather Brown. It's part of my majick-master's school for majickers."

"You see, gal? I told you he wasn't no apprentice of mine." Da sounded triumphant. You could never know what he would remember from moment to moment and what he would forget for a while and then recall when you didn't expect it. "Who do you say this master of yours is? I might know him."

"He is Madare the Benevolent."

"Can't say as I know him. Though the name's a bit much, don't you think?" Da chuckled. "Meaning to say that if a man's benevolent, well, he shouldn't need to say so in his name. His reputation ought to precede him."

I couldn't argue with that, but Raz gave off an offended air. To make amends, I thought of something more flattering to ask. "Tell us more about the Academy, Raz."

Raz took on the aspect of a travel guide, swelling with pride. "Our Academy occupies its own secret compound, a walled castle fortress isolated in the middle of the trackless Giltwood Forest. There, students from each of Blackwren's Three-and-a-Half Kingdoms study sorcery as taught by masters of each Majickal Guild."

"There's more than one Guild? I mean, not counting the Academy and the Society." I hadn't thought of that, but it made sense. "What are the Guilds?"

"Herbalism, folkmajick, sorcery, wizardry, and enchantments—but not necromancy or divination, which wicked rites belong to the Society of Mages, and not Healing, which is the domain of clerics and their saints."

Three and a half kingdoms. I mused. I knew Marwell, Ladenia, and the exotic land of Belibon across the sea, but what was the half? Probably the land of the dwarves, long occupied by one or the other of the larger two kingdoms.

I could see from up here why they called it the forest of gold wood: the braided tree trunks did resemble gold-leafed carvings, like a picture frame I had once seen. And the leaves were colorful, all shades of yellow and green.

Da's voice boomed over the breeze. "Funny how quickly this fellow can make time." Soon I felt no strong wind, for we rode the prevailing skyblow.

"Flying in was a very clever notion." Raz made it sound like his own idea. I did see places in the brush that could have hidden warriors, but only after Raz pointed them out, and I couldn't attest that they were, as he claimed, "knots of evil spies who are watching the approaches to the Academy." I shuddered anyway.

We started to lose altitude. "We're nearly there," I said.

"Tell him to spiral down and choose a nice clear place to land, probably the center of the Quad."

"I'm leaving that up to 'Spunky.'"

"Who?"

"The dragon. He can choose a perfectly good spot. Can't you, boy?" I patted his head-bumps. He sent me a picture of an open area with a questioning feeling, and I sent back my approval. "Looks good to me."

I was about to meet Raz's majick-master.

CHAPTER THIRTY-TWO

We were, apparently, coming in for a landing.

"Look out below!" Raz shouted. The amazement I read on the students' faces made me giggle as we swooped down over their ducking heads. The crowd scattered as my dragon splayed out his landing toes.

Unsteadily, one wing lower to the ground by barely a bubble, we approached the quad. At least I thought we were properly aimed for the greenspace, which was surrounded by tall brick buildings, some with spires, one with a clock tower.

A circle of faces watched us, gawking upward. Heads below bobbed as my dragon wavered, finding just the right spot. He decided to land in the center of the commons, next to a fountain. We thudded to the ground in a scatter of wet cobblestones.

Raz hopped off and reached to help me down. Da made no move to dismount; he sat, majestic as a king on an elephant, feeding Spunky carrots out of his pocket. I hoped they would agree with the dragon's astral digestive tract.

"Pardon me, Aspirant," Raz said to a gawker wearing a sky-blue robe, "but could you summon for us one of the stablehands?" To me he added, "I only hope they've studied up on the care and feeding of astral dragons." Then he chuckled to himself.

I studied the students—no, "aspirants" was what Raz had called them—a moment, deciding the wearers of light blue were the youngest. "What do the different colors of robes mean, levels of achievement?"

"Good guess. And the belts indicate the various disciplines studied." I hadn't noticed the multi-corded belts until he mentioned them. Tied around the aspirants' waists, the belts contained cords of various colors. I assumed he meant that each of the rainbow braids showed what kind of majicks the wearers could cast.

I took hold of the end of one of our harness ropes to use as a makeshift leash. A stablehand clad in leathers arrived and eyed me and my charge suspiciously. Apparently, when you were leading a dragon, you were automatically Noticeable.

Raz assumed his normal bossy manner. "Take us behind the stable to the fenced exercise yard. I don't suppose you'd have a stall this large." He meant to keep others away, not to keep the dragon in, I hoped. "And get the horses out of the area and into their stalls. I don't know what all it thinks of as food."

The stablehand maintained a discreet distance as we trudged across to the stable area. We entered a small fenced area stacked with hay-cubes. "Sit," Raz said.

I sat, and so did my dragon, looking hungrily at the horses. "No, Spunky. They're our friends. Our pets, like you." He gave me a sad-eyed beagle look, but settled down. Da slid down the tail and off the dragon's back; he searched his pockets for treats, coming up with another carrot, which Spunky carefully took out of his hand.

After we had sat a moment, I let a couple of fascinated blue-robers pet it on the neck. "He's tame, but I wouldn't get too close if I were you." I liked the looks on their faces when I teased them that way.

"She's exaggerating. It's perfectly safe, we think. But please do keep hold of the end of that rope," Raz instructed the blue-robed aspirants. They must have been first-years; they were sufficiently intimidated to cross their legs and sit down on square hay-bales with testy glances at the dragon. They were obedient to Raz, though, like those boys who've pledged a club first-year and feel they have to do what the older crew tells them, no matter how illogical. I stifled a giggle.

The dragon gave me a moony look. Absently I reached up and he brought down his great head. I scratched the eye ridge gently. He closed his eyes (I could have sworn I heard a sigh) and began to sing.

"Hrr, hrr, hnrr."

"I think he's purring." I couldn't keep the pleased sound out of my tone.

Raz looked a little sick.

Then I noticed how oddly the aspirants stared at me. "I was only kidding. Don't be afraid of him." For the first time, I saw the thick chains they'd already clasped around his tender feet, and the wide distance they maintained from him, despite their agreement to guard him.

"We're not afraid." The boy sounded less than sincere.

"Unchain this dragon this very instant. He's only a baby!" I snatched a key ring off the blue-rober's cord belt. "He'll stay if I tell him to." I turned to the dragon and unlocked the chains; they clanged to the ground. "Stay."

His eyes transmitted love. He tilted his head curiously. "Hrr?"

I raised my flute to my lips, enjoying the slackening jaws of the aspirants and Raz's pinching of the bridge of his nose as though he felt a headache coming on. Thinking of a simple melody, I fluted for it how nice the hay was for a nap, and how friendly the aspirants all were, and none of what he saw was at all good to eat. I told him how pleased I would be, and so would he, if he'd wait here for me to come back, which would be very soon. My tune slowed and gentled as I explained how sleepy he felt, and how it seemed just the right time for a nap.

He obligingly lay down—well, first he turned around three times, his great tail curling around him as if to tangle and trip him up, but it didn't; he scratched to fluff up the hay, coiled his tail around himself in the manner of a contented cat, snaked his neck around until he had it in a comfortable position, settled his head on top of his butt, and started to snore. At least I thought that was what that sawing noise must be, accompanied by little puffs of white smoke stinking of doused firewood.

"There." I snapped at the acolytes and tossed the keys back. "See how easy? Iron may be painful to majickal creatures, just as it confines majickers. Never again confine a tame animal with chains."

"Yes'm." One of the boys gulped as he caught the keys. It made me madder that, so far, I had seen only boys at this school.

"Furthermore." I pointed at the dragon's feet. "I see that he has short stout ankles that might tend to swell. See his front feet, how they're pigeon-toed, and just splay out into toes from those wide arches? You'd expect them to be long like jackrabbit feet, but they're not, just pudgy-looking. Anyhow, it means he mustn't stay on his feet too long. He's not made for standing in confined spaces or walking a lot." This was also one of the impressions the dragon had sent me as we searched for a landing spot. "Let him lie down, and don't ever force him to stand."

The expressions on their faces told me all I needed to know. My dragon was safe with them.

I dragged the drying-cloth through my flute. "And contact me immediately if he awakens and seems upset."

I turned and stalked away, enjoying their gaping. I could feel it on my back. I didn't realize until I felt Raz's footsteps behind me that they had no idea how to find me, nor where I was headed. Nor did I.

"Was that really necessary?" Raz murmured behind me as I made my grand exit out the stable gate. I stopped to wait for him—er, them. With him was Da, lagging badly, casting longing glances back at Spunky. Raz had jammed that ridiculous purple hat back on his head, only a little creased from having been smashed into a pocket—the hat, not his head. I stopped at the fence's end and crossed my arms, tapping my foot, waiting for them to catch up so I could follow Raz to wherever it was he planned to take us. Raz obliged me, shoving my upper arm forward in front of him as they caught up with me.

"Where are we going now? Stop shoving." I walked slowly, just to irritate him. I was still pleased with myself over the way I'd handled the dragon.

"First we shall head for the baths, where you can clean yourself up." He gestured, and an aspirant handed me a pink robe. Probably the color for visitors, I conjectured.

"Whatever for?" I yanked Raz's chain.

"So you can be presentable."

"For going where?"

"To the Master's study, of course."

"What did you tell me about 'of course'?"

"This time, it's fitting."

I pretended to balk, but I was eaten up with curiosity. What would Raz's majick-master be like?

# # #

The aspirant in the outer office poked his head into where we stood, fidgeting, awaiting the Master's summons. "You may go in now."

The Master Madare's study was dark and cool inside, smelling of old, beloved, crumbly book-bindings and spicy tobacco. A pipe lay on the polished greenwood desk, its bowl a carved likeness of a dragonhead. I took that as a good sign.

The wall of shutters covering the windows were partly open, admitting only enough sunbeam for my eyes to see comfortably. A large, squashy-looking chair hovered about knee-tall in the air behind the expanse of desk, its back to us. All we could see was the back of his gray head and his active elbows; he seemed busy, tracing the lines in a heavy book with his forefinger and going "Um-hmm, um-hmm."

We stepped on the blue expanse of something soft underfoot—a furlike, woolly carpet—and waited for him to turn and notice us.

His chair swiveled around and he stood. "So Raz the Wanderer returns at last." At first I cringed, but then I saw the twinkle in his grey eyes. His shoulder-hugging hair, sparse as it was, matched them save for a few streaks of yellow, and even his neatly trimmed grey beard, reminding me of a well-maintained stand of lawngrass cupping his chin and throat, had some yellowish staining; I judged that betrayed his liking for tobacco smoke. "Welcome home."

The Master Madare was of average height, yet even seated he seemed to loom over us. His round face beamed with a friendly light. I didn't feel uncomfortable, despite my majick-sense going off in myriad alarms because of the power that radiated from him, though he wasn't spellcasting, just energized with ability. He wore a dark orange robe with arcane symbols embroidered on it in silver thread, a belt of cords of every color, and soft black boots. On each sleeve was an elastic circling his upper arm at midpoint, holding in place a silver tassel. Except for the fancy clothes, he reminded me of a jolly-looking friar. His linked fingers were pillowed on his ample belly. He wore wire full-moon spectacles and a mysteriously pleased grin.

Raz bowed to the floor, holding it until the man waved him up. I belatedly imitated him, but only got out a brief deep curtsy. It was a wonder I didn't fall on my face. I hoped the master would bear in mind that I'd only recently arrived on dragonback.

Madare looked me up and down appraisingly, but with no coarseness, just curiosity. "So you are the woman in Raz Songsterson's life." His reedy, accented voice sounded amused.

Never before did I think I'd ever seen Raz truly blush. I stammered out something incoherent.

"I didn't mean to embarrass you. I merely meant that I have been wondering what could have managed to keep my prize scholar away from the Academy for the better part of a rotation." He smiled kindly, and I felt less self-conscious. "I trust you have brought him back to stay for a time."

Raz flourished that ridiculous purple hat. "Magemaster, may I present my friends, majicker-in-training Dulcinea Jean Brown, and her father—briefly my Magefather—Hector Otto Brown, both of Ladenia." Grateful to have the chance to redeem myself in terms of my dignity and manners, I sank into the formal curtsey I'd last used when I first met Raz.

Da remained standing, looking more addled than ever, hands flapping at his sides. He studied the books on the majick-master's shelves as though he were visiting a library and ignored our introductions altogether. Seeming vague, Da watched pink liquid roiling around in a bauble that apparently served as a bookend on the lowest shelf and nodded, as if to himself.

The majick-master seemed to sense there was something amiss with Da, but didn't raise an eyebrow, apparently preferring to wait for Raz to explain. Instead, he waved me up off the floor and returned my smile. "Dulcinea Brown, I greet you gladly." Turning to Da, he repeated the honorific, but seemingly expected Da's lack of response. "On your feet, please. I require no such formality from my visitors. Especially those brought to me by my favorite protégé." He motioned for us to sit in the velvet chairs at the edge of his desk, while he perched on its rounded edge, one knee bent and the corresponding foot jiggling back and forth.

My ankles and knees cracked as I stood back up, but everyone was polite enough to pretend they hadn't heard. I gathered the unfamiliar robe around my knees and settled in one of the chairs.

Raz steepled his hands into the position of prayer. "Majickmaster, sir, I have quite a bit of news to give you. Shall I tell you of my travels since I left on my mission?"

The master nodded. "Take what time you judge necessary. But first things first. Use terms that do not betray your loyalties." I was certain that meant Raz shouldn't tell too much in front of us, but the majick-master was in for a surprise.

"Worry not about what they may hear, sir. They have played significant roles in the completion of my mission, and are fully aware of everything I may discuss."

That brought a quizzical look from the majick-master. I heard shuffling of feet from the acolytes who stood at respectful attention behind us and at either side of the door, keeping a watchful eye on Da as he browsed the library. I sensed that if he reached out to touch anything, he'd be stopped in time. "I trust you have done nothing against your better judgment, Raz Songsterson."

"No, sir."

"Continue, please."

Raz straightened and cleared his throat importantly. "Yes, sir. First, the results of my mission." He told in sketchy terms about his infiltration of the Society of Mages and about their plan to terrorize Ladenia City at Festival time.

Madare's eyebrows drew together, and he looked grim.

Raz spread his arms majestically when he got to the part about the dragon. "They not only got their hands on a chunk of draconite, but they also used it to conjure a baby dragon to experiment on. Their plan is to get several mature dragons under their control, once they learn more." He smiled. "Unfortunately, to do anything, they need the stone."

"You have with you the stone?"

"More or less." Raz shot me a glance. I remembered where it was, and wondered if the dragon could digest such a thing. Apparently the treats and mice hadn't upset his astral digestion, but I didn't know what the jewel might do.

"And you have freed the dragon?" The master looked confused.

"We have it with us. Would you like to see?"

The master held up his palms. "Wait, wait. This story is not complete. I must know first how this all came about before I can understand. Is the dragon in a safe place?"

"He's in the stables. We flew in on him." I clapped my palm over my big mouth too late. The master quirked an eyebrow at me, appearing amused. "Sorry, sir."

"Don't apologize." He nodded my way. "Raz is not telling the complete story in order. That may be because I asked for the results of his mission without fully realizing what part you had played in it. For me to understand, I shall need to hear it all, keeping the details within reason, I think. Please, let us hear from the beginning this tale and its culmination in your arrival." He snapped his fingers and the acolytes stood at attention. "Serve our visitors some refreshments."

Glass clinked, and a silver tray with a pitcher and matching glasses materialized in one of the acolytes' hands. The Master gave him a pleased nod as he handed around large blue glasses with round tops and thick stems, then poured in a pastel fizzy liquid that I hoped was lemonade. When I sipped, I wasn't disappointed. But Raz seemed to get ale, and Da waved away the offer, clasping his hands behind his back and turning to the opposite wall to study the bookspines there. Out of the corner of my eye I'd seen him sauntering around the room looking up at the shelves, hands clasped behind his back. He admired the books from afar, but somehow knew not to touch the majickal tomes, short of sniffing the leathers. The aspirants assigned to chaperone him looked nerve-wracked.

The master sipped at something darkly amber and motioned for Raz to begin.

CHAPTER THIRTY-THREE

Raz had missed (or rather ignored) his calling; he should have become a bard. He told the story of how we'd come to be here, but he acted it out like a dramaturge. I could tell he'd inherited showmanship from his daddoo. He made it sound more exciting and less frustrating than I remembered, or maybe that was because he left out the tedious bits. Also, he made himself sound too important, but I forgave him that.

When Raz told of my fluting, the master gazed at me. I felt his majickal tendrils scan me; not invasively, as the monk's had done, but appraisingly. I had the feeling of being weighed and measured by a concerned healer.

"So you spoke to the dragon via your music." He quirked an eyebrow, but smiling, to let me know he was in favor of whatever I was up to.

I lifted up my flute from where it hung in its bag at my throat. "Yes, sir."

"I brought her here, Master, partially because I wanted you to hear and see her. I believe she has discovered a majick of an entirely new nature. It reminds me of what the evil ones do when they summon the elementals, yet it is not of wickedness, but seemingly of nature, like the herbal majick she knows." He swept his hand up and down me in a royal gesture, and I flinched, suddenly self-conscious.

"You seem impressed. I know you have good judgment in these matters, so I expect she has talent, as you say. But your thoughts on the subject concern me. An entirely new majick is difficult to accept." The master kept his face unreadable.

"We must study it. I believe she should be trained to understand and control her powers so she can grow in majicking."

"Certainly that is appropriate. Have you started training her?" Naturally, he knew Raz came from fluters.

"I don't believe I can train her alone. When you hear her, you will understand better."

Madare turned again to me. "All right, Dulcinea Brown. I imagine you're feeling pressured by now, what with the recommendation Raz has just given. But don't let yourself get shaky. He does lean toward exaggeration, and I promise not to be disappointed or make unfair judgments."

I ducked my head, realizing he was trying to be nice. I knew he meant well. But I was a little offended, knowing he thought me a mere slip of a village girl with whom Raz was infatuated. "Thank you, sir."

"I would be very curious to hear your music, especially if it's all that Raz claims it is."

What did he think—that Raz had done the majick himself, and was being modest? He surely knew Raz better than to suspect humility.

I stood. "Shall I play now?"

"Would you like to?" His eyes twinkled, meant to relax me, but I took it as a challenge.

Well, I knew I wasn't a fraud. I eased my flute out and stroked it with my forefinger, feeling majick well up inside of me. I had my chance to audition, and I wasn't in the mood to disappoint. "I'd like to try."

"Show me what you can do." He sat again behind his desk, smiling, rearranging his robes and folding his fingers over his belly as though waiting for a play to begin.

They hadn't brought me a thing to flute on. The dragon was resting, and there was no room in here to show him off. Besides, I didn't want to bring him to me for such a spurious reason. Nor to drag them out to the stables. What would I work my song around?

My gaze fell on a thick walking-stick behind Madare's desk. The handle was carved and painted to resemble a brown owl. It measured about the size of Da's two meaty fists one on top of the

other, and looked quite intelligent because of the talent of the
carver and decorator. Tease me and patronize me, would he? Well,
I could trick him right back.

I started a soft song about a huge, stately buttonwood tree,
and about its years in the forest deep and undisturbed. Then one
night there came a terrible angry storm. Lightning struck one of
the thickest limbs up in its top. The limb tore off and hurtled to
the ground, where it lay insensible under the leaves and moss until it turned petrified. Years later a young woodsman came walking
through the forest on a shortcut and happened to step on the end
of the limb. He picked it up and carried it home with him, where
his elderly father to pass the time began whittling things out of it.

I knew that my audience was seeing my imagery, for their
faces bore looks of fascination, if not slackjawedness on the parts of
the acolytes, whom I'd inadvertently drawn in right along with
the others. I couldn't grin because of my embouchure, but my
spirits soared with this evidence of my proper flutemagery. Now
for the extra persuading embellishments that Raz had just implied
only I could do (this I still couldn't believe, but I could accept that
he'd never met one like me before, and felt privileged to be the one
to show things off.)

Trillingly, I explained how the whittler first made a carved
brooch for his wife, and a dolly shaped like a bear for his daughter,
and several sconce-holders with faces of the Green Man who watches
over all gardens. He turned to doing scare-birds for the fence around
their squash vines, and became rather fond of the shapes. Soon all
that was left of the huge branch was a thick staff just the right size
for a walking-stick. So the old man made it into one, but where
there should have been only a handle, he carved the best bird he'd
ever carved, a wise owl to watch over the bearer and warn him of all
dangers as well as provide the proper pronunciation of words he
didn't know, just because it was so insultingly useful.

I made the stick in my song rise and dance around, and the
walking-stick leaning against the wall began to twitch. Humming
as I blew, I persuaded as strongly as ever I had since I made the

mice chew off my ropes and opened the door of the storeroom. I told the stick to rise up and twirl in the air, and sure enough the walking stick shuddered and then began to float. It twirled over the master's astonished-looking head and traced figure eights with its two ends, then rolled around to trace a circle on the ceiling. His fingers unsteepled; the look of astonishment on his visage was wonderfully fulfilling. He took hold of the arms of his chair and pushed it back a tad, staring up at the stick but getting out from under, just in case (I supposed) I decided to tap him on the head or do something equally disrespectful. I knew I wouldn't sink to that, but he had no way of knowing it. I felt like bursting out with giggles, but kept my airstream steadily flowing.

I made the stick horizontal now and had it float about the room, pointing out interesting things on the shelves with its pointy stick-end. Da followed it with his eyes, somehow knowing it was unnatural for the stick to call his attention to a porcelain unicorn, a glistening split amethyst geode, a deeply blue crystal bowl. I was careful not to touch any of the things. I peeked at the majick-master, who was nodding, mouth hanging open, as I once had in wonder at a skilled dancer in a traveling troupe I saw.

I grew a bit bolder. It wasn't very nice for me to have it ring that temple bell or tap on the chimes he kept, but I did each very gently so as to harm nothing. Impulsively, I told it to show me what Madare was proudest of on his desk; I figured if it was really his customary companion, it would somehow know.

The stick wiggled back and forth, then dipped its plain end into the inkwell on his desk and wrote my name on his blotter. Internally, I applauded its initiative, but hoped it hadn't gone too far.

I studied the majick-master again. He looked properly respectful; it was time to end. As a finale, I suggested the staff stand on end on the desk, where it tapped out rhythm to my tune. I ended with a long trill and made the stick take a bow, then float gently down to lie across the Master's desk.

The acolytes broke into applause. Raz was red-faced but looked quite pleased, whether with me or with himself for finding me, I couldn't tell. Da had even turned to watch, and was shaking his head in wonder. "What use is stuff like that to a practical man?" I heard him mutter. I let myself relax into a grin.

Madare took my measure again with a long look, then shook his head, adjusting his spectacles and having a long sip from his glass. "Indeed, Raz Songsterson, you did not embellish upon her abilities. I believe she must be trained immediately, and by us, before the Society realizes what she can do and takes her under that oppressively feathered wing. We must find the source, range, and limits of this new majick." Only then did he shake his index finger at me. "And Fortuna must have been watching over you when you chose those things to fiddle around with. Next time you are in a wizard's private study, be careful to ask first before you touch anything, even with your majicking."

Humbled a bit, I nodded seriously. "I apologize, Master. I was a bit carried away." I'd been incautious because I wanted to dispel his disbelief, but I would remember next time to control my ego, and not be prideful like Raz. If there was a next time. When would I ever need to display silly spells like that again unless I joined a traveling troupe? That was a novel idea, and I tilted my head a moment to consider it.

"You won't join a troupe with me, you silly girl. You're going to be a majicker. And you'll teach here. Won't she, Master?"

The voice was double-reeded, songlike, strange to my ears. I glanced around to find which acolyte dared to speak out to the Master, and furthermore how he'd known what I was thinking about the troupe. Madare picked up the walking-stick from his desk, and I realized what had spoken. The carved owl was animated, and now it spoke up again.

"She's good, she's good, don't you think?" It looked smug and slowly blinked its round yellow eyes at its master. "Admit it, you know she did well." If it had been a pet bird, it would have been stomping excitedly back and forth on its perch, to judge from the enthusiasm in its tone.

"Did you do that?" Raz stared at me.

Bewildered, I shook my head.

"Master, when did you animate the staff? And how did she manipulate it without being shocked senseless by your majick?" Raz seemed most excited about my possible ability to evade majickal shocks when touching others' personally majicked items; the idea both scared me and elated me. I didn't want a unique talent people would hate me for.

But Madare shook his head. "It's not majicked. I mean, it wasn't. This is no staff. It was merely a curiosity given me by the King of Marwell once upon a time as a courtesy in thanks for something I did to aid him in a diplomatic arrangement. A beautiful walking-stick, and for all I know its origins are exactly as she piped for it." He looked seriously at Raz, then at me, then at my Da. "She woke him from the wood." He looked back at me.

Words wouldn't form in my mouth. There was nothing to say. I had done that?

Good gravy!

"I didn't intend to. . . ." I couldn't think what I meant. "To interfere with your belongings. I was conceited enough to think that I needed to prove something to you. That was self-centered and ridiculous of me, and I see that I was being a very impolite guest. I apologize."

He was shaking his head. "No need for an apology. I think it's amazing. In fact, Raz didn't add sufficient emphasis to your talents. What I think we must do is make you the subject of a special study. Which I propose to undertake immediately, with the assistance of Raz and one other of my exceptional aspirants that I'll have to think on before choosing, because he or she will need to have whatever talents Raz and I lack in order to fully analyze you and your methods." He turned pensive, stroking his beard with his free hand.

The owl swiveled its head. "You know who you are thinking of choosing. Trust that instinct."

"Quiet," he instructed it. "I'm unused to being challenged by items in my wardrobe. What I am thinking is that she must start here right away in the elementary courses of majicking, in order to learn the control of her mind's power. At the same time, we will undertake our independent studies. She won't carry a full course load, but she can do enough to benefit her at the same time she teaches us."

"I couldn't do that." I burst out, attracting everyone's attention. "This is a beautiful academy, but I can see it must cost quite a lot to come here. I have no money for schooling."

The owl screeched. "Never mind that, never mind that." Madare put his hand on its head to quiet it.

"It's not necessary to worry about financing. I am taking you on as a study subject. Naturally, you will receive a full scholarship to the Academy. Including room and board as well as tuition. In return for what you can teach us, study anything you like for as long as you like."

I hesitated, overwhelmed. I looked into each of their faces as I tried to think what Raz and his majick-master might want to use me for, and concluded that they meant no harm nor manipulation. They sincerely wanted to learn what I could do and believed I could teach it to others with the same aptitude. "I'm flattered. I'm immensely flattered, and very pleased. But. . . ."

I knew I could not accept the offer. As wonderful as the Academy seemed, I could only spend a short time touring it before I must take Da home again. In fact, I wasn't sure how long I could keep Da corralled and out of trouble here. I had to end my visit and return home to run the family business, minding the store as best I could as Da allowed me, or else Da would go to the poor farm. The shop had already surely lost money by being closed so much, and Da couldn't run it alone. Furthermore, I had no intention of handing away my shop to that conniving Widder, even if she'd been a big help, and Da had grown fond of her. Especially if Da had grown fond of her. I remembered why we had brought Da here in the first place, and hoped Raz would think of a way to frame our request.

"I wish it were so simple." I glanced at Da, who had woken up a bit when I played. Now he stood in the back of the room staring at us, looking unsure of himself. "But my father is bespelled. I cannot leave him alone at home with a clear conscience. My duty, I'm afraid, lies with him."

Attention turned to the back of the room. Da gazed at the majick-master questioningly, almost fearfully.

Madare held out his hand as if to shake Da's. "Come, sir, introduce yourself. I am Madare of Alorraine, majick-master of this Academy."

Da shook hands with both of his clasped over Madare's, like the lifelong salesman he was. "Glad to know ye, sir. I'm Otto Brown." He ducked his head in a small bow, then gave us all a shamefaced look. "But I'll admit to you, I don't know why I've come here to meet you. These two"—Da waved his hands diffidently behind him, in our general direction—"why they keep laywaying me, I cannot fathom. The youth is a complete incoherent; I do not even know the girl. Yet here I am. What do you want with me?" He spread his palms plaintively and made saucer-eyes like the dragon.

"I see." Madare stood and came around the desk. "Do you have any difficulty remembering things?" As he spoke, he gently laid his hand on Da's forearm. I saw Da relax from within.

"Now that ye mention it—not that it's anything to complain about—but I do sometimes misplace things or don't recall why I am doing something. I'm not worried, mind you."

"Of course not." Madare's voice soothed, hypnotic in its persuasiveness. "Of course there's nothing to worry about. Simply relax."

As he spoke, he stroked Da's forearm with his thumb as if smoothing it out. With the other hand, he reached up to a close-by shelf and retrieved two greenish glass globes like the one Raz had "borrowed" from the majickers' storeroom. He placed one in each of Da's still-outstretched palms and gently closed Da's fingers around the globes.

On the cool glass, Da's oily fingers made slithery prints. The majick-master, his hands over Da's, brought the globes together, then slightly apart. "Repeat this action. Tell me when you feel a force pushing your hands apart."

Da bellowed his hands back and forth obediently, clinking the globes together delicately at first, then taking them wider, settling with them apart about a king's foot wide. "Ah. . . . About here, I think."

"Hold exactly thus, please." Madare muttered a few words, then began a soft chant:

> *I draw the power, drawing down*
> *From ley lines back into the ground*
> *From this man's heart I draw the spell*
> *Within this vessel to contain it well!*

The globes glowed with a dull light I instinctively knew was malevolent. They mesmerized all eyes in the room.

"Clap them together, then drop them." Madare gestured, speaking forcefully. Wide-eyed, Da smashed them into one another with force, using effort against their mutual repulsion. He apparently expected them to resist one another still, but they crashed hard together, then cracked all over, patterning themselves with crazed surfaces like a blue glass pitcher I'd once dropped in the basin. I expected them to shatter. Instead, they continued cracking all over, then deformed, mashing into each other and melding like clay into one ball two times the diameter of the originals.

I realized what was happening: Madare's spell grasped hold of the strings that held my Da and fed power to the angry spell of compelling, then drew the power out into the globes. That power had been in my Da, confusing his mind. The process was like drawing out a soul, except it was more like restoring Daddoo's soul, because I could see his eyes unglazing a bit. He stared into the glow, looking dizzy.

The ball made popping sounds and the liquidlike substance inside roiled as the globes combined, then grew brighter. Da gaped as it shaped under his hands without being under his volition. His hands slid around on the glass, despite his grip.

"Drop the ball, drop it now." The wizard repeated his instructions, almost shouting.

Hesitating only a moment longer, Da separated his hands, audibly peeling them off the ball. It hit the woven carpet with a thud and went dark. Only a few sparkles of life were now left in the sullen, shadowed globe.

CHAPTER THIRTY-FOUR

"The spell. It's trapped?" Raz broke the almost-reverent silence.

"What do *you* say?" Madare selected a set of tongs out of an umbrella-tin of tools, picked up the sphere, and carefully placed it within a leather sack that one of the aspirants hurried to hold out. "We shall study this power. It was an indwelling spell, yet outpowered from a hidden source off the majick-web. Very high-level and entwined, sophisticated. It had a tight hold on his entire personality. I've seldom seen anything like it outside of the spiritual realm. Not usually in majickwork. In the works of evil clerics—now, there I've seen things like this. . . ."

"Like being possessed," I burst out. I clapped my hand over my mouth, fearing I'd again spoken out of turn.

Madare should have scolded me for my lack of manners. Instead, he looked up at me, blinking. He nodded, solemn. "Possessed by majick."

The aspirants looked dazed, as though they had come to a Midsummer sermon just for the sake of appearances, but had suddenly ended up converted when the saints actually chose that gathering to visit in spirit form and make the ash marks upon their foreheads. Raz looked at Da, and I followed his gaze.

Da stared at his hands. Then he looked up and over at me. Recognition came into his hazel-gold eyes. "Dulcinea?"

"Daddoo!"

He held out his arms and I ran into them. We shared an old-fashioned bear hug at last as the tears splashed down both our faces.

"Where have I been? What's happened? I've been away such a long time . . . we're still away from home, it seems. But what happened? The last thing I remember, we were in Ladenia City to stay overnight."

"It's complicated, Da. I'll tell you later." My gaze met the majick-master's. "We can't thank you enough. How can I ever repay you?"

"Study with us." The master sighed. "Allow us to study you. You could benefit all of benevolent majicking if we can analyze your talent and determine how to judge others' aptitude for it. I have in mind quite a few challenges."

I looked up at Da. "Should I, Da? Should I stay here and study?"

Da ran his hands through what was left of his hair. "Hold your horses, child. First let me find out more about where we are and what's being asked of you."

Briefly Raz and I explained to Da about the Academy, leaving out how we'd gotten here and why we'd come, beyond saying that it was a long way from home, and promising to tell all later. We did mention the dragon, and his eyes lit up; maybe he remembered our ride dimly. But when we got to the part about the scholarship, he looked mystified.

"She has learned some majick? And she's needing training on the flute?" He seemed bewildered. "Fluting is for show people, traveling troupes, entertainers in taverns. I never knew it to be majickal. And stay here to study, by herself? But my Dulcinea is only a child."

"Think of the adventure she's just had, sir. Once you remember it, I mean." Raz grinned, shaking his head contradictorily. "I hope much of it comes back to you. She's done a lot of growing up."

I couldn't believe Raz would realize that, let alone admit it.

Da shook his head. "I can't remember rightly how this all came about, but I also don't believe in limiting what your children do with their lives. I always thought she'd want to follow me at the apothecary's trade and finish her studies in herbal majick. She's already learned much just from being around it." Then he shrugged.

"Whate'er she wants to do, she can do. Now it's coming back to me vaguely, how she made a story with her whistling, seems just a short time ago. But I never realized that had any value for majick. I thought it was just a hobby of yours." He squeezed my shoulders. "Dulcinea, I haven't let myself see how you've been maturing. I guess it's true that you're almost grown."

"I'm past the age of majickwake, Daddoo."

He grinned sheepishly. "Hard to see that my baby's now a young miss. Well, I guess if you can have an adventure like the one you're going to tell me about, I suppose you can take care of yourself." He scratched his chin. "If these gentlemen can explain the place more to my satisfaction so's I know it's a creditable true college of majick and that it's safe for you to stay, then. . . ." He shook his head. "Assuming that everything turns out to be the way they say it is, I suppose you can study here if you like."

"Will you be all right by yourself?" I didn't know why I felt like crying. Wasn't this what I wanted?

He frowned. "Now, why wouldn't I, lass? I feel better than I have in years. And it comes to me that I've been training that wonderful woman from next door, Juleida Groop, and she's turned out to be a right sharp merchant herself. She's somewhat of an interesting companion, as well." He grinned, and I thought I saw his cheeks pink up a little. "Can't remember when all that started, but she has learned how to keep hold of the business end of things and works well right by my side. No, you're not needed to work the shop at the moment, child—I mean, little lady." It would take him time to adjust to the idea of me as a grown-up. "I'll be just fine. You decide what it is you want to do, and you tell us."

I hugged him again.

He frowned. "I feel majicking on you of my own making. And it's not your wards of protection. What is it? What have I done while I . . . wasn't myself?" He seemed to sense that he'd been out of control. "I haven't done anything to you, have I?"

My Unnoticeability had mostly faded, but was not completely gone. I explained how he'd cast the Unnoticeable spell while he was "away." He looked sheepish, but Raz and his master laughed. "Well, I'm sorry for that, Dulcie. I wasn't thinking straight, that's one thing I know. But it's easy enough to take off." He laid his hands on my head and spoke a couple of unrememberable words. "There's it gone, all right. But I wager during your adventure it turned out to be useful, after all. Didn't it?"

"It did, Da." We all laughed. "I only wish I knew whether I want to come home, or continue the adventure. I'll worry about you. Those men in the Society had spies set to capture us from the shop. If it hadn't been for Spunky, they'd probably have gotten us."

"Spunky?"

"The dragon. I'll explain later. But I think you might need protection."

"You wouldn't be much protection, Dulcinea." Raz was speaking out of turn, so I gave him a look.

"Let me ruminate on that problem. I think I have an idea or two about how to keep them from molesting your home again." The head wizard winked, as though to let me know that Da would be all right. "Young lady, don't feel pushed in either direction. You have time to decide what you will do." He clapped his hands once. "But now, I think we have some other things to occupy us for a time."

There was one more thing pressing on my mind. Without realizing I was about to burst out talking out of turn—I seemed to do a lot of that lately—I suddenly said, "Our horses are still lost in the woods. I need to get them and bring them here or take them home."

The majick-master raised an eyebrow. Raz opened his mouth to rebuke me, but Madare lifted one palm. "Tell me where your horses are."

"I don't know exactly. We rode them part way here, before we found the dragon." In a moment I added, "It's near a hollow tree where I stuffed our rucksacks."

"I can show the acolytes, sir," Raz said. "I'll make a memory map for them."

Madare nodded. "We'll send someone for them, Dulcinea. There are several routes we've developed since Raz left us, ways we can send messengers out and receive students in. I'm sure you'll want them taken back to your father's house, and I'm sure he'll be needing a bit of extra help once he gets there, which I believe they might provide. In exchange for a bit of practical training, perhaps." He rubbed his beard. "I have just the pair of students in mind. Yes, they'll do nicely. Raz, get with my assistant right away and make that map." Raz ducked out the door, obviously knowing just where to go.

Madare rubbed his big palms together. "Who is ready for a brief tour of our facilities?"

Hands behind his back, but this time tapping his heels and bouncing a bit, Da cleared his throat. He was his own dear old self again.

Madare turned. "What can I do for you, sir?"

"There was one other thing before we leave. . . ." Da pointed up a shelf at a particular tome. The spine was marked in runes I couldn't comprehend, stamped on in gold on the black leather. "If I might take a closer look at that volume . . . I'll be quite careful in handling it. Just like to see something for a moment."

Madare took it down and handed it to him. "I can sense that you and this book are ready for each other." He smiled. "You are quite a powerful mage yourself, I'd wager, although the source of your wisdom is different from mine in that it is of nature. Yet we are men of like minds and abilities." I couldn't believe this great wizard saw my Da as a peer. "Why don't you keep this to study as long as you like, and return it to me along with the acolytes I'm sending. That should be long enough for them to learn something, shouldn't it?" His eyes twinkled. "Some practical experience away from the school will do the two I send a world of good. Whatever they ask about, or whatever you think they need to learn, teach them."

Da beamed. This wizard, a teacher of wizards, actually respected Da and his majicking. What else had I underestimated about Da, Raz . . . or myself?

"Now, for our tour. But first, I should like to see this Wyrm. Shall we pay him a visit?" He held out his hand and helped me up. Clapping Da on the back with the other hand, Master Madare put one hand on my shoulder and led us out. The acolytes followed, dogging Da's footsteps and worriedly watching his handling of the tome.

# # #

As we crossed the quad, I felt the ground vibrating. The dragon's head popped up out of a deep trench in the academy square's manicured grounds in front of the clock tower. He must have heard us approaching. His tail lashed around like a pup's, scattering several acolytes.

"Dragons love to dig, it appears." Raz's tone was unnecessarily droll. "Was he any trouble?" He addressed the question to one of the aspirants who stood guard, fists at his sides, near where the dragon lolled in his newly made mud.

"He needed to . . . do his business, sir. And we couldn't let him dig in the stable." The acolyte's face was red. "Sir."

"It's all right," said Madare. The students bowed and stepped out of the way so the majick-master could approach. "By Colin's stone, Songsterson. You weren't joking. I believe you've brought us an actual True Dragon. It's something I've never seen in all my travels."

Raz's cheeks and forehead pinked up a little. He bowed. "Please feel free to examine him, sir. He's perfectly tame."

I hoped Raz's confidence was properly placed. I also had my flute at the ready.

Behind us, Da lagged by the fountain, looking up at the buildings as if he'd never seen them before. When the dragon caught Da's scent, it raised its head and craned its neck back and forth until it found him. Da reached us and stepped gingerly toward the dragon, but before Da could flinch or duck, the dragon's head shot out and settled gently on Da's shoulder. "Hrrr, hrrr!"

Da laughed and pulled more carrots out of his pocket. "I remember you, fellow. Now I recall riding here on you, though I believed I was merely having a vivid dream. But here I am and indeed here you are. Dulcinea called you Spunky, didn't she? Well, Spunky, boy, how about a snack?"

"I see these two have taken a particular liking to one another," murmured Madare.

"Possibly because Magefather Brown has continually been slipping the dragon various little treats that he keeps in his pockets." Raz considered a moment. "Astral dragons, amazingly enough, it appears can eat while in this plane. Although, since they feed on majickal energy while here instead of foodstuffs, I forecast we'll find they don't absorb anything they chew."

"Excuse me, sir." Another of the acolytes guarding the dragon came to the master, bowing. "But that much is true. We've found during the course of watching the dragon that some items he must have swallowed have, er, passed unchanged through his system." He held out a handful of sugar lumps and carrots, stuck together and slightly damp, but recognizable. "The lads over there have caged the mice that, um, came out a while ago." I was relieved to hear the mice hadn't suffered a worse fate.

"Master!" Raz turned to Madare, excited. "That means that if we'll keep watch, and have the aspirants keep close track of his, er, digestion . . . we might well recover the dragonstone."

"Recover it?" The master hadn't, I remembered, yet heard exactly what the fate of that majickal jewel had been.

Raz turned. "Give this dragon the run of the grounds, accompanied by Magefather Brown, if he will, and his chaperones. Moving about will help it eliminate the stone." He added in a worried tone, "I certainly hope he hasn't assimilated it somehow or that it hasn't managed to get stuck."

"You will, I trust, enlighten me on this topic further." The Master regarded Raz sternly.

Raz explained about the tiny detail he'd skipped during the tale of our escape from the evil citadel. "But if the other things he's swallowed survived unharmed, the stone is likely to turn up."

Da roared with laughter. The dragon, not understanding but enjoying his new companion, joined in singing a happy purring tune. Da patted the dragon's neck and flourished his other hand. "Let us tour, then. Lead on, Spunk, but ensure we're followed by these uneasy droppings handlers." He winked at me. "Always remember, child. Curb your dragon."

But I knew it didn't matter. "It won't make any difference, really, whether we find that stone or not." Abruptly, I had their full attention.

Raz looked blank. "Why not?"

"Because no one knows how to use the dragonstone to send him back to the astral plane, even if he wants to go. I promised to take him home, but unless somebody figures that thing out better than Raz did, I won't be able to keep the promise."

Madare nodded. "The stone, if it turns up, will be put under guard in my personal control. We shall study it until we determine how to properly use or dispose of it, pledging of course never to use it for exploiting free dragonkind."

"It would have been a shame to UnConjure him and return him home before we met him. He's so friendly he would make a good pet." Da petted him on the nose, then scratched his eyeridge. The dragon made sounds of contentment. "I declare, boy, I wish I could keep you myself. Then we'd never lack for protection at the shop."

The majick-master looked contemplatively at the two. "I think you may get your wish."

"What's that?"

"Majicker Brown, you seem a man well suited to study the dragon. The most important thing is rapport, and you have that, I can see."

"Oh, I'm flattered, that I am." Da chuckled. "But I couldn't stay here. I've got to return to my business."

"I will vouch for Magefather Brown's abilities and the excellence of his facility for herbal majicking," said Raz quickly. "I learned much from him."

Madare stroked his beard contemplatively. "I could set up a study program for you, Majicker Brown, as well. Your study subject would be the dragon; you could take two of my advanced research assistants to help set up and run experiments. Of course you'll also have the pair of acolytes I already mentioned, and they can assist you as well. We'd require status reports every four to eight days, but I don't foresee a problem."

"How can you all communicate?" Raz was remembering his own troubles in contacting the Academy from outside. "By carrier pigeon? I thought the pigeon program had been suspended after Master Lapir retired."

"Some of the pigeons are still in use, but I have a better idea." Madare brought his palms together under his chin. "We do try to minimize ground travel, so we cannot communicate by messenger, but majick proves superior anyroad. I will send with you a new scrying device we have devised. It uses new methods that circumvent the Society's block on our surrounds. In this way we can keep communications open." He raised his hands. "As to how we get the research subject there, I would not object to your flying the dragon home, if Dulcinea can show you how to manage him—and I'm certain she can; you're plenty capable a majicker, if not with music, then with other talents. The tome you've borrowed should also help you with your majickal communications."

Da hugged the book tighter, grinning all the more. "I'll take good care of it."

"I sense you have plenty of room to keep and study the dragon, so I can't see why it wouldn't work." Madare smiled. "To be frank, I don't think we would be able to keep him properly here at the Academy. There are too many dangers to the aspirants and visitors who might try untrained majick on him. But where there aren't so many eager but incautious students who'd want to try out their skills, he'd be safer and happier."

Da looked happier than I could remember seeing him. "Let's talk about that further. That would be extraordinary."

Madare swept an arm forward. "We shall talk. But now, the tour."

"I think I'd rather go with ye than walk my dragon." Da chuckled, and the dragon made his happy sound. We left Spunky in the stable-yard with instructions to watch for the stone if they must, but to keep the dragon safe above all. Da slipped the last sugar-cake to the dragon, and Spunky sighed and purred.

As we walked to the laboratories, Da fell into step with me and put his arm around my shoulder. "Dulcinea, I am still pondering this idea, about your studies here. I am leaning in your direction. This Madare seems to be our type of person. It seems to me he has much to teach you. And it sounds like you may be able to teach all these highfalutin' scholars a thing or two." He shook his head. "Imagine that, my daughter teaching majick to the ivory tower. If, after this tour, I am satisfied that the Academy is legitimate"—he patted my upper arm—"I think you should stay."

"Oh, Daddoo." I didn't know whether to shout for joy or take to my couch in tears of mourning for the end of my childhood. Though I supposed it had actually ended some time ago, when Raz Songsterson walked into our workroom to take his majickal audition.

CHAPTER THE LAST

(Chapter Thirty-five)

The academy spanned an area greater than our whole village at home, with specialized buildings located in clusters at a distance from the aspirants' living quarters and the guilds' classrooms. They raised most of their own food and kept livestock for wool, eggs, and meat. They had dwarf fruit trees and berry bushes planted in what they called an agricultural ring, which divided the Academy grounds into large pie-shaped sections, but I thought it could have been done just for beauty's sake.

We walked through the stone building containing classrooms, shielded chambers, and majicklabs for one of the guilds—I think it was air majicking—and the large lecture room used for all the introductory courses. I would be spending some time in there my first rotation, if I stayed. One class was in session, and we stood quietly in the back while a boy recited the periodic table of majickal elements. I thought I did see two females in that classroom.

In the nicest of the stone buildings, the one closest to the advanced studies house, Madare brought us to the east wind's corner. He took out a key ring and unlocked a door leading to a stone staircase. We ascended the circular stair inside that turret to the third level.

Here we found a circular workroom with a radius of about a dragonslength (my new definition for two horses' lengths.) The curved wall was lined with windows, and I saw the entire of the Academy campus proper laid out beneath us, the rest of the grounds stretching all the way to the stone wall defending it. I could even see to the tops of the trees in the wood beyond. In the room's center stood a dais with a round worktable, and there were slates on easels to use for writing on. Shelves, drawers, and cubbyholes under the tabletop served as storage space.

Madare stood behind us. "This is the place I have in mind to devote to you." He laid his hands on our shoulders. "You two will study and analyze flutemajick. You must discover how to find those with the aptitude for it, and then develop a teaching method to draw out their talents. Not everyone will experience spontaneous development at majickwake, the way Dulcinea did."

"Is it really possible that others can do this as well?" Raz's voice echoed off all the hard surfaces.

"I believe it is probable. This new majick could revitalize our discipline. Attract new talent into our walls."

"Sounds like it could really put your place here on the map," Da put in.

"Da!" I was embarrassed, but no one contradicted him.

Madare reached up to hooks on the wall, where there hung several belts like the aspirants wore. These were unlike the ones I'd seen on the aspirants; these had different colors, orange and peach and cantaloupe and coral. "This would be your belt, one I'd saved for future discoveries. The shades of orange will be reserved for the music majickers." He handed me the belt. "You would wear the first one."

My cheeks burned. I bobbed a curtsy. "I feel honored, sir."

"Raz might earn his, as well." He chuckled as he handed Raz a second one. "You will study other disciplines, but your major focus will be to teach and to discover others with the same untrained gift. As full partners in the new Music Lab, you'd immediately start designing aptitude tests and a curriculum."

"Immediately?"

He nodded. "I would like that. But it is up to you."

I shivered. I couldn't deny the excitement I felt upon hearing these plans. What great potential these studies might hold. I hadn't realized it until now, but I was so extremely fortunate to have my powers. And now I'd be able to work with Raz and his circle in ways that might result in a completely new understanding of majick. While they, in turn, studied me.

And what irony in the thought of Raz studying me. Not to mention the appeal of being with him, close by, every day, again. But the suddenness of staying a long way from home for I didn't know how long slapped me hard.

I would have to stand here watching Da ride our dragon back to my home, knowing my place had been taken by that Widder; he'd go not with Raz and me but with two acolytes I knew nothing about, and I'd fret here, waiting for them to scry a message back upon their safe arrival. I had misgivings about being able to learn the majick here, along with worry that my majick might not be so fascinating once they got into the study of it. I might even lose it while being examined; I'd heard of many aspiring majickers who lost their abilities entirely once surrounded by doubters and challenged to perform.

But then Raz slipped his hand into mine. I thought he was going to shake it to congratulate me, but instead he squeezed. "I'm so proud of you, Dulcinea."

I went weak in the knees.

Majick-master Madare smiled. And I think he winked.

Da looked at me solemnly. "And I am even prouder. You are your mother's daughter."

He'd never said that before. I closed my eyes to keep from crying.

A quick prayer of thanksgiving was in order. While I was at it, I needed help. *Saints, any of you, please send me guidance.*

When I opened my eyes, I had my answer. All the shining faces surrounding me, the dear people I loved—even Madare already, with his quick approval of me and acceptance of my talents as worthy—they told me I must fulfill my destiny. I had been born for a particular mission and purpose, and this must be it. I could do this!

Besides, with an adventure such as we'd just had under our multi-corded belts, how could we help but do even more amazing things once we graduated?

Whether or not Raz Songsterson realized it, there was one thing I'd always known. I knew we would make a great team.

—*The End*—

—*of Book One: DULCINEA, or WIZARDRY A-FLUTE*
Read the Next Book!

Here's a preview of the first chapter of the next book in the Dulcinea and Raz series, *Dulcinea's Dragon*.

DULCINEA'S DRAGON

CHAPTER ONE

For what seemed like the eleventy-first time today, I scraped the enchanted chalk across the laboratory tabletop. The runes *thorn*, *gee*, and *yogh* already glowed dully in what would become the center of my hexagram. I held in my mind's eye an image of the lines of force traced green on the smooth slate, lines of majickal force replacing my dusty chalk lines. Briefly my tongue pressed against my teeth as I brought the chalk to the final vertex. I slowly retraced the entire figure, whispering the incantation; then I waited.

And for the eleventy-first time, nothing happened.

"Drat!" I dropped the chalk on the table; it clacked against the marble and broke. "What am I doing wrong?"

Perhaps I had mispronounced something as I recited the incantation. Or I wasn't, as Raz often teased, holding my mouth just exactly right. Raz Songsterson could be a trying mentor, one moment unthinkingly tagging me "Dulcinea the Dunce," the next patting my shoulder and calling me his best girl. In front of the class. Naturally, neither phrase was more than a taunt. I didn't think I received any special treatment while under his tutelage, because I was merely his student now, as I continually reminded myself. Raz was fond of me, but the kind of affection I had for him was not reciprocated. Sometimes I struggled to keep my romantic feelings toward Raz from clouding my thoughts.

The glow was already fading from the runes. I ran my fingertips lightly over the outer chalked marks, rubbing them out as easily as any stray lines. My fingers didn't tingle; the marks hadn't even a pinch of majick in them, then. For a moment I held my breath, then puffed it out slowly. I spread my fingers on the table, pressing gently, and took another deep breath. I had to relax before I tried the spell again.

I opened my commonplace book to the explanation of this first laboratory exercise, the one I'd flubbed in front of everyone the previous day. The one that I still hadn't gotten right yet. I reread it solemnly, running my forefinger under each line. The first few words illumined, indicating the initial step.

Carefully I copied the runes with a new stick of chalk. They took on a faint, almost imperceptible glow; I was definitely getting some majickal signal.

I sketched the six-sided figure first, then added the equilateral triangles, one bristling out from each flat edge like pointers on a blessed compass. This formed the hexagram in whose center my spellpower should be concentrated. I visualized the practice coin I was to summon into the center of the hexagram, the only coin still remaining in the laboratory supply room from where all my classmates had called theirs. Slowly I retraced the entire figure in one unbroken motion, without recrossing any line, always moving widdershins, and enunciating the incantation exactly as Raz and Majick-Master Nyessa had taught:

> *"That which I seek,*
> *Our attraction is weak;*
> *Let it grow stronger,*
> *And wait no longer:*
> *Come to me*
> *As I call thee!"*

Nothing.

"Blast!" My hand flew to cover my mouth. I knew better than to burst out with curses while spellpower might still shimmer invisibly in the area. Yet this elementary summoning spell was supposed to be simple, as it had been for my classmates. Why was I having so much trouble?

I'd made little progress in Spell Reading and Writing; I suspected I was flunking Introductory Incantations; and I knew I was barely hanging on in Foundations of Spellcraft. The only classroom I hadn't shamed myself in was Majickal Compounds, all about the uses and making of various preparations of material components for magecraft, but then compounding should come easily to the daughter of an apothecary: I'd been preparing, and sometimes inventing, herbal remedies since I could sit up unassisted in Daddoo's lap and tie a string around the mouth of a burlap bag.

Thinking about my difficulties made my head swim. Maybe it had been a mistake to come so far from home to the majickal academy, especially when they'd had such high expectations for me. Worse, I felt I must keep trying to prove that Raz had been right to vouch for my trainability and talent. I was beginning to fear that I'd never learn any mageworks but the flutemajick I already had, which had come so easily back home. How much longer the majick-masters would tolerate my poor performance was anyone's guess.

I couldn't let down Raz and Daddoo and the other majick-masters who believed in me. I had to get this right, and quickly. Rubbing out the failed marks, I started over.

Again I dragged the chalk around and dutifully chanted the incantation with all the confidence I could muster. As I brought the chalk to the final vertex and the chalked lines met, I held my breath.

Still nothing. I'd bollixed it again.

There should at least have been some glow, a spark, an echo of majick. "What am I missing? What's wrong with me?" My temples throbbed. I stuck my fingers into my hair and pulled it out to its length, catching several snarls, which I yanked at angrily. "Oh, for the love of majicking. I'm going to make this work."

Jerking open the door to the supply cabinet that formed the lab table's base, I rummaged through the numerous majickal instruments underneath, hoping to come across one that might help me find the problem. A blue glass scrying bowl, crystal titration cylinders, somebody's discarded athame with a rusted blade, the silver-plated iron damping rod Raz had stuck under here and forgotten about. I dimly remembered the function of each arcane-looking device from Majick-Master Nyissa's first lecture in Spellcraft.

What I needed was something to measure and monitor the power draw of a spell. I thought I saw something interesting behind the dusty stacks of previous years' notebooks. Reaching to the back of the cabinet (and getting a noseful of dust), I pushed aside a cracked cauldron and found a magerule. At least I thought that's what it was. I recalled copying down what Raz told us in class, and flipped to the proper page. The illustration looked right.

Constructed of slim, light solid rods of magemettle wood, a magerule is the most expensive and important instrument in the majickal laboratory. It consists of three nested globes that are not solid, but made of grids of flexible twigs. The globes are threaded on a thumb-thick branch of rowan-wood, and this stands vertically on a tripod stand. Placed in parallel with the linked material components for a spell, this device governs the drawing of power from the Web of majick, preventing one from pulling more power than that for which it has been set.

We hadn't had a demonstration of any of the equipment yet; first-form students apparently didn't use the magerule immediately. But I needed more help than the others, and I had special access to this lab because of the flutemajick project I was supposed to be doing with Raz; I would be extra careful. Biting my lip, I pulled out the magerule.

At Raz's last lecture, I'd copied down the suggested range of power to be drawn for this spell; if I remembered correctly, the magerule would rotate when power was being drawn, and then would glow to indicate the level of flow of the majickal force, with a brighter glow indicating a stronger force. I was sure that a trained eye could guess the levels fairly accurately. The best I could hope for, without asking Raz and revealing my continued difficulty in grasping the most basic concepts of Web majicking, would be to know exactly at which point the majick draw began, and where it failed.

I couldn't yet hold everything in my head. Someday, supposedly, I'd know how to properly monitor my own power draw from the web of majick, and I would not need any equipment. At the moment, I wondered whether the equipment would even help.

As I assembled the magerule and connected its grounding wire to the table's surface, I found myself humming a soothing tune, one I'd invented for my flute as a sort of celebration of summer evenings. I needed to calm down, so that my state of mind wouldn't interfere with my workings. I wondered if fatigue and irritation could prevent my mind from contacting the spellpower source, connecting with the web of majick. The proper attitude, as my Daddoo had always said, was the battle half won.

I rubbed down the tabletop, this time with a soft ceremonial cloth instead of my oily fingers, polishing it to a clear sheen until I could see my pale self reflected in it, all the while thinking determinedly positive thoughts. Maybe I should try to summon something closer, something that I already owned. What kind of majicker couldn't pull a coin out of her own purse?

I could flute it out in a candlemark. I glanced over at my things, hanging on their accustomed wall hook, my money pouch on its string behind the tunic and leggings, barely a kingsarm away. Maybe I was a little conceited about my special talent, but I could've fluted my purse-strings unknotted and sent a coin into the air, and if it hadn't come out dancing and flipping and spinning across the table, I'd have lain down with a cool cloth on my forehead, suspecting a spell of the ague coming on. But if the others could do it this other way, I could, too. I had to believe that.

I started the whole process over again. This time, I invented my own incantation.

"O ancient bonds
of chalk and ash,
Bring forth one coin
From my purse's stash!"

The very air lay still and silent. The fine transparent hair on my arms stood up as I felt the power I'd raised at last. The lines on the hexagram traced blue, a sparkle of light racing around like the beam of a majicklight and leaving its blue trail, as though touched by the toes of a fairy. It was like watching a parade of glow-worms.

Soon the majickal ikon glowed strongly. The runes within began to wriggle and form themselves into the word of power. My first spell was working.

But then everything stopped. The runes wibbled like dying worms, then froze. The blue faded like a doused cookfire. No coin materialized. I heaved a sigh and had just reached for the cloth once again when a faint popping noise directly overhead startled me.

Something wet splashed down onto my sleeve. I looked up just in time for another huge splash to hit me in the face, just above my right eye. I covered my eyes with my hands and peeked carefully out through the spaces between my fingers. Purple stuff on the ceiling. Purple and jiggly. The ceiling was covered with blobs of purple jelly. . . jam that didn't seem to be sticking up there terribly well. More splashes ensued, at a faster pace, and landing all over the tabletop and my clean lab robe.

The spell had misfired.

This was evil stuff, stinking like rancid yak grease or the fetid pulpy fruit of the yarbir tree, and sticky as any marmalade besides. I'd have a time of it, cleaning all that off of every surface in the lab. While holding my nose. But I couldn't stop to clean now, for the stuff continued to form at an alarming rate. New clumps formed by the moment, hanging just long enough to leave stains all over the ceiling before dripping down on me and my clean lab. Another sequence of pops, and liquid purple goop streamed down from the ceiling in slow tornadoes.

Maybe I could blame it on the upstairs lab, claiming someone'd spilled goop down through the floorboards. Into this shielded chamber? Nobody would believe me. I was a terrible liar, one of those people who'd start giggling or looking up at the ceiling the moment the lie hit my lips. I only hoped this gunk was washable.

The first order of business was to disconnect the wayward spell from the majickal Web from whence it drew its energy. Unlike the flute-majick that came to me naturally, for which the energy source was somewhere within me, this kind of working was dangerous if uncontrolled. Spellcasting in this fashion drew on a far larger battery, and though messy, this misfire had been lucky.

Taking a ceremonial cloth, I began trying to erase the lines of force, but of course I couldn't get my hand anywhere near them. They glowed with the spell majick they were drawing. I had to think, use the techniques I was supposed to have learned in class.

Pushing my sticky hair back from my face—and hoping the purple stuff wasn't harmful; maybe I could market it throughout the Academy as hair pomade—I tried to recall how to disconnect from the Web's power. I squeezed my eyes shut and concentrated, visualizing the Web as a core of molten majick just beneath the ground, glowing red at its center; I imagined its orange, pink, and maroon threads of power radiating out in all directions underfoot. To find the one that my spell was connected to, I would need to push the power until I could feel with my mind where to go.

Too bad I'd never yet felt any power with my mind in five moons at this Academy. I cupped my hands and began pushing in around the edge of the circle of force that theoretically should have formed itself above my hexagram. By the right-hand rule (forming my hand into a loose fist and following the way the thumb pointed as a guideline), I figured which way the power radiating from the hexagram was flowing. Now I should be able to push it into a skinnier cylinder and then "roll" it into a thinner and thinner log, like rolling dough for sweet-cakes. Turning it into a kind of snake. A snake containing not venom, but power. The effort was mental, not physical, but since my image represented a physical analogue to what I needed to do mentally, the visualization would work.

At least it would have for any of my classmates. I should have been able to feel the power pushing back. I should have felt it growing into a slimmer cylinder, and should have easily found the threads that led into the Web of majick, an ethereal latticework that is wrapped around the planet as ley lines of force. I could then stop the spell's action by following this power down to the first line of force, the spell's origination point on the Web, and unweaving it like a tangled bootlace until I could find where to snip it free. Then I should all at once feel the power pushing back at me, and I should catch hold of it with my arcane grip, the mental grip majickers use to manipulate the power threads. With my mind, I'd search, un-tat, and untangle the virtual energy cords; I'd majickally snap the string, closing the energy leaks and the connection.

Instead, another wet plop landed on my forehead and ran down in rivulets like sticky bangs.

Maybe I could untangle this majickally if I wanted to wait until I was knee-deep in the goo, and then yell for Raz. No, never for him; it would be less humiliating to call for one of the initiated acolytes, each of whom served as majickal lab assistants for a year before they took on apprenticeships, or even for a majick-master. I didn't want Raz to know the depth of my incompetence.

Reaching out with my mind, I felt nothing but an insistent warmth and the buzz of the energy, nothing like the arms or threads or whatever it was you were supposed to grab hold of. I didn't have any arcane grip or astral hands or anything of the sort. I had to squint my smarting eyes against the brightness of the blue lines, and defend my head against the continuing onslaught of wet purple weirdness. This called for drastic measures.

Fortunately, I was not a complete cudge. When I'd first started working in the lab, Raz had shown me an emergency disconnection to be used when one simply couldn't wait for it to work the proper way. I only hoped I didn't kill myself trying it. Of course, that outcome was mildly appealing, in that it would spare me the embarrassment of everyone knowing about my misachievements.

I reached under the table and grabbed Raz's damping rod by its rubber-sheathed end. Just in time, I remembered to wrap a ceremonial cloth around my hands to protect my forearms. I rapped the rod on the tabletop, wincing at the thought of scratching the smooth stone, and then rammed it into the majickal force field. The lines sputtered and snapped out sparks that burned tiny holes in the cloths. As soon as I could inch the rod further along—as the force field diminished in strength—I swept it slowly across the hexagram, erasing the figure in a shower of orange sparkles. Metal disrupts majick, especially iron, and this rod had been silvered, then bespelled to assist in the process without allowing damaging throwback to race down those threads I could never feel and back to the nexus of power. (If it had been just any iron rod, I could have been killed by the power, and it could also have disrupted spells all across the web. Thus, the method was not a spellstopper typically taught to beginners.)

Steam, then white smoke, rose from the surface of the marble. Like doused flames, the blue threads ebbed away, and the hexagram turned to chalkdust. The gel stopped forming, the remaining blobs quivering to quiescence. Their vibration stopped, and so did the sizzling. If there was residual majick, it wasn't reproducing.

It was the dullard's way out. But at least it had stopped the glop.

What a mess. I reached over to wipe the nasty purple goop off the magerule, but as I touched it, it creaked ominously. The innermost of the three nested spheres wobbled, and the outer pair rotated widdershins at odds with one another, restlessly, instead of in unison and careful motion together as would be normally expected. Reflexively, I reached out, but snatched my hand away immediately. The magerule was hot as a cinder. As I examined it more closely, I saw that it had started cracking at the majick-welds. That was ominous. It did, however, seem to be cooling down quickly.

I must have drawn an overload. Bless watchful Saint Alyncia (the healer, who served also as a guardian and protector of novices in any field) that the magerule's governance had prevented a worse mishap. I only hoped the rule could be repaired.

The smell was starting to make my stomach wrench. I tied a rag over my nose and wiped down my hair and face as best I could. Disgusting. I supposed it was lucky my hair hadn't grown out past my shoulders yet; if it were hopelessly ruined, at least losing it wouldn't mean wasting a whole year's growth. Perhaps it could be put aright by majick. Raz would probably tell me I should wear a hat until my skills improved.

"Why me?" I asked the ceiling as I mopped the revolting spills. I jumped when it seemingly answered.

"Perhaps you're rushing things."

I turned. Raz stood in the doorway, arms crossed. How long had he been there? His voice was mild, but his words had stung.

I exhaled. "Raz, I'm just trying to keep up with the rest of the class. I flubbed this spell in front of all those people at the trials yesterday. Now I can't even get it right alone in the lab. How can they let me work as a teacher when I can't even learn the simplest of brings?"

He just looked at me. "Dulcinea. . . ."

But I ignored his tone of voice. "I mean it, Raz. I may not be able to do this. I'm having so much trouble learning the basics of majicking as a first-year student, I honestly wonder if I'll even earn my first cord." Students were awarded silken-corded belts to signify their current levels. "What happens if I can't pass elementary level incantations?"

Raz was strangely quiet in response. He wore a loose indigo robe, its satiny sleeves rolled to mid-elbow on his lanky arms and tied in place with gold braid. Matching braid trimmed the tops of his best boots and tied back his long raven hair. He had reached

the second-highest level in the academy, as explained by the collection of cords woven about his skinny waist. His silver sigil
gleamed on its cord around his neck. It was odd that he wore such
formal dress just to stop by and visit me in the lab, but I was too
angry at myself to consider it.

"It's just not working out. If I were a quitter. . . ." I swiped at
the tabletop ineffectually, but I was ready for a full-scale temper
tantrum. Normally I could listen endlessly to Raz's mellifluous
voice with its Marwellian burr, deep without being raspy, but now
every word he said rankled me. Though he hadn't said much yet.
Where was his usual caustic wit? Buried in purple goop?

I shut my spellbook, muttering the wards and tracing a
snakestail with my forefinger as I tied it closed and set the latch
before stuffing it under my robe, into the inside pocket of my
student tunic. My purple-splotched lab robe angered me further.
Irritable, I held out my stained white sleeves. "Look at this. It's
simply ruined."

Raz looked, but I could tell he wasn't really seeing me. The
remoteness of his emerald gaze stopped me in mid-rant. "What is
it, Raz?"

He cleared his throat. "I certainly hope, Dulcinea, that your
problems with the coursework can be overcome. I have every confidence that if they can be, you will put your mind to doing just
that. If I can assist you in any way, I will. Still, you may, of course,
be right. Although you have adjusted well to student life over the
past three moons, there can be problems other than homesickness
that prevent one's complete devotion to the learning of the majickal
craft. You are the one in the best position to know." Raz's voice was
too quiet. He should have been mocking. And that was a strange
thing for Raz to say.

"Raz Songsterson, you're scaring me. What's going on?"

He stepped all the way into the lab and gestured toward the
lab stools, his flowing sleeves barely escaping being soiled by the
goop on the tabletop. His nose wrinkled slightly, probably in response to the overpowering stench of yak. "Sit down, Dulcinea."

I sank onto one of the wooden stools. "What's wrong?" For a moment I thought Raz was going to tell me I had failed so miserably I was to be sent home. But then I realized that message would more likely come from the head majick-master, and surely not before the end of the term. Suddenly my stomach filled with cold water. Something at home, my daddoo there by himself. "Is Da all right?"

Raz hesitated before answering. "As far as I know."

As far as he knew? That meant nothing. Ice gripped my vitals, and I started trembling. "Tell me what you know, Raz. You're really upsetting me."

He blinked his cat-green eyes. "Nothing has happened at home that I know of, Dulcinea." Just as my heart started beating again, he amended it. "I wouldn't know about anything like that, would I? I'm not privy to all the news. I only came to tell you that you're wanted in the Master Madare's chamber at once."

"I've been called to the head majick-master's office?" I grabbed the edge of the counter to keep from falling off my stool. "Raz, that means something's really wrong! What's wrong?"

"Nothing's wrong."

I knew I was babbling. I couldn't help it. "Of course something's wrong. Oh, saints. I know it perfectly well." I stood, beginning to pace; I had to work off my nervous energy or I might explode like the purple goop, flunking student all over the ceiling. "This is doubly ironic, because I thought I would do so well. Until I've learned the basics, I know I can't be allowed to teach. But that doesn't matter at the moment, because we haven't done nearly enough work on the new study sequence for flutemajicking to take on a student." I omitted any mention of Raz's neglected responsibilities. I sat back down as my knees became too wobbly to stand. "But that's not a reason for being called to see the head majick-master." Something else struck me. "Raz, something's happened at home. Hasn't it?"

"Dulcinea, please try to maintain a hold on your wild imagination. Nothing's happened at home. Not that I know about." He amended it quickly, making my breast tighten. Raz wasn't usually such a stickler for precision in honesty. "You have a gift, Dulcinea, for leading conversations away from the main issue. What I came to tell you"—his left eyelid drooped slightly, the way it did whenever he was about to tell me something he'd rather not—"and I would never have interrupted your work had it not been important, is that we're both wanted in the Master Madare's office. At our earliest convenience. Which would be now."

My teeth clenched, then prepared to chatter. They felt as though they might just drop out on the floor. "But, Raz. This must be something awful. Else why would the Master summon both of us?" Raz shouldn't have been made to take me to the head-master. He was not to blame for my shortcomings. I definitely couldn't bear to be disciplined—dismissed—in front of Raz. "He must understand that I have to stand on my own merits. You can't be held responsible for my mistakes simply because you recom-mended me." My grades; it had to be about my grades. "I know I failed the first trials yesterday, but they told me not to worry, that I could make them up. They said everybody has trouble at first, adjusting to life away from home."

In response to Raz's disapproving glance, I made a conscious effort to stop wringing my purpled hands. But I couldn't control the wavering in my voice. "Or it's the new course that I haven't finished. Oh, sweet Saint Alyncia. Now I'm going to get thrown out of the Academy." The townfolk would turn up their noses, and told-you-so would be in everyone's gazes whenever they met mine; they'd be thinking, "We knew you wouldn't make it. It's only fitting you were knocked off your high horse, little miss Dulcinea Jean Brown. Imagine, going to the majickal academy when you belong right here, helping your Da in his shop."

To Raz's credit, he didn't roll his eyes. "Dulcinea, I don't think that's it, either." Raz glanced at my clothes as though for the first time. "You'd best clean yourself up, and quickly." He reached up for one of the clean robes hanging on hooks on the back wall and threw it at me.

Worried now for sure, I swapped robes in front of him, glad I had a clean tunic and leggings underneath. I'd stop by my room and wipe myself down as best I could. I scribbled a note and stuck it on the lab door with a blob of putty, hoping everyone would respect my request not to open it until after I had a chance to clean up. Secretly I was glad Raz would be with me; this was my first formal call-down, and I could take comfort in Raz's proximity. But only if I could rinse the gunk out of my hair first.

# # #

The Master's smile was wan as he stood behind his desk to welcome us into his office. His purple robe with its tiny white stars shone softly under the sky-windows over his desk; his long graying hair was in a neat queue down his back, and his mustache and beard were as neatly waxed as though he were receiving foreign royalty. He gestured me out of my deep curtsy almost instantly. "Dulcinea Brown. I see you've been busy with your classwork. Having a spot of difficulty in the lab, are you? I mean, this morning?"

I felt my cheeks burning. He'd heard, all right. "A little bit, sir. But how could you know already?"

"I sniffed majick-singe on you first thing." Majickal burns were a dangerous phenomenon in spellcasting. But what he probably smelled was the rancid yak grease. I hadn't been able to get all of it off without a proper wash.

"I'm all right, sir. I've just come from having misfired a spell." I ducked my head, shamed. I was wearing a scarf to hide my sticky hair, but at least my face had come clean.

"You dealt with it properly, I'd wager. Come, sit down." He reached for a chair; gently he eased me towards it. "I have something I must speak to you about."

My heart thudded. All at once, his deferential manner toward me—which didn't seem to extend to Raz—struck me as odd. Raz had positioned himself behind me, perhaps to hide his expression from me. I'd been uneasy for good reason, it seemed. Why should Raz, instead of an acolyte, be sent to bring me here? And why was Raz going to be allowed to stay while we talked?

My knees buckled. I grabbed for the edge of his massive carved clearwood desk and lowered myself into the chair with caution. "Sir?"

"Dulcinea. . . ." His face softened along with his tone of voice. "I'm afraid I'm going to have to ask you to return home at once."

"Sir. . . ." My ears began to whine with my pulse. "Am I being removed from the course of study?"

His eyebrows flew up. "Nothing like that, no. It's a rather more delicate matter." He cleared his throat. "Something that requires your attention at home."

I suddenly felt my gorge rising in panic. "What is it? What's happened?" For the first time I realized that far worse news might await me, and everything started to fade to black. "It's my Da, isn't it?" I squeezed my eyes shut and swallowed hard. "Has he fallen ill?" *Oh, merciful saints, protect him.* Huge hands squeezed my chest as I started praying silently, on the verge of panic.

The Master reached across the desk and grasped my arm. "No, there's nothing like that." He put his hand over both of mine, covering my livid knuckles, which were clenched on the desk's edge. "Nothing like that at all. Your father's fine. I have just spoken with him, in fact."

I could breathe again. "Oh, thank the saints. I'm sorry for being so—um, you've spoken with Daddoo?" I looked around, but Da hadn't appeared.

The Master smiled. "Via a new voice communication spell, Dulcinea. We've constructed a majickal apparatus by which our voices may be first encoded, then transmitted along the Web to a similar apparatus at the destination, using a simple spell that was previously developed for maintaining contact between buildings within the confines of our own campus." He spread his arms expansively, his voluminous sleeves knocking the papers on his desk out of their neat stacks. (I saw a lot of Raz in that gesture, or should I say Raz'd picked it up from his mentor.) "Now that we have developed an encoding scheme to protect our communications, we've found it safe to communicate over longer distances, between certain of our extension campuses and laboratories." I had heard there were other locations where advanced students did field research, but Da's shop was the newest offsite lab. "Of course, I am the sole custodian of the spellcasting equipment at the moment, since it is still an experimental arrangement. And it's used only for professional purposes."

He should know I'd never ask to talk to Da on his fancy spell. I was perfectly content using the carrier pigeons for letters back and forth, and grateful that they were allowing me that privilege, which usually was reserved for upperclassmen. And I couldn't help but remember Raz's translation of "of course" as "as any jackass can plainly see." I felt a little insulted, but managed to compose myself enough to reply calmly. "Of course, sir."

"The spell is something that Raz took on recently as a special project for me." He looked over my head, presumably to smile at Raz. I felt a little swell of pride in Raz, despite myself. "We've been in frequent communication lately with your father, and we needed a more immediate method of exchanging information with him. You see, Dulcinea, the project that he took on for us has developed some problems."

"Yes, sir." I tried to make myself sound concerned, but actually my whole body was flooded with relief. Da was all right. I wasn't failing out of school. Still, caution was my middle name. "Um . . . which project would that be?" Da had taken home two novices to train in potions and poultices, but I suspected the trouble lay with his second project, the one for which the Master had sent along two advanced students to help Da—the dragon.

Madare's features relaxed a bit, and a chuckle escaped him. "Well, Dulcinea. I realize that when we were making our arrangements for your father to investigate this particular phenomenon for us, you were excited and busy getting settled in here at the school, so you weren't privy to all the plans. But you do remember that when your Daddoo left here, he took along something that he was going to help us out with."

I blinked innocently. "All I know is that he promised to study and report back to you about the dragon."

The majick-master's face lit up the way teachers' faces do when a slow student guesses something correctly. "That's right. This concerns the dragon, Dulcinea. Your Da and I both have studied the information he has gathered from watching it, and we are concerned that something is seriously wrong with it. In fact, I would go so far as to say that, although it still shows good rapport with your father, in all other respects our dragon is heading downhill, especially in regards to its health."

It took me a moment to mentally process all those fancy words. The dragon was sick? My hands flew to my cheeks. "Oh, no."

I loved Da's little pet. Spunky was a baby blue dragon we'd rescued from a group of renegade mages; they'd used a stolen dragonstone to summon it here from another plane (strictly forbidden by the Majicker's Oath) in order to terrorize the populace. We'd been trying to figure out how to send him back ever since. Meanwhile, my Da had been studying it and sending his findings back to the Academy. What we'd found so far was that it was only a baby dragon, and it didn't know how to tell us much about itself, let alone about the dragonstone and how it was used to cross the planes of existence. I hadn't realized they knew much more than that.

I folded my hands in my lap. "What can you tell me, sir?"

"He's not thriving, Dulcinea. We don't know why."

"Has he been eating? I mean, have they found things to feed him?" I hadn't been sure he could eat in our plane of existence. The last time I'd had a message from Da, he'd made no mention of the dragon or its habits, so I'd assumed things were going well.

The majick-master winced. "We have, but that has been a costly proposition." I guessed he meant they'd paid for plenty of livestock. "At first he thrived, and we thought we were serving the needs of his metabolism. But now the situation has changed." He stood, his voluminous purple robes a-swishing, and came around the desk, standing with his hands clasped behind his back. "Our dragon is growing stunted. His natural development has halted. We feed him a varied diet based on our research and majickal analysis of his bodily wastes"—I didn't envy whoever Da had assigned to that duty—"but despite our efforts, he seems to be starving." He perched on the edge of the desk and stroked his beard. "It can't communicate what is the matter with it. As with a human baby, all it can do is cry and look forlorn. Your father has good empathy with the creature, but what he can find out is limited to his observations and the results of the various tests we have run. Unfortunately, there is no one, not even your father, who has the ability to communicate with him as well as you can."

I thought of our flight between the Academy and our shop, when I had shown the dragon the way home with pictures I made majickally with flute music, and nodded politely. Back when we'd first found the dragon, I'd been best in figuring out what he wanted and showing him what we wanted him to do, but later he'd taken well to Da. Thing was, Da didn't know how to commune with him through music. He hadn't been the first one ever to come up with the majick of music, and although I thought he was proud of me, I also knew it bothered him a little that his own daughter had a talent he didn't have. Da had the resources of the Academy at his disposal, and pigeons and messengers traveled regularly between our two locations to deliver back and forth, yet he wasn't in tune with the dragon's mind the way he might need to be. And I didn't think I could teach that, nor did I believe my Da would take well to learning from his own daughter.

"What we need from you, Dulcinea. . . ." Madare cleared his throat and looked strangely uncomfortable. It was an expression to which his face was obviously unaccustomed. I couldn't imagine what the majick-master would feel awkward about asking *me* to do. "You must summon your natural talent once again, and hope your rapport with our dragon can be recaptured as before. You must try to commune with him once again, so as to verify what our research seems to indicate."

I rested my chin in my cupped palms pensively, hoping I looked more knowledgeable than I felt. "What does the research show, sir?"

"As best we can tell, some nutrient that is abundant in the dragons' normal diet is missing. There's something he needs to consume in sufficient quantities at this point so that he can move to the next stage of development. We believe it's time for his maturation from juvenile to adolescent dragon, and that this nutrient is the catalyst for the beginning of the change. We believe he needs to begin that change as soon as possible, or. . . ."

"Or?"

The master looked grim. "Or he will die. We can't figure out a way to satisfy this need, and we haven't yet come upon any way to return him to his own realm. You're our best hope."

"I don't suppose he can remain stalled at this stage for very long, then?" The dragon was so cute at his current size, and jolly large enough already; what if he became a behemoth, too large to be kept leashed to a tree in our back garden courtyard? How could anyone keep him fed once he'd attained full dragon growth?

The master shook his head. "He cannot. He must start his maturation, as Nature intends. What if you tried to remain a girl yourself instead of accepting your natural transformation into a mature woman?"

I briefly considered mentioning that I'd already become what Da called a "young lady," that I wasn't a mere wisp of a girl, but thought better of it. The majick-masters treated all students, even those with seventeen years of life experience—me—as if we were just out of short pants or pigtails. I cupped my chin in my hand, hoping I'd look studious enough to be taken seriously. "Wouldn't it make more sense for you to have some advanced students perform the rest of the research here, where you could monitor it easily?"

He sighed. "That would be nice. Obviously, the ideal arrangement would be to have your Da fly him here, but frankly we suspect the dragon is far too weak for that. He doesn't flail his wings
nor attempt to fly to the end of his leash the way he did initially;
he confines himself to wandering around the garden and allowing
people to take him on short walks." I figured a dragon that size on
a walk would have his choice of flowers and bushes from neighbors' gardens, then, if he were so inclined. He must not be able to
eat in our plane. "In addition, after studying the Society of Mages'
positions around our perimeter—as you must have been told, they
are watching our enclave more closely every day—we determined
that it would be far too risky to bring him here, whether by land
or by air."

The Society of Mages wasn't what the name implied: they
dealt in dark sorcery and pacts with demons, wearing the black
hats to our white. My knuckles were in my mouth; realizing I
shouldn't betray my alarm, I eased them out and instead cupped
my chin pensively, one finger on my lower lip.

"Our sources report that they took careful note of the dragon's
movements when he flew in and out of here last time, and they've
made certain preparations that are obviously intended to shoot
him out of the air."

I swallowed a gasp.

Madare's beard quivered a little. "No, the way to prevent their
finding where we are keeping the dragon is to send you there, traveling unobtrusively. You can't go overland by yourself, of course."

Of course not, a mere wisp like Dulcinea Jean Brown couldn't
be trusted on the road; I suppressed a sigh and nodded attentively.

"Since he knows the way and is well known to your Daddoo,
has in fact worked extensively with him, we have decided that Raz
will accompany you. He can keep you safe on the journey. Upon
his arrival, he can take care of a matter I've discussed with him." I
could have sworn he winked at Raz.

I glanced over my shoulder, but I couldn't gauge Raz's reaction. His expression was unreadable.

It was beginning to dawn on me that once I left the course of study here, I might not be able to return to it. "What about my examinations and my mage-trials, sir?"

He harrumphed. "Arrangements will be made for you to make those up." He fiddled with his sleeves and didn't meet my gaze. "Although it will interrupt your course of study, and regrettably so, you must concentrate for a time on our work with the dragon. You may take your books along with you if you like; they might help you. You'll have full remote access to the acolytes in the library, so you can have them look things up when you need to. And of course you'll be giving them plenty of new information. With this research, you might even earn special project credit."

Despite his carefully chosen words, it sounded as though I might not even be invited back to the school, after all. I didn't feel the disappointment that I'd expected, which surprised me. And Raz was coming along, at least for a while. I folded my hands in my lap and ducked my head momentarily, as a sign of respectful agreement. "I hope I won't disappoint you, sir." After a moment, I blurted out, "But how can I use the library from home?"

"Once you arrive, we'll use the voice communication system to monitor your progress and assist you in any possible way. You shall send us the results you obtain as soon as you obtain them, and we shall suggest methods for your research as they come to mind. Eventually, it may be possible to fly him back here. Should he remain too weak to fly, we can harness him into a majickal contraption I'll design to allow our advanced students, the apprentices and journeymen, to analyze data or operate on him from afar. Raz and your Da can work out those details once you're there. Does that answer your question?"

"Yes, thank you, sir."

"Do you have other questions for me?" The master seemed ready to wrap things up, to dismiss us to the road.

"No, sir." I was too worried about the dragon and still about Da, in case there might be things they weren't telling me, to think of any questions. Suddenly I couldn't wait to be home—not to start the project, but to be there. I wished there was major enough wizarding to send us there instantly, but I knew better than to even ask if there were such a thing. I knew they couldn't and shouldn't squander such power on a trip home for me, and besides, if there were a way, they'd have brought the dragon here. Majick was majick, after all, not miracle working. I whispered a prayer to Saint Alyncia and stood, hands clasped in front of me, waiting impatiently to be dismissed.

The Master nodded. He smiled. "You two may go now to prepare for your journey. I'll make the arrangements, so all you need to do is pack. Meet back here at third bell."

I curtseyed shallowly and turned to go. Behind me, Raz was rubbing his palms together. His face was wreathed in smiles, and his eyes twinkled like a baby's when it has just discovered its toes will reach its mouth. He seemed happy at last.

Raz, content to baby-sit me on my way home? That surprised me. Usually he got plum assignments, not this kind of menial chore. To see him so giddy should've pleased me, but it kind of worried at the corner of my mind. Something more to all of this— I knew there had to be.

But as I stepped out of the Master's offices, relief washed over me like a cool overhead pour of creekwater in suntime. My Da was safe. And I was going to have an excuse to see him.

To go home.

Da's letters were chatty and empty of serious news or information. More alarmingly, they contained far too many references to his new clerk in our apothecary, an untrained but eager helper who was also our widowed next-door neighbor lady. Da wrote mostly "Juleida this, Juleida that." I was already tired of that name. Juleida Churchman had chased Da for years and was nothing but an interfering old hen. I was trying to be grateful that he had help, but it still stuck to the roof of my mouth like salty nut-butter. The first action I would take as mistress of the household again was banish her. Raz and I could clerk while we did our dragon healing and studying. That was the way it should be.

Da must be upset that his project was taking such a rocky pathway, but he hadn't let on to me. That made me suspicious about what else might have been going on at home, and what else exactly he wasn't telling me everything about.

The tension had finally begun to drain from my neck and shoulders. Whatever happened with this sequence at school, the decision had been made for me, and I had a new task that I hoped I would be more suited to. By the time I got to my tiny bunk in the first-year aspirants' quarters, I almost felt like whistling, and as I pulled my packs out from underbed and started to load them, I was smiling.

Raz had seemed farthels and farthels away mentally for at least a fortnight. He hadn't paid one bit of attention to the majickal curriculum we were supposedly developing together, a sequence of courses intended for students who showed aptitude for the majick of music. The burden had consequently fallen heavily on me to not only complete my initial training on Web majick but to try to formulate a coursework sequence and contents for those when I had never done it before. At first I thought Raz was just testing me to see if I could shoulder the entire burden, but by now it appeared his mind had been occupied with something else. It certainly hadn't been on our work.

Now that I thought about it, the whole time I'd been at the academy, Raz had spent most of the time he was in our lab sighing and staring out the window. His distant expression and his gazing away off over the horizon whenever I tried to tell him things he ought to remember, or ask about things he ought to want to tell me, were a major problem. Though I'd loved Raz virtually from the moment we met—back home, when I knelt for him to do a majickal audition on me, of all things—I was actually glad we'd be putting this project aside and taking a break from all this tense togetherness. No wonder he was so pleased; he wouldn't have to work on the new courses with me alone, and he might be looking forward to working with Da. It was just as well, because I could not get his attention about the most important of things. It is a difficult collaboration when it is a team of one mouth and one earless mule.

It would be a relief to start on a new project with my Daddoo. I couldn't wait to show him all I had learned—well, mostly things I'd failed to master, but learned about nevertheless. He'd probably never heard all about majicking's long history, which I could quote to him now after all the reciting in class ("Majick was discovered in the Year of Peace 1593, Second Fredel, by the Ladenian Dalbo Applegate when his inept assistant, Wray Little, attempting to hang a clothesline, inadvertently crossed a majickal line of power and found the string empowered with a strange force of attraction.") He would be amazed at some of the strange ways taught here, such as the enchantments that worked with candles and the potions we'd never thought to brew. I had even learned why there were limits on the drawing of power from the majickal web, and how to circumvent the limits safely.

The headmaster had said I could take my textbooks. I already had my notebooks in their usual sack, but there wasn't much room in my luggage for anything besides what I'd brought; I thought it best not to leave anything personal behind, in case I didn't return. All my traveling packs bulged.

After a moment, I stuffed the precious books in on top of my clothes, thinking I could stash my drawstring of toiletries in a saddlebag and sling my extra pair of boots (which usually rode inside a pack) over my saddle by the laces. These books told all about the rules—natural law as well as human agreements—that governed the use of majickal power. In them were the makings for all kinds of new majick, some that I might never master, some that Da might like to study. These were things never thought of back home, where herbal majick was the norm. Wouldn't Daddoo be proud of me?

End of Sample

APPENDIX I : ACKNOWLEDGEMENTS

There wasn't room on the dedication page to acknowledge everyone who has helped me. I would like to thank Terry Deupree for reading each chapter as it was revised to be sent to the original Warner Aspect First Novel Contest in 1996 (in which the book placed as first runner-up, which was flattering) and giving important feedback about the story. I would also like to thank Fred Gohsman for passing the manuscript to friends, urging me to mail the book out, and constantly asking for the sequel. I owe a debt as well to three dedicated critiquers who read most of the novel (fifteen pages at a time) and contributed many good suggestions: Linda Donahue, Kathy Turski, and Julia Mandala. Most of all, I thank the members of the FidoNet International Writing Echo, who have supported and encouraged me for many years. Special thanks go to Dennis Havens, Rachel Veraa, and my alter ego, Denise Weeks. (Miss you, Hossie, Brianne, and Ma Ducks.)

Mama, thank you for everything. I wish my daddy, grandparents, mother-in-law, and father-in-law were here to see this book in print, but I am certain that all my balcony people are watching this with a smile.

And, last but certainly not least, a special thanks to all my readers everywhere.

APPENDIX II : SHALANNA'S READERS' NEWSLETTER

For a free subscription to the readers' newsletter that Shalanna Collins and her staff send out each quarter, send your name and address in an e-mail message to *shalanna@home.com* and state that you would like to receive her newsletter. If you have any feedback for Shalanna about her books or what you'd like to see from her next, feel free to tell her!